Dance
of the DANDELION

Praise for Dance of the Dandelion

Dina Sleiman is a beautiful writer. Romantic and gritty, *Dance of the Dandelion* takes readers on an epic journey of human failings, self-discovery, and second chances. Through it all God's love and forgiveness shines through.

JULIE KLASSEN
best-selling, award-winning author of *The Lady of Milkweed Manor* and *The Apothecary's Daughter*

This medieval romp of a book reads like a dance! Full of unexpected twists and turns, it displays the folly or joy of our choices and the God who enables us to find true freedom in Him. Dandelion Dering is a heroine you won't soon forget!

LAURA FRANTZ
author of *The Frontiersman's Daughter* and *Courting Morrow Little*

"The almost musical, lyrical writing of new author, Dina Sleiman, invites the reader to join in the Dance of Dandelion from the very first sentence of the book. I felt the raw poverty of the young peasant girl, Dandelion, and agonized with her as she searched to fill the empty places in her heart. A stunning debut novel, I look forward to what will be forthcoming from this talented author."

GOLDEN KEYES PARSONS
author of the Darkness to Light Series

"Dina Sleiman breathes new life into the written word with her exquisitely penned story, *Dance of the Dandelion*. I was instantly transported back to medieval days and into the heart of her heroine, gripped so strongly that I couldn't bear to put the book down. Though the medieval genre carries with it certain expectations, Sleiman transcends them with excellent writing and a tale as real as it is timeless."

ROSEANNA M. WHITE
author of *A Stray Drop of Blood* and *Jewel of Persia*

DINA L. SLEIMAN

This is a work of fiction. All characters and events portrayed in this novel are either fictitious or used fictitiously.

DANCE OF THE DANDELION

WhiteFire Publishing
13607 Bedford Rd NE
Cumberland, MD 21502

ISBN: 9780983455608 (print)
        978-0-983455-62-2 (digital)

Cover model photo by Christian Aghra Photography
Cover Design by Tekeme Studios (www.Tekeme.com)

This book is dedicated to my daughter Christiana Rose Sleiman,
who served as my inspiration for childhood Dandelion,
my first adoring fan, my faithful critic,
and my beautiful cover model.

Life is a dance,
from the swirling cosmos circling earth,
to the subtle harmony of bodies,
to the measured cadence of minute particles
hidden deep within.

While others stood aside and watched,
I embraced its gentle ebbs and flows,
dove deep into the divine current.

Within this dance,
its spins and dips,
its rhythmic leaps and sways,
I have experienced the deepest sorrows;
and I have discovered

We played a flute for you, and you did not dance...
Matthew 11:17

Chapter 1

Sussex England - 1327

The gray stone castle beckoned from atop the grassy hill, waiting, calling to me as always. Its turreted towers rose tall and strong as sentinels on either side—solid, dependable, so unlike my own wattle and daub hut down the lane. Pennants in the Worthing colors of garnet and gold swayed against a vibrant blue sky.

"Dreaming again, are you, Dandelion?" Alice's voice came from behind, jolting me from my trance.

I swiveled from the window. My eyes took a moment to adjust to the dim interior of Father John's kitchen with its wood-beamed walls. Alice's rosy face came into view. She held a basket of bright orange carrots against her ample hip.

A warm flush worked its way up my cheek at being caught musing yet again. "I was putting the bread on the sill to cool." If only my telltale cheeks would cool as well.

"Seems you left your mind in the castle courtyard near the ovens where you baked that bread." Alice placed the carrots on the table and picked up a long knife. She waved it toward the backyard where my closest friend, William, sat under a shady tree, studying a Latin text. "Perhaps you ought to turn your thoughts closer to home."

I huffed. William had ignored me when I walked by moments earlier. "To what? Latin? You're the one who told me a woman could go further in life with domestic skills."

"Indeed, my sweet. But well you know I am referring to that handsome boy holding the book and not the text itself."

"He is far too busy with his studies for the likes of me. Besides, well *you* know I plan to aim higher than William Ashby. Goodness, he might yet end up in the church if Father John has his way." I took the carrots and knife from her hand and began slicing.

"Oh, leave those." Alice offered me a basket instead. "Go and collect some flowers for your new kirtle. It's beautiful outside."

A smile tickled my lips. "Buttercup yellow with a sage green mantle. Oh, Alice, you are too good to me." I couldn't hold back a squeal. Nor could I wait to throw this tattered brown tunic I wore into the rag heap. The new kirtle would show off my subtle curves to perfection. Although I had learned the basics of weaving and sewing as a child,

I was anxious to continue my lessons in dyeing and embroidery.

Taking the basket from her, I gave Alice's plump shoulder a squeeze. How could I thank her enough for the opportunities she had offered me? Me, Dandelion, daughter of the crippled cottar. Alice claimed with my new skills I could work in a town or open a shop someday, but I dreamed only of working and living at the castle. There I would remain close to my family and provide for them as I always longed to.

She batted me away with an affectionate swat. "Go on with you now. And while you're at it, that fine young man beneath the tree might need some incentive to keep him from taking holy orders. Don't wait until it's too late."

Of course, everyone knew that "housekeeping" was the least of Alice's duties in the home of our village priest, but as the dear woman tended to the needs of the poor and the sick alongside Father John, no one dared complain. Such arrangements were common enough. I had seen with my own eyes the devotion they shared. Perhaps Alice wished to protect me from falling into a similar fate. But I highly doubted William was the man for me.

I crinkled my face and shook my head before walking out the door into the bright golden sunshine. As I passed by him beneath the tree on my way to the garden, I decided to heed Alice's sage advice nonetheless. "God give you good day, William."

He grunted but never even looked up from his blasted book. Beyond William's feet in the shade sat the smooth patch of dirt where Father John taught us our letters and numbers, where we later scratched complex mathematics equations with a pointed stick. Once, Father John drew a map of the whole world and gave us a thorough geography lesson on that patch. It was filled with fond memories of William, my baby brother Tim, and me, working side by side to make a better life for ourselves and escape this peasant village.

I continued the conversation on my own. "Yes, and a lovely day it is. Don't you think? The perfect afternoon for picking flowers. Remember when we picked flowers together, William?" We used to do everything together.

He raised his brow at my chatter but said not at word. Although William did indeed love to study, his behavior toward me seemed oddly rude of late. Had I evaded his veiled hints of marriage one too many times?

I proceeded to ignore him as well and settled myself in the garden, inhaling a deep whiff of the fertile Sussex countryside. Who needed the likes of William Ashby? Glancing across the valley, I took in fresh-turned earth bursting with life beneath the azure sky, sloping green hills dotted with fluffy white sheep, meadows of wildflowers, a gurgling stream, and the dappled forest beyond. I had danced through those fields as a child. My feet itched to spin and leap even now, but at sixteen, I grew old for such nonsense. Instead, I applied myself to the more pressing task of locating the perfect blossoms for my precious kirtle. I surveyed a cluster of blooms that looked just right and ran my fingers across the moist, silken petals.

"Dandy, come over here," William shouted. "Can you help me make this out?"

So now he wished to speak with me?

I bent over and continued my search for the ideal yellow blossoms.

A hair ribbon fell in my eye, and I swiped it away. Assisting Alice, I amassed quite a collection of them. My favorites were violet, sky blue, and sea-foam green. Each brought out a different shade in my exotic eyes, William said, and a different side of my personality. I wore the purple ribbon today. Purple stood for passion.

"Dandy, please."

I wished my brother Tim was with him under that tree hard at work at his studies. Unlike me, an academic education could in truth take him far in the world. Father John offered a priceless gift to William and Tim. The gift of a future. Yet more oft than not, the eleven-year-old boy tossed it aside to romp through the forest with his friends. I should set down this basket and drag his thieving behind back here this minute. He may not care about his own well-being, but I most certainly did. And I had no desire to see him tied to a whipping post.

"Marian, please don't ignore me. I need you."

William's use of the nickname made me laugh. It brought to mind that he and I had once run through the woods as members of Robin Hood's merry band of poachers as well. Perhaps I should not begrudge Tim the fun. It was a miracle the lad had survived 1315, the year of the great famine. His weak infant whimpers called to me over the distance of memory even now.

I ran my fingers across my brow to wipe the thoughts away. He was the last born boy and our family treasure. Surely Tim would be fine. After all, the castle steward remained our longtime ally.

"Please, come and help me. I'm truly stuck, and Father John won't be home for hours," William called.

"But I'm all covered with dirt. Goodness, William, you act as if you're the only one with anything important to do. Bring it over here." I brushed my hands on Alice's old apron.

He walked toward me. "It's unfair you have such a knack for languages when you don't appreciate it."

"It's unfair I cannot make good use of my knack for languages, thus I must content myself to sew."

William looked stiff from too much sitting as he joined me. "Right here, Dandy. It's right here." He pointed to the page. "I can't seem to wrap my mind around it."

"Hand it over." I snatched it from him. "'Est autem fides sperandorum substantia rerum argumentum non parentum.' Hmm. 'Now faith is . . . .' Well, that is simple enough."

"Yes, yes, I got that part, it's the next that puzzles me." He leaned in and took the other side of the book.

9

As he pressed close, I bade my errant heart to still and focused upon the words. "Well, I guess it says . . . being sure or being certain. Substance would be the easiest translation, but it doesn't make any sense."

He stopped and looked up at me for a moment. Some emotion I couldn't read flashed through his eyes. "Perhaps that's right. It does seem odd, though. 'Now faith is the substance of things hoped for and the proof of things not seen.'"

"No, no, not proof, it looks more like argument. Evidence, perhaps. It's all gibberish if you ask me. I don't think it was written down properly. Someone should fix it."

He pulled the book away from me. "You shouldn't talk that way about the Word of God. If we don't understand it, then I suppose we are the ones in need of fixing."

I glared at him. "Oh fie. Really, William, I don't know how much more of your piety I can stomach. Do you truly plan to become a priest? You could be a clerk or a bailiff or something practical with all you've learned."

"You're missing the point entirely. Give it a try. 'Now faith is the substance of things hoped for, the evidence of things not seen.' It's . . . as if faith is something we can touch or hold. Perhaps by our faith, we make things real, as if our very faith is all the proof we need. There, it does make sense. I can't see God, but I know He is real, and that very knowing is all the proof I need."

"Yes, yes, it's spellbinding."

He brushed off my sarcasm. "And look, there's more still I think, in the word *hope*. We don't have to hope God exists, that would be silly."

"Silly indeed." I rolled my eyes.

"It seems as if the hope may be bringing things into existence. Perhaps our faith is some sort of force to bring about change." He tapped on the page. "See, I told you, it is compelling if you just put some time into it."

"Truly, you give me a headache with all the time you put into it."

"Don't you understand at all?" He reached toward me but let his hand drop.

"Faith . . . faith is a force? Like fairy magic I suppose." I stood up and walked to a nearby tree. Leaning against it, I settled my gaze upon the castle. "Why, as a matter of fact, I do have faith. I have faith that one day a handsome prince shall gallop in on a black charger and sweep me away. He'll take me to a distant land, and there he shall build me a lovely manor of gray stones with flowers all about instead of an ugly old moat. It will be filled with books and beautiful fabrics. It will be quite charming, I'm certain. So there you are. Do you fancy I can hope that into existence?" I turned back to him and lifted an eyebrow.

He shook the book in the air. "God's teeth, Dandy, why must you twist everything and make it about your stupid dreams and your vanity? Why not say Lord Thomas Worthing? I know full well that's who you think of, that spoiled fool running around Scotland killing people for Lord only knows what reason. What an idiot you are. My mother is right. You are by far the most selfish, arrogant heathen on God's green earth. *That* I have faith of, indeed."

Thoughts of Lord Worthing never failed to rile William, but his shabby treatment of me had gone on long enough. "I've wasted quite enough time on this stupid conversation and the likes of you, William Ashby." I gathered my flowers, turned, and walked away, stomping my bare feet against the dirt lane.

I had last caught sight of his lordship five years earlier on this very lane. He indeed rode a fine charger, looking every inch the strong, handsome knight with his garnet and gold colors flying in the wind. Cantering past me, he had smiled and winked. Rather than remaining angry with William as I should, the memory made me grin. I turned my lips back to a pout before he could see.

William trotted at my heels like a kicked puppy as I turned upon a wooded trail. "Dandy, I'm sorry. Please don't be cross with me. I just worry about you."

"About my eternal soul or whom I shall marry?" I continued walking.

"Well, I wouldn't be much of a friend if I didn't worry about your soul, and if I get a little jealous, it's because I care so much. Fairy stories are fun, but those sorts of imaginations can only bring trouble. You're still my prettiest girl, though, pretty enough to be a princess." He spoke directly into my ear in his most charming voice, a deep manly voice that made me quiver.

I pushed him away. "Oh, stop it. I forgive you, I suppose. We both know I shall eventually."

"Come, let's sit by the river like we did when we were children."

I smirked. William fancied himself so grown-up. As we continued down the leafy trail, he used the excuse of climbing over a fallen log to take my hand, then never let go, gallant indeed. It felt so warm and safe in his large rugged palm. We had been best friends for so long I oft forgot how handsome his sandy hair looked falling in soft waves about his wide cheekbones.

A child squealed at a distance. William had given up poaching for religious reasons long ago. However, he passed the role of Robin Hood to Tim, who rounded up his own troop of merry men. The new crop of boisterous young hunters filled the woods with happy sounds of adventure and thievery.

At nineteen and sixteen William and I were children in so many ways, still learning and discovering the world, yet fully grown by everyone's expectations. I gazed up at William's face. It narrowed nicely down to a cleft chin and full lips. He stood tall and natural like the woods around us, slender but strong, a peasant girl's dream, but to me he was a friend. Wasn't he? Every girl in the village might long for him, swoon in his handsome presence, but surely I had higher ambitions than William. Didn't I?

My older sister Sadie planned to marry soon. She seemed happy enough with the prospect, and why not? It was the best she ever wished for, the best she could expect—marriage to a handsome young villein, working in his family's fields, raising his children, growing more peasants to work in more fields. Never mind they would both be old and gray within ten years. Never mind she would likely die in childbirth long before then. My brother Robert was ever slipping into the woods with a redhead from down the lane. No doubt he'd be on the path to matrimony before long. But that sort of life was far from enough for me.

I held tight to William's hand as we approached the Arun River, the namesake of the castle and the village. We sat on our favorite warm rock, and to my surprise, he wrapped his arm around my waist. With his free hand he took a springy lock of my wheat-colored hair and twisted it about his finger, causing my stomach to twirl as well.

I attempted to lighten the mood. "Not such the holy saint now, are you?" Yet, the quiet breathiness of my voice surprised even me, and the result was quite the opposite.

"Dandy, you asked about me becoming a priest, but you must know how much I love you. I would give it all up in a second if I thought you would marry me. It's just when you talk all wistful about some high, fancy lifestyle, I fear I don't have a chance." He caressed my cheek.

A tear filled my eye at his very nearness. I turned my head into his palm and rested it there. "Oh, William, don't—"

"No, please. I can't give you a castle, Dandy, and you know I'll never have a black charger. I'll be lucky to have any sort of horse at all. But, if I work terribly hard, I can make a life for us. I'll build you the prettiest little cottage right over there on the hillside by the river. I can see it now. I'll dig and gather the stones by hand. I will. I'll do it just for you, and we'll plant the loveliest ring of flowers around it you ever did see."

I could almost picture it. My head grew swishy at the tickle of William's breath against my skin.

"I'll build a bridge over the river, and I'll make a path of cobblestones going right to the door, so you won't get your feet muddy, or your shoes either. I'll see to it you have shoes and plenty of clothes and warm cloaks for the winter, you and every one of our children. And I'll wake you up each morning with a cup of fresh milk from our very own cow . . . a cup of fresh milk . . . ." His voice faded. "And kisses. I'll cover you head to toe with kisses each and every day of our lives."

My breath caught in my chest.

True to his word, he kissed my cheeks, my eyes, the tip of my nose with his full, soft lips. I thought nothing in the world could feel better than his velvet touch, until he tipped up my chin, and his trail of kisses reached my lips. They came alive beneath his and moved of their own accord. A bubbly warmth filled me to my fingertips and toes. I knew I should stop him, stop this fantasy, but he had drawn me in as well. It all seemed so real, so very real and possible as we sat kissing in the sunshine. Oh, how I wanted this moment to be true and last forever. I never dreamed of such bliss. In all of my planning and scheming, I never planned for this.

William pulled away, struggling for breath, and stared into my eyes. My heart fluttered in my chest. I could see my own amazement mirrored in his golden-brown orbs. He let go of me and lay back on the rock with a long sigh. We remained in our separate reveries, yet somehow one. I edged forward and dipped my toes in the cool flowing water, swishing them to and fro, reliving the kiss again and again, touching my lips where the tingle remained.

Then William roused me back to the present. He held in his hand a crown of cornflowers he had woven as I mused. He placed it upon my head and ran his fingers down the length of my hair. "Now you look a princess," he said. "The cornflowers match your blue eyes, and with those golden tresses cascading down your shoulders, who would dare deny it?" He reached for another flower and formed it into a tiny circle this time. He lifted my hand and slid it with ease onto my fourth finger. A good omen, Sadie would say. "Dandelion, fairy queen of all I see, I may not be a handsome prince, but will you marry me?"

"Oh, William, you've been reading far too much poetry for your own good." I gave him a playful shove, breaking the spell.

But it was midsummer, and we had discovered a new delight, sweeter even than the pink candy Lord Worthing had once given me. Day after day we were found kissing on the rock.

Tim and his cohorts teased us mercilessly. They snuck up behind us one day completely unheeded and pushed us into the water. We just splashed back up at them and continued kissing, soaking wet and knee-deep in the river. If only matters could have remained so simple.

Chapter 2

"Tell us again, William. Tell us the story of your brothers running off to London." Tim bounced on the bench beside me. I reached over to tousle his silken brown curls. Gracious, he was nearly as tall as me these days. A tear pricked my eye as I thought of the scrawny little boy he once had been. He would grow large and strong like William and his brothers, like the nobles at the castle, and someday his education would serve him well. Life held more for Tim than the path of a poor cottar.

William swallowed a bite of the chicken he had brought us for dinner. The scent of roasted fowl reminded me of a different story—the story of two pathetic peasant children who had never tasted meat until their dear friend William first took them poaching. Those days seemed so far behind us now.

"I'm sure you've all heard it a hundred times." William wiped his mouth with the back of his hand. "Are you sure you wouldn't rather me tell another?"

"No, no, please, William." Mum smiled fondly to him from her weathered face. She crossed her arms encased in rough flaxen fabric upon the pink embroidered cloth I had made for the table. "We always love your stories no matter how oft we hear them. Why, you could be a troubadour."

"Yes, yes, a troubadour." My sister Sadie clapped.

Da simply nodded his approval.

"Or an entertaining priest like Father John," my brother Robert added.

"Or run off to an exciting life in London." Young Tim bounced some more, causing the wildflowers and vase I had placed in the center of the table to tremble. Our hut had long been dreary and soot covered, but I had since managed to turn the one-room, mud-daubed place into something bright and cheery, akin to a home.

"Well." William sat down his fork to begin his long tale. "It was a warm fall day not unlike today. We had just finished the harvest in no time at all with so many grown sons to help. Despite our ample yardland, my two middle brothers had been itching for some time to strike off on their own and seek their fortunes in London town."

"But first they would have to get away and survive a year on their own without getting caught." Tim added into the story he knew too well.

"Precisely," William said. "And no doubt my mother would lose her coveted position as a maid at the castle, but we held a family meeting and decided the time was ripe, ripe as the grain we had harvested. Of course I loved the land and farming, as did my two eldest brothers . . . ."

While William continued the tale I could quote by heart, my mind floated away. William planned to travel to London this winter and visit his brothers, who had set themselves up as merchants and begun families of their own. I could barely fathom it. I had never traveled past the nearby market town of Chichester. The hundreds of people crowding the square had nearly overwhelmed my senses. I heard that tens of thousands lived in London and the streets went on for near eternity, lined with stores and houses. Could William and I run off and make a life for ourselves in such a place?

We had grown inseparable over the past months. No one questioned his arrival to dinner this evening with crock in hand. For so many years my family had lived upon pottage and stews of root vegetables. As Robert grew old enough to help in the fields, we added bread that Sadie baked fresh in the castle courtyard. Then we had tossed in a few squirrels, birds, and fish Tim and I poached in the woods. But now William oft supplied rich foods of meat, milk, and eggs to supplement our meager fair.

I gazed about the table at the rapt expressions. My older siblings Sadie and Robert laughed at William's tale while Mum beamed up at him. He had been Tim's hero ever since that first day he cooked us the squirrel he had shot with his handmade sling. Da was still and quiet as always. The crippled peasant man might not say much with his stuttering speech, but the sparkle in his eyes as he focused upon William spoke volumes.

Oh, how I adored my dear little da. Somehow he had managed to care for us all these years since the famine despite his physical ailments and our tiny allotment of farmland. No doubt he dreamed William might one day be his son. I would so hate to disappoint him.

I could almost imagine a future for William and me. A future of hard work, continuing to improve our lives side by side and take our place in what some were calling the emerging middle class.

William continued weaving the story. His deep, rich voice filled the room and tickled my ears. Warmth and comfort flowed through me. If only I felt certain. I had always hoped for a life safe and secure inside the castle. In my wildest imaginings, I longed for a nobleman to sweep me away, to protect and provide, to ensure I never suffered through another famine like the one of 1315.

Oh, that wretched winter, the winter when Mum's glazed eyes fixed upon the ceiling, the winter when Da shuffled away with Mary's small lifeless body, the winter when I collapsed desolate upon the ground, convinced he would never return.

But that haunting season was far behind me now. Perhaps William was right, and it was high time I put such childish dreams of castles and lords aside.

Once William, Da, and Tim left to celebrate the harvest round a bonfire with the villagers, Mum took the opportunity to tease me. "Perhaps we should plan a double ceremony, Dandelion. Seems to me Sadie may not be the only one with a belly on her if you keep up the way you've been going."

Sitting on the floor near Mum's feet by the hearth, I looked up from my stitching. "Oh, Mum, please. If it were anyone but William, maybe, but you must realize he's the holiest boy in the shire."

"As if I would tolerate it." Sadie crossed her arms overtop her swollen stomach. Plump with her first child, she could do little more than sit on her stool by the fire these days. While as yet unmarried, she was betrothed to a quiet young village man she flirted with for years. "I'll not have my wedding ruined by the likes of her. She'd probably come in one of her ridiculous costumes with ribbons and flowers in her hair, trying to steal all the attention."

I brushed my hand against my yellow kirtle with pride. Sadie could keep her plain brown tunic for all I cared. I had no need for such frumpery. "Merciful heavens, Sadie. It was a jest."

She huffed. "It shall be *my* wedding, and you shall come dressed like a normal, respectable girl. Did I not dance around the bonfire and throw pins in the brook to catch my Gilbert? I've earned this day."

Sadie and her silly superstitions. More likely her healthy appetite for "the sins of the flesh" had caught her beau. They planned to wed after the harvest was finished and their own small hut constructed—after she survived the childbirth, as was so often the order of events in our corner of the world.

I glanced up at my sister. In truth, Sadie looked rather charming with her round belly. She retained a sweet, freckled face—despite her tendency toward nagging—and had a hazy look of pregnancy about her to match her shiny brown hair. I continued my embroidery. "No need to get peevish. I don't plan to marry William or anyone else. You may have your precious day, and may it not give you a moment's peace."

"Don't be ridiculous, Sadie." Robert sat at the table and sharpened his sickle. "I assure you, Gilbert has eyes for no one but you and that big silly belly of yours. He loves you like crazy. Lord only knows why. You look like a great, grumpy brown cow to me."

Sadie attempted a dramatic exit but took several tries to stand and lost the effect. "Well, he'd better. And it's not my fault I'm so enormous.

This stubborn baby should have come long ago." She stomped out with tears in her eyes.

"Shame on you," Mum said. No one wanted to mention the concern caused by Sadie's overdue child. Large babies and late babies both meant trouble—long, hard deliveries and a higher risk of death.

"I'll go talk to her," Robert said. He pulled up his gusseted hood and followed her out the door.

Mum and I sat working on Sadie's wedding gown. It was not the finest fabric, but a huge sacrifice for our parents nevertheless. The creamy woolen tunic was the best Sadie would ever own. The material would be used again someday as a shroud to wrap her in the grave—our custom, sad but true. The rest of the villagers found it a beautiful tradition. I didn't know why I plagued myself over such things.

I perused Sadie's woolen wedding gown again. My embroidered floral touches at the collar and cuffs would turn it into a veritable treasure by Arun Village standards. How I loved watching the pictures form beneath my fingers, as if they flowed from the tips. I finished stitching a scrolling vine before I turned to my mother and asked a question that had been on my mind all summer. "Mum, how did you choose to marry Da? I remember when you were still young, before Tim was born. You were pretty enough to catch any man in town."

"Why, I suppose I loved him."

"But what does that mean, Mum?" I laid my embroidery to the side and turned, resting my arms on her knees. "Everybody says that. Then within half a year the men are beating and the wives are nagging, and before long both are looking elsewhere for love."

"Do you think that was the case with your father and me?"

"Well, no." I glanced away.

"So then, let me tell you what love is, dearest." She sat her sewing down as well. "Love is not when your heart beats too fast, and when you get sweaty and cross-eyed over some foolish boy. That's what most folks call love, but they couldn't be more wrong. That sort of feeling fades before the summer's out. No, love feels more like coming home. Love is being close to someone. It's two souls blending into one that can never be parted. Real love is not so much feeling as it is being and giving. It doesn't come overnight or in a glance. It's built over years of letting yourself go to be a part of something bigger. That sort of love, my pretty little missy, will never go away."

"So you have that with Da?" I laid my chin on her knees atop my hands like I had as a child. The position comforted me.

"I most certainly do."

"But how did it happen?"

"Well, this is something I never told you." She brushed her fingers through my hair. "It shames me to say it, though it was no fault of mine." Her voice trailed off.

"What? What is it, Mum?"

"My own Da, he was not as nice as yours. He used to beat me

terribly for no apparent reason. One day I was sitting out in the field crying, trying to wrap my hurt arm, when over hobbled the sweetest little boy you ever did see. He took one look at my arm and finished wrapping it for me. Then he sat down with me and cried. Many years passed before the boy confessed his own father had beaten him until he was addled and crippled. His mother ran away with him before it was too late, and they ended here with an old uncle as cottars."

"Oh, Mum, how terrible."

"We were bound through friendship and caring. Certainly I could have found stronger boys, richer boys, handsomer boys, but they would not have been my boy. Your da and me, we belong together. Can't you see?"

I sat up and searched her brown eyes. The surrounding sags in her skin added wisdom to their depths. "And was it the right choice?"

"How could you ask such a question?" Mum tensed and blinked. "Indeed, what kind of child have I reared?"

I took her worn hands into my own. "I'm sorry, Mum, but you know well enough we've had hard times too. I want to understand."

"Well, I suppose I can forgive it." She pulled her hands away and picked up the dress again. "Mind you never talk that way in front of your father, though. I won't stand for it."

"Yes, ma'am." My stomach clenched. I hadn't meant to hurt her.

She continued sewing in silence a moment as she waited for her temper to pass. "So, you are feeling serious about young William, then. It's no wonder. The two of you have been thick as thieves since childhood."

Sadie and Robert walked through the door in time for the teasing to commence.

"So is it to be William after all, little one?" Robert bent down to poke at my ribs. "I thought you two well kissed out by now."

I pushed his hands away. "I don't know if it is William after all, so don't go skipping to conclusions, Robert Dering."

"Why in the world not?" Sadie's smile attested that Robert had worked his magic upon her mood. "It's clear he's crazy for you. He's practically a part of the family."

"If he's toying with you, I'll teach him a lesson quick enough." Robert punched his knuckles against his open palm a few times.

I swatted his leg. "He's not toying with me. I'm just not sure about my own feelings. Besides, we're still young."

"Young?" Sadie plopped back onto her stool by the fire. "Why, you're never too young to snare the finest catch in the village. I can barely speak to him without blushing, given that handsome face and fine physique of his. He's kind and generous. And . . . and . . . rich!" She shook her hands in frustration.

"She has the right of it, Dandelion." Mum nodded.

Sadie pressed a palm to her cheek. "Goodness, you're more an idiot than I thought. All of his brothers are successful. Look at the two off in

London town. That leaves more land for William. You could crack an egg on my head. If you throw it in the well and see his face, it means you'll marry him for sure. It worked for me. I saw my Gilbert's face as clear as day."

Robert mimicked a girly trot and squealed. "By all means, let's run right down to the well. That's the most ridiculous thing I've ever heard. Truly though, Dandelion, might he still join the church?"

I picked up my embroidery to resume working. "I suppose it's possible," I said with a sigh. I dared not mention to my family the conditions that would keep William from taking his vows.

Robert settled back down to his tools as well. "But I see him in the fields all the time these days."

"Yes, more of his insufferable piety," I said. "With two brothers gone, he must be sure to contribute his share of work. I suppose eventually he'll do something with his life."

"What does that mean?" Sadie leaned forward and scowled at me, her mood again taking a turn for the worse. "Are you implying that Robert and I and everyone else in the village haven't done anything with our lives?"

I took a deep breath and considered my answer. "I simply think you could seek to improve yourselves, as Tim and I have done. I've told you, I'd be happy to teach you to read in the evenings. Goodness, invite your friends along. Just think of what you could do with an education."

"Peasants reading," Mum grumbled. "What use is that? Won't help you grow even one extra stalk of grain. Best to know your place in life, Dandelion. Leave reading to the priests and nobles."

"We're fine as we are." Robert ran his thumb over his sickle. "We're happy enough here in our little valley. Don't trouble yourself so."

"We all have lives, Dandelion—full and wonderful lives." Sadie wagged her finger toward my face. "If you go on thinking you're too high and mighty, life will pass you right by, it will, and then it will be too late."

"That's quite enough," Mum said. "I'm tired, and you shall give me a headache with this childish bickering."

We went back to our tasks in surly silence. Sadie's reprimand echoed through my mind.

Life will pass you right by, it will, and then it will be too late.

So similar to Alice's words of warning. I pushed them aside. No, I would not let my sister nor Alice rush me into a decision I could never take back.

Did I love William? Perhaps I did, but I could not risk committing myself to a life of deprivation as Sadie was about to do. As my mother once had. If she was correct, and love was indeed like coming home, then I supposed William would always be there waiting.

Chapter 3

A few nights after the fight with my siblings, I thrashed about on my pallet, tangled in dreams of cracking eggs on Sadie's head and throwing them into the well. I looked and looked for William's face. I thought for a moment I found it, but then it swirled and changed. For the life of me, I couldn't make it out. I started screaming again and again.

I jolted awake to realize it wasn't me, but Sadie who did the screaming. I offered to take Tim outside, desperate to escape the tortured, twisted look on Sadie's face and the awful, soul-curdling shrieks that stabbed into my skull, but Mum shooed all the men out instead. Robert ran for Alice. We had no midwife in the village, and we couldn't afford to send for one from Chichester, but Alice was skilled at nursing.

Alice took one look at my shaking hands and blood-drained face and sent me to fetch some water. I ran through the chill, misty night all the way to the well, so relieved to be away from the suffocating hut and the sticky wet mess that was my sister. Thank God William was a good boy after all. It could be me in there, if not for his self-control. Lord knows I would have given myself to him quick enough, if ever he had asked.

The well stood close to the castle walls. I dared not look into its depths after my nightmare. I continued on past the well and collapsed against the steadfast stones that I adored, pressed my hands against their ridges, my cheeks against their gritty strength. Over the past few years, I had read religious books, sermons and poems, a few short tales along the way. Never did I encounter the true-life story of a princess or noblewoman, and yet I saw glimpses everywhere, in every single book, glimpses of a different sort of life. Father John had supplied me with an education beyond my wildest dreams, but what had it truly accomplished?

At first I was enthralled, thrilled to learn about a world so foreign to mine. It brought me back to the day in the sun long ago when I first saw a gilded carriage emerge from the castle gates. As I learned more, though, I could hardly take it. Far beyond envy, it was cold and palpable, and I could taste it in my mouth, forcing me to lay my books aside before it tore me apart.

Now with the rhythmic echo of Sadie's screams still reaching out to me, I crushed hard against the castle wall, hoping it would pull me into it somehow, yet trapped as always on the outside. I didn't want to settle for second best. I was no fool. I knew I could never marry a rich lord like Thomas Worthing, but I needn't settle for the likes of William Ashby either.

No wonder peasants weren't taught to read—so much better to keep them stupid and complacent, to make them feel like some sort of inferior species, as if life inside the castle were nothing more than a fairyland meant for immortals. But, blast it all, I knew better.

Again I heard Sadie's screams; louder and faster they came. I leaned my forehead into the rough stones and covered my ears with my hands, thinking for the first time in years about my sister Mary who died during the famine. How cold and hard her flesh had felt.

I thought of Mum and the babies she lost between Tim and me. The years of ill health and mental imbalance she endured. The high price our family paid until father put his foot down and refused to partake in the nightly grunts and groans that came from our parent's pallet in the cramped hut.

I dragged fresh air into my lungs against their will. Tears ran down my cheeks and the night wind bit against their trails. My feet grew frigid in the damp grass. I wished I brought a blanket, or a cloak, or that I just wasn't here at all. I wished I were sleeping on a feather mattress with a silky coverlet, surrounded by filmy curtains on a tall bed inside the warm castle.

A strange shiver crept up my spine. Someone watched me from atop the guard tower. I'd felt those same eyes upon me often throughout the years. Should I be afraid, or was the castle simply awaiting my arrival? Offering up a quick wave, I shook off my despondency and hurried back to the well.

I would be strong for Sadie, for my family, for all of the villagers. Mentally, I added midwifery to the list of skills I wished to master as I hauled up a bucket of water. There must be a way to prevent such agony as I had witnessed this night.

To my wonder, by the time I arrived at the hut, I heard a small, sweet cry. "It's a boy," Alice shouted.

Gilbert, my father, and my brothers hugged one another and jumped about at the happy news that yet another man had graced the earth.

Once inside the door, the sharp smells of blood and childbirth assaulted me. Sadie looked far more a mess than when I left her.

"All is well, Dandelion. This one was in a hurry after all the waiting." Alice held up the squalling bundle. "Your sister's a bit ripped up, but he's out safe and sound now. Here, you hold him while I tend her."

I stared, gaping at the sheets covered with bodily fluids and the jagged tears upon my sister's wounded bottom. Surely such things did not happen at the castle.

Then, like magic, there he was in my arms. The tiniest little creature, looking up at me with big, round eyes. He stopped crying and studied me. I snuggled the warm bundle against my chest, happy he came from this awful night. I looked at Sadie with pity. "I was so worried."

Her lips trembled as she smiled. "It's all right. I'm fine now."

"Don't be afraid, little one," Mum said from Sadie's bedside. "The worst is always quick, and look what comes of it."

I did look at the soft face again. I rubbed my fingers over him. He felt like silk. I took the small, new human out to meet his family. They dubbed him Gilbert Jr. on the spot.

And none of the men would ever understand what lay behind that door.

The wedding proceeded according to plan after harvest. Sadie wore her creamy woolen gown with glee and didn't even fuss when she saw me in my yellow and green kirtle. She proclaimed me the prettiest bride's attendant ever. Gilbert stood atop the church steps with rapt expression and waited for his bride as she approached.

Thanks to Alice's excellent ministrations, Sadie had recovered quickly. At first Sadie balked at the daily cleansing of her wounds, fearing demons might enter through the water, but Alice insisted too many young women died of infections caused by such ridiculous superstitions, and she would have none of it. Thus my sister climbed the stairs with light and cheerful strides to stand next to her groom.

I took note again of Alice's wisdom. Before I sought employment at the castle, I would learn all I could from the woman.

The tall, rotund Father John was a bit tipsy, but at his most eloquent because of it, and so gave the loveliest wedding speech. "'Love', my dear sheep, 'is patient and kind. It is not prideful. It is not selfish. It always hopes. It always believes. It always forgives. Love never gives up.' Yes, my flock, this is the true nature of love, and our marital love is but a beautiful symbol of God's own love for His bride, the Holy Church."

He swung wide his arms in his black robe.

I held back a chuckle at his theatrical display.

"A bride without spot or wrinkle He will come to claim someday. So be ye ready for Him, and remember through the love of these two precious children, His incredible love for you. 'For now we see darkly, as a poor reflection in a mirror, but someday we shall indeed see Him face to face. Now these three remain,' I tell thee, 'faith, hope, and love, but the greatest of these is love.'" Friar John, as we so often called him, flowed neatly from his own sermon into the traditional ceremony.

Sadie glowed as Gilbert repeated the timeless words.

The speech left me misty eyed.

Afterwards, William caught me for a few kisses out behind the chapel. "When shall I see you walking up the church steps to marry me, my princess?" He nuzzled my neck with the manly prickles of his chin, clouding my thinking.

I shook my head to regain my senses and smacked his arm. "William, behave. I'm a mere sixteen years old. I have plans and dreams to attend to. We've plenty of time for marriage."

That odd sense of being watched flashed over me again. The cold shiver crept up my spine as it had so many times throughout the years. Perhaps I *should* be afraid. I rubbed my hands over the prickles on my arms.

Father John's chuckle offered distraction.

"Ahh, you must forgive the boy, Dandelion. A wedding makes us all a bit wistful. I must confess that I would gladly marry my beloved Alice on this day if my vows permitted." Friar John's bulbous nose and tonsured scalp glowed red from too much wine. His hair stuck out about his head in comical white tufts.

In the seven years since he arrived, Friar John kept our sleepy village amply entertained, both in church and outside of it. He had tried the austere existence of a friar early in his career and kept the nickname for its musical quality, although he took a position in a wealthy parish soon after he realized the pauper's path was not for him. He did, however, hold to the tradition of the friar with his inspirational, albeit long-winded, sermons in our native tongue to supplement his rattled Latin mass.

I couldn't help but ask, "Friar John, if you had it all to do over again, would you still become a priest?"

"Now that's a difficult one, lassie. I do so love my work. I can't imagine what else I might have done." The friar's sky blue eyes grew moist.

William gave me a little squeeze from behind.

I lightened the moment. "Why, you could have been a player. You have a flair for drama. I'd bet you could have put on the best morality plays in all of England."

Friar John sniffled and caught my cheerful mood. "But could a player's wages keep me so lavishly supplied with wine and ale as the holy church? I think not. Come, children, I hear a barrel of my finest calling me."

Alice rounded the corner just then with her plump, pink face and a generous rear to match. Her merry laughter rang out as she looped her arm in the friar's. "Looks to me as if you've had quite enough ale already, my dear. But the minstrels are warming up. Do you think it is permissible for a devout and upstanding priest to dance with his spinster housekeeper on a day such as this? It would be a fine display of Christian compassion."

He wiggled his brows at her. "That it would, indeed."

"You two are incorrigible. Will no one behave properly today?" I swatted William again for good measure.

He snatched my hand and pulled it to his lips. "What say you, Alice? Dandy suggests that Friar John abandon the priesthood and join a group of traveling players."

She gave the friar's arm a squeeze. "There is no other life for our beloved John than that of a priest. Never have I met a man who so dearly loved his Savior nor his flock. " She smiled, but her eyes looked misty as well.

I looped my arm through William's, and we all walked toward the field where the celebration was beginning. The sun shone bright and glorious. It was a warm fall day and perfect for a party. The cold look William's mother shot my way did not for one moment phase me. Gilbert's brothers played merry tunes on their pipes and lutes. William swore they were as good as the castle minstrels, having had ample opportunity to visit the castle in the years his mother served there. He spun me around the field over and over again.

I was dizzy from happiness and twirling and ale by the time William led me down the path to our favorite rock by the river. "Kissing rock," Tim dubbed it the day he pushed us in the water. William and I cuddled together, my back against his chest, fitting as naturally as sun to sky. He played with my hair, twining his fingers through it, as he always loved to do. "Hast thou will to have the woman as thy wedded wife?" He echoed the words from the ceremony and answered himself most assuredly. "Yes sir."

I gave a pleasant moan.

"May thou well find at thy best to love her and hold ye to her and to no other to thy lives' end?" He answered himself again. "Yes sir."

I kissed his arm where it lay draped across my chest.

"Then take her by your hand and say after me." William turned me in his arms to grasp my hand in his. "I, William Ashby, take thee, Dandelion Dering, in form of the Holy Church to my wedded wife, forsaking all others, holding me wholly to thee, in sickness and in health, in riches and in poverty, in well and in woe, to death us depart, and thereto I plight my troth."

I looked up at his face and saw this was a life-changing moment for him. This was no child's game. I pressed my head against his shoulder and bit deep into my lip. Thankfully, our traditional ceremony did not require me to respond.

I loved him—didn't I? But I wasn't ready to make the same devout promises about poverty and woe. I just wanted to sit with him on our rock, perhaps not until death parted us, but most certainly on that glorious autumn afternoon in the sun.

Chapter 4

"A monster lurking nearby the castle, fancy that." Tim's eyes drooped as he sat before the fire listening to the end of William's tale of the famed hero Beowulf and the fierce Grendel. Even through several generations and William's amateur telling of it, the poem retained rich Saxon language, rhythm, and alliteration that near lulled me toward sleep as well.

Robert nudged his younger brother. "Ah, but perhaps it is not a story. Perhaps a monster lurks near Arun Castle as well."

I snuggled deeper into William's arms next to the cozy fire in our hut and plucked at a russet string on his fine woolen tunic.

"More likely the monster hides within." William kissed my brow, then unexpectedly jumped toward Tim and growled.

Tim startled, and we all burst into laughter.

"Shh." I batted William's leg. "You'll wake Mum and Da. Let them rest. Da's joints do ache so this time of year."

"The infusions you've been making help a good bit, Dandelion." Robert nodded to the pallet spread across the floor in the far corner. The old peasant folks had drifted off while William told his tale. "I haven't seen Da sleep this well in years."

"You know, William," Tim said. "Family legend has it that we descended from some Saxon nobility not unlike your Beowulf."

"True." Robert's eyes shone with pride in the firelight. "One of the only stories Da ever told us, and by far the best."

I remembered that balmy summer night beneath the stars like it was yesterday. The night I first discovered my family had a surname—Dering.

"Little one." Robert gave Tim's shoulder a pat. "I think it's time we head to bed as well." Robert and Tim shared a pallet, but with Sadie married, I now had my own small one between my parents and the boys. William had supplied me with extra blankets to replace my sister's warmth. Just for this one winter, he had said with a wink.

"I suppose that's my hint I should be going." William hugged me tighter to him.

"No, no. Stay as long as you like. That wind will take a body's breath away." Robert shivered at the thought. "I don't blame you if you want to stay by the hearth a while longer."

"And the company's not bad." William nuzzled my curls.

I sighed and rubbed his arms.

"Just behave. I'm trusting you two." Robert wagged his finger at us.

As if William and I could get ourselves into any trouble here. I grinned.

The boys moved to the far end of the one-room hut and stripped off their worn outer tunics, readying themselves for bed.

"So Saturday is the big day." I turned to look at William and walked my fingers up his strong, sculpted chest. Such physical farm work did have its advantages. "Off to your grand adventure in London. I wish I could go with you." I couldn't believe winter had nearly past. William and his oldest brother Geoffrey would be back before plowing season began.

"That would be highly inappropriate. But who knows, maybe next year at this time . . . ."

I grinned. "Who knows? Now that I think of it, though, I can't imagine sleeping outdoors in this miserable weather."

"Perhaps we shall find an inn or two along the way. And there are other ways of keeping warm, my pretty."

I giggled.

"What shall I bring you from my trip?"

"Hmm." I pretended to consider the question, although well I knew the answer. "How about a wimple of fine fabric. I might not be a maiden forever. Someday soon, I might require the head covering of a married woman."

He kissed my temple. "No need for your trickery, my princess. Rest assured we shall cry the banns and make it official upon my return. I will bring you three wimples if you like and perhaps some shiny trinket for your finger. We'll be ready in time for a lovely spring wedding. "

"Oh, William. Have I told you how much I adore you?"

"Adore me?"

I looked deep into his golden-brown eyes. I could drown in those depths. Unable to resist, I pressed my lips to his with a moan.

Our steamy embraces may have cooled over the months, but they mellowed into something more tender and meaningful. I was no longer so hot to join with him, but I was filled with a subtler desire to be one with him in body, mind, and soul—to remove that slight space of otherness between us and become as close as two humans physically could. I longed to feel growing within my body a small human constructed of William and me and love. Over the winter something had gradually shifted in my way of thinking. I no longer hid from myself the truth—my heart had belonged to William since childhood. Now seventeen, I felt ready to give myself to him without reservation.

"I don't just adore you, William. I love you. I love you with all my being."

He closed his eyes as if to savor the moment. "Mmm." William smiled and kissed me again. "That's what I was hoping to hear. I love you too, my sweet, more than you can ever imagine."

I turned my back to his chest again and settled within his arms, not wanting him to see my happy tears. "So a spring wedding it shall be. And who knows, maybe I'll have my position at the castle by then. Life is good."

William tensed. "Dandelion, truly, I don't want you applying for a position at the castle. I only jested in part. That place is evil. Lady Worthing went a bit daft when her husband died, and when her younger son joined him in the grave, she lost all vestiges of humanity."

"Surely she's not so bad, William. Servants do love to complain about their masters."

"Perhaps. But I can take care of you. You needn't work yourself to exhaustion."

I frowned. "Your mother might want some say in this. I swear that woman hates me. She might not want me about the house day after day."

"Don't worry yourself about my mother. I can handle her. She'll adjust. Before long we'll have our own home. And you can start a little business if you like. Your handiwork is so skilled these days."

The thought did appeal to me, but it wasn't so simple. "Shall I sell my embroidered kerchiefs and tablecloths to the villagers? They're not likely to part with their hard earned coin for such fripperies."

"I'll take you to Chichester when I sell my produce. We shall set up a little stand for your wares. Why, you'll be the talk of the town."

Not a bad idea in truth, but William knew I longed to serve at the castle, had thought of little else for years. I bristled in his arms as a concern crossed my mind. "Would you prevent me from working at the castle then? Is this to be a condition of our betrothal?"

He rubbed my stiff shoulders. "Don't be ridiculous. I know you far too well to try to stand in the way of your dreams. But I wish you would consider my caution. I fear naught but regrets await you at that castle."

I relaxed a bit and smiled. How silly of me to worry. I always had been able to win William over to my wishes. "I will consider it, William, but I doubt I shall change my mind."

"Of course." He sighed his resignation. "I'm sure it shall all work out. Together we can face any obstacle." He kissed me once again. "But I really should be going."

I hugged his arms around me and held tight. "Please don't go. I can't bear to part."

He untangled his arms from mine and stood, setting me on my feet as well. "Not much longer, my sweet. Not much longer, and I shall never let you out of my arms."

I walked him to the door and wrapped myself around him to snatch a few parting kisses. Indeed, I never wanted to let him go.

"Aren't you going to wish me luck?" I stood at the edge of William's field that spring, wearing my prettiest pink kirtle laced tight on the sides over a lilac tunic. The air smelled of fresh-turned soil.

He stopped plowing and gave me a hard look. "Why should I?

"Perhaps because this is the most significant day of my life."

"I've made it very clear. I don't want you working in that Godforsaken castle."

I was about to tease him for being silly, still jealous of Lord Thomas Worthing, but I stopped short. William's glare displayed he was in no mood for jests. We had yet to cry the banns as he promised. Tears stung my eyes. I walked to him and rested my head against his chest, seeking familiar comfort. He faltered several times before placing his arm around my back. All winter long we had joked and laughed, told stories and sang songs while nestled by the fire.

That was before his trip to London six weeks ago. He climbed into the wagon next to his brother Geoffrey full of dreams of big city life, but returned two weeks later, a completely different person and hauntingly alone. Geoffrey, long the head of the family, caught a mysterious illness while visiting their merchant brothers in London, and there he died.

Of course, I expected William to reach to me for solace, but instead he shut me out. I couldn't fathom why. Why was he so cold and harsh? Had his mother turned him against me? I wished I could talk to his brother Ralph, but he had always held me at a distance. Now William pushed me away as well. It didn't make any sense. I hated pondering it, and so I had focused on preparations for my interview instead, but he seemed not to notice at all.

I braced myself and continued. "William, you're the one who told me such wonderful tales about the castle."

"Those stories were from my childhood. It's different now, and it's no place for the likes of you."

I jerked away. "I suppose you shan't be giving me a kiss for good luck then."

"Not likely. I have more important things to do."

That rude boy returned to his plowing.

I will not cry. I turned and walked toward the castle full of resolve. This was my big day, and I would not let William spoil it. The winter of 1315 yet haunted me, and the desires it stirred never left. I was willing to start as chambermaid and work my way up, hoping to someday rise to cook or housekeeper, even lady's maid or tutor. I would love teaching children as Friar John once taught me.

Of course, it would be years before the need arose. The younger

Worthing son, George, had not long survived the war in Scotland, and Lord Thomas Worthing seemed in no rush to start a family. When not on the battlefield, he lived at court in the favored company of the new young king, Edward III. It appeared he was too busy for marriage, although not, if rumor held true, for dalliance with the many noble women there.

I waved to a group of children playing hoodman's blind as I passed back through the village. The entire shire waited for Lord Worthing's return. While hot-blooded and arrogant to the core, Thomas Worthing was known to be a fair man, a man of his word and not without compassion. His tyrannical mother had ruled far too long. That he should run off to war with no heir in place was unthinkable. He should marry and come home to tend his estate. Like many other girls, I had allowed myself to dream of Lord Worthing. William was correct about that.

I continued with determined strides along the lane as it curved and climbed the hill.

Destiny awaited.

The castle lay before me now—the castle of my dreams, the castle that would one day be Lord Thomas Worthing's in truth as well as name. I imagined he remembered me; that he fell in love with me on that most significant day long ago when he gave me a coin and a piece of candy. The day I first awoke to a world of color and wonder.

Ludicrous. Indeed, my life would never be complete without my William. I would make my way in the world through hard work with William by my side. Thoughts of Lord Worthing were naught but fanciful musing. I shook them off as I reached the outer wall.

Eyes peered from atop the crenellated tower. I nodded to the guard.

My old friend Michael, the teetering, grandfatherly steward, met me at the gate.

"God give you good day," I called.

"And you as well." He winked at me. "Quite a big day it is."

I wished he could assign me work himself, but he lasted so many years only by deferring to the iron will of his mistress. He dared not hire me without her approval. The powerful women held all our fates in her hands.

Michael and I passed through the inner bailey and entered the immense great hall. Although I oft baked bread in the giant ovens outdoors, I had never entered the castle proper before. Clean and elegant, it smelled of the fresh, herb-strewn rushes upon the floor. The long trek through the corridor past fine tapestries, gilded vases, and polished armor took my breath away—but confirmed every suspicion about life inside the castle. I stroked my trembling hand against the gray stone wall, from the inside at last.

I never wanted to leave.

Taking a deep breath of the perfumed air, I followed the steward up the grand marble stairway. When we reached the lady's chamber, he mouthed, "God go with you."

I gulped down a lump filling my throat.

Lady Catherine Worthing sat looking out a window from her cushioned velvet chair. Smooth fabric in a surprising icy shade of blue hung from the walls. A brilliant oriental carpet like those in stories covered the floor. Her youthful appearance amazed me. I supposed she was late in her thirties, and yet her skin looked as beautiful and unlined as a village teen. Her face was sharp and pale but striking, and her long black hair, uncovered here in her private chamber, displayed only sprinkled wisps of silver. Our women were past their prime by twenty-five and generally gray and withered at her age.

I pressed my lips together to keep my mouth from gaping.

Yet another wonder hidden behind the castle walls.

Lady Worthing's everyday dress was made of the softest red wool. She wore an elegant over-tunic of some shimmering diaphanous material, clasped at the front with a richly jeweled brooch in the fierce Worthing dragon motif. Silken slippers adorned her feet, yet she sat unconscious of her finery—and of the fact its price could feed hundreds of people for months. She wore her privilege and wealth as casually as her expensive clothing, never giving thought to all those who would kill to be in her place, who likely died to put her there.

Somehow, I felt sure she neither knew, nor cared. To her we were merely drones, worker bees to keep her so lavishly bedecked. It was simply the natural order of things. I gazed at her petite pinky finger, the one with which she could easily crush me. The trembling in my own hands increased.

She turned from the window to acknowledge me. Lady Worthing gave one glance down her long tapered nose and seemed to take an instant dislike. "We have no position for dirty little peasant girls right now. Perhaps when we need a scullery maid to empty the chamber pots and scrub the pig troughs we shall look you up, but I doubt it."

Chapter 5

I couldn't suppress my gasp. I washed in the stream not hours ago, and I was sure the steward had put in a good word for me. The woman hadn't so much as asked my name. "But your ladyship," I said in all innocence, "did the steward not tell you, I can read and write, keep accounts, sew, and cook? I'm a very hard worker. Father John will vouch for me."

"You impudent little chit. How dare you question me?"

My heart sank within my chest. "I'm sorry, ma'am. I thought you didn't know who I was."

"Oh, I know who you are well enough. I see what's going on from this window. I know your type." Her contempt grew as she studied me. "You think curly blonde hair and a pretty smile will take you anywhere you want to go. You are worthless to me—beyond worthless, with your uppity airs and gaudy clothes."

I looked down at the pink kirtle I had dyed and stitched myself with the utmost love and care, but even I couldn't overlook the coarseness of the cheap flaxen fabric. I hid one bare foot beneath the other.

Lady Worthing's arsenal still held more. "And aren't you the very one who has been bedding down with the knights? Have you a favorite, or is it a different one every evening for the likes of you?"

My eyes grew huge. I pulled the collar of my kirtle up about my neck.

"Oh, so then that's how it is," the lady said with a suggestive lift of her sharp eyebrows.

The slander to my virtue made no sense at all. I had never heard of the depravity this wicked woman implied, but I continued with my plea, even as my voice choked in my throat. "Surely you have mistaken me for someone else, ma'am. As I mentioned, I am a well-educated young woman. I'm an excellent worker, and I come with very good references."

"You think reading and writing make you special. Why I've seen trick ponies do as much. You were born a cheap slovenly slattern, and you will ever remain one if I have my way."

Tears stung my eyes, but I would never give her the satisfaction. "With all due respect ma'am, if you would but give me a chance—"

"A chance, a chance for what? To have you seducing my guards for favors and ribbons? Look at you. You disgust me. Take her away," she shouted.

Thus ended my dream.

I spent the next three days crying near the riverbank, pressed against the warm rock where William had kissed me last summer, listening to the river trickle along with my tears. I dreamed of him whisking me in his arms. Of drowning my pain deep in his warmth and strength. The brush of his lips lifting me from my despair. But he never left his blasted plow long enough to offer so much as a word of sympathy.

Alice and Sadie came to me, but they were no comfort. They assured me Lady Worthing was a bitter, jealous old woman who couldn't handle competition from a pretty servant girl. Perhaps it was true, likely it was true, but it brought me no closer to my ambition of living in the castle. Alice promised there were plenty of castles where I might seek employment within a few days' travel, but they may as well lie on the moon.

Lady Worthing's cruel and thoughtless words had crushed me to the core. William did not jest when he described an insidious evil lurking within the castle walls. It lived and breathed in the very form of Lady Worthing. I should have felt relieved to be cast out from that place, but I could not. I couldn't live without that castle. It was branded upon my earliest memories.

Those memories from 1315, when I was a mere four years old.

The year of the great famine.

And a morning I would never forget.

Time, along with the green valley, faded about me. I found myself back in that horrid, frigid hut.

By that cold spring day during my fourth year of life, Da had arrived home at long last with a weary trudge and a small bag of grain, but he had yet to utter a word. Early in the morning, he grabbed up his hoe and dashed out the door as fast as his crippled legs could carry him, besieged with a need to beat life from the still frozen soil. Mum had rallied from the strange delirium which held her bound since the birth of Baby Tim, but only enough to stifle sobs with her fist and gaze forlornly at the remnants of her family from her pallet in the corner. I huddled near the hearth with my brother Robert, my head buried in his chest and bottom pressed to the frigid earthen floor, far too numb for tears myself.

A knock upon the door startled me. Eight-year-old Sadie opened it, and there stood the local reeve, the liaison between the castle and our peasant village. He stared into Robert's gaunt cheeks and hollow eyes from safe outside the doorway.

Sadie placed her hands atop her bony hips. "Yes, sir," she said, jarring the reeve from his discomfort.

He focused upon her dirty, freckled face instead. "Uh, yes, um . . . as you surely know, his lordship was recently killed on campaign. Lady Worthing requests all villagers assemble in the main street, to see how they fared the winter and plan for the year to come."

With a sassy tilt of her head, Sadie said, "We know little here, sir, except our own misery, but thank you anyway."

The reeve looked at his feet until Sadie took mercy and slammed the door. I found a long-lost giggle to reward my precocious sister. She alone had tended us during much of that haunting season. After wrapping Robert, Baby Tim, and me in whatever brown rags she could find, Sadie led us to the door for the first time since fall. Mum held Tim and sagged heavily against Sadie as they stepped out of our dim little hut with its mud walls and dingy thatched roof.

Then came my turn. For a moment, the light was too bright and everything went dark. I shaded my eyes and squinted against the glare. My vision cleared, and despite the icy, waste-filled muck clinging to my bare feet, I stood gaping at a sky the color of cornflowers and a flamboyant golden sun. Even the pure white clouds were food for my color-starved eyes. The village around me was dreary like our hut but, looking up, something sparked, awakened in my soul, something akin to hope or even joy.

As we took our place in the depleted gathering of villagers, bundled in their drab mantles and hoods, the castle gates sprang apart and out poured a profusion of colors as a carriage emerged and rolled toward me.

It pulled to a stop, and a footman in matching livery jumped down. He opened the door, and the noble family descended, flooding me with an entire world of rapturous shades. I barely knew the categories of red, blue, green, and yellow to separate them and bring some order to my over-stimulated senses.

And the textures, the fabrics—soft, lush, and deep, so unlike the rough flax chafing at my skin. Oh, how I longed to run my fingers against them. Roused from a bad dream, I knew this world of beauty was where I belonged. Every fiber within me tingled, crying out to join this optical dance.

Spellbound, I was drawn to the lady's velvet gown with sparkling silver threads. As the reeve heralded her, I started my limitless journey forward, tiny fingers outstretched—one step, two, even three before Sadie noticed and jerked me back. Lady Catherine Worthing addressed the villagers, but I heard not a word. I marveled at the unbelievable, warm ripple of fox fur peeking out from the lady's cape, as I stood shivering in the mud.

A whine sounded over her speech. "I'm hungry." It came from the plump, healthy face of a young lord, about my own age, although twice my girth. It took a moment for the meaning of the word *hungry* to register, so out of context, so forbidden the reference to the scratching of bird claws in our bellies all winter.

"Hungry?" I whispered up to Robert, only to be shushed.

The little lord now stamped his foot. "I'm hungry, hungry, hungry."

My temper flared, and I clenched my fist as an even plumper servant woman quieted his chant with a pink object from her pocket. His pinched, red face softened as she popped it in his mouth. His round cheeks molded about the heavenly treat. My own face must have betrayed my contempt, because the older of the richly clad boys now gazed directly at me, his eyes filled with amusement. He stood next to his mother, at that very moment being proclaimed the new Earl of Worthing.

The numbing drone of her ladyship's speech flew by me as I fought my way through an assaulting blaze of ideas and emotions. I didn't realize the adolescent earl had edged his way around the crowd until he stood but inches away, inconspicuously offering me something shiny and pink, pilfered from the servant woman's obliging pockets.

"Ahem," he said.

I looked up in wide-eyed wonder at the divine embodiment hidden in his hand—a pink sugarcoated candy. Truly, I never imagined anything so fabulous. What should I do?

After another, "Ahem," and a quick glance in my direction, he opened his hand to make the offer clear.

I reached out and took the candy. I swear to this very day that it buzzed and pulsed in my palm, that it glowed between my fingers as I held still to enjoy the mere possession of the object. When I raised it to my lips, I nearly dropped in a swoon from the intense burst of flavor. Sweet and sour mingled upon a tongue accustomed to nothing more than bland vegetables and gruel.

Once the speech ended, the young gallant turned and fell to one knee before me. Dark, wavy hair swung across his smooth brow in the most enchanting way, contrasting with eyes as blue as the day's clear sky. A dusting of amber freckles added the perfect touch to his boyish charm. He gave no regard to his emerald velvet hose and fine leather boots soaking in the mud. He clasped my hand and said in a voice rich as honey, "I beseech you, pretty maiden, deign to tell me the name of this delicate blossom I have the honor of serving this day."

Although I laughed at his antics, his elegant request left me baffled. Sadie's poke in the ribs did not help, for I had no notion what he wanted. And then came the greatest wonder on that wondrous day.

"Her name is Dandelion, my lord. Named her myself after the fairest flower in yonder fields." My father came up behind us and said each word with nary a stutter and amazing pride.

"Thank you, my good man. An apt name it is." The earl tugged at my curls. Even months of filth could not hide the beauty of my golden tresses. "You, little one, have brought me great joy on this sad day." Pulling a coin magically from my ear, he placed it in my hand. "Eat well tonight, my little Dandelion, and perhaps tomorrow shall be a brighter day."

"Look, Da." I held up the silver groat as the young Lord Worthing turned his attention to the press of villagers.

Da bent over to hug me. "Oh, my b-b-bonny child, in a month I did not earn as much as you did this day."

Late that evening in the heavy darkness, pressed tight between Sadie and Robert, I whispered again and again the word, "Hungry, hungry, hungry," although for once I was not. I thought everyone asleep, until I heard muffled sobs coming from my parents' pallet. I closed my mouth in silent shame.

So help me God, I would never return to that mire of browns and grays, and would most-assuredly never go hungry again.

I turned my eyes to gaze upon the bright vale surrounding me, filled with yellow buttercups, red poppies, purple foxgloves, blue cornflowers. Bees and butterflies frolicked among their colorful blossoms. Their scents wafted about me, a riot of sweet perfumes to match their stunning visual display. Across the rolling river sat the hillside where William had promised to build me a cottage.

How could he just ignore me here as I wept? He of all people should understand, having lost his own father during that haunting famine year. We had fought for a better life together. I had nearly arrived. Only to have it all snatched away.

And where was that stupid, careless boy? Piously hard at work, or happy to see me struck down with nowhere to run but him? Did he even know what happened? Did he care? Surely he realized I needed him to scoop me up and kiss all my problems away.

Instead, it was Friar John who at last pulled me out of my dark place with one of his brilliant, if somewhat hypocritical speeches.

He emerged from the wooded path with determined strides.

"Ah, lassie," he said, picking up my crumpled form in one clean swoop and setting me on my feet. "It's time to be up about your business once again. As the Holy Book says, 'There is a time to mourn and a time to dance.' So put on your dancing shoes, for you've wasted quite enough tears on that Godforsaken tomb of a castle."

"But all I ever wanted was to work at the ca-ca-castle." I hiccupped through my tears.

"The love of money is the root from which all evil springs. Why, look at Judas Iscariot. He betrayed our very Lord and Savior for a few talents of silver. Scandalous, I tell you. But I've seen a look about you, Dandelion, when you think no one is watching—staring up at the castle with lust in your eyes, like a starving person or a man obsessed with a woman. It will be your downfall if you let it, child. I tell you true, it's a blessing they rejected you, the very salvation of your soul, for which I've prayed."

My tears stopped, but my jaw dropped at his final comment. How dare he?

"Ah, you thought I didn't know," Friar John said. "It is not our blessed Lord and Savior you believe in half so much as that blasted stone castle." He pointed toward the object of his disdain. "But it is a house built on shifting sands. When the winds blow, it will be shaken away."

I crossed my arms over my chest as anger welled up hot inside of me. "That is where you're wrong, Father. The castle has stood for hundreds of years. It is our pathetic little huts and your own wooden house that will likely fall with the next strong wind."

"Ah, but, child, I speak not of earthly winds and storms, but of the wind and fire of the very Holy Spirit of God. When it touches you, you shall be forever changed, whether set alight or smoldered to ashes. There's no escaping its powerful grasp."

His words struck a chord, but I wouldn't admit it. I raised my chin. "You see fit to pray for my soul?"

"Aye, that I do, lassie. It's clear you find me unworthy, but with all my shortcomings, I understand my need for a Savior more than most. Young William prays for your salvation as well, and never a purer lad have I met."

"Indeed, Father. I was baptized. I keep the sacraments and attend mass. Is this not sufficient to save my soul as the church teaches?" I clenched my jaw.

He shook his hands above his head like the fiery preacher he was. "If thou shall confess with thy mouth and believe in thy heart, you shall be saved."

"Well, I believe you are a pair of cursed fools," I shouted at the priest. "William's thrilled I have nothing better to do with my life than marry the miserable likes of him."

"Now, now, Dandy. William bears his own cross of late. It's you who should be tending him, in my opinion. William and I both knew the answers to your problems did not lie behind those walls, and we both prayed you would be saved from yourself."

"You and William and your blasted prayers can go to the devil." I stomped away but heard him chuckling softly. I was so mad I could spit—but I wasn't crying anymore. I would deal with William soon enough.

Chapter 6

"William. Oh, William." I attempted a light tone as I called to him. It didn't help that he had stripped down to his short breeches and open shirt, looking more well-muscled and manly than ever on this warm spring day. My heart did a little flip. He stopped plowing and mopped off his brow with the back of his arm. Several weeks now passed, and still he avoided me. "Please, William, you need a rest. I've brought some water and an apple and your favorite book. Come read poetry to me beside the river like the old days."

"It's not the old days anymore, and well you know it."

"Please, oh please. Just for a few moments."

"Really, Dandy, it's time you grow up and get to work yourself. We're not children anymore, and life is not the bed of flowers you fancy it to be. The earth may well be the center of the universe, but you most certainly are not."

Not letting his comments deter me, I pressed against him and ran my finger over his rippled chest. He smelled of warm moist soil. I knew how to change his mood. "Come now, you know how I adore flowers. Flowers . . . and poetry . . . and kisses—kisses by the river with my best beau."

He laughed, an eerily hollow laugh. "Oh, enough. It is hot, and I could use a break. It's high time we talk, but you'll not earn my kisses so easily today." He pushed me away.

Blinking back tears, I handed him the water, which he downed before chomping on his apple and heading to the path.

"Fine," I said. "I have a few things to discuss with you as well. You've barely spoken to me in weeks."

"I have much on my mind. Issues you know nothing about." He kept his eyes focused ahead.

A spark of anger replaced my sadness. "Well, why don't you explain them to me? I'm truly not so dense."

"You are many things, but we all know dense is not one of them." He took another noisy chomp. "It's . . . well, I'm not quite sure how to explain."

"Oh." I waited for him to go on, but I was met by silence. "Come, William, we must keep talking. I'm still grieved you weren't there for me when I was cast from the castle. I cried for days, and you didn't even care."

"Of course I cared, but it's for the best, and you know it. You just didn't want to hear it. So, I had nothing to say."

"For the best." As that spark of anger flamed to a bonfire in my chest, I stopped and swung him around to face me. "How dare you suggest such a thing? I know nothing of the sort. I did it for both of us. Lord knows, I'm sick of your family treating me like some sort of rodent. If I secured a position at the castle, they wouldn't care that my parents are poor cottars or how small my dowry is. They would have accepted me then, and we could have been married."

"Why you stupid, arrogant, shallow little girl." He threw off my arm. "Tell me that isn't what you think. Tell me after all these years you know better."

"Better than what? It's true, every word." I smacked him against the chest. "Maybe you're the one who's too stupid to see it."

"Dandelion Dering, my family doesn't look at you oddly because you're poor." He turned away and raked his fingers through his hair. "They know you are smart and funny and beautiful. If you're good enough for me, you're good enough for them, and that is God's own truth."

I had endured their shabby treatment for years. He wasn't making any sense. "Then why? Explain it to me this instant."

He looked deep into my eyes. His anger faded, and he sounded sad, so sad, sadder than I had heard him in years. "They treat you that way because they're afraid. They're so afraid, and so am I."

His statement drew the air right out of my lungs. I took a step back. "Afraid of what? This is ridiculous. I'm just a girl."

"Afraid you'll break my heart."

I gasped for breath. I dropped down onto the nearest patch of grass alongside the path and choked out the words, "But why?"

"They think you only want me because I'm the best you can find. They think the moment someone richer, or smarter, or more successful comes along, you'll be gone quick as lightning."

"And you don't even defend me?" I loved William dearly, yet there was a shadow of truth to his words.

"It's right there in your eyes. You're so terribly ambitious. I'm not saying I blame you. I love you. You're my matching half, my reason for living. But it scares me. It scares me near to death."

He joined me in the grass, and we both sat silently.

I watched a bee hard at work collecting nectar for honey, caught in its tedious flight, flying round and round from blossom to blossom. So much like the worker bees in Lady Worthing's hive. It wearied me as I listened to it buzz and drone. It alit upon a golden-topped dandelion and sucked the juice right out.

I blinked away the image. "It will be okay. It will all work out. I love you too. Truly, I do, and you have a bright future ahead of you. You could still get work in the castle, or we could move to London with your brothers. I'll open a little shop like Alice always wanted. It will be all right," I said, crying now.

I pulled his face to me and kissed him. "It will all work out, William," I said as I cried and kissed his face.

He gathered me tight to him and kissed me full on the mouth.

It was a desperate kiss, the loneliest kiss I ever experienced. It felt for all the world like a kiss good-bye.

I looked up and saw tears in his eyes too. "What's wrong? Talk to me, please."

"But, the problem is . . . ." He let go of me and paused for a long, long time. "I'm not so sure it will be okay. Not after you hear what I need to tell you."

My hands still clung to his cheeks. "What? Say it. Whatever it is, we'll work it out. I promise."

He dragged his face away. "I don't know if we can."

"Can what?"

His mood shifted. He was anger and tears all at once. "Can survive staying here and working in these fields for the rest of our lives."

A buzzing began in my ears, so much like the droning bees. "But why? Why would we have to survive that? You're being silly now. The world is changing and expanding every day. We're not tied to the land the way our ancestors were. The world is full of opportunities." I grabbed his arm. "The rising middle class they call it, remember. We read a pamphlet. Look at your brothers. I know I wanted to live in the castle, but London will do just fine, as long as we're together."

He picked at the grass by his feet. "You don't understand. I don't want to live in London with the rats and the soot and the stinky, dirty streets. It's a disease-ridden hellhole."

My world began to dissolve, like our pathetic mud huts in the midst of a deluge. There had to be a way. "Fine then, not to London, south by the sea—on a ship—in Wales—in Italy—on the moon. I don't care where, as long as we're together." I threw myself against his back, embracing him from behind.

"You don't care where, as long as it's not here."

"But I would be thrilled for you to work at the castle." I murmured it against him, tasting the salt on his skin.

"Darn it, Dandy, you're not listening." He shook me off again. "You never listen. I'm not moving to London. I'm not going to be a clerk or a merchant or a bailiff in a castle. I'm going to live here, in this village, for the rest of my life and work that very field you dragged me away from."

"What in the world are you talking about?"

"If I don't stay here and sign papers to work the land, my family will lose it all. Not only me, but my brother and my nephews too, Geoffrey's children. When he died, everything changed. They're too young to sign for it, and Lady Worthing won't give an entire yardland to one grown son. Especially when she knows two of my brothers escaped her clutches. She'll cut us back to cottars just to spite them.

My father lived and died for that land. He taught me to cherish it. I can't let him down."

The desire to cling to him fled me. I pulled back, distancing myself from him and his horrifying words. "Then let your other brothers come back from London. They've had their fun. They've made their fortunes. For God's sake, it's your turn now."

"No, it will be me. It has been decided."

Blood rushed to my head, threatening to explode, and my hands began to shake. "But why in the world? It's just a stupid, muddy field. It's not even yours to own. Once we're settled, we'll send for your family. We'll not abandon them."

"But I love that stupid, muddy field. I love that field and the river and the forest surrounding it where we played as children. I love the little lane where my mother lives and your family and Friar John and Alice and everyone we care about in the world." He veritably flung the words at my face. "This village needs me. I don't want to move away, Dandy. Don't you understand? I don't want to work in a dreary office for the rest of my life. I can't, and I won't."

I scooted farther back from the assault. "You can and you will, William Ashby. You will if you love me. You will if you ever want to marry me."

"That's what we've been afraid of all these years."

"Shut up." I pressed my hands to my head to stop the ringing and the pain. Dark walls closed around me. I could barely breathe the smoky air. I stood up and took several deep gasps, still clutching my head. "Just shut up. Shut your idiotic mouth and let me think for a moment. You didn't sign the papers yet, did you? It's not too late, is it? William, tell me it's not too late."

He sat unswerving and stared me down. "I didn't sign them yet, but I've made up my mind. I will sign them, and there's nothing you can do to stop me."

"Like that . . . just like that you make a life-changing decision for both of us." My heart raced, like a war horse storming off to battle.

"This is what I've planned all along, Dandy, but you never wanted to hear it."

"What about me? I thought you wanted me." I sobbed, nearing hysteria. "I thought you loved me."

"I do. I do, but it's not that simple."

"Oh, it's quite simple. It's all about you and what you want and what you need. None of it is about me. I've been such a fool." Pain sliced through my brow, stabbing again and again like a dagger. I dragged precious woodland air into my lungs, but it tasted acrid and sooty in my mouth.

William bent over, shaking his head between his knees. "I'm going to say this once, knowing full well you'll never understand. This is not about duty or guilt. It certainly isn't about selfishness. I'm doing this because I prayed long and hard, and I know this is God's path for my life. I hope that you are a part of God's path for my life as well, but you have a decision to make. It is a hard one, and neither God nor I can make it for you."

I stood and paced in a circle, continuing our perverse courtship dance as the sky fell in above my head. Pressing my hands against it, I shoved it away. "I have a decision to make. Hah! You and your precious God have made all the decisions around here. What could possibly be left for me?"

"You know the truth now, every last bit of it." He rose to one knee in front of me and grasped my hands in his. The movement that should have been utterly romantic was aggressive and angry instead. "Dandelion Dering, will you marry me?"

Something shattered inside of me. Hunger pangs seized my stomach. "If you sign those papers, William, not only will I not marry you, I will never so much as speak to you again."

"I'm signing them. I've made up my mind. Will you marry me?"

I ripped my hands away with finality as I gasped for breath. "Don't do it, William. I'm warning you. Don't sign those papers."

"I'm signing them. Will you marry me?" He said it distinctly, loudly, one word at a time.

"If you do, I swear I will never forgive you." The birds scratched mercilessly at the pit of my belly. The giant, angry talons of a falcon. How much longer could I bear it?

"Dandelion," he said, standing but no longer shouting. He gripped me by the forearms and stared straight into my eyes. His voice was quiet as death. "I'm signing the papers. It's a simple question I'm asking. Will you marry me?"

"When hell freezes."

He let go of me.

I turned my back to him and stalked away.

Chapter 7

Unlike my pitiful weeping after being rejected from the castle, upon ending my relationship with William I remained in a dazed stupor for days—weeks—it could have been months or even years as far as I was aware. He had stirred so many awful sensations from my childhood. Being trapped on this land, trapped in these awful mud huts, the air filled with smoke and soot. Hungry, hungry, always so hungry. I could never return to him now. Instead I numbed my mind to the pain, moving ever forward, never back.

Somehow, I continued my normal routine on instinct. I must have behaved reasonably, because no one seemed to notice. William must not have mentioned our fight either, for nobody seemed aware. One night as Robert and Da shared a pint of ale in our small hut, I heard William's name and perked up; but they discussed the papers William signed that day, tying him to his damnable yardland for what could well be all eternity.

"We haven't seen much of William lately," Robert said. "I'm sure the decision weighed hard on him if he's managed to do without Dandy's cooking all these days. Don't you think so, Dandelion?" He said, taking note of my presence.

"William and I have parted ways." I heard myself mumble the words before standing up and walking out the door. Robert called to me several times, but I registered nothing, saw nothing. I just walked and walked, forward into the dusky night, silent as a ghost. Perhaps I was a ghost.

It was too much. My mind could not conceive it. Although I long fought my feelings, I could no longer imagine my life without William. Far beyond being my intended, he was my best friend, my playmate, my closest confidant. He was simply my William. Life contained no more right answers—only wrong ones anywhere I looked.

My heart lay dead within my chest, and so I floated as a ghost down the lane and into the forest. I had to escape that horrible, suffocating hut.

My feet led me to a strange dark path. I think I tripped and fell several times, but my feet kept moving and then running, onward into the night for hours. A small, detached part of myself wondered where they took me.

Finally, I stood on the edge of a precipice over fifty feet high. Sight and sound rushed back. I looked at my bare toes covered with blood and dirt, dangling over the edge. I took a deep breath of the cold night air, shivering in my muddy pink kirtle. In the shadowy moonlight I distinguished a pile of sharp boulders at the bottom of the cliff. Nearby I heard the joyful crash of a waterfall slamming against the rocks.

I know this spot. William brought me here once. It was miles from the village. However did I end up here? Did I come to remind myself of happier times? No, for surely my feet would have led me to kissing rock. Perhaps they planned for me to join the water in its joyful plunge to oblivion.

The thought appealed to me—one simple step over the edge. Eternity stretched before me. I wiggled my toes, feeling the cool air beneath them. There was nothing but air and space and rocks—hard, sharp rocks to crash my body upon.

Then the clouds parted, and the moon shone before me. It was huge that night, so full and glowing. I reached out to touch it. I longed to press my lips against it, but as I stretched forward, the ground shifted beneath my feet.

For a second lasting a lifetime, I debated my fate. *So this is what my feet intended—to float away into nothingness.* It would be so easy to end it all, to escape that horrid little village forever. But why did I wake at this precise moment when I might have fallen? Why did I now remember I had no reason to live? No employment, no castle, no William . . . and yet there was life within me still compelled to fight. With or without them, I would make a way for myself through this Godforsaken world of tears. And I would yet find love. I would do it. I could.

My feet stepped back even as pebbles and soil slid over the cliff. More seconds passed before I heard them hit the rocks far below. "It isn't too late. It isn't too late for anything," I said to the moon.

As instantly as I came to life, I realized how exhausted I was, bone weary and near collapsing. I stumbled backwards to a grove of trees and nestled myself into a soggy pile of leaves. Wrapped in a cold wet ball, I slept.

When I awoke, the sun was high. I assumed it was the next day but wasn't certain. Sitting up, a wave of dizziness overtook me, and for a moment the world went black. Fiery daggers stabbed my throat, and my head throbbed. This was no mere lover's pout, I was truly sick after my bizarre late-night trek. I tried to stand, but my legs buckled beneath me. In addition to my many scrapes and scratches, I saw a deep cut on my right calf, wide as my fist and throbbing to match my head. I couldn't remember how it got there. It was purple and angry, spreading into red streaks across my leg.

I surveyed my surroundings—a thick bier of trees, smelling of mildew, amazingly dark on this sunny day. A clear, bright blue sky peeked through the veil of green. Speckled shadows swirled in mesmerizing patterns as the leaves swayed in the breeze. Ancient, gnarled trunks mocked me with their weathered faces.

Some instinctual part of myself must have remembered the way home, but my conscious mind could not recall the paths. Last night I chose to live, but the realization emerged that now I might not make it after all. I spied a large, thick stick nearby and crawled to it. Managing to prop myself against a tree, I found I could hobble through the pain with the help of my makeshift staff. It would be slow going, but if I could determine the right direction . . . . The sun was overhead, not much help. I searched for landmarks, but could see nothing beyond the dense trees.

The joyful gurgle of the waterfall called to me again.

That's it.

If I could find a safe path down, I could follow the stream. It would surely take me to civilization. I stuck my tongue out at the fiendish trees and stumbled toward the cliff. I would make a way for myself. Find a road to a better life. Starting right here and right now.

Daylight revealed a winding pathway down the side of the cliff. I struggled, digging my stick deep into the ground with every step, my feet skittering all the way. My head pounded, and my vision blurred. Drops of cold sweat fell into my eyes, from exertion or fever, I wasn't sure. I attempted one more step, but it was one too many.

I tumbled, flailing down the path, then off it completely, plummeting the last ten feet to the ground. I landed with a thump upon a flat patch of dirt behind the jagged rocks. The pain seemed little worse than before I fell. However, my strength was gone, and I could barely lift my head.

Then my eye caught sight of a stray patch of blue cornflowers nearby—cornflowers like William twisted into a coronet for my head—cornflowers like the ring he placed on my finger. After two months, the floodgates opened and the tears flowed . . . prettily and daintily at first . . . then in wails and moans and torrents.

Hoof beats were upon me before I noticed them.

I froze, knowing not whether to scream or rejoice. Cold terror and warm relief fought for dominance in my chest. High atop the rocks, a large shadow sat upon the even larger one of a mammoth warhorse. The dark beast snorted its annoyance at this interruption to its lovely afternoon jaunt as the human figure dismounted.

I must have looked like a madwoman, but as he walked to me, the man showed no fear. He appeared a knight by his height and broad shoulders, although he wore simple brown leggings and tunic. His hair was cropped short with a sprinkling of silver throughout. His face was stoic but not unkind, with a strong, square jaw—a deadly serious face, lined with worry and grief more than age. A handsome face in its own way. I couldn't recall seeing it before, although his deep brown eyes were familiar. Warmth won the battle raging within as relief overtook me.

I tried to speak, to ask who he was and however he had found me. The daggers in my throat were merciless. The man motioned for me to relax but uttered not a sound. His hands searched my body. I was again tempted to panic, but he went about it with such methodical efficiency, I realized he merely checked for injuries. He nodded until he came to the gash on my leg. Then he frowned and placed the back of his hand to my forehead. His frown deepened, but he shook it off and gave a small smile, no doubt remembering my resonant screams moments earlier.

My self-appointed healer lifted me into his huge gentle arms, and I sighed against his chest. He carried me to the stream's edge and proceeded to rinse my wound. He poured clear, frigid water over my leg until it grew less purple and angry. He wrapped it with a clean white cloth from his satchel and used another to rinse my face and neck. Lifting my head, he put a flask of water to my mouth.

I took a few painful sips.

The man shot a sharp whistle to his horse, and the grand stallion obeyed.

Trotting over from a tasty patch of clover, the horse shook his head in complaint, his graceful mane swinging. Then the beast looked at me with searching eyes, with sympathy if possible, and understood his master's intent. The man lifted me from the ground and, securing me with one arm, mounted the great beast. Unlike the few battered workhorses I'd sat upon, this one exuded power, strength, even intelligence. Though taller than most women, I was thin and lithe, and doubted the horse even felt my extra weight.

The man pulled me tighter to his chest. He guided the horse through the rocks and then on through the forest. Before long we reached a broad path. The horse settled into a comfortable canter. I took a deep breath and closed my eyes, not at all concerned about where he might be taking me. Rocked smoothly, sweetly as a babe in a cradle, my aching body relaxed, knowing somehow I had found the road I was searching for. Soon I was sound asleep.

I awoke as the gentle man pulled me from his horse. The scenery looked familiar. The worn, gray stones of Arun Castle surrounded me, although I had never seen them from this angle before. We were in a corner near a tall circular tower. My rescuer carried me around the side and ducked through a doorway. It was dark, but I no longer feared anything in the arms of this sweet and caring giant. After several spins up a spiral staircase, we reached a landing at the top.

As he opened the door, I gasped. Just when I thought this day could grow no stranger, I was transported to some glimmering paradise. The walls and floor were simple gray stone, but they were swathed with shimmering silken fabric in a soft rainbow of soothing colors. Spicy colors, spices from some distant land—cinnamon, curry, chili, and paprika, accented with a deep eggplant purple. Plush rugs fringed with twisted silken threads lay scattered in a pleasing arrangement about the apartment. A refreshing breeze blew through several big open windows into the sunny, circular room. My rescuer carried me to a wooden bench topped with an embroidered crimson cushion and gingerly settled me upon it. I thought I rested on a cloud.

Noticing still a greater wonder upon the opposite wall, I bolted upright, but regretted moving as pain cut through my head. The man directed me to lie back down, and from my feathery perch I delighted at the marvel of an entire wall covered with books. There were over a hundred of the miraculous treasures, their smooth leather spines more gorgeous to me than all the finery of the room combined.

The man, whom I decided to call Gus, as every man surely needed some sort of name, climbed up another set of stairs circling the apartment to the second floor. It must have been his sleeping chamber, although this one room was already three times the size of my family's home.

Surveying the apartment, I noted a huge fireplace with two square-shaped armchairs facing it, and a large table carved from wood with both golden and amber hues. Matching benches sat tucked beneath it, and a silver candelabrum adorned the top. A desk covered with half-burnt candles and writing supplies nestled in a corner next to a small closet. I was awed by the wonderful sense of openness, for the ceiling was a good ten feet high. I had grown weary near to death of watching my tall, strong William slouch beneath the low beams of our homes. I took a deep breath and smiled through my cracking lips.

When Gus returned, he carried an ornate urn and more white cloth. He walked to an area beyond my vision. I heard a metallic pumping sound and the surprising splash of water into a basin. A chuckle emerged from my belly, but barely made it past my fiery throat. Water indoors! Would these wonders never cease? He knelt upon the rug beside me and lifted my skirt with a questioning glance. I nodded for him to continue, and he washed my legs with cool, soapy water smelling of lavender.

He lifted the urn and opened the cover. "Healing salve." He spoke his first words with a low voice, gruff from lack of using. "From the orient."

The clear waxy substance smelled warm and wonderful. It stung, and I bit my lip against the pain as Gus bound the wound loosely. Never had I been so well cared for in all my life. After completing my medical treatment, he set about the generous task of bathing my arms, neck, and face with soothing sweeps, more for dirt than fever this time. The scent of lavender lingered on my skin. He studied me for a moment, then ran up the steps again, returning with a jeweled hairbrush.

I felt my hair. As I guessed, it was full from top to bottom with snarls, twigs, dirt, and leaves. I reached for the brush, but he pulled it from me with a "tisk."

"Rest," he mumbled and brushed it for me. He did it just right, using smooth, gentle strokes, even holding tight from above as he dealt with difficult tangles. Once the dirt and snarls were removed, he continued brushing with practiced strokes. Had I been a kitten, I would have purred at the comforting warmth spreading from my middle to fingertips and toes, but settled for a pleasant moan instead.

I must have dozed. In my next waking moment the brush was nowhere in sight. Gus lifted my head onto a pillow and spooned warm broth into my mouth. It tasted of chicken, onions, and salt, and it soothed my searing throat. I longed to reach out and squeeze his strong, nurturing hand, but kept eating the delicious soup instead.

He fetched a thick, warm blanket, soft like a baby lamb, to lay over me. "Sleep now. We will talk later," he said.

I complied with all willingness. Already, slumber dulled the edges of my vision, invading my head like a fog as thick as the blanket atop me.

When Gus woke me again, I noticed the setting sun. I had been missing at least a full day. Why didn't he fetch my parents? Although I didn't recall seeing him before, he could have discovered who I was easily enough. Perhaps I guessed wrong and this was not Arun Castle. I imagined my family in a frenzy of worry. Robert's intended, the red-headed Daisy, expected their first child. She was my friend as well. I'd hate to cause her distress. They must have been looking for me at that very moment. And William . . . .

Gus sat on the cushion in the space between my curled-up legs and arms. I felt so safe and relaxed with him. He held a cup to my lips. It smelled odd and biting but good. "An infusion of healing herbs. To help the fever."

I trusted him enough to drink it down. "Wh . . . ere i . . . s," I tried to ask about my family, but I couldn't get it out.

"Shh," he said, "tomorrow will be soon enough." Then a flash crossed his eyes, and he realized something that made him turn a comical shade of pink. "So sorry. I didn't think of . . . ." Words failed him now as well. He carried me to a closet near the indoor pump. He pushed aside a curtain of functional gray wool and sat me upon a stone bench with a surprising hole in the center about the size of a dinner plate. "The garderobe." He said the mystical word as if it explained everything. I must have looked baffled, for he added, "To relieve yourself."

I was stunned, but did indeed need to go. My full bladder clutched at the very thought, although in my haze, I hadn't noticed it until now. After he closed the curtain, I shifted my dress and positioned myself over the hole. I remained nervous until I caught a whiff of waste material far beneath me. I emptied my bladder and heard a splash somewhere under the tall tower. I made a funny sound that should have been a laugh. I fancied myself so sophisticated, but I had never heard of, read about, or even imagined anything like this. *Garderobe.* He said it so simply, as if surely I used one every day of my life.

"Finished?" he said through the curtain.

I managed an affirmative sound.

He gathered me up and tucked me back in bed. "Would you like to eat?" The very thought of passing more than liquid through my throat stung, so I shook my head but smiled my thanks.

Gus took a peek under my bandage and seemed satisfied. He started a fire in the big hearth, picked up a book, and settled into one of the carved armchairs with a crimson cushioned seat. The crackling flames turned the room even more magical as fabrics swayed in the flickering light. I fought sleep to enjoy this paradise a few moments longer.

I couldn't make out all the words on the book Gus held, but I read *"Fides"* written in large letters across the top. *Faith.* It brought me back to my William and the fight we once had in Friar John's backyard. The oddest thought struck me. My rescue today was remarkably similar to the story I used to taunt William.

"One day a handsome prince will gallop in on a black charger and sweep me away. He'll take me to a distant land, and there he will build me a lovely manor of gray stones with flowers all about instead of an ugly old moat. It will be filled with books and beautiful silken fabric."

A haunting little shiver shot through me.

Could I have believed this whole day into existence? Surely this was not wrought by faith? My prediction was more than a little wicked. I didn't know for certain if I even believed in God any more than elves or fairies.

Gus was a benevolent protector, a guardian angel of sorts, not a handsome prince. I studied him in the molten firelight. Actually, he was not bad to look at, and he certainly had proven himself kind. Wasn't he exactly the sort of man I planned to catch all those years ago? Older perhaps, late in his thirties, I guessed, but there was nothing scandalous about a man his age marrying a young girl.

Marrying? Why was I thinking about marriage? Just yesterday I registered that I would never marry my William. Surely I wasn't ready to ponder wedding this man. Yet, how neatly packaged and providential the situation seemed. Even with my most aggressive scheming, I could never have concocted this.

I cast Gus a flirtatious smile and watched his eyebrows rise in astonishment. He flushed pink once again.

Chapter
8

As morning dawned, Gus slept in the chair beside the fireplace with a small pillow behind his head and a blanket tossed overtop him. He heard me stirring between the silk and wool and opened his eyes.

I managed a cheerful, if raspy, "Good morning."

He smiled his small, stoic smile, of which I was growing fond, then stood and stretched. "So your voice is back. How fares the rest of you?"

I sat up and placed my bare feet on the cool gray stones. No pains stabbed through me this time, and the world shifted only slightly. "Much better I think."

"Good. Shall I fetch breakfast?" He rushed down the stairs before I could answer.

I found his shyness amusing. I had many questions to ask and much thanks to offer, but I didn't mind waiting a few more moments. My rescuer seemed a man of few words. I liked it. There was something mysterious and romantic about it.

Other than my leg, I felt remarkably well thanks to his remedies. I stood up cautiously as the room tilted and righted once again. After a few seconds all dizziness passed, and I hopped on my good foot to the window to learn if I was indeed at Arun Castle.

The view was breathtaking. I saw my entire village spread before me like miniature toys. A knot I hadn't noticed in my belly untied, yet I didn't feel ready to return to my family. Rather, I longed to further explore this paradise. A small walkway and a crenellated wall stood outside the window.

Through the second window I viewed the entry to the castle gates on both sides of the wall, and through the third the entire bailey. No wonder I felt eyes watching me so many times. I assumed the guard changed regularly, but by the domestic look of this place, Gus lived here, keeping constant watch over the castle. *Why, he knows precisely who I am. What a mystery he is.*

Thinking the books may hold some answers, I hopped over to the shelves. His collection was huge, and I wondered how in the world a mere castle guard acquired so many. Some titles were in English, but most were Latin, and yet others foreign tongues and alphabets I did not know. Gus must have traveled extensively, likely as a soldier or a knight, but possibly as a merchant, a sailor, or even a pilgrim. It seemed despite his few words, he might be skilled in several languages.

I trailed my fingers along the costly leather spines and noticed a broad variety of subjects—farming, astronomy, theology, poetry, and philosophy. Upon his nearby writing desk I found accounts kept in a log and a lifelike sketch of a blue jay sitting on the crenellated wall.

Goodness, he's a scholar and an artist.

I opened a book on the desk and saw it contained dates, times, and short entries of events. I turned to the last entry of the book. It read, "Sunset on June 2nd." Although I had lost track of the days, it appeared recent. Reading on, awareness dawned. I knew precisely to what it referred. "Pretty blonde village girl enters the woods at nightfall—odd—will continue to monitor."

I jumped when I heard footsteps and rushed back to the window overlooking the village. The picture before my eyes jolted me even more than the entry in the book, tying my stomach back into the knots that had dissipated only moments ago.

Gus entered, carrying a tray laden with food and a steaming pot. He sat the tray on the dining table and scooped me in his firm arms, as was becoming his custom. I liked the feeling of them, and his strong broad chest, but couldn't shake the guilt the glance out the window had stirred. Setting me back on the couch, he said, "Rest."

I was, in fact, tired from my brief adventure around the room. I leaned against the cushions and closed my eyes. I needed a moment to process what I had seen—a large gathering of men assembled in the middle of town. As "Gus" pulled me away, the men scattered.

Were they looking for me? Surely I should make my presence known, but I needed more time in this secluded retreat. I wasn't ready for their questions, their prying eyes, their dreadful neighborly concern.

Gus pulled a little table in front of my seat and placed the breakfast upon it. Did he know what was going on out there? Did he see? Was he oblivious, or did he have his own reasons for hiding me away?

We shared a silent and companionable meal. The food offered so casually was full of delicacies. The bread was near white, the grain crushed finer than any I had ever eaten. I had sampled butter, cheese, eggs, and bacon, but never so much or all at once. The sweet fruit compote and cup of spiced cider were entirely new to me. Ravenous, I applied myself to the nourishing meal.

Now this was the way one should live.

After eating my fill, I spoke. "I don't even know your name."

"Gottfried," he said.

"Gottfried." I stared at him, seeking to unravel the mystery in the dark depths of his eyes. "I've never heard it before."

"It is Bavarian. My mother was from the Germanic people."

"Oh. I had begun to call you 'Gus' to myself. I suppose I wasn't too far off."

Looking down into his cup, he said, "Gus is good. You may call me Gus."

I found his reticence endearing and longed to stroke his pink cheek, but feared such brazen behavior would only increase his discomfort. "My name is Dandelion."

He did not respond.

"However did you find me?"

He looked up and smiled his little smile. "Thank the good Lord you wail so loudly. The path had run out, and I never would have spotted you."

So he *was* searching for me. "You are a castle guard?"

"Of sorts."

I had so many questions earlier, but sitting with him, things seemed simple. *Gus searched for me and found me, and now he's taking care of me. What else could possibly matter?* I reached out and patted his hand. "Thank you, kind sir."

He turned pink again but continued to look me in the eye. "You should sleep. You shall need your strength."

My eyes were feeling heavy. He checked my bandage one more time and covered me. I watched him tidy our breakfast, impressed by his efficiency. Most men waited for women to do the cleaning. Clearly years alone had taught him to take care of himself. *I would like to take care of Gus*, I thought as I drifted to sleep. Surely he deserved it more than any man I had ever known.

I would like us to care for each other.

After an equally pleasant and quiet midday meal, Gus said, "Do you feel up to a bath? I have salts from the Holy Land for your leg."

I fidgeted uncomfortably. Although I rarely worried over decency or appearances, I felt unsure about a bath. Certainly it was time for me to head home. I should splash off fully clothed in the stream, as I normally did. Even that put me at risk of demons according to the ever-superstitious Sadie. I never took a "bath" before and wasn't entirely sure what it entailed, but felt fairly positive nudity was involved. A warm flush blossomed from my chest. Surely he should never suggest such a thing.

"I can call for a maid servant if you like."

The mere offer of a chaperone was reassuring and calmed the patter of my heart. I truly didn't want to give up our solitude yet, and a bath sounded heavenly. Yet another taste of the castle riches. Oh, but I could adjust to this lifestyle. The scent of his costly lavender soap lingered in my memory. "I . . . I don't think that will be necessary."

"Good. The water is cooling in my chamber."

So, he set up the entire thing as I napped. What a thoughtful gesture.

He lifted me and carried me up the stairs. I resisted the temptation to wrap my arms around his bulging shoulders, longing to press my fingers into those dense muscles that made me feel so secure. He set me on my feet near the steaming wooden tub. "There is a towel and soap on the table. You may don the clean tunic on the bed if you like. Will you be all right?"

"Yes, I'm sure I'll be fine." I barely noticed him leaving as I perused the room. It was very much of the same style as the chamber below, but featured a huge bed surrounded by velvet curtains. A menacing bearskin rug lay on the floor. Gus's polished armor stood displayed in one corner.

So he is a knight.

Next to a large armoire sat an ornate table with a basin of water. A shining piece of glass hung above it. I hobbled over to take a closer look.

A very pretty girl with curling blonde hair stared curiously back.

I never saw myself in a looking glass before. I appeared tired and my hair was unruly, but still the beauty of the girl who stared back shocked me. I knew I was pretty, people always told me so, but I never expected this. I looked at the girl again. There was a perfection to her features that astounded me. Her face was heart-shaped and ever so poignant, her eyes wide-set and haunting, her lips full and bowed. I was overwhelmed at the sight. That face bore testimony to a divine creator far beyond myself. Good grooming, pretty clothes, even flowers and ribbons could only take one so far.

It humbled me. Indeed, it frightened me.

My fingers trembled as they ran down my sculpted cheekbones. Such a girl would ever be at the mercy of the men around her. How on earth had I remained safe thus far? Flouncing about town, flaunting my figure with tightly laced mantles? Running through the woods like a forest nymph? No doubt William's hovering presence had offered protection. Rumors of our impending engagement might have deterred unwanted suitors.

But no more.

William had cast me aside.

Chosen his damnable yardland over my well-being.

I had much to think about as I stepped into my first steaming bath. How easily I was becoming accustomed to these luxuries. The warmth soaked through my skin and calmed my shivering. I mused about a life here with Gus as the hazy steam floated around me. I felt so safe with him.

The water had long since cooled when I heard Gus call. "Dandelion, are you all right?"

"Yes, I'm sorry, it just felt so marvelous. I'm getting out now." I enjoyed the last slosh down my body, and reveled in the softness of the thick towel. I expected the tunic Gus left for me to be brown and far too large, but I was wrong. On the bed lay a woman's tunic, straight and slim, made of soft rose-colored fabric with scrolls embroidered about the collar. There were slits up both sides for freedom of movement, and matching trousers with a drawstring and narrow ankles. Where did they come from?

I donned only the tunic for the moment, my leg still needing bandaged. After brushing my hair, I called for Gus.

When he entered and saw me sitting on his bed in the short oriental tunic, he gasped. He blinked several times and cleared his throat. I managed not to giggle. Pleasant butterflies danced unbidden through my stomach. He should react so. I didn't want him to think of me only as some wayward child in need of rescuing.

He opened a trunk and took out the same urn of salve he used the day before. He knelt in front of me and raised the hem of my dress over my knee, not at all medically this time. He opened the urn and ran his fingers through the salve, reaching it tentatively toward my leg. I watched him graze the wound with the lightest touch—once, twice, three times, warming but not burning or stinging. Then his rough fingers ran along my skin. He caressed my leg ever so carefully, almost worshipfully. I listened as his breath grew heavy.

My own heart beat rapidly in turn.

He bandaged my leg and nodded toward the rose-colored trousers, then turned his back while I finished dressing. He was about to pick me up as usual, but then straightened. "You look well. Can you manage the stairway?"

I smiled. "Of course."

He allowed me to lean against him as we descended. His reluctance to carry me confirmed both that he was at the edge of his control, and that he was a gentleman determined not to pass the barrier.

Oh, Gus, could you be the man I always dreamed of?

I sat down on the cushioned bench. I was feeling very well now and didn't want to sleep. "These clothes," I said. "They are not from England, are they?"

He made a sound almost like a laugh. "No, they are not."

"So you've traveled."

"I was a soldier, a mercenary, through the Ottoman Empire and the Holy Land. Much later I met Lord Worthing, the old lord, James. We fought in Scotland. I brought his body home. I promised to watch over his lady wife before he died." The speech wearied him. "Rest some more." He headed down the stairs and out of the tower.

It explained much. A mercenary could well have amassed some wealth, collected foreign goods and even books. My eyes swept the room. It still looked a bit grand for a mere soldier, but I would take him at his word. So, Gus traveled through Saracen lands. That would have meant little before Friar John educated me. He loved to ramble on about the crusades and the barbaric Moslem infidels. He even drew a map to show us the geography of the Mediterranean region and the Arabian Peninsula.

Perhaps the odd alphabet on the bookshelf was Arabic. I wondered how a "barbaric" people could have woven such beautiful fabrics. I ran my fingertips over the embroidery around my collar and pondered what sort of "infidel" had sewn it. Was the salve so quickly healing my leg a Saracen invention? I remembered reading that they thought us barbaric infidels as well. Friar John scoffed at the thought, but it struck me as significant. I would love to discuss the matter with Gus—rather Gottfried—sometime and hear his thoughts.

I felt sure a wealth of knowledge, sensitivity, and passion lay below the surface of his quiet exterior. He brushed my hair so expertly, caressed my legs with such knowledgeable strokes.

I went to the window. Somewhere out there my family and friends searched for me. Likely my mum cried beside the hearth. Sadie was probably snipping at everyone and being unduly harsh with little Gilbert as she always did when distressed. She had another child on the way.

I should have felt far guiltier than I did, hiding away within sight of the village while they feared for my life. But alas, not one of them in that stifling place had ever understood me. Indeed, they found my entire life bizarre. I should have been sorry that William likely thought me dead, but in fact I couldn't help feeling some perverse satisfaction. He had brought this upon himself. A smile niggled at my lips, but I pressed them firmly together and sought some diversion from my sinful thoughts.

Hoping to bide the time until Gus returned, I perused the bookshelf and settled upon a volume of English poetry.

I was sitting cross-legged on my little bed, book in hands, when Gus returned.

"You can read?" It sounded like an accusation.

"I hope you don't mind. I've never had so many manuscripts to choose from, and I truly wasn't tired."

"No, not at all." He shook his head in wonder. He busied himself at the desk for a few moments before turning. "What else should I know?"

I smiled. "Well, I can write. I know a little Latin, and I'm quite good at sums."

"How?"

I considered the question. The patch of dirt where we held our lessons would be blocked from his sight by the chapel. "Friar John was teaching my brother and allowed me to listen. I can also cook, sew, weave, and dye fabrics. I've so enjoyed the beautiful ones you have here. Are they from the Orient?" I grazed my fingers over a wall curtain. I didn't want my list of accomplishments to sound too much like I was petitioning for a job, although I hoped perhaps I was.

"Yes, and you love to dance." So, he had been watching and taking note.

I hoped the impression was favorable. I wondered what he knew about William. I hadn't seen as far as kissing rock from the tower window, but surely we snatched plenty of kisses in the village as well.

What about the poaching? Gus may well have been watching all those years. I looked at him with suspicion as tension gripped my neck.

"Never fear," he said with a true smile that reached his eyes. "I'll not tell if you'll not." Again he alleviated the need for a myriad of questions with one simple response. The tension spreading through me dissipated, replaced by a warm syrupy flow.

No longer able to resist, I rose and walked toward him. Even with a limp, I could sway my hips alluringly. Arriving to his side, I stroked my hand down his arm.

"You're nearly well." He sounded disappointed.

"Yes, it seems I am. How shall I ever thank you?"

"Being here is thanks enough," he said with so much meaning. His hand clenched and opened again, as if he wanted to reach out and touch me as well. "I thought that dress would bring out the pink in your lips." He mumbled the words as if to himself, then his eyes shot up with alarm.

I didn't want him to run out the door again, so I laid my hand against his arm once more and smiled. "It's all right." I too must have succeeded in saying much with a few words, for he reached up and took my hand in his.

He lifted it to his lips and kissed it, his lips surprisingly soft against my skin. That syrupy sensation grew thicker.

I shook my head to gather my senses. "I suppose I should be heading home. Mum and Da must be beside themselves with worry."

"No!" He snapped out the word, then recovered himself as well. "We need one more night. For your wound to heal. I don't want my hard work ruined by foolish English superstitions."

The point was valid, and it revealed a respect for foreign culture that fascinated me. As I snuggled against Gus's rough-hewn side, I looked forward to years of stories told by the fire. Gazing up into the brown depths of his eyes, I anticipated philosophical discussions about the comparative merits of various societies. He placed his firm arm around my shoulder, and I fancied tales of his adventurous voyages, perhaps enticing accounts of veiled Saracen beauties.

"One more night," he repeated in his gruff voice. I imagined him reading Arabic poetry to me with that voice, and teaching me the secrets of their cryptic alphabet.

Maybe he would teach me about their God. I felt newly drawn toward some sort of deity I had yet to encounter. I forgot about my worried family and gazed deeper into his eyes as he stroked my brow with his knuckle. I would gladly spend one more evening in this lovely little hideaway before dealing with the consequences of the last two days.

Chapter 9

"**A**re you ready, Dandelion?" Gus called from upstairs.
"Yes."

This morning he announced it was time to speak with my parents—like that, "to speak with your parents," not time to go home or back to my parents. It boded well.

"I'll be down in a moment," he said.

While waiting, I explored the bookshelves once more. In addition to the huge library, they held a collection of interesting trinkets from his travels—a curved knife in an intricate sheath with a horse head cast in bronze, a strange beast with a hump on its back embellished with sparkling jewels, across from it another creature I didn't recognize with a long, curling nose and big, flopping ears. I ran my fingers over the rough, translucent earth-toned glass of a mosaic vase and a smooth bunch of marble grapes in shades of peach, cream, and rose. The world held a wide array of wonders, just as I always believed.

Gus approached from behind and laid a gentle hand upon my shoulder. "Let us depart."

I wore my own everyday dress. It was ripped and stained, but my family would have enough to digest without me looking vaguely like a harem girl. Nervous twitches gnawed at my belly as we descended the stairs. Gus lifted me onto his grand warhorse and walked beside me as we traversed the castle courtyard.

Halfway to the village, the first cries rang out. There was a flurry of movement around the little huts as people ran toward me. I thought I might be sick.

Sadie reached me first. "Oh, Dandy." She fairly dragged me off the horse and clenched me to her.

I thrilled to see her familiar freckled face, but dared not trust this welcome. Not when I hoped to be leaving again so soon.

She held me at arm's length and studied me before she yelled and shook me. "You fool girl. Where have you been all these days? Why, half the village is searching the woods for you as we speak, and here you come trotting down the lane as if you haven't a care in the world. You stupid, selfish little girl. I could beat you straightaway."

I shielded my heart against her attack. She would not wear me down on this of all days.

Others gathered round. Mum shuffled forward as fast as her old legs would carry her. "Dandelion, my baby." She pushed Sadie aside and pulled me into her arms, weeping fiercely. Her welcome was no doubt sincere.

Guilt settled upon me like a cloak—yet a portion of myself remained ever so slightly detached, hidden behind that metal shield. No, I would not let them deter my plans.

Sadie looked ready to launch into another attack when the church bells sounded. They rang out the joyful notes for Sundays and weddings, not the sad knoll of death.

"Hurry, hurry," Mum said. "We must go see your da. He's spoken barely a word since you left."

Sadie took Mum's silence as an invitation to proceed. "And just where have you been, you selfish little strumpet? Taken up with some fool soldier I see. Oh, you'll be sorry." She shook her finger at Gus with disdain. "This one's a heartbreaker, I tell you true. Not a week ago she broke faith with her intended, and already she's taken up with the likes of you."

"Begging your pardon, ma'am," Gus said. "The young lady was lost in the woods and wounded. I stumbled upon her while hunting. I would have returned her sooner had I known who she was. She was delirious until this very morning. You best watch your tongue, I think, and thank the good Lord she's still alive."

Sadie did close her mouth but eyed Gus with suspicion.

I kept my face from showing shock at this long and eloquent fabrication Gus had spoken on my behalf. I exaggerated my limp and leaned upon my hero as we headed toward home. Gus hunched over as we passed through the door. "Da," I whispered to the broken old man crying before the fire.

He looked up as if he saw a ghost. "You're alive. I had a d-d-d-dream and saw you dead at the b-bottom of a cliff. I had-had given up hope."

"I'm so sorry, Da." I knelt down to embrace him where he sat. Da would understand. He would never try to keep me here. "But you dreamed true. I was hurt badly, and I did fall down a cliff. I would have never made it, were it not for this gentleman here who saved me."

"My thanks to you, good sir." Mum rushed over to shake Gottfried's hand. "However did you find her? We've been looking for days. They spotted some tracks, but nary a trace of our Dandelion. We thought her gone for good."

"Humph." Sadie rolled her eyes. "I thought her gone to London."

"Hush, girl." A neighbor lady pushed further into the hut. "I told you I saw her with my own two eyes floating off like a phantom in the night. She weren't herself that evening. Your father and brother bore witness."

"Yes, but if this man found her two days past, why is he only now returning her to us? Fresh as a flower I might add. You were always given to high drama, Dandelion. Why must you make things difficult?"

"I'm so sorry, but I had a horrible fever, and I have a deep gash still in my leg." I pulled up my skirt to reveal the bandage. "My friend Gus is a fine healer, or I may never have made it home."

"Your friend is it?" Sadie examined him. "Wouldn't it be difficult to make friends while delirious?"

"Stop it, Sadie." Mum took hold of her arm. "Your sister is home. Why must you carry on so?"

Sadie gave Mum's hand a soft pat but glared at me. "I must carry on so because my husband and my brothers and half the village wasted two good planting days looking for this ungrateful chit who was not nearly as lost as we imagined. I'm sick to death of her theatrics. How dare you leave William and never even mention a word? He was one of the family, and I know for a certainty you love him, you shallow, vain little girl." Turning on Gus she continued her tirade. "Where, may I ask, sir, did you tend to my sister? I've seen you before, surely. You are a guard at the castle. Why didn't you alert the village?"

Gus never wavered. "I keep to myself, ma'am, in my own quarters atop the tower. I found her miles from here. How was I to know?"

"So you tended her in your own quarters?"

"Enough, Sadie," my father shouted uncharacteristically. "We thank you, kind sir. Our sons sh-sh-should return soon. You must j-j-j-join us for some ale."

We settled around our family table. The neighbors bade farewell. Robert's intended, Daisy, joined Mum as she fussed over me, and Sadie sulked in the corner. Da and Gus exchanged a total of ten words until Robert, Gilbert, and Tim returned with the search party. An exuberant Tim entertained us with funny tales of my wayward childhood, his arm around my waist the entire time. I held a tight smile in place. Tim was not to blame for any of this. Gus was quiet throughout, absorbing everything. Sadie whispered with angry gestures to Gilbert and Robert. William passed by the open doorway, but once he spotted me, walked away with his head hanging low. A part of me longed to follow him down the lane, but I held it firmly in check along with my smile. That portion of my life was finished. No turning back. Forward. Ever forward.

Robert, well known for his tact, found a polite opening to voice Sadie's concerns. "Sir, our family is forever in your debt," he said to Gus. "However, I do fear there may be some questions, which should be addressed. Could you not have informed someone sooner of Dandelion's whereabouts or taken her to the castle for help?"

Gus stood straighter. "I had only her welfare in mind. I feared for her life. I promise, though, my intentions were honorable. I planned to ask for her hand in marriage until I learned she might be betrothed."

"No, I am not. I was never betrothed," I said to him and the family at once, clutching my throat. "It was merely assumed."

"But you did, in fact, recently end the courtship," Robert said.

I shook my head as I fought back tears. "No, that's not precisely true either. We parted nearly two months past, but William and I were too heartsick to speak of it."

They all looked stunned.

Tim was quick to open his mouth. "How could you keep this a secret? William was part of this family as much as you or I. It's not right, Dandy. You and William are meant for each other. Everyone knows it. Like fish and water, I always said. I thought this was a lover's quarrel, a spat. Now you tell me it's finished for good. How dare you?"

I had no answer for him.

He pounded his fist on the table and stomped out in search of his good friend with one last hard look over his shoulder. How could he desert me like that? Who would stand up for me now?

"Dandy." Sadie shook her head and backed away as she spoke. "I am truly and sadly disappointed in you. This is a mistake you will forever regret. I know we fight, and I fuss at you unmercifully, but underneath all of that I love you. If you do this, though, if you leave William for this man, I know not if I'll be able to bear the sight of you." She didn't raise her voice during the entire speech. Somehow that hurt worse than her typical hollering. She gathered up her husband and son and walked out the door.

They were all abandoning me. No one was on my side.

Nothing new in that.

"My humblest apologies," Gus said to the remaining family. "Perhaps I should leave. I didn't intend to cause a stir." He looked at my father. "If I might speak with you outside."

"Of course." Da rose from his chair with Robert at his elbow and shuffled to the door. They nearly crashed into Friar John and Alice who rushed in to welcome me home.

Sensing the mood of the house, they slowed their pace and greeted me. "We would have come sooner, lassie, but I was saying the last rights over the old miller down the river." Friar John planted a kiss on my forehead. "Oh, you are a sight for sore eyes."

"We were dreadfully worried." Alice hugged me to her. "We've been praying day and night."

"I'm fine." I rested my head for a moment upon her plump shoulder. "I have a serious wound on my leg, and I was sick, but I'm healing nicely thanks to the man who just left with my father."

"Indeed, what was that all about?" said Friar John.

I paused, unsure of what to say. I supposed everyone would know soon enough, but Mum spared me the telling of it.

"It seems Dandy's rescuer may want to ask for her hand in marriage."

Alice pulled back and held me by the forearms. "Why ever would he do such a thing? Dandelion, surely you told him that you were promised to young William. You two have been in love for as long as I've known you."

I extricated myself from her embrace, shaking off her statement. "Everyone keeps saying that, but I don't think it's true. We were never officially promised to each other. William is set on following his own path. He gave no thought for my feelings. I cannot in good faith make a life with such a man."

"Oh, Dandy." Alice implored me with her eyes. "Tell me you jest. I can't imagine you without your William."

I sat down and rubbed my throbbing leg. "No, Alice. I'm terribly serious."

"And do you plan to accept this old soldier's proposal?" Mum's voice was cold. "You've said not a word about that."

I added another plate to the iron enclosure about my heart. "I do."

Friar John and Alice knew my tone well enough to drop the discussion. With a sympathetic nod to Mum, they left. Before he ducked through the low doorway, Friar John turned to me. "Don't ask me to perform the vows, Dandelion. The good Lord knows I could never bear it."

The entire village was against me. Their ill will permeated the walls of the house. How could I ever explain it to them? Who amongst them would ever understand?

Da and Robert returned, looking solemn. "It sounds like a sincere offer." Robert helped Da back into his chair by the fire. "He's a decent sort of fellow. He comes from noble stock and is a man of some means. Has Dandelion spoken on the issue yet?"

"Yes," I answered for myself. "I plan to marry him."

"Well, you needn't jump into anything," Robert said. "The last few days have been upsetting. You should take some time for matters to return to normal."

I knew well Robert's stall tactics. This morning everything was so clear, but now Tim and Sadie had betrayed me, and Robert seemed inclined to join their ranks. The dingy, thatched walls of the miserable little hut swirled about me. Chills ran up my arms and acrid smoke threatened to smother me once again, although the hearth was bare on this warm day. I was overwhelmed by an urge to curl in a ball beside it and weep. I had to escape. A baby whimpered in the background. Hunger pangs stabbed at my belly. My heartbeat quickened. I could barely draw a breath. It took several attempts at inhaling before I was able to speak. "No, I plan to marry him, and soon." My voice sounded harsh even to me.

"Your father and I do have some say in this, Dandelion," Mum said.

I heard prison bars clanging, driving into my skull. I winced against the noise. "Da?"

"Oh, Dandy, you've always been your own person." He wrung his hands in his lap. "I can't tell you what to do, but I w-w-wish from the bottom of my heart that you'd stay with dear William."

The clanging continued, loud and clear all around me. "So you all agree. You plan to oppose me." My voice was shrill and tight, about to shatter.

Robert attempted to calm the situation. "Come now, Dandy, this Gottfried seems a decent fellow. He didn't even ask for a dowry. The only point against him is . . . is he's not William."

"Please, Dandy," said Mum, "don't you do this evil thing."

It was too much. A red tinge overtook my vision, and my head threatened to explode like a canon. " Is it so evil to want to escape poverty and deprivation? To secure a better life for myself and my family? For my children? Why can't you understand? I want to help. To care for you. Why on earth will no one let me? Not a one of you has ever understood me. I don't belong here. I never belonged here. I can feel it. I don't know what obscene twist of fate landed me in this Godforsaken hellhole, but I'm done with the lot of you. Truly. This is the end. You may have your precious William. Adopt him for all I care. You love him more than your own flesh and blood. I'm leaving, and I'm never coming back. I'll be long gone, and I swear you shall never see me again." I stomped out the door, ignoring the pain shooting through my leg. Then I ran, my feet stumbling the best they could toward the castle walls. I fell against them and collapsed into tears.

Whatever came over me? Where did those horrifying words come from? I never spoke a harsh word to my parents in my life, but I was suffocating in that awful little house. Each mention of William pounded like a spike into my skull. I had to get out of there—away from all of them. I needed to get on with my life. I made a decision, and I would not be deterred. Ever forward, never back. William was my past. Gus was my present and my future.

Before long he heard me crying through the tower window and came to sweep me again into his arms. My knight in shining armor carried me to my exotic hideaway. Gus would take care of me.

"Dandelion, wake up." Gus shook me the following morning. It was barely dawn. "We must go find a priest."

"A priest?" I rubbed my drowsy eyes.

"Yes, we cannot wait to marry. Your reputation is at stake."

"To marry?"

"Yes, to marry." Gus lifted me from the pillow and swiveled my legs to the floor. "It must be today. Go upstairs and dress. I'll pack the supplies."

I repeated the wondrous words in my head. *Yes, to marry.* I hugged my arms about myself and squealed. After trotting up the stairs, I examined the room. Tomorrow morning I would awake in the giant bed. This would be my very own home. Not questioning him, I donned the beautiful rose-colored tunic and trousers once again. I brushed my hair with the jeweled brush in front of the priceless mirror, soon to belong to me. Me, Dandelion, the crippled cottar's daughter. The outfit did indeed bring out the pink in my complexion, enhanced even more by a flush of pleasure.

When I reached the bottom of the stairway, Gus too was flushed and smiling. He wore his chain mail and a knightly surcoat for the journey. A bright golden dragon was embroidered in sharp relief against a field of burgundy velvet—the Worthing coat of arms. Matching burgundy hose hugged his muscled legs. His shoulders appeared broad and strong in his armor.

My face felt hot from the surprising thoughts filling my head, good thoughts, as it would soon be my wedding night.

His horse, Roman, was saddled and waiting downstairs. He remembered me and whinnied his greeting. Gus looped one arm around my waist and swung us both upon the horse. He held tight to me while he took the reins in his free hand.

We galloped off toward the neighboring castle with a thunder. Servants stopped to watch us blaze past. Villagers gawked and stared, no doubt, but the faces were mercifully a blur. I thrilled at the breakneck pace, the wind blowing through my hair. I felt utterly safe on the huge beast with Gus's powerful arm about me. The forest flew by in a whir of green and brown from either side of the smooth road like a dream. The nearest castle was much closer than I imagined—little more than two hours by horseback. It was held by a squire in service to Lord Worthing, in the region west and north of his primary holdings.

We arrived at a pretty little chapel in the castle courtyard. The resident priest owed his commission to the Worthings. With a few gold coins from Gus's purse, the good clergyman was willing to overlook that we failed to cry the banns, and that no male family member gave me away. He found two villeins to witness the holy event. After a quick word about wives being submissive, the priest said the vows, Gus repeated, the priest signed and sealed a legal-looking document, and we were on our way again—this time as husband and wife. Only seventeen years old, and already I'd made Arun Castle my home.

I was Mrs. Gottfried Westover. I didn't even known his last name until I heard the priest say it.

Chapter 10

Arun Castle – England 1329

"What to do? What to do?" I spoke to my reflection as I rubbed rich silky cream onto my skin. I scraped my teeth clean with a small sharp stick and added a hint of berry stain to my lips. No doubt the same beauty rituals that kept Lady Worthing looking so young. Black kohl around my eyes seemed a bit much for morning, but I brushed my hair one hundred strokes as Gottfried had taught me. "Come now, surely you have some ideas for the day." But the blonde girl in the mirror didn't answer. Her silence made me frown. I continued to watch as she wound her curly hair into fashionable twists and secured them with pins at either side of her face.

Who would have thought? Dandelion the cottar's daughter was a lady of leisure. I slept until the sun was halfway up the sky that very morning. Gottfried had brought me breakfast in bed. Nine months of easy living had softened me for certain. How quickly I adapted to this lifestyle. The delicious food seemed almost passé. I picked up the tray of dirty plates and headed downstairs. Sitting it in the basin, I waved out the window to my husband. As usual, he sat on the crenellated walkway keeping watch over the castle. He nodded in my direction without actually looking away from the courtyard.

Perhaps a book would keep me occupied. I wandered to the shelf and ran my fingers across the leather spines. "Hmm, I've already covered these on farming." I wished I could share the innovations with the villagers. They would have been so very helpful. I sighed and continued my perusal. "Poetry . . . philosophy. I've read all these." Oh, how I longed to engage Gottfried in a debate on the new ideas I had discovered.

"Sermons," I said and rolled my eyes. Worthless indeed. So different than the vibrant relationship with God that Father John taught. I raised my voice a few notches. "It certainly would be lovely if Gottfried would help me with these Latin texts."

If he grunted a response, I did not hear.

"Of course not, he's far too busy," I said to the long-nosed trinket on the shelf, which I now knew was named an elephant. He winked back with his emerald green eye. I could try the Latin on my own. I could treat it like a puzzle, as I did in the old days with Wil . . . . Well, anyway, it would be a challenge, and Lord knew I had plenty of time.

I took a book down and flipped through the first few pages. What I understood did not by any means interest me, so I crammed it back onto the shelf and huffed away in disgust.

Next, I turned my attention to Gottfried, perched as usual on a wooden stool scribbling into one of his mysterious book. I had a sinking suspicion they were handed over to the treacherous Lady Worthing. In the early days of our marriage I sat on the wall with Gottfried and made small talk. I chattered constantly—while he worked, during meals, as we sat reading by the fire at night. I asked about his journeys, his battles—his answers were rarely more than monosyllabic. I continued throughout the summer in my quest to draw Gottfried into conversation, sure it was only a matter of time before his reserved demeanor cracked and the depths of his soul came rushing forth.

He took notice of me watching him through the window and cast me a hard glance. Little wonder I was reduced to conversing with mirrors and decorative animals. I crossed the room to the desk where my paints sat and gave the pot an angry flick. Why waste my time? The paint never cooperated. And any attempt at writing turned out nearly as disastrous. My journal was no doubt the most boring piece of literature in all of England, and my poems rang trite even to my own ears.

So, I went back upstairs to gather my embroidery instead. Since moving to the castle, I finally had the needed supplies to properly develop the art form. I was working on a tapestry with local flora and snippets of my favorite poetry to be a birthday surprise for Gottfried. Usually, I found great joy in watching my ideas spring to life on the fabric beneath my fingertips, but today it seemed tedious work. I paused for a moment, trying to think of other options for my time—no, just reading and sewing. Gottfried had snatched the rest away from me. Other than the few dishes in the sink, there was nothing to be done.

I cried out as I pierced the needle into my finger and sucked a drop of blood before it could spill onto my blue linen dress. What was wrong with me? I loved to sew.

Constructing my new wardrobe out of the oriental fabrics Gottfried had fetched from the mysterious attic provided weeks of joy. Now in addition to a full collection of shoes, hose, chemises, and headpieces, I owned five kirtles with matching mantles, and two silk gowns for special occasions. They were ever so lovely. I allowed my mind to wander back to Gottfried, the source of my bounty; much time had passed since I called him Gus. I wished I might talk with him out on the sunny walkway once again, but by the end of summer he was no longer amused with my chitchat.

"Dandelion." His sharp retort had come to my incessant questioning one evening over supper. "Enough. I am not a young man. I have found it is frivolous to waste words. Silence is the safest course. I speak only when I have something important to communicate. I would appreciate if you do likewise."

I had no idea how to respond, and realized he would prefer no response at all. I pressed down those thoughts along with the lump in my throat and whispered to myself, "I do truly love him, though." I tried to focus on his kisses, which felt so nice, even if they did not quite stir me with passion. I enjoyed sleeping in his safe embrace with my back pressed against him. His lovemaking was sweet and gentle, although not quite as fiery as I imagined, but being cherished by such a generous man was all that truly mattered, right?

I wandered over to the window facing the village. The cottages looked like little toys. I yearned to play with them, and with that teeny-tiny cow and miniature wagon over in the field. The morning was beautiful and sun-filled, smelling fresh like spring. The air nipped at my face, but Gottfried had given me a fur-lined cloak made of amethyst velvet for Twelfth Night.

He did take such very good care of me, I reminded myself. I ran my hand over the window ledge. Perhaps the new cloak wasn't quite appropriate for traipsing through fields, though. Not that it mattered. I remembered all too clearly the day I wandered outside, looking for plants and herbs.

I had hoped to make some healing remedies from one of his books. It was early fall and the first time I ventured outside the castle walls. I didn't want to face the villagers, but the lure of nature was too strong to resist. On the deserted side of the castle, I searched for herbs in the beautiful fall foliage without fear—until Gottfried came stomping out of nowhere.

He yanked me by one arm, hauled me over his shoulder and marched toward the tower.

"Stop it," I cried. "You're hurting me." But I pushed down the fear and anger that rose up within me. This was Gottfried. My protector. My provider. Surely he had a reason. Surely he would explain.

He continued stomping.

In our apartment, he dumped me into a chair. He leaned over, trapping me with fists pressed into the armrests. "Don't ever try that again."

I curled against the cushioned back. "Why? Whatever did I do that was so wrong?"

"I don't want you leaving the castle walls again. Do you hear me?" He grabbed my chin and locked eyes with me.

Again, I swallowed down my indignation, searching his eyes for some meaning, some explanation.

"It's not safe out there. God only knows what could have happened to you alone in the woods. Women should not be traipsing about the forest unaccompanied. This is our home, and I expect you to stay here."

"But I only wanted to—"

"I don't care what you wanted. I mean it. Do not leave this castle. I can't protect you out there. It's to the kitchen and back, and that's all. I'll lock you up if I have to, Dandelion. I swear it. Don't test me." His voice was commanding, but he looked oddly defeated.

I nodded my consent. He scooped me into a tight embrace, and I shivered within his arms, attempting to convince myself all was well in the world. For whatever reason, Gottfried truly feared for me. The fear was mutual. I vowed never to wander off again.

I speared away at my embroidery until it seemed like a reasonable time to fetch our midday meal. I looked down at the purple foxgloves added that day. I dreaded working on the blue cornflowers needed to finish the design. They were sure to bring to mind memories best forgotten.

I scrubbed the few breakfast dishes in the sink with a vengeance, banging to my heart's content. It was a wonder of superior craftsmanship that they didn't break. I was about to walk out the door, when I remembered. "Good Lord, I mustn't forget my cursed wimple." Gottfried insisted upon it. I ran upstairs, pulled on the blue veil, and wrapped the strangling end around my neck, securing it to one side. The long flowing scarves looked elegant and lady-like as they hid the golden curls already escaping from my ramshorn twists. I lifted my chin to match the regal—almost royal—appearance the headpiece presented, but I dreaded the coming summer. Would I never again feel the wind blow through my hair and cool the back of my neck? A bitter taste filled my mouth.

Although I had little appetite for our midday meal, I rushed down the tower stairs and into the open air. I took a deep breath and smiled, glad for a moment to be alive. I twirled in a circle and began a skipping little dance across the courtyard until I heard a cough high above my head and looked up at Gottfried. For heaven's sake, what crime did I commit now?

Gottfried gestured ahead and to my left. Two stable lads watched my impetuous performance.

They were good-looking boys of my own age. Last year at this time I would have winked and waved, but instead I looked down at my tray and took brisk steps to the kitchen building with the weight of Gottfried's eyes pressing against my shoulders.

Inside, I convinced my tense muscles to relax. I stood for a moment, enjoying the noise of busyness, the clank of pots, the warm shouts, the joy of mundane conversation. Several of the maids curtsied as they passed, although they had once treated me as a friend.

"Afternoon, ma'am," Betsy said with a polite bob. "Lovely weather we're having." And with that she was back to work.

My marriage to Gottfried elevated me to some nether region between peasant and nobility. It seemed I was above typical domestic servants but still far beneath Lady Worthing. My old pal the steward was now appropriate company for me, as was the lady's maid, although she snubbed me the few times we'd crossed paths. The soldiers may have been acceptable friends, but Gottfried would never allow it. If only I could enter the castle beyond the tower and the kitchen, things might be different.

I spotted my childhood cohort sampling the mutton stew. He was an adorable, teetering old man.

"Well, if it isn't my favorite girl. How are you today?" The steward continued without waiting for an answer. "Come and try this stew. It is a work of God."

He shoved the giant spoon in my face, and I took a bite of the savory concoction. "It's delicious." I wiped my lip. "You're awfully lively this morn."

"And why shouldn't I be? That tyrant has agreed to give me a pension. Only four short months and I'll be living in my own cottage beside my daughter in a town by the sea. Why, I may even build a fishing boat."

"That's wonderful." Catching his happy disposition, I took his hands in my own. I wished to be in his shoes. "But gracious, I shall miss you. Whatever will I do without you?"

"Her ladyship has her eye on some charming young chap to take my place. No doubt that's why she's so agreeable." He winked at me. "I think you'll manage to get along with him well enough."

"Oh, I don't know. I don't think my husband would approve." My feet shuffled beneath me.

"Gottfried. Come now, child, he's all bluster. You'll learn to handle him soon enough."

"Perhaps." Or perhaps he would lock me up.

"Gottfried is an honorable man, just set in his ways. All he needs is the right woman to challenge his stubbornness, and I'd say he's found her."

"I hope so." I bit my lip.

"What is this? Where's the spark, the fire I've always admired in you, Dandelion?"

I attempted a giggle. His speech should have cheered me, but instead tears stung my eyes. "Well, I suppose I should get back to the business at hand," I said. "I'm very pleased for you, though, only a few more months. Indeed, it is wonderful news." I could have chatted another ten minutes without getting into trouble, but I had lost my appetite for conversation.

He rapped on the counter. "One quick game first? I'm feeling lucky."

"No, not today," I said, although I always enjoyed our checkers matches. The steward, whom I now called Michael, wore a twisted smile as I went about gathering our midday meal and a basket of supplies for supper. Why must Gottfried so adamantly refuse eating in the great hall with the rest of the castle folk? Not that I minded cooking. I surely had nothing better to do.

I paused at the door before taking my last step. I listened to the happy hum once again. My entire life I took voices for granted. Sometimes during the dead of winter in our tiny cottage it seemed I would never escape them. Now I could barely stand to walk away.

Outside, I turned on impulse into a narrow alley. My breathing was rapid and raspy. I leaned backwards on the smooth stone wall and beat my head against it. "I miss those voices like crazy. I miss my family and my house and all of the stupid nosy villagers. I miss William, my best friend. I am miserable and bored and lonely near to death."

Tears overflowed. "Oh, whatever have I done?"

Chapter 11

On the morning of Gottfried's birthday, I awoke before the sun to cook him a special breakfast. Carrying the tray of bacon, eggs, and honey cakes up the stairs, I wondered at the marvel of the occasion. I had never met anyone aware of their actual calendar date of birth before. Villeins knew only the season, possibly the month they had been born along with the year of the reigning king. Mine fell somewhere in late winter. Thankfully, Gottfried had shared the information of his birth with me when we were still speaking. May third in the year of our lord 1289. Surely such a day deserved a grand celebration, but I would make do with a reserved one.

Gottfried rolled over and cracked an eye as I entered. An actual smile spread across his face. "Dandelion, what a pleasant surprise."

"Happy birthday, my husband."

"Breakfast in bed? You shall make a sluggard of me." He rubbed his eyes.

"I imagine your soldiers can do without you for a few moments on such a special day." I sat the tray in front of him on the bed.

"True enough."

"And I've brought you a present." I drew the rolled tapestry from the pocket of my apron.

He pulled it open. "How thoughtful. Flowers and poetry, your favorite things. Lovely. It shall bring you to mind. We shall mount it over the fire straightaway."

Once the sun had risen and Gottfried had finished his food in relative but pleasant silence, he surprised me by speaking again as I gazed forlornly out the window.

"Let's go for a walk in the forest, Dandelion. We can take a picnic lunch. I'll stop and tell the soldiers along the way."

On that morning we walked through the woods and even splashed in a stream. Gottfried suggested I take off my shoes and wimple, and it was glorious. He spread a blanket under a shady tree. After our luncheon, I laid my head upon his lap and stared into the inviting blue sky for what seemed like hours.

"I'm sorry I've kept you inside," he said. "I of all people should know how you love the outdoors."

Shocked though I was, I kept silent in hopes he would continue.

"Perhaps we should do this again. Make it a Sunday afternoon tradition. Would you like that?"

"Oh yes! Thank you, husband." I stopped myself from rambling on.

Just when I thought he wouldn't speak another word, he said, "I still can't quite believe you're mine. I've lost so much in my life, Dandelion. I hope you can forgive me."

"Certainly." I sat up a little and pulled his head to me for a kiss. Gottfried could be so sweet sometimes.

Later, he let me ride Roman alone through an open field. Society may not have considered such skills ladylike, but since Catherine Worthing was an infamous equestrian, Gottfried saw no harm. I even tried a few small jumps. Roman hopped over them and flipped me a condescending look, as if to ask if this were some sort of joke.

I could hardly wait for Sunday afternoon. Dare I hope Gottfried might keep his word?

And one day, one day soon, I would approach him about my family. Oh how I longed to see them.

It was a balmy summer afternoon a year after my arrival in the tower before I worked up the courage to make my request. I stirred together a batch of sticky plum sauce and rubbed it over the hearty pheasant. I made certain not to miss a single cranny. Dinner tonight must be perfect. So much was at stake. Through the window, I watched distant villeins hard at work in the fields below. I could no longer deny it. Despite the many troublesome memories of my childhood, I missed my family terribly.

Oh, I'd managed to make some sort of life for myself here in the tower. I had indeed unraveled some of those Latin texts, and they proved well worth the effort. Each Sunday afternoon Gottfried now took me for walks in the woods or long rides on Roman. Occasionally, he even told me legends about the forest. I learned not to press him and to listen more than I spoke. But, if the conversation remained light and pleasant, he would allow some chitchat on Sunday afternoons.

It was almost enough.

I removed the boiling vegetables from the fire and set to work dousing them with butter and salt, luxuries I never dreamed of as a poor peasant child. Who was I to complain about life with Gottfried? He oft played chess with me at night, and I visited with my good friend Roman daily in the stables. It was the most blissful little love affair, and my husband actually approved. Still, try though I might, that didn't erase my longing for my family. How could one lone man ever take their place?

I simply must earn Gottfried's approval to visit them. Never would I dare risking their safety by sneaking away from the castle to see them. My parents remained helpless as always, although I could now forgive them for it. Next to Lady Worthing and her absent son, Gottfried was the most powerful man in the shire. No, I was a grown woman, and as such should protect my family.

I missed going to church as well, and wished to hear one of Friar John's sermons, although I never much appreciated them before. I was in just such a mood to hope they might be true.

My mind drifted back in time as I sliced a batch of shiny red apples to bake with cinnamon and honey. Apples had once been such a rare treasure. I had come so far. My thoughts faded to the rolling countryside and the day I had first bit into the juicy fruit.

"Dandelion, look. I'm a knight." Baby Tim bellowed his war cry.

"I see you, precious. Indeed you are." I waved to the sweet boy with his russet curls and big brown eyes.

Although a mere nine years old myself, I guarded my last-born brother with great care as he galloped down the lane, his plump legs astride a stick turned mighty steed in his fertile imagination. Who would have guessed he began his life in the direst circumstances? Thank God our Mum never pushed him away during that awful winter. The desperation of 1315 did not last long in the hearty Sussex countryside. The pain of Mary's death faded, and our patterns fell back into the tedious complacency of peasant life. Robert worked the fields with Mum and Da, and the ever-practical Sadie tended our home, but the riches of the castle yet called out to me.

Watching my five-year-old brother left me free to roam the village and the rolling green fields dotted with fluffy white sheep. I followed Tim on his fine *horse* down the lane and splashing through a gurgling stream. In a patchwork cluster of wildflowers, we squealed as butterflies fluttered about us. I spun alongside them through the blue cornflowers, red poppies, yellow buttercups, and purple foxgloves. My bare feet glided and leapt to the tune in my head. Tim joined in with his own energetic stomp. There were no walls, no ceilings, only space and air and movement. I thought I might float away.

Tired from all the exertion, we lay down for a few moments, quiet and still on our fragrant, grassy carpet. We watched a bee gathering nectar, listened to it buzz against the whisper of the breeze. In those hushed moments, I heard my own heart beating and matched my breath to the rhythm of the fields. I took a moment to teach Tim names for all the wonders around us. Next, I wove a flowering rainbow of blossoms through my hair, turning it into a crown of crinkling wheat-colored curls atop my sun-kissed face. I was a fairy, a nymph, the queen of the fields. My faithful knight, Sir Timothy, played along, bowing before me as the rest of my subjects bleated and chirped their cheerful homage.

Moving onward, we reached the gray stones of Arun Castle. I grazed my fingers across them, feeling texture and strength. A warm, thick aroma I suspected to be meat cascaded over the walls. Oh, how I yearned for it. The steward on his rounds stopped and smiled to us. By the tender gleam in his eye, I sensed the grandfatherly man who ran the entire castle enjoyed watching us skip and prance through the fields as I enjoyed the butterflies.

Feeling particularly bold and saucy, I meandered over to the closest apple tree—forbidden fruit to all peasants. There the red orbs hung, shining rubies, property of "his lordship" as all treasures in our corner of the world. I reached up, looked the steward in the eye, pulled one off, brought it to my mouth, and took the biggest bite I could manage. Its tart sweetness caught me unexpectedly. My lips puckered about the tasty surprise.

Over the distance I heard hearty laughter as he threw his head back and hugged his arms around his belly. He wagged his finger at me in playful disapproval and walked back toward the castle gate, scratching his head and chuckling all the while. Enthralled by my new power, I squealed and grabbed a half dozen more. Eyes peered down from the watchtower. I wrapped the fruit in the loose end of my tattered brown tunic and dashed toward home with a perplexed Baby Tim close at my heels.

One second my bare feet beat against the rugged trail, and the next something flew out of the bushes and tumbled me to the ground, knocking the air right out of me. From my pinned position, I saw a shadowy face and the outline of wavy hair against the dappled sunlight. Tim stumbled into the fray, and terror seized me, my heart about to beat right out of my chest, until I recognized a familiar voice.

"I saw what you did, Dan Dee Lion. You're in for trouble." While I admired William Ashby's courage and dash for years, he rarely spared time for an "irksome" little girl such as me.

I managed to catch my breath. "Now look at what you've done, you horrible boy." I pushed him away and brushed the hair out of my face. "You are a spoiled imp, just like everyone says."

William set about helping me gather my dusty batch of apples. The sturdy fabric of his clothing displayed the truth. Although his father had passed away the year of the famine, his family held a valuable plot of yardland, over thirty acres to our meager cottar's five. His mother's service at the castle afforded him unique opportunities and luxuries, but he was good-hearted and fun loving above all else, forever running away from his older brothers and the hard work of the fields.

"Spoiled, says who?" He ruffled Tim's hair. "Do you think I'm spoiled?" William scooped Baby Tim into his arms, and started down the path.

"No, sir." Tim said. "You're real nice, and strong too."

"You see," said William. "As the friar oft quotes, 'out of the mouth of babes.' I thought you looked ripe for a good teasing. That's all. I didn't mean to knock you down so hard. Awfully sorry about that. Those apples do look lovely, though. I can't believe he let you get away with it."

"Well, clearly you know not who you are addressing." I stopped, lifted my chin, and attempted to peer down my nose at him. "Allow me to introduce myself. I am Dandelion, fairy queen of all you survey. Cross me again and you may wake up missing a toe, or with a giant wart on that ugly snout of yours." Although in fact, he had soft sandy hair and warm golden-brown eyes. I was quite charmed in spite of myself.

William feigned a look of outrage but couldn't hold back a laugh. "You're funny, Dan Dee Lion. I like you. You have spirit. Not nearly the annoying little girl I remember, but that name of yours is quite a mouthful. I think I shall call you Dandy."

A nickname! High praise from this well-favored boy three years my senior.

William continued toward home. "You're different than the other village children, you know that? A far cry smarter, I'm thinking. We should team up, you and I."

Baby Tim tugged on his sleeve. "And me?"

"Why, of course, you too." William winked my way. "You and I and Baby Tim. I think it's nigh time we joined forces. I've been considering starting myself a poaching band."

Suspicion filled my voice. "Poaching?" It was a dangerous endeavor, yet the idea held allure . . . free reign over all the bounty of the forest.

"Yes, like this rogue Robin Hood and his merry men I heard a tale about once at the castle," William said. "I think you're just the folks to join me. If, of course, you're so inclined, your royal highness."

Any doubts were banished by mention of the castle. I longed to live out a story told within those mystical walls. "Well, I shall have to consult my advisors, of course. I'm certain I would be an excellent addition to your band. What I'm wondering, good sir, is how I shall benefit?"

William hiked Tim up higher on his hip. "Let's see. You already saw an impressive display of my strength and speed, m'lady. I have my own knife, and I've been working on a slingshot in my spare time. Then of course, you must take into account my amazing cunning and craftiness. Add to that a little of your fairy magic, and we'll be unstoppable."

I maintained an air of indifference as I considered the offer.

"Think of it—squirrels, rabbits, birds, maybe even some fish." William tilted his head. "Can't you just taste it?"

I looked down at the root-knotted trail a moment before whispering my confession. "Well, I've never actually eaten meat before." I shot a timid glance up at him.

William gaped. "Never? Not even a goose on Twelfth Night?"

Tim bounced in William's arms. "No, me neither. Please, oh please, Dandy, can we?"

How could I resist my joyful little brother?

"It will be quite a grand adventure." William looked hopeful.

I recalled the enticing scent of meat wafting over the castle walls. "I suppose it sounds fun enough. When do we start?"

William glowed with triumph. "Well, those apples are a fair start for today. What say you? Can you spare one for your new partner in crime?"

"Actually, I do have an extra." I unraveled my tunic and offered one toward him. As he reached, I snatched it back. "Do we have a pact?"

"Indeed, a pact. Meet me here tomorrow at noontide." He pried the apple from my fingers. We shook on it, and he bit into the juicy fruit, sealing the agreement and our budding friendship.

I took a luxurious bite of the fruit in my hand. I would never go hungry again. No one could take my new life away from me. Yet I couldn't help missing vestiges of my previous existence. This evening I would ask Gottfried about attending the small castle chapel and about inviting my family for supper in the tower. I dared not risk encountering William at the village. I had no idea what I could ever say to him. Could I even bear the sight? My heart still shut down merely at the thought. Thus, supper tonight must be perfect.

I selected a special flask of wine upon the steward's suggestion earlier that morning. Once the bread was finished, I moved to the medley of summer vegetables, arranging them artfully upon the tray. I would serve them with a side dish of smoked fish. The cook even gave me the recipe for Gottfried's favorite baked apples. I hoped the meal would put him in the right frame of mind for my request. I stopped my frantic preparations and pressed my hand to my mouth.

How could I ever bare if it did not?

I surprised Gottfried by wearing the rose-colored tunic he loved so much. I rarely donned it now that I had my own clothing. The mystery of its origin still plagued me, but on that evening I would go to any lengths to please him. When he returned from his rounds, his eyes lit up.

Halfway through supper he opened a conversation about the plans to hire the new castle steward. "I shall miss Michael. He is a good man. It's a fine line he walks, keeping in Lady Worthing's good graces while being fair to the servants."

I breathed a long held sigh of relief. Gottfried was speaking to me of his own volition. "I will miss him too. We've been friends since I was a child."

"I know." He took a generous bite of pheasant.

My fingers shook as I refilled his wine goblet. "Gus, I've been meaning to mention . . . I miss my family so. Do you think we could invite them to supper some evening?"

"Dandelion, after all they've done to you? Where's your pride, your self-respect? Why would you put yourself through that?"

Evidently, during my months of chitchat, I complained overmuch about my family. I braced myself. "They aren't so bad. We had a disagreement. That's all. I'm sure they will forgive me."

He swept some invisible crumbs off the table. "Forgiveness is an illusion, Dandelion. The past always catches up. Grudges are real, always simmering beneath the surface. It won't be worth it. Trust me concerning this."

I wrung my hands upon my lap. "But they're my family. I love them. I miss them. I need them." And I certainly hoped Gottfried's pessimistic view of the world was wrong.

"You have everything you need right here." A cold edge found its way into his voice.

Needing to soothe him before another violent outburst ensued, I grasped for his hands over the table with my own trembling ones. "And I appreciate it, I do. Don't misunderstand, but please, can't I see my family? Just once. If it doesn't work out, I promise I won't ask again."

He contemplated for several minutes before responding. "No, it's out of the question. I won't allow it. Perhaps you can forgive them, but I cannot." He let go of my hands and continued eating.

I stared down at my empty palms, tempted to argue, but doubting it could help. More likely it would send him into another rage. My stomach twisted in knots. I struggled to hold my emotions in check, as I knew Gottfried expected, but began shaking with sobs nonetheless.

To my surprise he rushed over and scooped me into his arms. I cried in earnest against his unyielding chest.

"May I at least go to mass, then? Sometimes?" I hiccupped through my tears. "Here in the castle chapel, not in the village."

"Why must you torture yourself? Father John was more irate than any of them. If it were up to him you'd still be living in that hovel with your parents. He's made you the wayward topic of his sermons for months."

I didn't want to believe Gottfried, but for as much as I loved Friar John, he certainly could be irrational, and he had made it clear his loyalties lay with William. There was nothing left to say on the subject, but I cried in Gottfried's arms for a good long while. My husband was right. I was being childish. I tried to push aside the sick feeling in my stomach, the ache in my heart. Where was my pride? I had vowed never to go back to them. Was bringing them to me any better? "But I'm so, so lonely." I sobbed against Gottfried's rock-solid shoulder.

"I'm sorry. I'm too set in my ways. I've forgotten how to live with others, but I'm trying. And soon, there will be a little Gus or Dandy. You can talk to them and teach them and play with them until your heart's content. Forget about your old family, Dandelion. We shall make our own."

I smiled, still teary-eyed. The knots in my stomach untangled. Why hadn't I thought of a baby? Of course, a year had passed already, but Gottfried was not forceful with his lovemaking. He waited for some sign of willingness, and those were few enough after the first several months.

A baby, of course. I would apply myself to the task with all diligence. I reached up to kiss my husband full on the mouth.

A few days later Gottfried arrived in the morning with a sheepish look on his face and his hands hidden behind his back.

I sat up in bed, not ready to leave the soft blankets behind yet. "Where is my breakfast?" I pretended to be peevish.

"I brought you a surprise." He pulled a basket from behind his back. At first I thought it was breakfast after all. Then a funny little mewling sound emerged. He laid the basket on the bed, and the cloth napkin wiggled. I lifted it and squealed. A tiny, fluffy white puppy with a pretty red bow about its neck stared up at me with enormous eyes.

I didn't know whether to hug Gottfried or my precious gift first, but somehow managed to scoop the puppy in one hand and reach for my husband with the other.

He chuckled. "I thought you would like it. A baby may take a while, but this I can give you right away."

"Thank you, thank you, thank you." I bounced on the bed. "I love it. I love you so much. What is its name? Is it male or female? Whatever do I feed it?"

"Whoa, settle yourself. She's a female, and you may name her whatever you like. She can eat scraps from the kitchen, meat and cheese primarily."

My skin buzzed with the excitement of it. I stroked her soft curly hair. "Oh, I think I shall name her Cloud. She's so beautiful." She felt so warm, alive, and wonderful.

"She'll keep you busy." He reached over and let the puppy nip at his fingers. "You must train her not to relieve herself indoors and keep her from chewing the furniture."

"I will, I will, I promise. Oh, thank you, Gus."

"I was beginning to think you would move Roman into the house. This will work much better."

Gottfried made a joke? I lost my grip. Cloud nearly squirmed away.

I surveyed my elegant surroundings, again taken aback by their grandeur. I snuggled the frivolous pet beneath my chin while lounging within the pile of luxurious coverlets. Precisely how my faith and ambition had brought me to this place, I still did not understand. It was all I ever hoped it to be, yet at once so much less.

But I had a puppy. I had a puppy, and Gottfried made a joke. If I could only have a baby, things might just be complete.

Chapter 12

Midsummer brought with it two secret delights. That hazy golden season had long been my favorite. The entire earth slowed down in some sort of heat-induced lethargy. It forced one to stop and take deep breaths, to pause and contemplate the glowing sun and ripe fields bursting with life, to splash in a stream and listen to the gurgle of the water. Midsummer was always glorious, but none compared with the summer of 1329.

My first surprise came one afternoon while dusting the books. As I attempted to return a small stack of them, something blocked their path. I pulled them out and reached to the back of the shelf. There I found a small volume covered in brown leather pressed flat against the wood.

As I picked it up, I knew in an instant I held something monumental in my hands—a book burnt about the cover and along the edge of the pages. No title was discernable. I opened it slowly. On the first page, written in Gottfried's own handwriting, the inscription called out to me. *"Words that have changed my life from the woman who is my life."*

I slammed the book shut. I nearly dropped it, thinking flames might burst out and burn me as well. Gottfried would never want me intruding upon something so personal. I thrust it onto the shelf and covered it again. I pressed myself against the wall and took a few deep breaths. Who could the woman be? Was it I? Perhaps she was the woman of the rose-colored tunic. That little book could hold so many answers. Gottfried must never know I found it.

The next morning I hopped out of bed long before Gottfried returned from training with the soldiers. I went downstairs and removed the book from the shelf, sliding it deep within the hidden pockets of my kirtle. I replaced the other volumes, leaving a slight space between them and the wall.

It was difficult going about my day as though nothing was amiss. Gottfried was surprised to see me up when he returned. I was playing with Cloud and an old stocking and told him the dog woke me early.

He laughed and said I shouldn't spoil the creature so. I managed to remain calm during breakfast and even worked on my embroidery before announcing I was off to visit Roman.

Alone in Roman's stall, I found the courage to open the book again. "This is it, boy." I read through the inscription. "There's no turning back."

He whinnied his approval.

I turned the first page.

The unfamiliar script shocked me. It looked like some of the Arabic texts Gottfried kept on the shelf. I had never even heard him speak the language. However was this supposed to help? Then I flipped through and found a page I could read. "Translations of Poems by Samia." Well, it wasn't exactly what I hoped for, but at least I could understand it.

> *I dream of the day that I die,*
> *when at last I am held*
> *in God's ecstatic arms.*

> *Distance will fade, our hearts pour together as one.*
> *I will cup His cheek in my hand*
> *with passionate disregard.*

> *I dream of the day*
> *when He shall adore my exquisite beauty,*
> *and at last I may meld into His flesh.*

I closed my eyes against the intensity of the words. They vibrated somewhere in the inmost core of my being. Almost against my will, I slammed the book shut. No wonder Gottfried hid this. Surely it was blasphemy. And yet . . . somehow the sweetest blasphemy ever written. I stroked my fingers over the worn leather.

I ventured to open the book again. What a beautiful thought—to be held in the arms of God—for your hearts to pour together—to meld into God's flesh. My eyes filled with tears. I wanted to read more, and yet I was afraid. Who was this Samia? Had Gottfried known her? Had he loved her? Was she the woman who was his very life? Was she the woman of the rose-colored tunic, or was she some faceless poet from the ancient world?

The words spoke of God almost as her lover. I never heard of such a thing. I knew people were supposed to love God, but wasn't it to be some sort of spiritual or perhaps intellectual love—something sterile almost? It wasn't intended to be this sort of passionate intimacy, was it? Yet I could almost feel it. I held the book to my nose and inhaled the earthy scent, pulling it deep within my lungs.

Turning the page, I saw more English poems written in Gottfried's bold hand. I wasn't ready to read them, though. The one had nearly burst my mind to shreds.

"Well, I think that is quite enough for today. Isn't it, boy?" I slipped the book back into my pocket and walked forward to snuggle with the sweet horse. I hadn't discovered any new information about Gottfried. Yet the mere fact that he owned such a book contained startling insight. The Gottfried I knew only scorned and mocked religion. He avoided emotion and intensity. He hated wordiness. Who was this Gottfried? What had changed him? Or was he merely hiding this side from me?

Those thoughts spun through my head for days. I barely noticed all the bustle and commotion at the castle until my old friend Michael, the steward, caught me in the kitchen.

"Dandy, Dandy my girl," he shouted, tottering over to catch me. "You're not going to let an old man leave without saying good-bye, are you?"

"My goodness, is it time already? The new steward hasn't even arrived." I glanced about the kitchen, not entirely sure how I got there.

"Well, of course he has. He's been here for days." Michael squinted at me. "In truth, the question is where have you been? Off somewhere with your head in the clouds, it looks to me."

"I suppose you've caught me. Oh, Michael, I'm happy for you." I gave him a long and heartfelt hug. The sort only appropriate for a man of his advanced years. "But I will miss you so." I whispered the last part in his ear, choking back a sob.

He gave my shoulder a pat. "It will be all right, dearie. Indeed, you're stronger than you realize."

"I hope so." I let him go and stepped back, swiping my eyes. "So then, where is the handsome new steward you promised me?"

"I believe I promised he'd be charming, not handsome. Not quite the same thing. He's busy down at the village right now. Got to work right away, he did. Wanted to meet everybody and get a feel for the place. I think he'll do a fine job." As Michael spoke, he made his way over to the checkerboard and tapped it.

He found time for one last round, which he won, before setting off to pack his bags. I moped my way about the kitchen, fetching food for supper.

"So, you must be the pretty little soldier's whore I've heard so much about."

I gasped. The words stung like a slap, but as I spun around to face my attacker, his cheeky grin soothed the blow.

"I . . . I . . . ." I noticed the most charming glimmer in his dark eyes. "I am married to the head guard, if that's what you mean." I pressed a hand to my burning cheek.

"Yes, I've heard that rumor as well. Quite a bit of mystery surrounding you Miss . . . Dandelion, isn't it?"

"That's Missus Westover, to you, sir," I said cheekily in return. Something about his cheerful bluntness was refreshing.

"If you say so." He leaned against the heavy kitchen table and folded his arms across his chest. "Although, according to your sister, that would be either 'Missus Heartless Strumpet' or 'Missus Selfish Little She-Wench.' Would you care to hear what else they are calling you in the village?"

"I'm not so sure I would." I turned away to fetch a loaf of bread for my empty basket.

He followed close at my heels. "Ahh, but knowledge is power, my pretty. Don't worry. 'Heartless Strumpet' is likely the worst of it. 'Hermit's wife' is bandied about. Oh, and 'Whore of Babylon' I believe."

"Yes, that sounds like Friar John."

"Well, clearly I didn't believe a word of it, or I would never tease you so."

I searched his glimmering eyes, finding only merriment in their depths. "I would certainly hope not."

"I've been looking forward to meeting you. You're the most exciting thing this rustic little town has ever seen."

"Did you hear I have fairy magic?" I tossed over my shoulder.

He resumed his casual position against a nearby ledge. "Ah yes, but it seems it turned to dark magic when you moved into the dreary castle tower."

"Dreary, hah. You would laugh your breeches off if ever you saw it. It's prettier than Lady Worthing's own chamber." I placed a few boiled eggs into my basket next to the bread.

"Shh! Hush this instant, fairy child." He looked from side to side in an exaggerated and comical fashion. "Her spies are everywhere." He held my full attention now. "I think I've failed to properly introduce myself. Richard Wright, second son of the third son of the fifth daughter of some ancient earl somewhere in bloody old England, named after the late great King Richard the Lionhearted, at your service, my lady." He followed the recitation with a deep bow.

I could see why Michael described him as charming but not handsome. His features were a bit too sharp and angular. He was thinner than most women preferred, but he had dark wavy hair and the most beautiful eyes, nearly black. His smooth, pale cheeks sported a flush of pink in the center of each. His lopsided grin was enough to make any female tingly and weak in the knees. I was not as impervious to it as I wished I might be.

I executed an embellished curtsey of my own. "I'm pleased to make your acquaintance, Mister Richard Wright, second son of the third son of the fifth daughter of some ancient earl somewhere in bloody old England."

He arched one brow at my perfect imitation of his affected speech.

"I am Dandelion, formerly addressed as the crippled cottar's daughter, now known far and wide as 'Heartless Strumpet,' 'Selfish Little She-Wench,' 'Whore of Babylon,' and purveyor of the dark magic arts."

"Ahh, a quick one, aren't you? No one mentioned that. This is going to be even more fun than I imagined."

"What is going to be even more fun than you imagined?" I feigned irritation as a pleasant flush flowed over me.

"Well, I was informed by my predecessor that one of my most pressing duties was to befriend one Dandelion Westover. That is you, is it not?"

"Yes, I forgot that one in my litany of titles, as well as 'Soldier's Whore' and 'Hermit's Wife.'"

"You did indeed." He watched me out of the corner of his eye with the lopsided grin in place. It warmed me in places it should not. My blood hadn't coursed through my veins like this since William. Oh, how I missed the sensation. It brought me right back to that summer and kissing rock. Something about Richard's easy manner reminded me of my William. Surely that explained the reaction. Or at least I hoped as much.

Richard and I stood locked in a silent exchange for several moments before he shook his head to break the spell. "So what do you say, then? Friends?"

"Absolutely." Of course, friends. I was a married woman now, no longer a village maid. I chided myself.

"Good, for I was beginning to despair there wasn't a decent bit of conversation to be found anywhere in this Godforsaken valley."

"Godforsaken?" I resumed collecting my supplies. "I may not be well traveled, sir, but I remain fairly certain this is one of the prettiest places on earth." Surely there was no harm in enjoying his entertaining banter.

"Touché. You have got a point there. What shall I say then—culture deprived, lacking in sophistication?" He stayed put this time but followed my progress with his provocative eyes.

My own remained locked to his. "Yes, well with those I can heartily agree. My husband and I have a very nice library, though. Do you like to read?" A reminder of my husband would set the proper tone.

"I do indeed, but I think I shall be too busy for a time. You are quite an original, Missus Westover. This promises to be fun."

"I think you may be right." I turned on my heel and sashayed away while I still could, needing time to recall my wedding vows and consider how to maintain a proper friendship with this charming young man. I spared one last glance at my second secret delight of the sun-drenched season of midsummer.

As harvest arrived, I begged Gottfried to let Richard come to supper one night, certain that he liked the fellow after all these weeks. I had, in fact, already issued the invitation. With Richard running the castle and Gottfried guarding it, they had much opportunity to work together, and did so quite well. Although Gottfried smiled at my comment that he owed Richard a great debt for saving him hundreds of words a day, he insisted he was in no mood for company. Noticing tears in my eyes, Gottfried suggested I dine with Richard in the Great Hall. "It is customary, after all. I'll eat early. You can sit with me and then be off for a bit of fun. You aren't cut out for solitude."

Was there a bit of indictment in that statement? Who on earth cared if there was?

I dashed upstairs to change into my newest silken gown made of the deep purple I so adored since my first glance of Gottfried's home. I topped it with a short lavender cotehardie featuring long flowing sleeves that reached to my knees and split from top to bottom to reveal the slim under-sleeves of the tunic beneath. It was quite an elaborate creation of ribbons, embroidery, and adornments. Supper in the great hall was an even better premier than I imagined.

Supper in the great hall! I covered my face with my hands, suppressed a squeal, and beat my toes gleefully against the floor. After all these long months, I would enter the castle proper. The entire staff would be there, along with Lady Worthing, any visiting nobility, and their retinues. Richard had mentioned her sister and family were passing through this week, but I had never dreamed to meet them. There could be as many as a hundred people on a single night. Perhaps there would be minstrels and jugglers, even a troubadour to sing songs about legendary heroes. I itched to dash over there this instant. However would I wait?

I suffered through supper with Gottfried, a false smile glued in place. His eyes widened at the sight of my new dress, but he was talked out for the day. I jumped a foot when the knock arrived, so foreign was the sound in this place. Gottfried nodded, and I darted for the entrance, giving my floor-length kirtle a final fluff before opening the door.

Richard's usual expression of casual boredom switched to something far different when he saw me. He stood gaping for a moment before recovering himself. "My, my, I was completely unaware what a fashionable woman I would be dining with this evening." Entering and seeing Gottfried's half-eaten plate in front of him, Richard was crestfallen. "I'm so, so sorry. Am I late?"

"No, Richard," Gottfried said. "I'm not feeling up to company tonight. Dandelion will join you in the great hall, if that meets with your approval."

"Absolutely." Richard winked at me. "But are you quite certain you trust me with this lovely lady of yours?"

"Why not? I'll slit your throat if you don't treat her with the utmost respect." They both laughed, but the message was clear.

"I'll be right back." I ran upstairs to fetch my headpiece. Looking into the mirror, I fastened it just right. The creamy gossamer scarves of the new barbet were held in place by a thin golden headband. This latest fashion concealed very little. Tonight was the first time Richard had seen me with my hair uncovered. In the mirror I watched the blonde silken swirls falling over my shoulder and down my bodice. No wonder the strong reaction. The first day we met, we were unfortunately smitten with each other. Since then, though, we managed to be nothing more than companions, chums. The relationship was important to both of us, so we made every effort to keep the tenor light and friendly.

I tucked my hair into the netting and headed back down to the men. "I'm ready."

Richard offered his arm as we descended the steep tower stairs. I wore flimsy satin slippers and was happy for his extra support. If a slight hum and crackle flowed between us, it was no fault of mine. We maintained the contact as we traveled through the courtyard toward the great hall. Walking to the castle proper arm in arm with Richard . . . it was almost more than my heart could bear.

Rich smells of venison and vegetables met us at the huge double doors. The room was indeed full of boisterous life. Rowdy soldiers mingled in one corner. A few children ran about. I squeezed Richard's arm. "Oh, look." I nodded toward the dogs and falcons resting near their owners at the long tables. As we entered, the serving maids arrived through a different door and were greeted with a hearty cheer.

On the raised dais in front of the room, Lady Worthing and her guests enjoyed themselves. She leaned over a table covered with a burgundy cloth to match the coats of arms along the gray walls. Was that relaxed and pleasant woman the same Lady Worthing I met on the day of my interview? She chatted with another lady I guessed to be her sister and even stopped to catch one of the children in a hug as he dashed past. The lady of the castle gave the little boy a gentle reprimand and pointed him in the direction of the bench, where she wanted him to sit.

Richard led me to a quiet trestle table in the back. I noticed one of the soldiers pinching Betsy on the rear as we passed. She rebuked him as expected, but her eyes were smiling the entire time. We were able to slip by unnoticed. But things were not as relaxed after that. People whispered and some pointed directly at me.

How could I blame them? I had lived as a stranger here for over a year now. Their curiosity was only natural. I clasped my trembling fingers about a goblet of red wine and took a bracing sip, determined to prove my place among them.

The volume decreased as the castle-dwellers settled down to their meals. We were served our food on a trencher of bread. My family could never spare bread for such a treat, and Gottfried preferred to eat from plates, so already the evening was an adventure. Richard and I sat close on the wooden bench, but that was expected since we shared our trencher. He took out his own small dagger to cut our meat, offering me the best pieces, feeding me from the tip of his knife, finding opportunities to graze my lips with his soft fingers. If I enjoyed his warmth and spicy scent a bit too much, surely I was not to be blamed.

We talked and joked every day for months. Tonight, we were oddly without words, gazing instead into each other's eyes, his so dark and fathomless. The silence between us was strikingly different than the type I shared with Gottfried.

Minstrels strolled about, playing dreamy music as we ate. Flickering torches and candles added to the mood. A fiddler stopped and sang a love ballad directly to me. Richard looked proud as the room took notice. "You're the prettiest girl here," he whispered.

I ducked my chin to hide my smile. Surely the swishing in my head was from the rich wine, not from his compliment. I dared not respond.

After the last course, Lady Catherine Worthing called for the dancing to commence. I hadn't danced in so long. I did so miss it. Tables were cleared away and stacked against the wall before the first number began. Although the men vastly outnumbered the women, a few fortunate soldiers snatched up girls from around the room. A nobleman and his wife, the woman I suspected to be Lady Worthing's sister, joined in the fun. They were well-coordinated dances. Everyone seemed to know the steps and patterns, but I had never seen them before. I watched, my body swaying of its own accord to the pulse of the music. My toe tapped against the fresh rushes on the floor, releasing the perfume of the dried flowers mixed among them.

"Would you care to dance?" Richard spoke into my ear over the noise.

"I don't know this style. In the village we just sort of jumped around to the music."

"But look at you. You can hardly sit still."

"Indeed, I admit it. I would love to dance, but don't get mad if I mess it all up and step on your big feet. You've been fairly warned."

He stood, bowed, and offered his hand to lift me from the bench.

The dancers welcomed us and opened a spot within the swirling circle. I stumbled at first. I did indeed step on Richard's big feet and giggled up at him, but the dance was repetitive. Before long the tune seeped into my being, and I performed the moves with flair.

The next piece was slower, accenting my graceful posture and slim lines. I followed Richard and the flow of the music with an instinctual ability. Those moments when he caught me in his arms for a spin or took my hand in a promenade were nothing short of magical. I felt I might float away upon a cloud.

When the dance finished, a tall friendly soldier named Gerald whisked me away from Richard, declaring Gottfried's bride had been hidden in secret long enough. He made me laugh and feel right at home. I danced with many of the soldiers before Richard managed to reclaim me.

"I thought they'd never let you go." He tried to sound perturbed, but I could tell he was pleased for me.

Once the music slowed to a halt, the dancers wandered toward their

tables. A sharp, clear voice cut through the din of the room. "Richard."
It was Lady Worthing.

Richard tensed.

My stomach fell among the rushes at my feet.

"My lady." He managed to respond in a bright voice. "How may
I be of service?"

"I thought you weren't going to make it to supper tonight."

He turned to address her. "A change of plans, m'lady. I trust I have
not caused you any inconvenience."

"No, none at all." She was smiling, but I was not convinced. "Bring
your companion here. We should like to meet her."

"By all means, noble lady." We walked to the head table and stood
before them.

I held tight to Richard's hand and fought to keep my breathing
steady. This was the moment I had waited for. I would not muck it
up this time.

"May I introduce to you Dandelion Westover, my dear friend and
wife of your guard, Gottfried Westover."

"Indeed. It's high time you show your face, wench. I was beginning
to think you were merely a figment of Gotty's warped imagination."
She and her friends laughed.

Not quite the verbal slap she had given me the last time we spoke.
Lady Worthing sounded almost cheerful despite the barb to her
words. Still, I remained on my guard. I wasn't sure what to say when
Richard nudged me.

"Bow," he whispered between clenched teeth.

My mind clicked into action. "I'm honored to make your
acquaintance, m'lady," I said with a curtsey. "I apologize for my
oversight. I am new to courtly manners. My husband does not much
like to socialize, but I meant no offense. This evening has been truly
lovely, and I am so sorry I've missed out on your generous hospitality
all this time."

"Listen to her, is she joking?" said the woman to Lady Worthing's
left. "New to courtly manners? I wish my own daughter could
give a pretty little speech as you did." She shot a glance at a lass of
marriageable age down the bench.

The girl rolled her eyes and returned to a sullen pout.

Lady Catherine Worthing took a smug sip from her wine goblet.
"I assure you she's completely in earnest, my dear sister. She was
nothing but a slovenly peasant mere months ago. The name alone is
proof. Dandelion. Hah, could a more common and crass name possibly
exist? Whatever did Gottfried do to you? Is it true the two of you are
involved in black magic?"

I stifled a gasp. Would she charge me with witchcraft and be done
with me for good?

The sister flicked Lady Worthing on the shoulder. "Oh hush up,
Catherine. Don't listen to her for a moment, dear. Why, you're a

natural. Anyone can see. I for one commend a young woman who can better herself and move up in the world. Lord knows, we did a bit of that ourselves, Catty. My sister gets all worked up when she isn't the most beautiful woman in the room."

Daggers flew from Lady Worthing's eyes toward her sister.

Richard diffused the situation. "Ah, that is where I must chance to disagree with you, Lady Tallanger. Your lovely sister shall forever be the most beautiful woman in any room. Only you yourself hold a candle to her."

Lady Worthing relaxed and smiled her thanks to Richard.

I realized I had been holding my breath and let it out with a quiet swoosh. "Oh, that silken tongue will get you far in life, my boy," Lady Tallanger's husband said. He lifted his glass of wine. "But since that is my wife you're speaking of, let's agree we are blessed to be in the presence of three extraordinarily beautiful women."

That should have appeased everyone, but a shriek came from the mouth of the pouty lass, who was otherwise quite comely.

Lord Tallanger tipped his glass toward his daughter. "I stand corrected, four extraordinarily beautiful women."

"Here, here," said Richard. Everyone agreed to the sentiment, drinking a toast to it.

"Do sit with us a moment, Dandelion." Lady Tallanger motioned to the empty bench across from her. "I must ask about that dress you're wearing. Wherever did you find it?"

Richard and I slid onto the offered seat. Did she like the dress? Had I done something to offend?

Before I could answer, Lady Worthing cut me off. "I don't know where she found it, but clearly I've been paying Gottfried far too much." She sounded more like the pleasant woman I saw when I entered. "I've only seen a dress like it once before, and that was on the wife of a duke."

"Is that your story then, Dandelion?" said Lady Tallanger. "Is Gottfried a duke in disguise?"

I sat up straight. "Not that I'm aware of, m'lady. He does, however, own a collection of exquisite fabrics from his time in the orient. I designed the dress myself."

"Completely on your own, out of your own head?" Lady Worthing eyed the dress up and down.

"Well, I may have caught sight of the duchess you mentioned." I adjusted the sleeve and smoothed the skirt. "We do have a bird's eye view from the tower."

"I thought so," said Lady Worthing.

"Still, Catty, look at the craftsmanship of it, and the girl has a brilliant eye for color." Lady Tallanger reached across the table for my hand.

It took all my self-control not to jump at the unexpected gesture.

Lady Tallanger took no notice. "Dandelion, you simply must come sew with us tomorrow and teach us how to make this dress."

"Oh would you?" The pouty daughter sparked to life. "My friends would be so jealous. The tournament in Southampton is only a few weeks away."

Again, words failed me. I so wanted to get this right. That they admired my dress made me thrum with pleasure. That Lady Worthing might turn on me at a whim caused my throat to clutch.

"Wait one moment," said Lady Worthing. "We have a very busy schedule organized for your visit. Tomorrow I've planned a hunt. I can't cancel it for sewing lessons from a peasant girl, and the next day we have a picnic." Her face was tightening back into the icy expression I associated with her.

"Oh dear, you're right." Lady Tallanger let go of my hand to rub her sister's back. "Well, what about the day after tomorrow then? Are you free, Dandelion?"

I almost laughed out loud at the funny look Richard shot sideways in reference to my pathetic social calendar. I caught myself and said, "The day after tomorrow should be fine. No doubt I can free up a few hours. I would be delighted to teach you."

"I don't sew, Sarah, and I certainly don't take sewing lessons." Lady Worthing's voice was colder than ever, her sister's calming strokes not delivering the desired effect. Yet my fear diminished in the ongoing support of the noblewoman.

Lady Sarah Tallanger was not swayed by Catherine's harsh tone. "Well, join us anyway. It will be fun."

"Please, Auntie Cat." The teen crooned, melting Lady Worthing's demeanor. "Perhaps Dandelion would be willing to demonstrate on a dress for you to keep."

"If I must," said Lady Worthing. "You know I can never deny you children."

"Good, then, it's settled." Lady Tallanger turned back to me in triumph. "Dandelion, meet us in the solar at noon. We'll have luncheon together while we work. See if you can get that old warrior of yours to part with a few bolts of fabric. I'd be happy to pay him market value."

"Certainly. I'll be there, and I'll bring whatever materials I can. I'm looking forward to it."

As Richard walked me back to our table, I realized it was true. These women may be intimidating, but I so missed female companionship. Already they treated me more like an equal than any of the women at the castle thus far. Lady Tallanger was a friendlier, softer version of her sister, and I looked forward to spending time with her and learning better my new place in the world.

A final set of dancing began as we reached our table. "Shall we?" said Richard, spinning me around once for effect.

"Oh, Richard, I'm far too tired. Those soldiers nearly danced my feet off."

"Well, you've accomplished plenty for one night." We settled side by side upon a bench, facing outward to better enjoy the view. "Not only were you the highlight of the party, you've been invited to luncheon with the lady of the castle. You're practically a peer of the realm."

"Don't be silly." I longed to rest my head against his shoulder, but would never dare such a public display of affection. "They only want me to sew. I'm little better than a shop girl to them."

"Ah, now there you are wrong. Nobles are very strict about manners and customs. Luncheon in the solar is code for 'you are one of us now.' They are treating you as a lady."

I gazed at him for a while. I looked at the head table and back to him again. Candlelight glimmered in his impish eyes. "What do you think, Richard? Do you see me as a lady now?"

"Dandelion," he whispered into my ear. "On your worst day as a peasant girl in the fields, I have no doubt you were a finer lady than any woman in this room." His warm breath feathered over my ear as he spoke.

I felt tingly all over, the tingles extending as I melted into his eyes. The secret lingered on my skin like a kiss. I licked my lips and bit down on the bottom one in spite of myself.

Richard cleared his throat. "Friends?"

I steeled my heart against these mounting sensations and echoed my answer from the day we first met. "Absolutely." I smiled up at him, but the smile was bittersweet.

"We'd better be going before I get in trouble with that brutal husband of yours."

I laughed, although it wasn't funny. "Yes. It's past time for me to get home."

The next morning I found myself longing to read more of Gottfried's secret journal. The books so sent my mind reeling the first time, I had not yet mustered the courage to look at it again. All of a sudden, I wanted to learn more—more about Samia and Gottfried and more about Samia's God. I felt ready. And so I hid myself away in Roman's stall, reading against the soothing backdrop of the horses nickering.

I sat awestruck upon the sweet-smelling hay as I thumbed through the pages. Lines and tidbits swirled through my head like a spell.

Spinning between earth and sacred praise,
my body sings, like the sun . . . .

Upon Your breath, I watch the leaves enthralled in dance.
I too shall flutter and twirl
within the enchantment of Your divine spirit . . . .

How could Gottfried experience these magical words and still be the cold and rational person he was? Not only had he read them, he had studied them, translated them, written them down in his own hand. It didn't make sense.

You pull us toward your lips,
extending like the moon in all its radiant splendor . . . .

I will stretch my arms to feel
the raindrop dance upon my palms,
feeling life, feeling You in a wild and watery rush.

My Lord. Who was this woman Samia to know her God so, and why didn't I? Was her God my God too? Surely she was a Moslem infidel. If this was the God of the infidels, perhaps I should become one.
I continued to ponder Samia's poems.

I dive deep into the clear pool of God.
I am enraptured
by the cool silken liquid molding to my bare skin.
I glide effortlessly, set free
from earthly weights. My ears are filled with the gentle swish
that washes away memory and desire.

I am now.

Were these the words of an infidel? Must one become godless to truly find God? Nature reflecting the grandeur and wonder of God was a theme repeated throughout these verses. How foolish was I? For years I danced and played within the essence of divinity, and I never even noticed. How blind could one girl be?
It all seemed so clear now, but perhaps it was too late. I could no longer romp and roam through creation, through the very soul of God. I was restricted to stone towers, castles, and wooden barns. Oh, occasionally I walked with Gottfried for a few stolen moments in that mystical paradise, but those walks were like the brief ones I gave Cloud for her to relieve herself.
"Good Lord, Roman." I looked at the horse aghast. "My life is amazingly similar to Cloud's. The pleasures I convince myself to appreciate are nothing more than the table scraps of life. But is this truly living? Most certainly not."
My mind buzzed and brimmed with new thoughts and desires. I wished I could talk to William about them. I still missed him desperately. Even if Gottfried allowed me to visit him, though, it wouldn't be fair. William wanted me to be his wife, his partner. I wouldn't toss a few scraps of friendship to him and make matters worse.

93

With whom could I discuss these ideas? They were too intricate to process on my own, stirring something deep inside of me, but I didn't have a clue how to tap that inner well. Oh, how I wanted to. Father John might know the secret, but I would not talk to him if my soul depended on it, although likely it did.

"What do you think of this one, Roman?" I read it aloud. "'Bless me, oh Beloved, with those timeless enshrouded moments.'" Roman crooked his head to the side, as if puzzled.

"I know," I said. "I shall be pondering that for a long time—timeless moments. Can such a thing exist? And yet, I can almost glimpse what she means." I closed my eyes and allowed my mind to drift. "Yes, in fact, I do know what she means. In the presence of her God time ceases to exist, and yet each moment seems to last forever as she basks in the radiance of her Beloved. Look, here she describes love as at once the 'greatest stillness and the most vibrant act.'"

The horse did not reply. Instead he bent his head to gather a mouthful of grain.

I pulled at my hair in frustration. "Don't you see, Roman? I want that kind of love. I want the intimacy and intensity Samia wrote about. I need it in my life, but will I ever find it with Gottfried? Hah! You know him better than anyone. It's hopeless. My life is hopeless."

He looked at me with sympathy.

"It's not fair, Roman. It's just not fair."

Roman, always the skeptic, shook his head from side to side.

"Good God in heaven, help me. I've been reduced to discussing the status of the universe with a horse. And worse yet, he's right. It is entirely fair. I brought this upon myself but, oh God, how I regret it."

Tears pricked my eyes. I wished at that moment I knew how to pray and truly talk to God. The prayers I memorized as a child didn't seem to work. Once again a new kind of world glimmered before me, but stretch as I might, I couldn't reach it. I should have left the book in its secret hideaway and never opened this celestial sphere of my awareness, but it was too late.

I stood and walked to the horse before my frustration overtook me. "Well, old boy." I stroked his mane. "I've been here far too long already, but I'll be back tomorrow with treats. Yes I will. That's my good boy." I snuggled with him a moment longer before returning to the tower.

Chapter 14

A mere two days later nothing could have been further from my mind than the nebulous world of mystic poetry. I was caught up in a blaze of cutting, pinning, sewing, and female companionship. Lady Tallanger was ever so much fun, and even her pouty daughter, Lady Jane, brightened at the thought of new clothing. I was taken aback to realize she was close to my own age. I felt so old of late.

We worked in Lady Worthing's solar in the opposite tower from Gottfried's. It was an airy, sunny place, more casually and warmly decorated than her official chamber. She looked at ease in this environment. The large windows offered a bird's eye view equal to the guard tower, and I had no doubt Lady Worthing kept her own observant eye upon her holdings.

When Richard made his way to the solar, he found plenty of cause to tease and banter.

"What then is this?" he shouted in dismay. "You all have taken my favorite political analyst and turned her brain into a mush of ribbons and bows. Why, I haven't had a decent conversation in days, and now I fear I never shall." He walked about the room picking up trimmings and tossing them down in disgust.

I smirked at him and continued my work.

Lady Worthing rolled her eyes and ignored him as well.

Lady Jane and Lady Tallanger giggled over their fabric.

We had begun by dismantling my gown to copy. All four of us were of a similar size, making the task fairly simple. I was the tallest, and Lady Tallanger was quick to point out with a chuckle that she was both the shortest and plumpest of the group. Those were not good qualities to have at once, she assessed.

Over the past two days, I had grown comfortable with Lady Tallanger, and even Lady Worthing seemed relaxed and content. I had never interacted with educated women before, but found our personalities fit nicely. I was more well-read than any of them and the only one skilled in Latin, but they were all far more worldly wise and spoke French nearly as well as English, floating in and out of the two languages with urbane sophistication.

Supposing we couldn't ignore Richard forever, I removed some pins from my mouth and took up his challenge. "Really, Richard. You should thank these ladies, for this sewing may well reduce my intellect to a level you can more easily comprehend."

"Ouch." Richard clutched his heart. "That was hurtful indeed, Dandelion."

Lady Worthing's sly grin gave me the encouragement I needed to continue.

"Are you implying, sir, that I, Dandelion, crippled cottar's daughter and heartless strumpet, might hold the ammunition to wound one Richard Wright, second son of the third son of the fifth daughter of some ancient earl somewhere in bloody old England, named after the late, great King Richard the Lionhearted?"

"I am indeed, good lady." He bowed before me.

"Bravo, Dandelion." Lady Tallanger clapped in delight. "I've known this impudent boy for years, and never before has anyone bested him at a match of wits."

I picked up a new piece of fabric and began pinning. "Wits, hah! You should see me on the chessboard."

"Alas, it is true, and not only chess. Any game I teach her, she swiftly turns it against me." Richard settled himself upon the window ledge.

"Indeed," said Lady Tallanger, her interest sparking. "Do you know how to play Catherine's card game, my dear?"

I surveyed my handiwork before answering. "I must confess, Richard has taught me to beat him soundly at several variations."

Even Lady Worthing giggled at that.

"Catty, you foolish girl." Lady Tallanger gave her sister's knee a little shove. "You've been complaining for months about how lonely you are, and here was the perfect companion under your nose all this time."

Richard crossed his arms over his chest. "I've tried to tell her as much."

"Yes, Auntie Cat, that's perfect." Lady Jane jumped up in her excitement. "You could fire crotchety old Tillie and hire Dandelion as your lady's maid instead. Don't you think that would be perfect, Dandelion?"

I hated to disappoint her, or myself for that matter. No, I dared not hope for such an improbability. "Well in all honesty, Lady Jane, in the past there has been some tension between Lady Worthing and me."

"True enough," said the lady herself, but with no malice. "More importantly, Tillie is a distant cousin, and I promised your uncle I would always have a place for her."

A look of impatience passed over Lady Tallanger's face. "Well, it needn't be as lady's maid. You don't enjoy her company one whit. With Dandelion you'd be one of the most fashionable women in all of England, and you'd be much happier." She leaned forward and met Catherine's gaze directly. "Sisters know these things, Catty. You should trust me."

Lady Worthing turned away and eyed me warily. We had grown closer over the last carefree days, but she still did not look convinced.

"I'll take it under advisement." She busied herself untangling ribbons, although she had not shown much interest in the project all day. "Besides, we've not even asked Dandelion if she is open to employment."

"Well, don't make any official request until we see her at cards." Lady Tallanger raised her eyebrows. "Join us at our table tonight for supper, Dandelion, and afterwards we shall play."

"I should love to. If it meets with your approval, Lady Worthing."

"Certainly." The ribbons in Lady Worthing's hands were more of a tangled mess than when she started. "Only, don't plan on winning tonight."

"I make no promises," I ventured to joke.

Richard winked at me from his resting place by the window.

When I awoke the next morning, a crisp fall chill tinged the air. I sat up and stretched luxuriously, recounting the evening before. Gaming at the castle had been more fun than I ever imagined, although it pained me the first time I placed my stakes on the table. I laughed, I squealed, I bantered—all to the tune of strolling musicians. Oh what an evening, almost too good to be true. After Lady Tallanger and I trounced several of the soldiers at cards, they begged a round of dancing to restore their good spirits. Only my second dinner at the castle, and already I felt like a part of the inner circle. I never shared such camaraderie with the villagers.

Cloud perked up from her pillow and came rushing over to smother me in kisses and happy whelps.

"You silly little puppy." I cuddled into her fur. "You were waiting for me to wake, weren't you?" I picked her up and turned her toward one of the broad windows. "Try and be still for a moment and look what a beautiful day it is." Sitting on the bed, we saw straight past the village to the forest of autumn trees. It was a canvas of warm colors dotted together in swirls of orange, gold, plum, and russet. "I bet you can't wait to get out there, crunch through those leaves, and dive into great piles of them. Truth be told," I whispered to her, "I would love to join you. Tomorrow is Sunday. I'll be sure to talk Grumpy Gussy into a nice long country stroll for both of us."

Suddenly, the downstairs door slammed open with such force that something crashed to the floor. Heavy footsteps rushed across the room and pounded up the steps. I pulled the covers high up to my neck and sat shivering in my chemise.

Gottfried stormed into the room. My stoic husband had been replaced by a red-faced, seething man. Cloud yipped for a moment before she flew in fear across the bed and down the stairs.

My eyes grew wide, and I pressed my hand to my cheek.

Gottfried stopped short a few feet from me. He clenched his fists and twitched. "You whore. You slut. Not only do I let you go to supper, but I send you with a purse full of money, and this is how you repay me." He looked as if he wanted to dive upon me and strike me, perhaps even strangle me. For a moment his hands reached toward me. He ran for the dresser, swiping the washbasin from the top with one fell swoop. It went crashing to the floor in a shower of fragments. My peace of mind smashed to bits along with it.

Who was this fiend?

Terrified, I pulled back against the headboard even tighter, gathering my knees to my chest, the covers to my chin, and squeezed closed my eyes. I thought his anger was spent, until I heard another great metallic crunch. When I opened my eyes, his armor was strewn willy-nilly across the floor.

He kicked it once more, and then sat at the foot of the bed huffing with his back toward me. "Why? Why would you do it?"

"My husband, I do not know. Whatever have I done to offend you?" I couldn't keep my voice from trembling. Gottfried would not like it. Not one bit.

He turned and sneered at me. "Oh, you know what you did. Your own sister tried to warn me. I was a fool not to listen."

"But Gottfried, I swear to you I have done nothing wrong. Why do you accuse me so? What has happened to make you angry?"

"Nothing wrong? Nothing wrong." He lunged closer to me.

My stomach clenched and roiled.

"Why then did I catch my soldiers bandying about your name like some common harlot? 'Did you see her eyes?' 'Forget her eyes, man, did you see those breasts? Ah, I could barely resist reaching up to grab them while we danced.'"

I hugged a pillow to my chest, covering the offensive breasts. "I did nothing to provoke that, Gottfried. Surely you know how soldiers talk. I was the very picture of propriety last night. I behaved no differently than the other ladies." I blinked back tears, knowing they would only anger him further.

Gottfried reached out and shook me by the shoulders. "You fool, you are different, and every one of them knows it. Without me you'd still be nothing but a peasant whore. You cannot afford to joke and cavort like the Tallanger ladies. No one would ever dare sully their names. And of all people, Lady Worthing should be no role model for you." Gottfried let go and stared straight at me, waiting for a response.

"I'm sorry, Gottfried. I'm so sorry. I had no idea. I'll do better. I'll be better. I . . . I . . . ." My voice dissolved, and I stifled a sob.

"Better is not enough."

"But . . . but all I did was play games and dance. You knew as much when you sent me."

"All you did was play games and dance. Ahh, but I have not yet told you the rest. I nearly jumped out at those fool soldiers and bashed their heads, but then I thought I better wait lest there be more. 'Plan to lure her into your bed, do you?' Then, 'Good Lord, no. I'm terrified of the old captain. I'll content myself to leer from afar.' But that's when it got even more revealing. 'Wise man. Besides, it's clear she has eyes for no one but that pretty boy, Richard Wright. Did you see them mooning at each other? Oh Richard, look,'" Gottfried repeated in a bright feminine voice, "'I've done it, just like you taught me. You're the very best, Richard.' Then they went on to speculate what Richard had taught you, and what Richard might be the best at. In the name of all that is holy. I trusted you. What a fool I've been."

I pulled away from my pressed position against the headboard and reached toward him. Poor man. No wonder he was so upset. But none of it was true. None of it was my fault. "Gottfried, I swear you have not trusted me amiss. There is nothing between Richard and me except friendship. There never has been, and there never shall be. He's a charming boy, everyone knows that, but you are my husband, and I love you."

He shifted, and his muscles began to relax. His back was to me once again. "Be that as it may, this friendship was a mistake. It is over. There will be no more meals in the great hall and no more fooling about with Richard in the afternoons. It doesn't look right. People are already talking. You are confined to these quarters. I will have a kitchen maid bring our meals from now on."

Hot anger replaced my fear. How dare he? I threw the pillow down with a huff. "So am I to be punished like an errant child, then?"

"You are an errant child, Dandelion, only I was too blind to see it."

There would be no fighting him. Well I knew that tone of voice. I sat still and quiet for a moment to bring my temper under control. "But what of the dresses?"

"God's teeth." He slammed his fist against the mattress.

I jolted.

"The cursed dresses. You shall have to finish them. I'll not give the servants more fodder for gossip. If I hear you spoke but one word to the likes of Richard Wright, though, I swear I shall strangle you with my own bare hands." He left the room.

I had no doubt he meant those last words. I recalled murder in his eyes, clear as the bright-colored leaves outside my window. Tears streamed down my cheeks. The room was filled with memoirs of his furor—the smashed basin, the strewn and dented armor.

I saw glimpses of this bitter Gottfried months ago and braced my heart against him. How horrible of him to charm his way back into my good grace only to return to this monster at the slightest provocation. Why ever did he permit the friendship with Richard in the first place? Why did he let me go to dinner in the great hall? If he wanted a docile and silent Dandelion, he molded her months ago.

Cloud leapt on the bed, jolting me from my self-pity. She licked up my salty tears and danced about on my mattress, signaling she would soon piddle upon it if I did not take her outside. "All right, girl, I understand. I still have a day to face. No more wallowing about." So I donned a pretty dress and attempted to shake off my hellish morning.

Chapter 15

"Dandelion." Lady Jane sounded dismayed. "Where in the world are you today? I've called your name three times. I need help with this stitch. I can't get it right."

Lady Tallanger looked up from her sewing. "You certainly are quiet today, Dandelion. Is something wrong?"

I helped Jane correct her stitch. "No, m'lady. I'm sorry. I'm in a dreamy mood, I suppose."

"Yes," said Lady Worthing, "and I'm still waiting on your opinion about this evening's entertainment." She looked bored from watching the rest of us sew. "Should we employ this traveling troubadour, or shall we stick with cards?"

"Cards will more likely pull her out of her dreary mood, Auntie Cat," said Jane. "Let her play with Richard tonight. That should do the trick."

I had started off into yet another daydream about a little boy named William listening to a traveling troubadour tell tales of a hero named Robin Hood, but Jane's comment jerked me out of my reverie. I felt a flush rise to my face. "Oh, Lady Jane, you mustn't say such things. Richard is my friend. That's all."

"I know." She looked puzzled. "I only mentioned it since you seem to have so much fun with him."

Lady Worthing and her sister remained silent, but sent each other knowing looks, making me blush all the more. I sat back down.

"So." Lady Tallanger broke the awkward moment. "What is your vote then, Dandy?"

I crouched over my sewing again. "I would vote for the troubadour. I love stories. But I'm afraid I won't be at supper tonight. My presence is required at home this evening."

"Well, we'll save him for tomorrow then," said Jane. "I suppose we'd best not make too merry until Gerald and Henry recover from their accident."

My eyes shot open, but I managed to keep my jaw from dropping. How horrifying. I never thought to ask about the conclusion of Gottfried's encounter with the soldiers. I fought to keep my voice steady as I spoke. "Gerald and Henry, whatever happened?"

"Oh, you know soldiers." Lady Worthing snickered. "They get to showing off their manliness and get carried away. The two bumbling idiots managed to bash heads this morning during drills. It was quite a nasty mess."

I pressed my lips tight together. The bashing of heads implicated my husband beyond any doubt.

"Auntie, be fair. They are not idiots. Why, I think they're both quite brave. So then, Dandelion, tomorrow for the troubadour?" Jane watched me expectantly.

"No, dear." I attempted to maintain indifference. "I'm afraid I shan't be returning to supper for a while."

Jane looked puzzled yet again. Lady Tallanger stared down at her sewing.

"Gottfried." Lady Worthing supplied the one word answer to her confused niece.

"Oh," Jane said and looked down at her sewing, as well.

What do they know of my husband? They seemed to share some family secret in the uttering of his name. I was tempted to be angry, except they were right.

We all stitched in silence for some time. Lady Tallanger continued the conversation without preamble. "All the more reason to hire her."

Lady Worthing ran her fingers through her hair. "We've already discussed this, Sarah."

"Well, under these circumstances, I should think Dandelion would be thrilled with the duty."

I didn't respond, but glanced up, a spark of hope flickering.

"And what about Tillie?" Lady Worthing asked.

Lady Tallanger sat straight and tall. "I've been thinking about her, Catherine. Our small manor near Bath is in need of a housekeeper. I could settle Tillie there. Lord knows I dread inflicting her upon the servants, but better them than you."

Lady Worthing pondered that for a moment. "Actually, I think she would do very well as a housekeeper. She's neat as a pin, you know, and I think she'd enjoy ordering people about."

"Yes." Lady Tallanger returned to her laughing self. "That's what worries me."

"Don't worry, Mummy," said Jane. "The bailiff will keep her in line."

"Old Weathersby." Lady Worthing laughed with them. "I'd nearly forgotten him. Oh, it's just the thing, Sarah. They'll either kill one another or fall madly in love." They all dissolved into giggles at the thought. I found myself smiling, as well.

"In all seriousness." Lady Worthing turned to me. "I have come to enjoy your company, Dandelion, but Tillie's been with me for decades. I can't imagine life without her. Perhaps we could give you a different title, maybe Mistress of the Wardrobe. I'm sure Gottfried would not want you gone as often as lady's maid requires."

"I'm sure you're right, m'lady." I swallowed down a hard lump in my throat.

Lady Tallanger caught the wistful note in my voice and cast me a sympathetic look.

I laid down my needle. "Speaking of which, if you will please excuse me, I should be heading home. Gottfried wasn't feeling well this morning, and I promised not to be gone long."

No one questioned my obvious lie. I wrapped up my sewing and slipped from the room.

There was no country walk on Sunday, just a sullen, sulking interlude with Gottfried in the tower. At least I had several more days to sew with the ladies before my imprisonment became official. On the last afternoon we finished early and decided to play a few rounds of cards for trinkets and favors.

After the first hour Lady Worthing looked appalled by the heap of collected trinkets in front of her sister and me upon the small wooden table. Jane and I chatted while we played, but the two elder ladies treated the game with all seriousness.

Lady Worthing interrupted her prattling niece. "Jane, do focus on the game."

"Ignore her, Dandelion, and do tell where all the handsome men are hiding in this valley. I fear I shall see none until the tournament in Southampton."

"I must confess, other than the villagers, I've met few men myself. Gottfried keeps me quite sequestered. What about Gerald? He's a fine-looking fellow."

"Please. A soldier is no appropriate match for Jane," Lady Worthing snapped.

I frowned. "Of course not. I'm sorry, m'lady. I didn't realize she meant as a potential husband."

"No, Dandelion, you have the right of it. I'm just looking for some fine lad to daydream about, perhaps dance with tonight."

"Well, if we're simply dreaming, what about that handsome farm boy you saw on the way in?" Lady Tallanger raised her eyebrows over her splayed cards.

Lady Jane blushed. "Now, that's more like it, Mummy. I finer form and face I've never seen on a knight in all the realm. Might you know him, Dandelion? Tall, strong, cleft chin, sandy hair, brown eyes. Surely there's not another like him."

The room shifted. My throat clenched. I couldn't bear to hear them speak of William, especially not after this horrible week with Gottfried.

"I know who you mean." Lady Worthing flicked her cards as she considered her move. "William Ashby is his name. A fine young man. I've been impressed by his hard work. He's done well for a serf, and he's never married. Lord only knows how he's managed to fend off the village girls all these years. Almost makes me wish to be peasant." She giggled.

Jane put her card on the table in a move that ended the game. Lady Tallanger cheered and clapped, scooping another pile of winnings our way. I managed to recover myself and prayed the conversation would take a different turn.

Lady Worthing threw down her remaining cards in disgust. "For God's sake, Jane, you are the most dreadful partner today. Where is your head?"

Jane regrouped her cards and handed them to me. "I'm sorry, Auntie. That's what comes of dreaming of young men, I suppose. I was picturing this William as a knight in the tournament. I would dress him in red and gray, I think."

"Well, go dream elsewhere, child." Lady Worthing waved her away. "And fetch me Tillie. She shall help me win back that pot."

"Yes, ma'am," said Jane, unperturbed.

I shuffled the deck to prepare for a new hand, glad that Jane did not seem upset by the dismissal. The cards clicked against my palms. "But come back and tell me stories about the tournaments while we play, dear Lady Jane. I love your tales of the jousts. The one about the Black Knight, perhaps." That should turn her thoughts safely from William.

Tillie was not so fun to tease as Jane. She was astute and no nonsense. The game took a serious turn. There was no time for storytelling, and the pot went back and forth rapidly. Once we were back in control, Lady Tallanger made a passive sounding announcement. "Well, that was an excellent game, Dandelion. I'm sure you should be getting back to Gottfried now."

I was surprised and disappointed, but she was correct. I stood and gathered my winnings.

"Wait a moment, young lady. Where do you think you're going with *my* winnings?" Lady Worthing sounded angry, but when I looked up I saw a twinkle in her eye. "Sit your pretty little bum back in that seat this instant. I'm not finished with you yet."

"But alas," said Lady Tallanger still in her oddly passive voice, "you have nothing left with which to bet."

"Hah!" Lady Worthing snapped up the cards. "I have an entire castle at my disposal. Name your stakes, my tricky sister, for I well know when you are up to something."

"Fine." Lady Tallanger rose to the bait. "I want Tillie."

"Me," shouted Tillie. "Whatever for?"

Lady Tallanger leaned over the table, reeking of earnestness. "I have a small keep near Bath, Tillie. I rarely visit it, but every time I do I find it in utter disarray. I need a good woman there as housekeeper, and I've been asking Catty to turn you over to me for months."

The sisters shot several silent messages back and forth. Jane made a funny little noise from where she sat observing. Tillie caught none of it. What a masterful move on Lady Tallanger's part—her own manor to tend. Tillie may well throw the game for such an opportunity.

"What then shall I do for a lady's maid?" said Lady Worthing.

I answered right on cue. "Why, I suppose I could help until you find someone, m'lady."

"And if we win?" Lady Worthing sat the cards in the center of the table but did not let go.

Lady Tallanger placed her hand atop her sister's. "The entire pot plus my new gown from London you've been lusting after. Do you agree?"

Lady Worthing removed her hand and sat back. "Deal the cards."

At that moment Richard stuck his head in the door. "Oh goody. High stakes, can I watch?"

Everyone looked at me. I shook my head. Richard noted my serious expression and excused himself.

As preordained by the very manipulative Lady Tallanger, fifteen minutes later Tillie ran off to begin packing. She would leave in a few days when the Tallangers departed and travel with them to the tournament in Southampton. They would drop her at the small castle in Bath along their journey home. She almost looked happy.

"I'll speak with Gottfried the day after tomorrow, Dandelion," said Lady Worthing as I packed away the cards. "I doubt he will like this, so do all you can to pacify him before then."

"Yes, m'lady. I most certainly will. And m'lady." I looked up to meet her straight in the eye. "Thank you."

She held my gaze for a moment, then growing flustered looked down again. "You're very welcome, Dandelion."

Two days later Gottfried arrived to dinner with his anger reined. Throughout the meal, delivered by the kitchen maid, he said not a word. After everything was gone, Gottfried sat swirling his spoon back and forth across the bottom of the empty bowl. "It seems your services are required at the castle."

"Oh?" I feigned surprise.

"Tillie's about to bolt, and you are the only suitable companion for Lady Worthing until she can find a permanent replacement."

So she would ease him into the idea. The noble sisters were truly artful manipulators. I had much to learn from them.

"You will sleep here, though." His voice thundered. "You will prepare her for supper and return for the remainder of the evening. I will not negotiate on that."

"Certainly." I scooped up the dishes from the table and carried them to the basin. I smiled to the silent stone wall.

Chapter 16

I sat snug and warm as I watched glimmering snowflakes fall against a gray sky through the windows for the first time of my life. Even in Gottfried's luxurious tower suite, we shut tight our wooden shutters against the cold winds of winter, giving the entire season a dark and shadowy feel. Lady Worthing's imported glass windowpanes allowed the light and pretty snow-covered scenery into her solar while still blocking out the chill. They were a modern marvel called "cristallo," almost completely clear and only available since the reign of Edward II.

Lady Worthing detested sewing, but she loved the elegant embroidered touches on my clothing, and enjoyed this artistic style of needlework far more than the tedium of stitching dresses. Today we worked together on a wall hanging similar to the one I designed for Gottfried. It would be larger to fit the grand scale of the great hall, but we used my original as a guide for the project.

"This will be the talk of the region," said Lady Worthing. "Never before have I seen a tapestry featuring local flora. And poetry on top of it. What a creative idea, Dandelion, and how fortunate we've no men about to insist on battle scenes or coats of arms."

"Yes, m'lady. We are lucky indeed." Of course, the villagers were not at all lucky to be under Lady Worthing's oppressive thumb, but I had come to appreciate this female domain, and the villagers were far from my mind on that shimmering day.

"I hope we have this done in time for Christmas." Lady Worthing tied off a scarlet thread then picked up a sage green one to continue.

"I expect it will be done in a week or two if we keep up this pace. I can always take it to the guard tower in the evenings if needed, Lady Worthing."

"We discussed this, dearest. You are to call me Lady Catherine, or Auntie Cat if you must, but no more of these formalities."

I smiled, feeling ever so much like a member of the family. "I think Lady Catherine will suffice. My apologies. I'm just so happy to be here with you."

"Which reminds me, Dandelion, I must have another talk with that Grumpy Gotty of yours. I will require you at supper during the Christmas festivities. You can still sleep at home, but you must attend me at such major social events."

I looked up to see if she jested, but she was still sewing with all seriousness. "Well, good luck with that, m'lady. Gottfried is still harping on when you shall find a replacement."

"Oh, I think he knows better. It's his way of pretending he has some control over the matter."

"Perhaps, but he was quite adamant I return for supper each night."

"Don't worry, my dear. I know how to handle that husband of yours."

I held my needle poised over the fabric. "By all means, tell me the secret, for I've little enough success getting my way with him."

"Ah, I will tell you, Dandelion, but I doubt you will much like it." She leaned close and whispered loudly, "The secret is, nothing puts Gottfried in an agreeable mood quite like a good whipping."

"You would have him whipped over this?"

"Of course not, I meant he would do the whipping. I have a young houseboy who's been asking for trouble. This will be the perfect opportunity to kill two birds with one stone." She continued embroidering as if nothing was amiss.

I remained confused. "But why Gottfried?"

"Has he not told you after all this time that he is my whipping man as well as my chief guard? Good gracious, girl, do you not know the man at all?"

The tapestry fell unheeded onto my lap. "Apparently not." I studied her face. "And so, are you suggesting he enjoys the task?"

"Absolutely, nothing puts him in a finer mood," she said. "Except an execution of course, but I think that would be a bit drastic."

"Very funny," I said.

Lady Catherine responded with an evil giggle. "I'm not entirely joking, Dandelion. Of course I would never have anyone killed to have my way, but I've truly never seen Gottfried happier than after a beheading. I was forced to execute a villein last summer who murdered his local reeve. You should have seen the gleam in Gottfried's eye. Chilling. Then the very next day he came and asked me where he might purchase a puppy. A puppy of all things."

"I think I shall be sick." I blinked back tears as my stomach churned.

"That's how I felt, until he told me it was to be a gift for you. He was quite funny trying to put it into the little basket." She held up the fabric to examine her work more closely.

I glanced over at Cloud snuggled near the fire. Lady Catherine had fancifully put ribbons in her hair and dressed her in a miniature pink woolen tunic, protection from the chill in the drafty castle. Thank God I kept her with me today instead of returning her to Gottfried's care in the afternoon as I oft did.

"I'd never seen him handle any living creature other than that monstrous war horse of his," said Lady Catherine, "and of course me—back in those days."

I gasped, causing Lady Catherine to laugh at me.

"So, you didn't know that either." She looked up and at last noticed how upset the conversation had made me. "Good Lord, child, what do you know about him?"

I sat silent and still.

"Don't worry, my dear," she said. "I tired of him long ago. Truly, I thought you knew, or I wouldn't have brought it up so casually. Everyone knew. It was years ago. You were still a child. After my husband was killed in the war, Gottfried brought his body home. I was so lonely and sad, and Gottfried was a handsome man of noble descent and so very dear to me. I thought, why not? It didn't last long, I promise. We were not well suited—other than in the bedchamber. We've been nothing but friends ever since."

"Oh."

"Please, Dandelion, don't be cross with me. I sincerely thought you knew."

I managed to pull myself out of my stupor. "I'm not cross with you, m'lady, just very surprised. It seems you are correct. I don't know Gottfried at all."

She reached over and patted my hand. "Well, there is a huge difference between your ages, and he's become so silent over the years."

"So then, you probably know him better than I do."

"I must confess, much of what I know is through second-hand stories from my late husband."

I picked up the tapestry and focused on my sewing for a while. I considered asking Lady Catherine questions about Gottfried, although I wasn't sure I wanted the answers. After covering several inches of fabric with a huge red poppy, I could resist no longer. "M'lady, did Gottfried ever mention a woman named Samia? I think she was a Saracen."

"Well, he certainly never talked to me about other women. Where did you hear of this Samia?"

Guilt washed over me. Should I tell Lady Catherine about the book? Surely not. It was my best-hidden and most-beloved secret. I wiggled around the truth. "I umm . . . I found some old letters with her name in them. I know I shouldn't have been snooping, but I got the impression he was in love with her once. I thought if I knew their story, I might understand Gottfried better."

She pondered a moment, seeming to run the facts through several mental computations before answering. "I almost hate to tell this story, for it is very private, and I know only my husband's version of it. But I think it may hold the secret for which you are looking."

She proceeded to tell me this story, which shall haunt me to the grave. Gottfried and two young friends had set out from Europe in the early part of the century to seek fortunes in the East. Although the crusades ended several decades too soon for their taste, mercenary soldiers were being paid handsomely by the Ottoman Empire to hold their conquered territories around the Holy Land.

The exotic culture of the Saracens appealed to them—the mysterious veiled women, the fine clothing, the flavorful food, and the sunny, temperate weather. They even picked up the language, and planned to stay for many years to come. Everything was fine until Gottfried met a girl. A girl, who must have been Samia.

Samia's family was killed during the invasion of her village by the Ottoman Empire. She was a stunning beauty with long, waving blonde hair, sun-kissed skin, and golden-brown eyes. Blondes were rare in that part of the world, and thus very valuable to the distant "uncle" who was her guardian. He began selling her to the highest bidder for short-term "marriages" when she was a mere twelve years old. The girl was rendered little better than a prostitute.

Somehow Samia managed not to let this break her spirit. She loved nature and life and laughing and poetry, and she loved her God deeply. Gottfried fell madly in love with her. He considered kidnapping her and escaping back to Europe, but after weighing all available plans decided there was no way to go about it without putting Samia's life in terrible jeopardy. Not willing to risk even one strand of her golden hair, Gottfried approached her guardian to ask for her hand legitimately and permanently in marriage.

The amount the uncle suggested as the bride-price was staggering, but Gottfried would not be deterred. He had met a group of European men in the Holy Land as rich as Arabian sheiks. They were bitter veterans of the final and failed crusade. Gottfried went to them for advice on how to earn the money to buy his bride. They were happy to oblige the naïve young man. He knew they dealt in spices and holy relics, but the men taught him other ways to turn a fast profit. Dishonest ways—violent ways.

Gottfried was still an idealistic Christian man and wanted nothing to do with thievery, so he began his own business, buying and selling spices, cloth, rugs, and books. The turnover was quick, and he amassed a fortune. Because he was good and honest, many merchants dealt only with him, and he cut into the business of the old crusaders. They threatened his life, but once again, Gottfried was not deterred. For after all, what was life worth without his precious Samia?

It took him well over a year, but he earned enough money to purchase his bride, as was the Saracen custom. Gottfried sent word to his English soldier friends to meet him near the outskirts of Samia's village. He wanted two strong knights with him when he faced her guardian. Gottfried was near delirious with glee. He had enough money to pay Samia's bride-price with plenty of goods and gold left over to open a business in England. The three thundered into town like the same carefree youths who first arrived in the Holy Land, until they heard the screaming coming from Samia's home.

They ran up the stairs, across the porch, and through the door, following the screams. It seemed miles to reach Samia's chamber and run through that final doorway where they saw a servant woman holding a body in her arms. The body and the servant were both covered in rivers of blood, fresh red blood still in motion. The woman's echoing screams came like heartbeats, like the blood spurting upon her.

When they made their way to the body, their eyes told them what their hearts already knew. The blood-soaked body was Samia. Gottfried could tell by her long tapered fingers, the curve of her ankle, the swell of her breasts, but they were faced with the gruesome reality that her head was entirely missing—no wavy golden hair, no warm amber eyes, no sun-kissed cheeks, just the horrifying source of the river of blood. In that blood upon the wall behind her was written, "for Christ and the Church," the blasphemous slogan of the crusaders-turned-criminals.

I dared not repeat the ways Gottfried rewarded each of the murderous fiends with a slow and torturous death, after which his eyes reportedly glazed over and he lost all reason. The friends scooped him up and made their way back to England. For months, he never spoke a word and remained in that same demented trance. Then one night in a tavern near London, they met Earl James Worthing. He was giving a passionate and inebriated speech about the evils of the Scottish from atop the bar.

Something Worthing said struck a chord within Gottfried. Lord Worthing gave Gottfried's life a purpose once again—perhaps not a meaning, but at least a purpose. That was where the story ended, really. He fought bravely in Scotland, but with little joy. He and Lord Worthing became fast friends. Upon Lord Worthing's death, Gottfried returned his body to Lady Worthing and took up residence in the guardhouse to protect her. He was her lover in the early days and then a faithful friend. He grew more and more reticent with each passing year and was nearly a hermit by the time he shocked the castle with news of his sudden marriage to me.

When Lady Catherine finished her story, it was dinnertime. I arose and left with my eyes glazed over much as Gottfried's must have looked so long ago.

Chapter 17

Days passed before I found a chance to lock myself in Roman's hay-scented stable, press myself onto my favorite bale, and ponder the history of Samia, reading her poems over and over. I found it compelling and a bit frightening to learn how much I looked like her. I feared my marriage was nothing more than the result of a man long obsessed with a dead woman.

The woman, Samia, was disquieting as well. What sort of person could endure such a life yet remain hopeful and bright and God-fearing? Did the poetry sustain her? I doubted pretty words alone could have such an effect, but if she truly understood the words, if she herself experienced such an encounter with the maker of the universe . . . .

If indeed Gottfried once loved a woman like her, and if he married me under some delusion I would be like her, he must have been incredibly disappointed. I was nothing like his precious Samia at all.

I felt tempted to be hurt that Gottfried did not love me as he once loved Samia, but the horrible truth was, I didn't care, for I never loved Gottfried either. Oh, perhaps I loved a figment of my imagination called Gus for a brief moment, but not Gottfried, my true-life husband. I tried to love him, pretended to love him, even convinced myself for a time. No, as I further studied my feelings, I realized that although I mourned for Samia and the loss of the passionate young man who had once been Gottfried, I was not jealous at all.

Gottfried and I committed a grievous wrong by marrying.

He in chasing after a ghost, and I in running away from one.

A creak outside the stall startled me. The gate opened and in walked Richard with his typical alluring swagger. He shot me a look from beneath hooded eyes. He leaned against the closed stall door and crossed his arms in front of him. "You'll not have Catherine to run interference for you today, Dandelion. Whatever shall you do with me?"

Lady Catherine had ordered Richard not to socialize with me. He obeyed, although he oft visited while I was in her company. He sent wistful looks my way when he thought no one watched.

"Oh, Richard." I surprised us both by running over to clutch him near. "I've missed you so."

"Whoa. What is this? I came here today prepared with no less than five searing reprimands about your behavior and at least ten witty arguments as to why you should speak with me. You can't just jump up and embrace me. I shan't have the chance to use even one."

I chuckled against his warm chest, already moist from my tears. "You always did know how to make me laugh. Oh, I need you today, Richard. I'm so glad you're here, but it's terribly dangerous."

He nuzzled my hair. "Not too terribly. I took a back route, and I tipped a groom to whistle if anyone approaches."

I looked up at him and smiled, still safe within his embrace. What a good friend Richard was not to give up on me. "I'm so sorry I've been avoiding you. I should have been braver than that."

"So this is truly about Gottfried's orders. You aren't mad at me? I haven't offended you?"

"Not at all. Gottfried overheard Gerald and Henry gossiping about us. None of it was true, but it sent him into the most frightening rage. I fear it was he who caused their 'accident.' Gottfried threatened to kill both of us, and I believed him." I bit deep into my lip and fought to steady my breathing. "I'm so afraid of him. I had to escape the tower. He would never let me work for Lady Catherine if he thought I would be near you."

He gazed deep into my eyes. "So leave him. Run away with me."

I swatted him on the shoulder and laughed again. He always did know how to break the tension. "Richard. Would that I could. And to where precisely would we run?"

"Hmm, I've always wanted to see Venice, or perhaps we should travel to the Holy Land. There's much money to be made there, I've heard."

I pulled away and took him by the elbow to lead him to my precious book. "Come here, there's something I want to share with you."

"What is this, an old manuscript?" He sat me down on the hay bale and knelt before me, prying the book from my fingers. "I don't need stories and fancy words. Don't read me poetry or philosophy. I have you again, and that's all that matters."

I was stunned by his vehemence.

"I love you so. I do, Dandelion. Not as a friend. I've wanted to say that to you for months, but thought as long as I never spoke the words, we could still be close. Now that Gottfried's stolen you away from me entirely, it doesn't matter anymore." He leaned in and kissed me directly on the lips.

My body stirred and awakened as it had with William. It swayed toward him of its own accord, but my higher self found the resolve to pull my mouth away. "Richard, no. This is a terrible idea. If Gottfried learns we were alone together, there will be trouble enough, but if he hears of this, surely he will kill us first and ask questions later."

Richard trapped me against the wall with his hands on either side of my shoulders. "Then let's run away. I love you. I must have you. These last few months were nearly the death of me."

"I can't. I can't do that. I'm a married woman. I made vows. I gave my word."

"Please, Dandy."

"I can't," I whispered with tears returning to my eyes.

Richard jerked away and strode to the opposite side of the stall, raking his fingers through his black hair in a way so attractive, it almost caused me physical pain.

"Don't walk away from me," I whispered fiercely. "I just got you back. I can't bear you walking away from me so soon."

He turned and took a single step toward me, shaking his outstretched hands. "What then shall we do? What is to become of us? We cannot live with each other, and we cannot live without each other. Is that what you're telling me? That is not a solution."

"Please be patient with me." I hid my face in my hands. "This is all so sudden, and I've had so much on my mind recently, horrible things on my mind. I need time to think. Ten minutes ago we weren't even speaking, and you want me to declare my undying love for you and run away upon a moment's notice?"

"This has been on my mind for months. It is not sudden to me. I don't want to continue living like this."

"Can we be friends for now, Richard? I don't know quite what to do with the one man I have in my life, but I am in terrible need of a friend." And with that I broke into sobs.

Richard pulled me up onto his lap and held me like a beloved sister. "We can be whatever you want. Just please stop crying. You shall ruin my new tunic."

I laughed through my tears, and he held me for a long time.

And so began an even more treacherous secret habit. I would dash off to Roman's stall as often as opportunity arose, and if at all possible Richard would meet me there. Our visits were sometimes cut short by his whistling stable boy warning of visitors, but Gottfried was always busy spying from the far side of the tower that time of day. When Richard couldn't make it, my faithful equine friend and my book of mystical poetry comforted me. They were almost as fulfilling, although they could not hold me in their arms and stroke my hair or sprinkle kisses along my cheeks and forehead.

Two weeks after our first encounter, I sat once again in my hideaway reading my book and pondering the spiritual universe, hoping for Richard to join me. On Sunday mornings I now attended the small chapel in the castle with Lady Catherine. Friar John and I maintained a civil and mutual silence. If he was using my moral decline as a sermon topic, he ceased to do so in my presence. In fact, his sermonizing in the castle was far briefer and more infrequent than in the village entirely. Lady Catherine preferred a simple, traditional Latin mass focused on the liturgy and was quite vocal about her opinion if ever the good priest strayed. She found the Blessed Mother a comfort during a crisis, but otherwise had little use for religion.

Richard entered Roman's stall quietly with something perched under his arm. "Here I bring you a present, and I find you reading that same old book again." He held out the hinged box, inlaid with different shades of wood and polished to a shine. "It's the new fox game everyone's been raving about. I hoped we could play for a while. Either you are a very slow reader, or that is a very fascinating book. I catch you with it every time I come."

I put the book down. "For me?" I took the box and stroked the pretty pattern. Wooden pieces rattled within. "Thank you, Richard. It's beautiful." I hugged the box. "Teach me how to play."

"No, no, first I must learn about this captivating manuscript."

"I tried to read it to you once, but you were too busy seducing me to listen."

"Well, I'm all ears now, my pretty." He sat down beside me on the bale of hay and leaned back against the wall. He stretched his feet in front of him and cupped his hands behind his head. Looking me in the eye, he waited for me to begin.

I was delighted to have such an attentive student. I picked the book back up and read.

> *I dream of the day that I die,*
> *when at last I am held*
> *in God's ecstatic arms.*

> *Distance will fade, our hearts pour together as one.*
> *I will cup His cheek in my hand*
> *with passionate disregard.*

> *I dream of the day*
> *when He shall adore my exquisite beauty,*
> *and at last I may meld into His flesh.*

He still sat looking at me, perplexed.

"Would you like to hear more?"

"Yes, please, go on. I need more information before I give my thoughts on the matter."

I continued to read my favorite passages. After several silent moments I said, "What do you think?"

"Well, the words are undeniably beautiful, but the ideas are rather odd. Aren't they? Who wrote them?"

"A Saracen woman. Her name was Samia."

He nodded. "Well it makes sense, then. She's not talking about god in the sense of the actual God at all."

I closed the book on my lap. "Why would you say that? Could not she have found God in her own way? Father John says God is always speaking to our hearts in a thousand small ways. Or, perhaps she is the true believer, and we are the infidels."

"Good Lord, Dandelion, you'll be burned at the stake for heresy. Then whom shall I have to hold and kiss? Wherever did you find this book?"

"It belongs to Gottfried." That would have been explanation enough, but I felt a need to share the entire story including the tale of Samia's violent murder. Recounting it brought tears to my eyes, such an awful story it was. How had Gottfried ever survived it? A fresh wave of pity washed through me.

"Good gracious," Richard said when I finished.

"Gottfried might never have loved me at all. I think I merely remind him of this woman, Samia."

"Good gracious."

"Is that all you can say?"

"Merciful heavens." He winked.

I slapped the book against my thigh. "Seriously, Richard, do you not find it unbelievable that the same Gottfried who translated these captivating spiritual poems has turned into a bitter, cold hermit?"

"Perhaps these very pagan ideas made him into the man he is today." He shifted on the hay bale and turned toward me. "Aren't all of the Moslems hateful and violent people? Perhaps that is where such thinking leads. I've no doubt Catherine told you a pretty tale, but it's not likely true anyway."

I shook the book in his face. "Come now. How could you call these ideas pagan? They are the most glorious descriptions of God I have ever read. This is the God I want to worship, be He Moslem or Christian."

"In truth, I fear they have bewitched you. Young ladies should not be filling their heads with such ridiculous notions. The Church should guide your thoughts about God. Take my advice and return this book to its hiding place at once."

"I will not, Richard, and you can't make me."

He stroked my cheek. "I would never 'make' you do anything. I'm just looking out for you."

His words and the light touch of his fingers upon my skin relaxed me. I reached up and cupped his hand against my cheek. I peeked over the rail and made sure we were alone before I scooted closer on our bale of hay, close enough that my leg pressed against his. "So you don't like my book at all." I pulled my bottom lip into a pout.

"Well, tell me this. What draws you to it so?"

I stroked my beloved book. "There is something on those pages I want, and I don't know how to get."

He placed his hand on mine. "Then perhaps it isn't meant to be gotten."

I was about to argue, but then a bell rang somewhere outside.

"Ahh, just what I was waiting for," Richard said. "I have something I'd like to share with you today, as well."

"But we haven't played our game yet. I can hardly wait to beat you." I tapped the wooden top of the gift beside me.

"There shall be time for that later. This is quite important."

"What is it? Shall I like it?"

"I'm not certain, but I think in time you shall come to appreciate it. After I leave, wait one minute, and then walk out the front door of the stable to the soldier's practice field." He gave my cheek a final stroke and stood.

"Richard."

"Trust me."

Tension seeped through my body. Something I may not like at first, but would grow to appreciate? Richard disappointed me once today. Would he yet again with this surprise?

I picked up my new board game and followed Richard's directions, not difficult as every living soul in the castle headed that way. The field looked particularly barren in the middle of December—barren and desolate, despite the many people milling about. A cold shudder shimmied down my spine.

I saw Richard bantering with the servants. I shot him a questioning glance, but he shrugged his shoulders. Before long, an official-looking procession approached. I recognized Lady Catherine from her regal walk and extravagant clothing. Next came Gottfried. He wore his surcoat with the Worthing insignia. A burgundy hood covered much of his face. *Odd.*

Gottfried swept past, dragging a boy, about fifteen years of age, and threw him against a rough wooden pole. Several soldiers stripped the boy's tunic from his back. They pulled his hands high over his head and strapped them to the pole.

At first I heard only murmurs and gasps, but then Lady Catherine's powerful voice surfaced. ". . . are charged with insubordination toward the governing authorities and are hereby sentenced to twenty lashes."

A chilling glee flashed through Gottfried's eyes. I felt more than saw the malicious grin hidden behind the hood. He swung the whip with a zeal that sickened my stomach, savoring each lash. I glanced at Richard again. The blood rushed from my face. Surely every ounce of my agony was displayed upon it. Richard responded by twisting his own face into an expression of sympathy, not at all sincere.

Chapter 18

I found myself in my favorite hideaway on a frigid January afternoon pouring yet again over Samia's book. I hoped Richard might come warm me, perhaps play my cherished fox game, but he did not. I cuddled with Roman, drawing from his heat and burying my red tipped nose in his soft, hay-scented mane. "I so wish it were Christmas again," I whispered to the great beast.

The holiday season had arrived with a flutter of parties, hunts, singing, and dancing. True to Lady Catherine's prediction, Gottfried was in fine spirits after the public whipping. It required incredible strength of will not to betray my revulsion toward his good mood wrought of violence and humiliation, but hide it I did. Knowing now the true depravity of my husband's nature, I was desperate not to provoke him. Gerald at long last recovered from his head bashing, but the physician suspected Henry never would. No, I did not want to earn my husband's wrath. I could not, however, allow him bed-sport any longer. I told him I was with child—a blatant lie—but it would gain me some time.

Without a doubt, Lady Catherine put on the finest holiday celebration in all of England. Although the church frowned upon excess during the remembrance of our Savior's birth, she cared not one whit. The castle dripped with holly and garlands. A giant evergreen tree decorated with bright red apples stood in the courtyard. From the burning Yule log, to the carolers, the troupes of players, the hunts, snow fights, and sleigh rides, it seemed the festivities would never end. We stuffed ourselves with an unending supply of wassail, mincemeat pies, and Christmas pudding.

Our tapestry of native wildflowers and poetry caused quite a sensation. Truth be told, I was quite a sensation myself. Every man wanted to dance with me and challenge me to chess. Every woman wanted to dine with me, and several copied my new hairstyle. I worried Lady Catherine's famed jealousy would rear its ugly head at this outpouring of attention, but she seemed to view me as a natural extension of herself these days. I was just thankful to be away from the tower. All too soon, our guests returned home.

Thus, here I was hiding away in Roman's stall once again. I cuddled with the huge beast until he lost patience with me. My fingers grew numb, even encased in leather gloves. I could not wait for Richard much longer. I stared down at my book, but I was far too frozen to study it further. Richard had pled his case several times now for me to be rid of it. Perhaps he was right. It was an odd obsession, and it brought me no real peace, only an empty sense of dissatisfaction. Perhaps I was bewitched.

Blowing on my frigid hands, I longed for summer and the forest and my old poaching companions. I longed to be far away from Gottfried and even from the gray stones of the castle. I longed to dance through the essence of divinity. I was so tired of the games of the nobility and longed for the simple games of childhood instead. My thoughts melted deep into the past.

William had been good to his promise that day after we made our pact in the forest. Tim and I met him back along the shadowed trail early the next afternoon for our first adventure as Robin Hood and his merry men.

"So first of all, we have to take an oath of secrecy," said William, standing straight and tall against the backdrop of trees. "Repeat after me. 'I do so solemnly swear before God and the King and his most high holiness, the Pope of Rome, that I shall never break the secrecy of our poaching society, or may lightning strike me down, so help me God.'"

We repeated as best we could, stumbling over the words the entire time.

William shook his head and smiled. "Well, I guess it shall have to do. Next, we'll each need a secret name. Naturally, I will be Robin Hood, since I'm the oldest and the leader."

I was contemplating protesting this when he continued, "And Dandy, you will be the beautiful and infamous Maid Marian." I had always wanted an elegant name like Marian, so I decided it was acceptable if he were the leader after all. "Last but not at all least, Tim, your name will be Little John, one of Robin's favorite merry men."

Five-year-old Tim let go of my hand and nodded his head with all seriousness.

William gave him a pat on the shoulder. "Good man. Now, when we're on a mission, we must always be sure to use these names to protect our true identities."

I sniggered a bit at the silliness of it all, as if anyone within three shires wouldn't know exactly who we were, but it sounded all too fun, so I went along. "Fearless leader, Robin Hood, what is our first mission?"

"Well, I have here in this bucket everything we'll need. Maid Marian, your job is distracting and charming. We'll stay near to where the steward is working each day since he is our best ally. You will dance and sing in the fields prettily, just as you always do. Little John and I will sneak into the woods with this bucket. Little John will help scare the small game out of the bushes, and I'll use my trusty slingshot, and we'll have dinner before you know it."

He rubbed his hands together. "Dan—I mean Marian, we'll be relying on you to pick a big bunch of your wildflowers. As soon as we come back out from the woods, you act as if you haven't a care in the world, skip over to us, and put your flowers in the bucket on top of the day's kill. From there we'll head to my secret hideaway in a cave by the river to skin it and cook it. Mmm mmm, I can almost taste that roasting meat now."

"What's it like?" asked Tim.

"You shall find out soon enough for yourself, little one." William took his hand.

"I can't wait to get started, but William . . . ." I said.

He shot me a glare. "That's Robin Hood to you, Maid Marian."

"So sorry, Robin Hood, but can't I help at all with the actual hunting?"

"Not yet, Marian. Poaching is a chancy endeavor. Why, we could all be whipped or worse. No, Maid Marian, your job is the most important of all. Without you, I would never even risk it."

At that, fear niggled in my chest. I was responsible for Baby Tim after all. Maybe this wasn't such a good idea. Then I looked into Tim's big hopeful eyes. William and I were old enough to get in trouble, but surely small Timmy would never be held accountable. I remembered the smell of roasting meat drifting over the castle walls. I thought of the steward's hearty laugh at my antics, and I suspected it would be all right.

Everything went just according to plan. "Robin Hood" proved to be quite handy with his new slingshot, and less than an hour later Baby Tim and I sat at William's rocky outcropping along the Arun River and bit into our first savory pieces of roasted squirrel.

The meat was weighty and substantial as I held it before me on a stick, watching juices slide down the striped pattern. I tested it first with my tongue. The rich, bold, wood-smoked taste washed over me like a flood, every bit as delightful as the aroma promised. I took a bite, and it felt oddly stringy against my tongue while I worked to chew it. As I swallowed it down, the thick mass slid through my throat and landed heavy in my stomach. Tim's face reflected my own wonder.

To think, the nobles lived this way every single day.

I ate a few more mouthfuls before pointing to the turreted tower rising over the trees with the Worthing flag of burgundy swaying on top. "Do you see that castle?" I said to William. "Someday I plan to live there."

"There, in that heap of old boulders? You know, they say it is haunted." He took another hearty bite himself.

"I mean it, William."

"Why ever would you want to live in a dark and drafty castle?" He swept his hand across the forest and river before us, turning to include the rolling meadow at our backs. "The land, Dandy. Just look at it. That's the place for me. Row after row of grain growing high, all from my hard work. I can almost feel the soil in my hand right now. What more could anyone want?"

"You . . . work hard?" I gave him a sidelong glance before turning my eyes out over the horizon. "What rubbish! There's a whole world out there, and I intend to find it."

Tim ignored our argument, chomping with zeal. I bent over to plant a kiss upon his curly head.

"Dreams and fairy stories," William said. "You best learn to live in the actual world. What if you decide to settle down and marry some handsome village lad?" He ducked his head. "Say for example, me?"

"Why should I marry the likes of you when there are two noble Worthing sons to choose from?"

He raised his face. Hurt flamed across it.

It tugged at something deep inside me. I laid my hand atop his for the briefest moment. "I'm sorry. It was a silly jest." I took another bite of the squirrel William had caught. "I owe you much."

His cheeks turned pink.

"Of course I wish to fall in love, but if I'm trapped in this village forever, I might just die." A cold shiver crept over me, and for a moment I could barely find my breath despite the flowing sunshine and whispering breeze.

"Castles aren't meant for such as us. You may as well accept that."

"Just you wait and see, William."

He gave me a tolerant grin and reclined upon the rock.

Tim and I ate our fill and then joined him, all three of us moaning on our backs, sunning as snakes near the river. Tim looked so satisfied after his first truly nourishing meal. He would have the opportunity to grow tall and strong like William and his brothers, like the nobles in the castle. Life held more for Tim and me than the path of poor cottars. I felt it when I tasted my first piece of candy, and it came back again as a wave. We were meant for more.

And I had more. So much more.

Why couldn't it be enough?

Perhaps because Tim and William were not here to share it with me. I would never risk subjecting them to Gottfried's wrath. I shivered yet again and cuddled against Roman in the frigid stall.

But something in my life most certainly needed to change. I supposed the book was as good a place as any to start. I brushed it with my leather gloves. Solving my problems must begin in the here and now. Clinging to ancient ghosts was no help at all. Lord knew it hadn't helped Gottfried in all these years. I decided to follow Richard's advice and return the book to the back of the shelf where it belonged.

Needing to do it before I lost my resolve, I rushed back to the tower and up the circling stairway. I peeked out through the shutters before approaching the bookshelf. Gottfried was engrossed in his work, as I expected. Taking the book in hand, I planned to replace it, but once I gazed upon it, I fell into its hypnotic spell again. A driving need to read one last poem tore through me. I opened the worn cover and stared at the words I knew so well, hoping to draw them into me for the long days ahead.

The next thing I knew, I flew upward and smacked hard against the cold stone wall, sliding down into a heap upon the floor as pain shot through me. I clung to my book and curled in a ball with it pressed against my throbbing cheek as Gottfried screamed at me. "Where did you get that book? Who said you could read it? Give it to me."

"No!" I heard myself answer.

"Give it to me now, you ungrateful little whore."

"No," I screamed back as Gottfried began a tugging war over the book. "No!" I continued to shriek. He hurled me into the wall once again. Still, I did not let go. Cloud barked in the background. She growled at Gottfried as he continued lashing me about the room. We crashed into a costly vase and sent it smashing to the floor. A shard sliced my foot, and I yelped. Cloud lunged at Gottfried and bit deep into his ankle.

Gottfried kicked her away. The tiny white puffball careened through the air and into the wall with a sickening thud. She slid down it into a heap on the floor much as I had, but she did not get up.

"Cloud." I wanted to run to her, but Gottfried still held tight the book. I gave it one last longing look, and released it to dash toward my beloved little dog. I picked her up, and she cracked an eye open.

A fiendish chuckle erupted behind me. Gottfried tossed the book into the raging flames of the fireplace. "That will teach you both," he said, and returned to the walkway as if nothing more happened than twisting the ear of a naughty child. I bundled Cloud in my cloak, intending to run back to the safety of the castle proper, until I felt the magical lure once again. Still clutching my dog, I grabbed the poker and knocked the book to the floor. I stomped out the flames and scooped up the charred remains before escaping.

I tore down the tower stairs, past the courtyard, and through the great hall.

The moment I entered Lady Catherine's chamber, she gasped. "Dandelion."

Richard's back was to the door. He tossed a glib comment over his shoulder. "What has my little heretic gotten herself into now?" The moment he looked up and saw Lady Catherine's ashen face, he spun around in true concern. "Good God, Dandelion, what happened to you?"

Cloud poked her head out from my cloak and whimpered. Their gazes turned downward, and I began to whimper as well. "He kicked my puppy into the wall."

Richard dashed to my side with an arm of support. We carried Cloud to the table. Catherine came to my other side. I sat Cloud down and unwrapped the cloak an inch at a time. She still whimpered and trembled. Her white curls were smudged with blood. One by one she tested out her little limbs, and we were all so relieved to see they were in working order. She gave a hearty shake and leapt into my arms again.

Catherine stroked Cloud's soft head and then ran a concerned hand down my arm as well. "Richard, go fetch the surgeon at once."

"It's all right." I gave Cloud a kiss. "Really, I think she'll be okay now."

Catherine cupped my cheek in her hand and turned my head toward her. "Not for the dog, Dandelion, for you."

Blood ran down my cloak, surely the source of Cloud's smudges. I hurried to the mirror. My hair was matted with the sticky red stuff, and one entire side of my face was purple and swollen. I sank to the floor and cried as the pain seared through me afresh.

"You're safe now. You don't ever have to go back to that horrible man. I promise." Lady Catherine knelt down to hug me despite her spotless gown. "Richard, go quickly."

Richard took off in search of the surgeon. Lady Catherine was so tender with me. She treated me like her very own daughter. Before the men returned, she washed my face and hair and changed me into one of her own bed robes. After a thorough check-up, the surgeon said I needed only rest and time for my wounds to heal.

Could there ever be so much time in all the earth?

Catherine herself tucked me into a guestroom bed with Cloud nestled at my side. Only then did she ask me to tell her everything.

"He found me hiding a book . . . a very personal book he had written with the girl . . .with Samia."

"His book." Lady Catherine covered her mouth. "I forgot all about his book. No wonder. He tried to burn it when he was with James. James rescued it from the fire, and Gottfried actually dared to punch the good Earl of Worthing. I can't believe he still has his book after all these years. Wherever did you find it? Was it hidden in that eerie old attic?"

I pulled the covers a bit higher about my chin. "It was hidden right in the back of the bookshelf near the hearth. I've had it for months.

I've been obsessed with it. Richard told me I should put it back. He said it was evil."

"He may well be correct, Dandelion, for look what it has done now." Catherine looked away and clenched her jaw. "Not only did it drive Gottfried into a rage, it caused you to lie to your mistress, as well. There were never any letters, were there? You knew about Samia from the book."

I bit my lip against the indictment and stroked Cloud for comfort where she lay beside me on a pillow. "Yes, I'm sorry. It seemed like such a weighty secret—a sacred trust almost. The writings are so mystical, so powerful. I wanted to tell you, but I wasn't quite ready to share it with anyone."

She stood and walked a few steps away. "You shared it with Richard." She sounded sad, almost hurt.

"I'm ready to share it with you now," I whispered, pulling it out from under the covers where I had hidden it.

Truly I wanted to share it with her now. Lady Catherine had grown so very dear to me.

She took it into her hands and examined it. "So what is in this book?"

"Poems." I took it back for a moment and turned to a sample. "The translations are in Gottfried's own writing."

She swatted at the book. "Poems. All this trouble over poems. And what, may I ask, is so special, so powerful about these poems?"

"Well, they are love poems, but not typical human love poems. They are love poems to God and even, it would seem, from God. They are the most beautiful, magical words I have ever read. Would you like to hear some?"

"Not now, Dandelion. I think I should put away this book for safekeeping. It has caused quite enough trouble." She took it from my hands and closed it.

I longed to reach after it but resisted. Hadn't I decided as much myself?

"These are very private and personal to Gottfried. You should have never snooped in them. I could have told you they were dangerous if you hadn't lied to me in the first place."

I struggled to hold back tears while a guilty lump formed in my throat. "You will take his side then."

"Don't be ridiculous." She tossed the book into a chest rather carelessly. "There is no excuse in the world for a chivalrous knight to bully a woman so. There's nothing you could have done to deserve this. I'm simply pointing out you did contribute to the situation. If you're going to be married to a man like Gottfried, you must tread carefully and be wise. It is the only way to survive."

"I suppose you are right about that."

"I suppose so, unless . . . ." She sat down in a chair near the fireplace and gazed into the flames.

"Unless?"

Catherine turned to me. "How many people witnessed your wedding to Gottfried?"

I sat up to look at her. "Only the priest at the nearby castle and two peasants."

"Hmm, easy enough to deal with." She waved a hand dismissively. "Father Cedric will say whatever I instruct him. And you never cried the banns?"

"No, m'lady. It was rather sudden. I'm afraid Gottfried paid the priest to ignore the banns."

"Good, that's very good." She gazed into the fire again, and I could almost see her manipulative mind hard at work.

"Is it?"

"And did your family know you were getting married?" She turned to me again. "Rumor has it they opposed the union."

"They knew of our intention, but nothing of the actual ceremony. Rumor also has it we were never truly married."

"Yes, yes, that's perfect. It sounds as if the legality of your union was tenuous at best. It seems the only thing tying you to Gottfried is a piece of parchment." She paused before walking out the door.

Whatever could she be up to now? I clung tight to Cloud, not at all sure that I wished to know.

She returned a few moments later holding a scroll sealed with wax. "A piece of parchment," she said, "which I happen to have in my possession."

"M'lady, however did you get it?" I leaned forward. Cloud jumped up from her pillow to hop around Catherine's legs and see what prize she held.

"Gottfried gave it to me to keep with the other legal documents. For all the man has been through, he is surprisingly naïve." She walked back to sit beside me and placed the scroll in my hand. "I will toss it in the fire, if you wish, Dandelion."

"Oh, I don't think so. Despite the fact half the village thinks I'm a whore, I'm in no hurry to make it true. Gottfried is my husband for better or worse."

She picked up a little mirror from the side table and held it to my face. "And this is the worse, I suppose."

"Perhaps I should. I'm not certain." I held the rolled parchment and turned it over, remembering the seal from the day of our wedding. I was so happy that day—that foolish, foolish day. The parchment felt so fragile against my fingers. Would it be so easy to make it all go away, to pretend the wretched day never happened?

But I would know the truth, and God would know the truth. No, it was not that simple. It was not that simple at all. "Please hold onto it." I handed the scroll back. "The time might yet come when I am desperate enough to do it."

"Are you certain?"

"Yes," I said, lying back against the pillows. "I don't think this will happen again. In truth, he only struck me once, and if he hit Lord James for the same crime, then I suppose I'm in good company. The rest of the bruises came from fighting over the book. I brought those upon myself. It was foolish. Besides, it is a husband's right to beat his wife, or so I've been told. Even when he kicked Cloud, it was because she bit his ankle and wouldn't let go."

I took a deep breath. "I should have realized. I've seen enough of his dark side. You are correct—if I'm going to stay married to Gottfried, I must tread carefully. So yes, unfortunately, I am certain."

"Then you should get to sleep. You'll be needing your rest to survive such a decision. But until you're better, you are not leaving this room, and that's an order." She tucked the covers around my chin.

Patting my cheek, she said, "And you shall tell him you lost your fictional baby in the fray. A bit of guilt will do the man no harm. I shall instruct the surgeon to forbid marital intimacies for a good long time. There are ways to punish a husband, my dear. You shall learn." With that, Lady Catherine drew the curtains about my bed.

A warm fire crackled in the hearth. Light flickered through the fabric of the drapes. I watched the mesmerizing, hypnotic display until my eyes grew heavy. I succumbed to dreams of dancing pagan fire gods calling out for a sacrifice and luring me toward the molten flames.

Chapter 19

Meandering through the woods on a gentle mare named Pegasus, I could hardly believe it was spring again. Lady Catherine galloped off ahead today, as she so oft did, giving us each a moment of solitude. She would be sure to tease me later, but in truth, her own soldiers could not keep up with her on horseback. I would find her in the clearing ahead, but for now the woods were all my own. They were glorious indeed on this day, fairly bursting with life and color. Buds poked out from tree branches that were frosty and barren only the week before. Songbirds chirped, and I heard the skitter of animals running free after hiding for their long winter's nap.

Mine was a winter of hiding as well—hiding in the castle, suffering through brief silent dinners, burrowing deep into the blankets, wrapping myself tight so Gottfried could not touch me in the night, covering my head with my pillow to drown out his snores and his scent. *Is it truly planting time already?* Had I actually survived another three months with that cursed and hateful husband? Wasn't it only yesterday when he pelted me against the hard stone wall?

In the daytime, life seemed so normal. I could almost forget this beautiful afternoon ride was little more than a waking dream, and at dusk I would face the horror that was truly my life. Richard was not much comfort. We no longer dared tempt Gottfried's temper. Besides, I was in no mood for games. At least Cloud remained pampered and safe inside the castle. She would never have to return to the tower again.

I shook off my depressive thoughts. I should live in the moment as Samia's poetry recommended. I should embrace the now in which I exist and not worry about the terrors of the night. Perhaps this was life after all, and that other place the dream, the nightmare. The air smelled so crisp and clear and sweet. Surely this was the better place to live.

Lady Catherine lazed up ahead on the grass. She must have watched me approach for longer than I realized. As I slid off my horse, she chastised me. "Dandelion, every time you think I'm not watching, I catch you with that sad, faraway look on your face. It's been months, dear. You must shake off this thing, and if you can't, then burn the Godforsaken parchment and be done with it."

I sat down beside her. "I'm sorry. I try to be a good companion, m'lady. I hope it hasn't bothered you overmuch."

"That's not the point. You are an excellent companion. The very fact

126

you manage to paste such a convincing smile on your face each time I walk into the room is proof enough. I simply can't abide watching you live this way."

I pinched at the pain over my eyebrows. "The smiles are not entirely false. Sometimes the world seems so normal, but when I'm alone with my thoughts it turns sinister and dark. I'm never quite sure which is real." I plucked at the grass beside me. She tipped up my head. "Reality is what you choose, Dandelion. You make your own reality. You choose your destiny. Why you continue to live like a victim to that man is beyond me."

Maybe because I deserve it, whispered a little voice inside my head, but I would never share the thought with Lady Catherine.

Later that night, back in my nightmare realm in the tower bedroom, tucked tight within the soft covers that no longer soothed me, I allowed myself to continue the line of reasoning. I pulled the blankets tighter over my ears to block out the sound of my husband's heavy breathing.

Maybe I did deserve this. I was the worst sort of faithless witch to William, and so destiny landed me here with Gottfried. I thought it was some grand design, even wrought by faith, but it was punishment for what I did, and I deserved it. I deserved every moment of it. What sort of monstrous woman turned her back on true love when it was offered? What kind of hideous creature must I be to walk away and never look back?

And did I face my punishment with dignity? Did I choose to be a faithful wife? Did I stay the path to find Gottfried's softer side? Of course not. I lied and sneaked and invaded his privacy. I went running into the arms of the first charming man who came along and tossed a few flattering words my way, although Gottfried never betrayed me.

And what did that bring me? Nothing but more pain. Richard was the one who lured me to the whipping. Richard was the one who made me return the book. Was fate laughing in my face one more time? That very act brought out the most hideous side of my husband's nature and severed any shred of relationship we shared.

And so now did I hate Richard? Did I snub and ignore him? Did I holler and spit in his face? No. Of course not, for those would be the choices of a healthy, sane woman, not a monstrous lunatic. No, instead I fell deeper and deeper in love with Richard each passing day. I tortured myself with thoughts of him all night long. I punished myself with furtive glances, secretive touches, and private jokes. My life was a living hell, and I deserved every moment of it.

Exhausted by such thoughts, at last I fell asleep.

I woke the next morning to the sad realization it was Sunday. I would be expected to spend the entire afternoon in my tower prison. The colorful fabrics draping the room that once looked so lovely and luxurious, now appeared angry and sullen—the browns like puddles of mud, the reds like bloody gashes, the purples like swollen bruises. The big open windows and view beyond were a reminder of everything withheld from me. Even the books gave no joy, for they brought to mind the one tragic book that destroyed my marriage. And now, yet another dreary Sunday loomed.

I went through the motions of breakfast and mass. I almost enjoyed the tasty meal in the great hall. I pretended up to the very last second that life was fine, but as I walked toward the tower a shattering headache struck me. They came more and more oft these days. I didn't know how much longer I could take them. Not only my mental stability, but my very health was falling apart. Before long I'd be no good to Lady Catherine at all, and I'd be trapped in the tower forever. Already there were entire days when every light seemed too bright and each little noise screeched within my ears. How much longer could I hide it?

"Dandelion," came a voice from the side of the courtyard. "I'm so sorry, lass." It was Father John, perhaps the last person I expected to be calling me, let alone apologizing.

I turned and waited silently. I was not willing to make things easy for him, but I was curious. The priest must be drunk.

He sat on a stone bench with his head low. "I'm sorry. I thought I would be happy to see you so down-trodden, to see justice and calamity fall upon you, but, in fact, it brings me no pleasure at all."

I lifted my chin a bit higher and looked at him from the side of my eye. "Why do you say that? I am doing just fine. I am exactly where I planned to be."

"I'll let you hold on to your pride if you must." He shook his head. "But truly I've never before seen you walking as if your shoes were made of lead and you bore a heavy yoke about your neck. I thought it would make things right if you suffered for turning your back on William for a richer man, but I'm thinking now that the sweet little Dandelion I knew since childhood could never deserve this."

I realized he wasn't drunk at all. He was lucid, sincere, even penitent. I dropped my head from the haughty angle and allowed some of my pain to pass through my voice. "It wasn't about money. It wasn't that simple. I wish you could understand."

"Looking at you in this moment, I think I do. Only remember this, Dandelion—happiness is not so much about our circumstances as it is about how we perceive those circumstances. The poorest, crippled beggar on the side of the road can have joy in his heart; and the richest, most influential man surrounded by people who love him can be caught in the throes of despair. You can't choose your circumstances, but you can choose how you will face them."

I made a sound somewhere between a snicker and a sniffle. "A private sermon just for me?"

He smiled and held up his hands. "As you well know, I'm a bit given to sermonizing, but I hope that won't keep you from hearing the truth. And for whatever it's worth, I forgive you."

There was nothing left to say. If possible, my head pounded even harder. I gave him a swift nod and turned back toward the tower. He chanted in Latin as I walked away.

"Sed et gloriamur in tribulationibus . . . ."

It was no work for me to translate, as it was one of his favorite verses. "But we rejoice also in our sufferings, because we know that suffering produces perseverance; perseverance, character; and character, hope. And hope does not disappoint . . . ."

Hope.

How dare he speak to me of hope. The last time I heard that verse I was full of hope—hope of a life with William. Even later I hoped Gottfried and I could work things out despite all odds. *Hope does not disappoint.*

Ha!

I went to bed straightaway, although it was mid-afternoon. I heard Gottfried stomp out of the tower at some point, I supposed to take Roman for a walk without me. I didn't sleep, but the dark quiet from the pillow over my head soothed my frayed nerves. In that quiet I was struck with an odd impulse. Peeking at the ceiling past the bottom of the pillow and staring at the door to the attic above, I heard the words.

Open it.

The words rang clear in my mind.

Open it. Look inside.

The refrain came again and again.

I listened to the chant for an hour. If Gottfried beat me merely for reading his book, what would he do should he find me digging through an entire treasure trove of secrets? But that was what hid in the attic. In that moment, I knew it as if I had known my entire life. Gottfried's secrets were within. The clues to his past lay beyond that door. I had to try.

I got out of bed and put my plan into action, pushing a trunk under the attic and placing a chair on top. It was still quite a scramble to hoist myself through the narrow hole, but years of tree climbing stood in my favor. Before long I sat in the dark attic, my feet still dangling through the opening.

Dark. Drat, I hadn't thought of that. I despaired clambering back down and starting all over again with a candle in hand. Then I remembered the last time Gottfried climbed up here for fabric. He hadn't taken anything with him. After several moments, light appeared as if by magic. He must have kept a candle somewhere. My eyes began to adjust, and I was able to make out the shadow of a small table, which did indeed have a candle upon it. I felt about and found the box of tinder and flint. I lit the candle, but in an instant, I regretted it.

There, right before me, on the wall behind the table, was a life-sized painting of myself sitting on Gottfried's huge bed dressed in the rose-colored tunic. That he should choose to paint me should be flattering. That my husband was so artistic should have pleased me, but my stomach clenched at what I saw. The pinching pain over my eyes turned to daggers and I pressed against it.

The Dandelion in the picture was not a young wife in her prime, she was a wide-eyed, innocent little girl, about seven years old I guessed from the proportions and the missing tooth. Yet she smiled up at the painter seductively, while the rose-colored tunic hung loosely and suggestively off her shoulders.

Bile rose in my throat, but I knew I must face this. This was the moment. I must face it all, whatever "all" might entail. I picked up the candle and followed the curve of the wall. The next discovery was not nearly as shocking—a painting very similar to the first, but of a woman with large round brown eyes wearing a yellow tunic. It must have been Samia. I settled a bit, for that was the sort of thing I expected to find.

Next to her was a line of smaller paintings of me in different stages of growth and development. The sensual pose looked more benign as I matured and filled out the tunic appropriately. In the last painting my legs were bare with a deep gash on one. He must have painted it after we were together. Whenever did he find the time? Of all the paintings it was the most poignant. Instead of mirroring Samia's alluring expression, I looked lost and a little afraid but smiled up hopefully nonetheless. I remembered that Dandelion. I shed a tear for her.

I sat down and paused. It was so much to take in, so much to figure out. The realization sank in—Gottfried was watching me, obsessed with me since childhood. What sort of unbalanced man did such a thing? I looked back over at the seven-year-old Dandelion. I felt violated, dirty. How dare he? Did he fantasize about an innocent little girl? And then there was the line of Dandelions, all in a row, set up like a shrine with a rug tossed in front. Was I some sort of warped religion to him? It seemed all too likely and all too disturbing.

I found more paintings, paintings of a headless Samia, of the maimed and disfigured crusaders. They sickened me, and I lost my midday meal in a corner. Why had this happened to the hopeful young Gottfried with the soul of a poet and the hands of an artist? It was almost too painful to bear.

Then, in the middle of that dark, depraved attic, warmth covered my skin as if beams of sunlight flooded me. Everything was beautiful and bright and crystal clear. Months of clouds and confusion vanished in the blink of an eye. I was so light and airy, I thought I could float away.

I am not the lunatic, Gottfried is.

That was why the attic called to me. It was filled with ghosts, and it needed me to know the truth—I was not to blame. I was the victim of a sick, deranged man. Perhaps seventeen-year-old Dandelion deserved punishment for betraying William, but certainly not seven-year-old Dandelion. I remembered her well—clean and shiny as a new coin, pure as freshly fallen snow, merry as a dancing butterfly in the field. Surely she never did a single thing in her life to deserve this.

I almost laughed out loud. I imagined Gottfried would protect me from the world, when all along he was the very world from which I needed protection. He was a deluded, sad, and bitter man, and I had done nothing to deserve this. Amazing how one moment I could believe something with all my heart, and the very next be equally convinced of the precise opposite. That one instant when I struck the tinder changed everything. Another one of Friar John's quotes flashed through my mind. *"He will bring to light what is hidden in darkness and will expose the motives of men's hearts."*

Was I a bit greedy? Surely. Shallow? Of course—but not evil, not crazy. All I ever wanted was a better life. William had not understood. He was determined to take his own path. Why did everyone expect I should follow him? I was my own person. I had my own destiny, and the time had come to take charge of it once again.

I hopped down from the attic, landing on my feet like a cat. If someone were watching, they would have guessed me the gleeful thirteen-year-old Dandelion, never the jaded, depressed nineteen-year-old version.

I skipped down the stairs and toward the front door, not giving more than a passing thought to the wardrobe of beautiful clothing or the fur-lined cape I left behind. I threw open the door to the outside world with relish. I lifted my hands over my head and took a deep breath. I turned my toes toward the castle and danced forward for the first time in months.

A few minutes later I shocked Lady Catherine by bursting into her chamber with all the excitement and energy of a naughty child. I had only three words for her, but they were words that changed everything.

"Burn the parchment."

It would be years before I questioned her authority to do so.

Chapter 20

The next morning dawned anew. The whole world would be different. For months I woke and dressed and ate breakfast with Gottfried before going to the castle. Today, I woke in my own small chamber down the hall from Lady Catherine's. It was a simple room with whitewashed walls, decorated in soft shades of pink, yellow, and lilac. I was relieved by the stark contrast to the tower.

On this new day I planned to fetch Lady Catherine's morning meal myself. It was the least I could do in return for the monumental favor of the afternoon before.

The cook was preparing Catherine's tray of bread and jam when I arrived in the kitchen. There were already two goblets of warm spiced wine on the tray. I added oatmeal, honey, and eggs, as I was used to a heartier breakfast than the noble lady ate.

Walking up the mammoth stairway, it occurred to me what this change might mean for Richard and me. All these months I had fought with myself not to dream of him. What might this mean for our future? My heart flipped in my chest. It was too soon to consider such thoughts. I must adjust to this new situation first.

When I opened the door to Catherine's chamber, I blinked twice. Richard sat inside, reclining at the foot of her bed in only his short breeches and the shirt he wore under his tunic. His over-tunic, hose, and cloak were thrown casually across the bedside table. Richard and Catherine were chatting and looked surprised to find me enter instead of the chambermaid.

"Dandelion, darling, I'm so glad you are up and about and feeling well this morning. We weren't expecting you for another hour at least, were we, Richard? I asked Richard to join me early this morning to discuss how we should best proceed with your situation."

"Yes," said Richard, still recovering from his shock. "I think first, though, we should apprise Dandelion as to last night's incident." He stood and grabbed his clothing from the table. I never saw him lazing about half-dressed before. Although Lady Catherine seemed at ease, he uncomfortably donned his tunic.

My head spun at the unwanted information. Lady Catherine's explanation did not suffice. But clearly, it was not to be discussed.

"An incident last night?" I broke the silence.

Lady Catherine brushed her hand in the air as if it were nothing.

"Yes, after I sent you early to bed, Gottfried showed up at the great hall in a full-blown rage. It took several soldiers to detain him."

I placed the tray of food on her bed stand. "Oh, heavens. I'm so sorry, m'lady."

"It's quite all right, Dandelion. I actually anticipated it." She picked up her wine goblet and took a sip. "He demanded I return you at once. I fibbed and told him your female injuries were acting up again, and I would send you home as soon as you were better. I didn't want to cause a scene in front of the servants, and I thought adding a bit more guilt might help. We shall have to confront him today, though."

I was thankful to have Lady Catherine on my side in all of this. She made a wonderful friend, but a ruthless enemy. Richard was sitting now, lacing his shoes. "We were planning what to tell him this morning. If last night was any indication, he will be furious and violent."

A shiver ran through me. How silly I was to believe I had escaped him.

"Yes, I think we'll have to give him the truth directly and sternly." Lady Catherine took a dainty bite of bread and jam before continuing. "He must know the marriage document has been destroyed and no records remain. He has no authority over you now, Dandelion. He lost this match, and the sooner he acknowledges it the better. As for everyone else, I think it is best they assume you are still married."

I shot Richard a questioning glance, but he stared down at his hands.

Lady Catherine took a long draught of her wine before continuing. "The situation puts us in an awkward position, you know. If you were never legally Gottfried's wife, then you were indeed only his peasant mistress, and not at all a suitable companion for me."

Richard stood now and moved closer to us. "I agree, we should keep that part to ourselves for as long as possible. I will start a rumor they've had a tiff and Dandy will be staying at the castle proper for a while."

"Oh, this is horrible." I fell into a chair, dizziness overcoming me. "I didn't think past burning the document. Gottfried may well kill me yet. Whatever shall I do?"

"Settle yourself, child." Lady Catherine enjoyed another bite of her breakfast. "I know how to handle Gottfried. I always have a few tricks held in reserve for moments like this."

I could barely unravel my thoughts. "So now I'm not married, but I'm to pretend I'm married to insure my position, which I only earned because I was married? This is terribly twisted about. We should have thought it all through more thoroughly, m'lady. I don't want to bring any dishonor to you or your household."

"Dandelion, it will be fine," she said.

"No it won't. It's a horrible mess." I covered my face with my hands and a sob gripped my throat.

Richard knelt beside me and placed his arm about my shoulder.

"Don't worry, Dandelion, it will all work out."

I laid my head against his chest. "Oh, Richard, we should have run away after all," I whispered.

"Enough of this pouting." Lady Catherine snapped, her mood taking an unexpected turn. "That is not at all amusing, Dandelion. This castle has just undergone a major transition, and I'll not listen to you joke about stealing away their new steward." Richard jumped away from me.

Lady Catherine glared at him and then me. "This is no time for self-centered daydreaming, you fool girl. We must keep our wits about us and make a quality decision." She wiped her hands on her napkin in a threatening manner.

Looking into Lady Catherine's steely gray eyes, I realized I made a terrible miscalculation. I spoke past the lump in my throat. "Of course not. I didn't mean it, m'lady. I swear. I'm so sorry. I didn't intend to be selfish. I would never try to steal Richard from you or anyone else. I'm just so overwrought."

"Catherine, don't be silly." Richard sat on her bedside and crooned in her ear. "You know I live for you alone, my sweet." He reached across for her hand and kissed it most gallantly. "She's right, Dandy, you shouldn't jest about such things," he said, but turned to toss me a wink that Catherine could not see. "Neither the fires of hell nor floodwaters could take me from your side, my good lady. I am completely your devoted servant."

Lady Catherine smiled up at him now. "Of course you are, Richard." His lopsided grin worked its magic on her, making her giggle like a young girl under its powerful spell.

He ran his finger down Lady Catherine's cheek. "Dandelion is frightened, and rightfully so. You may yield considerable influence with Gottfried, but sometimes I wonder if he is in his right mind. Such a man can be unpredictable."

"True, Richard. True enough." Lady Catherine seemed calm again. "I adore Gottfried, but there is something not quite right about him. I thought Dandelion might change that—but she's only a young girl after all."

"Be that as it may," said Richard, "the man is unstable. Perhaps we could have him jailed for a time."

"No!" I moved to sit at the foot of the bed, leaning toward them both. "Don't put him in jail, please. He's done nothing to deserve it."

"I beg to differ, Dandelion." Catherine leered at Richard, then turned back to me. "Committing a fraud against his liege lord. Claiming to be married when he was not. I can cause considerable trouble for Gottfried if I so choose—but I will not jail him. No, I cannot place Gottfried under arrest. He is too important to me."

Richard did not look pleased with her answer. "Well then, do you have a better plan?"

"Give me a moment." Catherine patted Richard's hand and gazed out the window. I swallowed back my fear. If anyone could come up with a scheme, it would be Catherine. Thank the good Lord she remained on my side.

"Perhaps I do. Perhaps running away wasn't such a bad idea after all. Some time and distance may be required." She paused and thought for a moment longer.

Did she jest? Was she toying with us? Richard and I dared not even look at each other.

"Yes," Catherine said. "I think we should take a trip, Dandelion. It's just the thing. I haven't traveled anywhere in years. I didn't feel I'd be leaving the castle in secure hands, but now with Richard so well established, I would love to go on a trip. It would be just the thing to cheer you."

My face twisted in confusion. "You and I, m'lady? On a trip?"

"Yes, don't you think so, Richard?" She turned to him and smiled.

He gave her hand a squeeze. "Actually, it may well solve everything. Lady Tallanger has been begging you to get out and see the world."

"My thoughts exactly." Catherine gestured toward the window. "The weather is lovely, and I have no pressing commitments. It's perfect."

"Indeed, m'lady," said Richard. "I think it is."

Catherine turned her attention to me. "What do you say, Dandelion?"

I could barely fathom her words.

And like that it was decided.

Lady Catherine sent word to the Tallangers in Bristol to meet us at their small keep near Bath the following week. Catherine had grown up down the lane. Her excitement was contagious. I pictured the grand Lady Catherine as a small child running through the woods as she hopped about the room flinging dresses and jewels into her traveling chest.

Soon, I forgot about the confrontation with Gottfried. I forgot I was afraid and upset. I forgot my husband would likely be scheming my murder by nightfall. I forgot Lady Worthing, although my closest friend, was still a powerful and threatening woman with whom I should maintain certain boundaries. I forgot all of that and skipped about the room like a child as well.

I was going on holiday!

"Oh, m'lady. I'm starting to wonder if heading southward was such a good idea after all. Perhaps we should have taken the direct route to Bath." I stood up in the stirrups and leaned forward over Pegasus's bouncing mane. Dusk was settling about us.

Lady Catherine looked both regal and relaxed upon her own stallion. "Well, it is too late now. We're nearly there."

"You may be accustomed to all this riding, but my bottom hurts. Can't we stop for a moment?" Indeed my rear had fallen asleep, and was now riddled with pinpricks.

"No, we cannot stop. Don't behave like a grumpy goose, you spoiled chit. We're doing this for you."

I bit my lip against a sharp retort. My sore rump was playing havoc with my mood. I wondered if tomorrow I might ride in the wagon with the luggage instead, perhaps atop our soft bedding.

I was still daydreaming when I dismounted. As I followed Catherine over the sandy dune and first glimpsed the turbulent waters spreading before me, everything else faded away. Lady Catherine received her just reward in my awestruck expression.

"I've heard about the sea," I murmured, "read about the sea, but I never came close to imagining this." My heart welled within my chest.

How shall I describe the scene? Powerful and elemental, expansive and vast in a way I never dreamt, extending for near eternity before melting into the sky. As I watched the rhythmic waves crash against a huge boulder and the mist rising against the horizon, the wonder and grandeur of God took on entirely new dimensions. The mystical poems I had read flashed again through my mind, causing my head to swish like the water at my feet, but the words took on even greater depth and proportion. I felt at the same time insignificant and yet a part of something more enormous than ever before.

Lady Catherine, always a master of the dramatic, had brought me to the western side of a jutting peninsula at sunset. I watched the giant fiery ball descend toward the water. The sky was an artist's pallet of thick orange and yellow brushstrokes streaked by puffy gray clouds. My feet twitched to step out upon the glimmering pathway to the sun. The tall swaying grass along the beach made an elegant silhouette against the striking panorama. It was a moment to embrace the divine.

I danced along the shore in the center of the ever-expanding universe.

Lying on a crusty pallet in a corner of a great hall along our trip, Catherine made a face and pressed an elegant hand against her slim nose. "Good heavens, it stinks in here."

"I suppose we must be thankful for shelter." I glanced about the room shadowed by dim firelight. Our host "castle" was in fact little more than a military barracks. After nearly a week of traveling, the place provided much cause for disappointment. The rushes upon the stone floor smelled of rotted food.

"Ugh, this is what happens when there is no lady in the manor."
Swatting at some bedbugs, Catherine nearly growled.

"But we must be gracious, m'lady. Lord Grayson is still a powerful
earl."

"Well, we had best leave early in the morning, for my graciousness
is wearing thin. We shall most certainly skip this stop along our journey
home." With a frown, she laid her head on the pillow and pulled the
covers to her chin.

While I grew up in such conditions, many years had passed since I
dealt with such stench and vermin. But I managed to settle myself for
sleep. I was surprised by the differences between the castles we stayed
in as we journeyed—some made of sandstone, some of shining black
rock. They could sprawl across a valley or rise straight up toward the
sky, contain elegant, extravagant furnishings, or even the look and
smell of a barnyard.

Perhaps some of the castles were larger or grander than our home,
but none so full of modern wonders and conveniences. Lady Catherine
said we must journey toward London to find anything rivaling our
advanced plumbing systems, cristallo windows, and fashionable
furnishings.

I noticed the villages surrounding the castles, as well, and was
taken aback to see the level of affluence in the attached communities
was in no way related to the wealth of the ruling noblemen. Some of
the simplest castles featured towns with pleasant cottages lining clean
streets filled with robust youngsters. Yet the grandest castle along
the way hid in its shadow a village full of poverty and desperation.
Although Lady Catherine was not particularly generous, I saw cruelty
along my journey that would have shocked the healthy, happy
villagers of Arun.

Batting off bugs, I couldn't help but wonder.

Whatever might await us in Bath?

Chapter
21

Several days later we reached our destination in a rolling vale near the famed town of Bath. Dismounting my horse, I surveyed the pretty country manor, built surprisingly of wood with only an ancient pole fence surrounding it. Lady Catherine and I left our belongings for the servants and stepped through the front door.

The place smelled crisp and clean like the surrounding valley, and the furnishings shined with a fresh coat of wax, evidence of Tillie's excellent housekeeping. It was small, little more than a great hall and kitchen downstairs with a loft that must contain the sleeping chambers, but it was cozy, warm, and natural. The large timbers overhead gave the feel of the outdoors, and a mosaic of colorful local stones surrounded the giant hearth. Big shuttered windows were thrown open to the sunshine and warm breezes.

"Oh, Lady Catherine, it's just lovely."

Her smile was small and serene. "It brings to mind my childhood."

I was surprised that Lady Catherine chose such a rustic spot for our final stopping place. The Tallangers were renowned for their enormous wealth. But like her own casual solar, this manor fit Lady Catherine, and she seemed more herself than ever, as if she took off some party masquerade.

The passel of rowdy Tallanger boys careened down the wooden banister to greet their favorite auntie. "Auntie Cat! Auntie Cat is here!"

Lady Catherine's face lit up like a candle. The years slipped away as she hugged them, jumped up and down and spun one in broad circles. Lord Tallanger chose the steps over the banister. Lady Sarah and Jane sped from the kitchen to greet us in an affectionate but most unladylike fashion.

"You made it at long last. We could hardly bear to wait." Lady Sarah gave her sister a warm embrace and giggled like a lass.

"Look, Auntie." The smallest lad tugged at Catherine's mantle. "Papa made me a slingshot." He held it before her, his chest puffed with pride. The boy's grin revealed several gaps from his missing teeth.

"A fine weapon indeed." She tussled his hair.

And finally, standing amid that flurry of greetings, I understood. Underneath the titles and the fancy clothes, this was a real family. For a few short weeks, they could romp through the woods, hunt with slingshots, and swim in streams as I had every day of my charmed childhood. Here they would play a game of make believe in which they were a normal country family, and I was invited to join.

They wore simple linen kirtles and tunics. Lord Tallanger actually sported a patch on his hose in a comical striped pattern. After traveling for days into the unknown yonder, I ended up at home—more at home than I had ever been in the cramped hut or the exotic tower or the elegant castle.

As I folded Lady Catherine's burgundy velvet mantle and placed it a chest that eve, my wonder still had not diminished. Smoothing down the soft fabric, I took a deep breath of the woodsy air. I had learned in the very first day more about this family than I had in all the previous months combined, including the names, ages, and distinguishing characteristics of each boy. The Tallangers' oldest son and heir, Jamey, was named after Lord James Worthing and off to court with Thomas and the new young king, Edward III. The two noblemen were taking the palace by storm, but Lady Sarah hoped Jamey would soon choose a favorite beauty and settle down to give her grandchildren.

"I thought you knew about Jamey," Lady Catherine said as I tucked her into bed in our tiny loft chamber.

"No, oddly enough I didn't. You don't speak of your son. Perhaps that's why Jamey never came up." I crawled under my own cozy covers.

"He was born first, three years after Thomas. Then tragically, Sarah suffered a series of miscarriages. Ten years passed before Jane made it safely into the world. She seemed to work some sort of magic, for the rest of them came tumbling out one on top of the other."

Cloud burst into the room at that moment. The funny little dog was dressed in a burgundy surcoat with the golden Worthing dragon embroidered on it by Catherine's own hand. Cloud barked an angry reprimand at us for leaving her sleeping alone by the fire in the great hall. Then she hopped onto Lady Catherine's bed and snuggled into a ball next to her legs, giving us a disdainful look as we laughed at her expense. "I hope you don't mind, Dandelion. She's become accustomed to sleeping with me."

"Not at all, m'lady. She's as much yours as mine by now."

Catherine didn't respond to my comment about Thomas, and I let it go.

"Oh Catty, what a beautiful day. It brings me right back to the time you first met James," Lady Sarah said and took a bite of apple tart.

We all sat under a shady tree eating a picnic from a blanket. The boys had long since finished and were swinging from a rope extending over a nearby pond. Lord Tallanger was gone on business. Only Lady Sarah, Lady Catherine, Jane, and I were left to pick at the remnants of the delicious beef pie and roasted chicken.

"Yes," Catherine whispered. "I can feel the happy memories again, instead of just the pain of losing him."

"I wish Papa were here to tell the story." Jane flopped over onto her belly and propped her head upon her hands.

We had spent the last days picnicking, riding in hay wagons and even milking cows. The landscape was similar to my Sussex home, yet distinct with its countless rambling thistles and its tall limestone cliffs in place of our chalky outcroppings. I felt closer to Lady Catherine and the Tallangers with each passing day.

There were no minstrels or mimes or troubadours at our remote hideaway, but the children entertained us with songs and dances much as my own siblings and I in our tiny village hut. Lord Tallanger turned out to be an expert storyteller, rivaling William in his narrative eloquence. We played games and frolicked as if none of us had ever set foot in a formal dining hall.

Lady Sarah dusted off some crumbs as she finished her tart. "I've heard the story so many times, I think I can tell it myself."

"Oh please, Mummy. Why, I don't think Dandelion's ever heard it."

"All right then." Lady Sarah arranged herself more comfortably.

Lady Catherine leaned back against the tree with a serene smile on her face and closed her eyes.

"Well, Catherine and George and I grew up in a little farmhouse not far from here. We were about six, eight, and ten years old, and we were swimming in this very pond in our undergarments, when we heard a sneeze from behind those bushes right over there. 'Halt, who goes there,' shouted George in his squeaky little voice. Out from the bushes poked the head of the cutest red-headed, freckle-faced boy."

"It was papa," shouted Jane, unable to contain herself.

"Indeed it was. It was the young Lord Edward Tallanger we had heard so much about but never seen. His family visited their small keep next door only once every few summers. He had managed to escape his mother who was ever worrying about his health. We formed a little club and even made a blood oath."

Jane could not keep herself from interrupting again. "Every few years they would meet again and pick up the friendship right where they left off."

"This is my story, Jane." She sent a teasing smile to her daughter. "So, anyway, the years went by, and one summer I was sitting right under this tree with Eddie. He leaned over, kissed me, and declared his undying love for me. Oh, what a glorious day, the most wonderful day of my life, of Edward's as well, and yet also the worst. You see, I was an innocent country girl without a clue that destitute squires' daughters did not go about marrying future earls."

"Forgive me for interrupting," said Catherine, "but I thought this story was supposed to be about me."

"Ahh, right on cue. The next summer Edward returned with his cousin James on their own private holiday. James knew of Edward's crush on the poor little country maiden. Eddie thought James came along to help him, but James planned to talk his foolish young cousin out of the attraction."

Jane reached over and took my hand in her own. She wiggled her eyebrows at me.

"The very first day the two of them came to call," said Lady Sarah, "Catherine answered the door. Her flowing black hair and flashing eyes mesmerized James. The four of us shared a picnic right here that day. James was near daft chasing after Catty, and quite a chase she led. I thought for weeks that she didn't care one whit about him. I thought she only spent time with James for my sake, but in fact, she was weaving her own masterful web."

We were distracted from the story by a loud splash as one of the boys fell from the rope and into the pond. The others jumped about and hollered in a frenzy, tugging at tunics and hose, until they stripped down to their breeches and jumped in the pond alongside their brother.

Sarah merely rolled her eyes. "In August, Catherine informed James she was to marry a young squire from across the county come winter, and she bade him farewell. I had never heard of such a squire, but James bought every word and was beside himself with jealousy."

Jane tugged hard at my hand.

"Now, I must point out that James was eight years Edward's senior and already a powerful earl." Lady Sarah wagged her finger at Jane. "He was used to getting whatever he wanted and let nothing stand in his way. One week later, James showed up at our door with the hugest ruby ring you've ever seen and asked for Catty's hand in marriage."

Jane sat up and clapped.

Her mother frowned. "It caused a massive scandal at court. Edward II should have refused the match, but he and James were close friends, and somehow he was persuaded."

"So," Jane said, "a few years later when Father asked permission to marry Mother, she was not just the daughter of a squire, she was the sister of an influential countess."

Her mother gave her a playful shove. "It turned out to be an excellent match for everyone."

"And so . . . ." Jane moved to Lady Catherine and gave her a quick hug. "We are all extremely grateful to have such a conniving, scheming, social climbing, money grubbing . . . ."

"Oh hush, you silly child." Lady Sarah turned to look me in the eye. "Don't let anyone fool you, Dandelion. Catherine and James were truly in love."

"Yes," said Catherine, clinging to Jane's hand, "but in the end he loved his detestable war more than he loved me."

Lady Sarah shifted positions. "Don't say that, Cat. He was a fiery and passionate man. He was as loyal to you as he was to his country. It was an honorable thing he did."

"And yet, he's gone, and all I ever wish is to have him back again." Catherine seemed so real, so vulnerable—exquisitely human and utterly defenseless.

I had long ago dismissed the myth of nobility as some superior race of gods and goddesses, some anointed species. Until that moment, though, I didn't comprehend that they were complete and rounded human beings like me, with dreams and heartaches like mine.

After the picnic, we visited the old farmhouse where the sisters grew up. Their brother George died in the war not long after James, but his widowed wife and children still lived down the lane from the Tallanger manor. The cottage had a pleasing kitchen gathering area with a generous dining table and plenty of comfortable chairs nestled about the hearth, as well as two roomy bedchambers. That was all. Granted it was several times larger, taller, and better constructed than my family's thatched hut, but I was amazed nonetheless to learn the stylish countesses grew up in this place. Once Lord Tallanger returned, we took a jaunt to the ancient town of Bath. The hot thermal pools were linked to worship of the Celtic goddess Solis, and there was a decadent, pagan feel to the place. To me, the town was a wonder and veritably teeming with life, like a colony of ants busy at work. The family proclaimed me hopelessly provincial, and warned Catherine never to take me to London, lest I fall dead of shock on the spot. Along the way home, Lord Tallanger regaled me with childhood tales of Thomas and Jamey, but Catherine stared into the hills. I determined to get to the bottom of this Thomas situation.

Chapter 22

Several nights later, I faced Lady Catherine with the question. I would challenge her if necessary. I needed to know the truth.

"Catherine," I whispered into the small, dark space between our beds. "Are you awake?"

"Yes. What is it?"

I heard her rolling toward me. "Please tell me about your son Thomas. What happened? Why don't you speak of him?"

"Oh, Dandy, must we really?"

"Yes, we must. We've grown so close, and yet there's a huge part of your life I still know nothing about." I propped myself upon one elbow.

She took a deep breath. "It's so hard to know where to start. He was such an adorable little boy, but even then there was a distance between us. I was terribly in love with his father and often away at court." She sighed. "Then George came along. What a whiny, demanding creature he was. Anytime I visited the children he took all the attention, and Thomas just sort of endured, but it was hellish on my nerves, Dandelion. I know it sounds horrible to say about your own child, but I was beside myself in those days with worry over James off to war, and I could hardly take the noise of the screeching little thing. I started to avoid the nursery entirely. Then I was off to court once again."

I couldn't believe what I was hearing.

"I should have made more effort with Thomas. When I did spend time with him I wanted to hug him and never let go, but after a while, he didn't hug me back anymore."

Little wonder.

"By the time James died, Thomas was training as a knight near London. He came home briefly for the funeral, but once he was announced as the new earl, he couldn't find a fast enough horse to carry him away. Apparently, word of my affair with Gottfried reached Thomas. Thomas had always adored Gottfried, but he felt we betrayed his father, and he was livid. He sent me a scathing letter demanding I end it at once." She paused and took another deep breath.

I was beginning to understand why this story was so difficult for her to tell. My face heated at the reminder of her and Gottfried. I was thankful she couldn't see me through the thick night. "So that is why the two of you broke it off."

"I wish I could say yes, Dandy. I wish to God I had been so strong. I just never wrote him back. I was barely coping through life without my beloved James. I couldn't bear the thought of giving up Gottfried too."

That struck me as odd. "But you . . . you said you were only together a short time."

"Well, I may have understated a bit. It was actually several years. When we did end things, I wrote to Thomas, but he was off in Scotland. After a time, he came home for a visit. I had my own life by then, though. I had grown accustomed to being a widowed lady in a castle with all the power to myself, and Thomas was happy being a warrior. Things were tense between us, and he didn't stay for long. I guess in our own ways we're happy enough with our arrangement, but I'd trade it all to be close with him as I am with you, Dandelion."

I laid my head on the pillow and stared up at the ceiling, compassion and anger battling inside me. "I'm so sorry."

"Yes, I am as well. And now Thomas and Jamey are up to some foolish plan to overthrow the regent and set up Edward III as a proper and independent king. If this coup fails, I may never get a chance to make things right."

Best keep a level head where Catherine was concerned. The poor woman had been through so much. I turned back toward her. "But if it succeeds, he may be one of the most powerful men in England."

"Yes, if it succeeds."

"I remember Thomas," I said dreamily, wishing to reassure her. "He's so handsome and brave and good-hearted. I'm sure he will be fine, m'lady."

Through the layers of darkness and blankets I felt her bristle. "And how do you know my Thomas?"

It seemed I had made another serious miscalculation about our relationship. "He gave me a piece of candy once when I was a little girl. It was the year of the famine. He seemed so grown up and heroic to me at the time. I hope you don't mind."

"About the candy, no. About you taking liberties in speaking of my son, I suppose I do mind. You are a married woman as far as the world knows, Dandelion, and you have no business talking about any man, let alone the Earl of Worthing, in those longing and familiar tones. It's not right, Dandelion. I shan't stand for it."

I reached across the space between us and found her hand. The roiling emotions settled into a sadness spreading across my chest. "I'm so sorry. Speaking of him has spoiled your mood. I regret bringing it up. I see now it is an upsetting subject for you."

She pushed my hand away. "Yes, well don't bring him up again—for any reason."

I lay holding back my tears in the warm bed in the small, cozy room of the homey manor and realized it was neither my home nor my family after all.

Before we bade our final farewells, Lady Sarah pulled me outside to a private cove in the garden surrounded by the perfume of daisies and lilies.

"I do so adore flowers." She took a lily into her fingers and took a deep whiff. "But, of course I didn't come out here to speak of the foliage. Dandelion, I'm concerned over this decision you made to burn your marriage certificate."

I twisted my head sideways. "Oh, I assumed Lady Catherine informed you of the circumstances."

"She did, but I must say this puts you in a rather vulnerable position. If I had anticipated this, I would never have encouraged you to be her maid." She stared into the distance.

"I don't understand." I followed her gaze but found nothing of interest.

"Oh, this is difficult for me to say." She turned to me. "I love my sister dearly, but she is a ruthless woman, and her jealousy is legendary."

I considered the statement. "So, you think I should be worried about Lady Catherine."

"I hope not, dear. I truly hope not. She's mellowed over the years, and she does care about you, but it's a possibility I cannot discount. You're no longer a married woman. Eventually it is sure to get out. That makes you competition, and Catherine will not stand for competition."

"Oh." I squeezed my hands in front of me.

"And then throw Richard into the mix, and it is a messy situation."

"Richard?" Whatever might Richard have to do with anything?

Lady Tallanger tilted her head. "Why of course Richard. She's never liked how intimate you two are, but she knew Gottfried terrified him. Now that you're free, oh my, this could get ugly indeed."

"But why would she . . . ?" The truth dawned on me. That morning in her room, Richard hadn't arrived half-dressed before me. He never left from the night before. My face grew hot. I pressed my hand against my cheek. How could I have been so naïve?

"You didn't know? That was the arrangement from the beginning, dear. I thought everyone knew."

Thoughts tumbled about my head. Memories I had discounted time and time again. "Now that we're discussing it, there've been all sorts of clues. I feel so foolish. Does she love him?"

She reached for my hand. "No, of course not. She was melancholy and needed a handsome young man to brighten her spirits. There have been others in the past. No, she adores him, but she doesn't love him. As I mentioned, this was the arrangement all along."

"Why didn't she tell me?"

"Perhaps she tried. To jaded and worldly people like ourselves, you appear so fresh and innocent. Perhaps she didn't want to disappoint you."

The conversation rang in my head as we galloped toward home through forest trails. On the surface things were normal, but an underlying tension brewed between Lady Catherine and me. This holiday proved quite a looping emotional journey—first seeing Catherine as a vulnerable and sympathetic person much like myself, and then seeing her reduced to something even lower and worse. Of course I was reared to think her wicked, but wicked on a grand and elevated scale, not in the base and common manner I viewed her now.

I thought of sweet young Thomas with his waving chestnut hair, his sky-blue eyes, and the light dusting of freckles across his nose. He deserved so much more than the cold and calculating mother he got. I remembered George, every bit as whiny and petulant as she described, but might not a kind and engaging mother have molded and guided such a willful child? And then to think of Thomas, the novice knight far away to the north, hearing of his wayward mother sleeping with his childhood hero on the heels of his father's death. It sickened me.

As did picturing Lady Catherine coupling with Richard. Here I thought him all my own. How foolish. He was her personal toy, her private plaything all along. Had he ever loved me? Did he truly care? Did it bother him to wake in her bed and flirt with me the very same day? If he suffered the least crisis of conscience, he was masterful at hiding it.

Oh, I still loved Lady Catherine. She had done so many kind and charitable things for me. How could I forget as I galloped home through the leafy paths of amazing distant lands from my very first holiday? I merely wished she could find it within herself to be a better person, a stronger person. I wished it for Thomas and for the long deceased George. I wished it for Richard.

And I wished it for me.

We were back at Arun Castle a full week before Richard sneaked into my bedchamber late one night. I awoke with a start, heart in my throat. "Richard, you terrified me. Whatever are you doing here?"

"Must I explain?" he said, closing my door and leaning against it with a devilish grin glinting in the moonlight.

"Yes, you must. Did Lady Catherine fall asleep in your arms before you finished with her?"

"Ahh, so you know, do you? I wondered how long it would take. I thought you seemed rather cool. I fancied you took up with some farmer boy while on holiday."

"Yes, I know, and I'm repulsed." I pulled my covers up to my neck. "It disgusts me to think you kissed me with lips come fresh from hers. Really, Richard, I thought you had better taste."

"I do indeed my pretty, which is precisely why I've come."

"Well, you've wasted your time. Get out before someone sees you here. I'll not be losing my position, my home, and my best friend over the likes of you."

"So you think Catherine a friend now, do you?" He crossed his arms over his chest. "Charming. This thing between Catherine and me . . . it's nothing, really. You are the one I love. How could you doubt it?"

I glared at him. "Because that's the type of simple-minded peasant girl I am. I highly doubt it when a man says he loves me en route from tupping my mistress."

"It means nothing, and she didn't want me tonight. Things work differently with the nobility."

"Get out. Just get out now." My stern finger pointed to the door.

He opened it but paused a moment before exiting. I thought I saw a shadow gliding through the dark hallway beyond. He chanced one last lopsided smile. "This is far from over, Dandelion."

Chapter 23

Despite Richard's warning, I thought the matter closed. Weeks passed, and life returned to normal. Gottfried accepted his defeat and hadn't emerged from his tower quarters, becoming more of a hermit than ever. He no longer emerged even to drill the soldiers. A small part of me feared for his state of mind, but I could not afford sympathy on his behalf. The man had nearly destroyed my life.

As for Richard, I was unable to maintain my grudge against him for long. He was too much fun. Our work kept us in close proximity, both at the beck and call of the ever-demanding Lady Catherine—fellow victims of her whims and impulses.

Even now, I was rushing off toward the kitchen to fetch a goblet of cider for her most noble bossiness. As I entered the expansive great hall, a familiar form sent me dashing back toward the shadows of the doorway. I peeked around the edge. Indeed there stood William, as tall and handsome as ever. My heart fluttered in my chest. My feet itched to run toward him and fling myself into his arms, beg him to save me from the insanity that was the castle, but surely he would push me away.

I gathered my resolve and took another look. What was that on his shoulder? As he turned, I saw it—a bag of grain, grain from the land he remained tied to, grain that he had tossed me aside to grow, grain that he toiled after only to hand over to his betters. The benign bag took on a sinister glow. The sensations flooded me again, the clanging, the pressing, the smoke, the hunger. I shook them off and hurried to the kitchen by a different route.

"Dandelion," Richard called to me as I entered. "I need your help. Lady Worthing most cruelly raked me through the ashes last night for my poor wine choice. I daren't make the same mistake two days in a row. Come down to the cellar with me. You know what she likes."

"So should you by now, Richard," I said, raising an eyebrow at him.

"Funny. Just help me or we shall both be sorry for her mood."

I fell into step with him. "Speaking of which, have you seen her pearl drop earrings? The ones Lord James gave her for their tenth anniversary? They've been missing for weeks, and she's quite upset."

"No, but I shall keep my eyes open. She's always leaving things about." He waved a hand dismissively.

As we descended the steps to the wine cellar, the sweltering temperature dropped, cooling the sweat along my neck. I still longed for my old, light, airy tunics on such hot days. I wished to throw off my headpiece and stomp through a creek with William and Tim once again.

I was deep in my thoughts and off my guard when Richard swept me against the cool damp stones and clamped his mouth to mine. At first I struggled. I pushed. I fought. I swear I did, but my resolve stood no chance against the frenzied onslaught of his lips. Once I ceased fighting, he lightened his grip and switched to slow, lazy, torturous kisses, which left me little more than a puddle of pudding against the wall.

When he drew away, an actual cry of disappointment escaped my molten lips. We were both breathless. He backed against the wall beside me to catch his bearings.

My hazy mind cleared. Still rasping for breath, I said, "Richard . . . how could you . . . we discussed this."

"I can't do it. I cannot live without you."

"But you are still with her."

"Yes." He spat the word. "And I hate every single moment. At first it was all a game, but I can't abide it any longer. I hate every strand of wiry, gray hair. I detest the feel of her loose and wrinkled skin. I want to gag when she presses those crinkly, sagging lips against mine. I can't take it anymore."

A wave of sorrow passed over me, the last thing I expected. Poor boy, caught in the trap of that manipulative woman. I ran my hand along the smooth contours of his face. "Surely you exaggerate. Surely it's not as bad as all that." Lady Worthing was going through the change of life and had aged in recent months, but she was still a comely female.

"No, it's true. I can't take it anymore. I need you. I need your lips to wash me clean. I need your scent to drown her stench. I need to bury myself in you and come out new and fresh once again. Please, Dandelion, don't deny me."

I turned toward him. "I want to. I so badly want to, but I can't. I love her still, and I can't do this to her. I'm completely at her mercy. Only you and she know the truth about me. Blast it all; she plotted this supposed truth herself. She writes our fates, Richard. We are but puppets in her hands. Think you Gottfried will come to my rescue now, and over this nonetheless? Will my peasant parents save me? They can't even save themselves. I can't risk it. Surely you can see that." I reached to him again.

He grasped my hand. "She doesn't care, Dandy. She doesn't love me like that. As long as I'm there to warm her bed at night, what does it matter if I'm in love with you?"

"It matters. Are you truly so foolish? It matters greatly. She's made it clear you are hers alone. In case you haven't noticed, Richard, I'm cursed with beauty and my youth is doing me no favors at a time when hers is fading. I'm in a precarious position as it is. I can't afford to make it worse."

He leaned his forehead against mine. "Do you love me, Dandelion? I've told you so many times, but you never respond."

"Of course I love you, Richard. Of course I love you." And we were inexplicably a tangle of kisses all over again.

When Richard came up for breath he said, "Then it's worth the risk."

"Perhaps, I don't know. I'm so confused. Maybe we should run away like you always wanted."

Those words hit his lust like a splash of cold water. He leaned his back against the wall once again.

"And that I cannot do."

My heart plummeted. "But why? You're the one who suggested it, begged for it if I rightly recall."

"It was nothing but a silly fantasy. I knew you wouldn't leave Gottfried. It was fun to dream. That was all."

I swallowed down my anger. "And now that I'm free?"

"She would ruin my career. In London, in Scotland, in France, it matters not where we would go, for she has friends and her friends have friends. I would be blacklisted for all eternity." Richard walked a few paces away and turned his back to me.

"And you care about your position more than you care about me?"

He raked his fingers through his hair. "Of course not, I love you. It's not so simple. Nothing's as blastedly simple as you try to make it."

I embraced him from behind. "Oh, but I think it is. Let's do it. We can run away together. Surely you can find inconsequential employment somewhere."

"No." He kissed my hand upon his chest. "We cannot."

The housekeeper's shrill call interrupted from upstairs. "Master Richard, Master Richard. Where are you? I need a word with you."

Richard swiped the back of his hand across his mouth to remove the last moist traces of my kiss. He shot me one more longing glance and dashed up the stairs.

To this day the progression of the matter from that point remains rapid and disjointed in my memory. First, I delivered Lady Catherine's cider. She pulled from behind her back the missing pearl drop earrings, twisted with straw. "Dandelion," she said. "You shall never guess what the stable boys found in Pegasus's stall. Who could have hid them there, but you? You're the only one who rides her."

I stood gaping and confounded until I looked into her cold, hateful eyes. I remembered those eyes. They first greeted me in this very chamber years ago.

"Guards."

The men materialized on cue.

"I've heard tell Dandelion is fond of cellars. I think perhaps she should cool off for a while in the dungeon."

I saw shock on their faces.

"But good lady . . . ." Gerald, my old dancing companion, sounded horrified.

"Silence." She spewed her venom at him. "I will not tolerate another word from you on behalf of this lying little thief. Why I didn't trust my instincts and leave her in the peasant village where she belonged is beyond me. A few days in jail will be just the thing to remind her of her place in the world."

The guards took me into custody, but faltered as we began the trek to the hateful dungeon.

Catherine stomped her foot. "Move it, you fools, or you shall be joining her."

I next found myself locked in a cell in the basement of the castle. The floors were damp, freezing cold, and reeked of urine. There was a skeleton in the corner I dared not investigate. Rats squeaked in the darkness.

I curled myself into a ball, and I waited. I waited for Richard to come to me either as fellow prisoner or rescuer, but he never did. I waited for days I think. It was hard to tell in the incessant blackness. I might have heard Father John praying outside my cell, or perhaps I was dreaming. Some brave and compassionate soul tossed a blanket and a flask of water to me while the guard slept.

There was so much I should have thought of during that time, so many questions should have plagued my mind. There was so much betrayal, so much treachery, but instead my thoughts floated away from the place. I dreamed of running through bright open fields with William and Tim. I dreamed of swimming in the river. I dreamed of a time when I never failed to charm my way out of trouble. A time when the consequences of my actions did not involve the likes of dungeons, rats, and deprivation. My mind drifted far from the awful dungeon.

After that first success, our poaching became a daily habit. William, Tim, and I would hunt, play, dance, sing, and eat. Oh how we ate! It was two weeks later when we met with our first mishap.

We were walking home from our hideaway when we crossed paths with Michael, the castle steward. "Well, hello there children, and how were his lordship's rabbits today? I think I still see a bit on the wee one's face if I'm not mistaken."

The three of us froze in abject terror and shame. Thoughts of wooden posts and whips flashed through my head. An executioner's axe glinted in my mind. William managed to nudge me from behind, and I quickly turned on the tears, which were not far from the surface at that point. They ran in warm rivulets down my cheeks. "We're so sorry, sir, so, so sorry. But we've been ever so hungry, sir, and the baby here . . . ."

"Enough already, little missy, you can turn off your fake tears. I know your type. Not that I'm troubled by it, mind you. Why . . . do you think I spent my entire life in a castle like that? No indeed. No, I know what it's like to wonder where your next meal is coming from. Don't bother me a bit if you want to catch yourselves a little dinner now and again. Actually, it looks to me like you've put a lot of hard work and planning into it."

"Yes sir, we have," I answered. Hope welled. Perhaps we would escape the whipping post after all.

"I figure no real harm's being done here. Just wanted to make sure you knew I was onto you. That is my job, after all. It always seemed a little unnatural to me that all this land and all those creatures should belong to a spoiled few sitting up there, hidden behind the castle walls."

I sighed in relief. "Yes, sir, that's exactly what I was thinking. It's like Robin Hood, you see."

"Robin Hood, eh? Well, mind you don't end up dead like Robin Hood. Poaching is still a dangerous game. Stick to the small stuff—squirrels, rabbits, birds, maybe a few fish. I'll cover for you the best I can, but be on the lookout for the castle guards. Enough of them have daddies with titles in front of their names that I'm sure they wouldn't find it as amusing as I do. No, those titled folks, they care a whole lot about deeds and ownership and whatnot."

William spoke up. "We planned to stay away from them sir, and to stick to the small game."

"Well, all right then, you'll probably fair well enough. You be sure to come by me first, though, so I can give you a nod. I always do my rounds right about noontide. There are hunting parties out in those woods some days. Why the king himself used to hunt here when the old lord was still alive. Heaven help you all if the Lady Worthing ever finds out. She's a cold one indeed, she is. There'll be nothing I can do to help you if she does." He walked off with that.

There was nothing left to say. We were happy to have a confirmed ally, but scared at the same time by our close call and his stern warning.

"You never told us that Robin Hood died!" I whispered.

"I wasn't aware that he did."

A cold one indeed. My friend Michael hadn't known the half of it. How could she do this to me? A large creature scurried over my foot in the dark. I allowed my mind to slip back to that other place.

Before long we regained our confidence. We were careful to wait faithfully for the steward's nod, avoiding the woods when he indicated. We enjoyed every minute of that summer, and went home with full bellies each night. Occasionally William's brothers would catch him and put him to work, but we made a game of that too, and with our help he was quickly done and back to poaching. Mum gave Tim and I suspicious looks when we couldn't finish our food, but since we were clearly growing stronger and healthier by the day, she didn't say a word.

Over dinner one night in the mud-daubed hut, Sadie had enough shrill complaints for everyone.

"These two urchins don't appreciate my hard work and cooking. That's what you get for letting them run around the countryside like a couple of heathens. They should be out in the fields helping like all the other children. It's that Ashby boy, I tell you! He's always up to no good." At fourteen, Sadie seemed to think herself our parent as well.

"Oh be quiet already, Sadie," Robert answered. "Just be happy for them. We don't have enough land to keep them busy anyway."

"Happy indeed!" She huffed off in a snit. "Ungrateful, selfish, spoiled little brats. Why I never—"

Mum cut into the argument. "The bread and pottage certainly are delicious, Sadie, but I can't help thinking that a rabbit or two in here would top it off just right. Don't you think so, Dandelion?"

I choked on my food and looked up in horror while everybody laughed. After my coughing fit passed I replied, "Well, I'm sure I wouldn't know anything about it. I've never even tasted a rabbit."

"Is that so, child?"

Five-year-old Tim twisted his adorable little face in confusion and said in a squeaky voice, "Sure you have, Dandy, remember, rabbits and squirrels and fish. William catches them for us almost every day."

My stomach dropped. "Tim! How could you? That was a secret," I scolded.

"Not from Mum and Da," he said with tears in his eyes, "I can't lie to Mum and Da, can I, Dandy?"

"Shame on you, Dandelion," Mum said. "Your brother's right, you shouldn't be keeping secrets from your parents. Just exactly how long has this been going on?"

"Since midsummer," I mumbled, looking down at my plate.

"Are we in trouble, ma'am?" Tim asked.

"Well, I haven't decided yet. Are you being careful?"

I clutched my roiling belly. "Yes, ma'am, ever so careful. I would never put Tim at risk. The castle steward knows all about it. He's in on it with us, and we're always on the lookout for problems."

"Hmmm," Mum said. "What do you think, Da, are they in trouble?"

"I-I-I think they will be," he stuttered, "unless they br-br-br-bring some meat home for my stew tomorrow night," he said with a straight and serious face. It was a moment before he burst out laughing and we all knew it was safe to join him.

My family enjoyed a fine dinner of rabbit stew the next night. We gathered around a big fire in the backyard, and William joined us. I felt like a princess in a castle courtyard. I couldn't have been prouder. It was truly cause for celebration. We had no instruments in our home, but Robert tapped out the beat on the bottom of an old pot and William hummed a happy tune as Baby Tim and I danced our favorite jig for the family's entertainment. It was a homemade concoction of spins, skips, and bows. I felt the blissful freedom that always came with the dance, and everyone was delighted by it. After a long and exhausting show, we collapsed to whistles and a thundering round of applause.

"Who would have dr-dr-dreamed of it," my father said with tears of joy, "a family of dancers. My children are dancers!" I walked over and bent down to give him a kiss on the cheek. He was so endearing when he smiled.

"Da, about families," Baby Tim said, climbing carefully up on to father's lap, "what is our family name? William over there is Ashby, and my friend Dennis is Burr, but nobody ever calls us by our family name. We're just 'the cottars,' always 'the cottars,' or worse yet the 'crippled cottars.' I don't want to be 'the cottars' anymore, Da. Who are we?"

We sat hushed by Tim's jarringly honest and profound proclamation.

William shot me a questioning glance and raised his brows, but I merely shrugged my shoulders.

Who? Who indeed were we? Not a question most peasants had time to stop and ponder, and yet there it was. We waited patiently to see if he would answer, if he could answer, for surely the question had hurt him most of all.

After a long pause my father cleared his throat, "Dering, son, our family name is Dering."

"You mean like brave and daring, like courageous?"

"Well, in a round about way, Tim. Family legend has it that in the old Saxon days it meant just that. Who's to know f-f-f-for sure? It just always seemed so odd-odd and unfitting for us, b-b-but not anymore. Why, look at you all. You could very well hale back to some old Saxon chieftain like my granddaddy used to say. The world is a funny pl-pl-place. Just when you think things have changed for the worst, they c-c-come around full circle, they do."

We had never heard so many words from our dad in a week before, let alone in one monumental, life-changing speech.

"Thank you Da," I said simply and walked over to give him another kiss on the cheek. My siblings each followed suit. William bade us a good even, and we quietly readied ourselves for bed. We had much to think about on that balmy summer's night.

Finally, I was roused from my delirium and dragged upstairs into the great hall set up for matters of government. A crowd had gathered for the occasion and filled the gray stone walls. I could not register a single face, except the evil one of Lady Worthing as I was thrust toward her feet, crumpling upon my pain-wracked knees. She accused me in an official manner of thievery and disloyalty, but then fell into a ranting litany of my so-called crimes. I shall never forget her icy voice.

"Fraudulently claiming to be married to an aristocrat, fornicating with the captain of the guard, prostituting herself to the soldiers in the garrison, murdering her unborn child, treachery, treason, witchcraft . . . ."

As the list of lies grew longer and more bizarre, I experienced a lucid moment. Looking into those hateful eyes, I realized she knew. She knew about far more than a tryst in the wine cellar. Somehow she knew it all—the passionate kisses, the proclamations of love, Richard's disgust, my pleas. This was more than punishment for betrayal; this was revenge for each insulting word Richard uttered in my presence. She was bent on making me suffer, making me pay in full for every ounce of grief we caused her.

In my next sentient moment I was being strapped against the whipping pole in the soldier's field, my arms stretched high over my head, the muscles in my shoulders straining. Someone ripped the back of my kirtle in two to the waist. I clenched my jaw and waited with my eyes closed tight, and then nothing. Where was Gottfried? I thought perhaps I fainted and missed the entire event. Yet, I felt no sting across my back.

I could hear Lady Worthing's mad shrieks in the distance, but my mind could not make sense of them. Then I was being cut down from the pole and Richard was supporting me as I stumbled toward the irate noble woman. She was livid, shaking, and red-faced.

She shrieked more than spoke, but I remained in my numb stupor. "Whipping would not suffice for her crimes. It's for the best, I tell you.

She shall pay for this, the brazen little tramp. Richard, since you are so fond of her, take this slovenly slattern and dump her in the gutters of London where she belongs. Take her to the stews where the whores ply their trade. She'll fare well enough there. She's had ample experience."

Her voice settled into an official tone once again. "Dandelion Dering, I hereby declare you are now and forevermore banished from my holdings. If you so much as set foot on my soil again, you will face the executioner's axe. Do I make myself clear?"

I think I nodded my head. I think her perverted speech was followed by yet another diatribe to Richard. Then I think I fainted dead away.

The next thing I knew for sure, I was on a horse surrounded by guardsmen, weeping in Richard's arms. He covered my torn dress with his own cloak somewhere along the way.

The wooded scenery passed by in a haze. It took all my strength to turn my face up toward him. "Now, Richard? Now shall we run away?"

He made shushing noises as he stroked my back.

Then my mind grew sharp, and I knew. He would not help me. For all his charm, for all his wit and warmth, Richard was a coward. It was his fatal flaw. He would not risk what little wealth and power he had fought so hard to gain, sacrificed his very soul over, for the sake of love. Let alone risk his life.

Richard would always put Richard first.

We had traveled at breakneck speed for nearly a day. We would reach the outskirts of London soon, and my fate would be sealed. I relaxed in Richard's arms and took what little comfort they offered.

After a time, our pace slowed. A tall, never-ending line of buildings surrounded us. The number of people milling through the streets was dizzying. I may well have fainted as the Tallangers predicted, were I not sitting secure within Richard's arms. I sat up straighter, not wishing to miss a thing. And we hadn't even entered London proper. The gates had closed at sunset, and Southwark, our destination, lay on the outskirts to the south of the city proper and across the Thames.

"Dandelion," Richard whispered into my ear for the first time on the long and historic journey. "It is imperative I follow Lady Catherine's instruction to the letter. Not merely my employment, but my very life may depend on it."

Lady Worthing had sent along ruthless guards who barely knew me. I turned and looked into Richard's liquid brown eyes.

Without moving his lips, he said, "Do you see that large cathedral to the left?"

I tried not to be distracted by its immensity and grandeur. My mind still struggled to stay in the moment, longing instead to drift away from my awful circumstances to the beautiful church.

"That is Southwark Cathedral. It belongs to the Bishop of Winchester. In a little while we shall enter the area where the brothels lie. I shall leave you in the gutter precisely as Lady Catherine commanded, but remember the way to the cathedral, and remember you are never without hope. It may be too late for me, but you can still save yourself. And . . . and . . . and know that I am truly sorry."

We came to a stop on a street bright with torches. There were indeed painted women on every corner. At first glance they looked a cheerful lot with their brazen clothes and bright, yellow headscarves to denote their trade. The Winchester Geese to be sold to the highest bidders. But I detected a hardness in their eyes, despite the seductive smiles.

Would I soon join their lot?

Richard gave me a shove off the horse for effect. "Farewell, Dandelion."

I hoped the guard did not notice the tear in his eye.

Richard looked away from me. "This is your home now."

I turned with an unexpected smile and returned Richard's cloak.

He reached toward it but stopped short. "Are you sure?"

"Yes." I hung it upon his outstretched arm. "I'll not be needing it here."

A guardsman tossed a ribald joke to his cohorts.

I did not even look as they trotted away.

So here I am, literally in the gutter with nothing to my name but the stinking, torn dress upon my back and the muck-covered slippers on my feet. This is by far the very most tragic and demeaning moment of my life. And how do I feel?

The surprising answer came—*free.*

I was no longer a villein tied to the land. I was free of entangling romances and manipulative friends. For perhaps the first time in my life I was just a girl, a girl with an entire world of possibilities open before her.

I could be the richest harlot in London town if I chose. I could turn to the church for guidance and help. I could find employment or even become a nun. The choice was mine—empowering and liberating.

I remembered Friar John's words. *"Happiness is not so much about our circumstances as it is about how we perceive those circumstances."* In what should have been my moment of greatest despair, I was free. I was free and alive and full of hope. And I knew exactly where to go. I turned my feet and headed onward with purpose. Brushing past gaudy men with their furs and jewels, I broke into a dash.

Chapter 24

The swirling rails outside the towering cathedral might have been the very gates of heaven itself. Watchmen stood nearby, but I slid through with nary a squeak of the hinges to give me away. Spires and steeples grazed the sky. Glimmering candlelight called to me through colorful panels of glass. Massive torches illuminated the entryway to the grand chapel, yet again the guards failed to notice my slight form slipping past. I attempted the enormous gilded door to the right, and it seemed ordained to slide open easily and silently.

I stood gaping at the lofty arched ceilings, soaring a hundred feet over my head, expecting to see angels flying about. I never imagined such a place. The scent of incense echoed through the air, filling me with tender joy. I could barely breathe. I filed past the endless rows of pews, my slippered footsteps whispering against the polished stone. Straight ahead atop the altar hung a mammoth carved crucifix, depicting the Christ in striking detail. Authentic-looking drops of blood dripped from His thorny crown and toward the torturous twist of His mouth. Brilliant and radiant, He extended toward me, leaving me mesmerized and frightened. I wasn't ready to face Him on this emotion-ridden night. I turned away, drawn toward a shaded alcove instead.

In it hid an evocative painting of Madonna and child. Despite the glittering halo around her head, she reminded me of my own mum—nurturing and maternal and shimmering with light. I felt soothed in her presence. The babe in her arms was rosy-cheeked, plump, and content. Many years would pass until He suffered His fate on the cross. I prostrated myself upon the narrow wooden bench at her feet and fell into a blissful, dreamless sleep.

The next morning I awoke to find an open-faced novitiate staring down at me in his black Benedictine robes. The sun streaming through the stained-glass windows burst into a myriad of colors upon his skin. This young priest could not stifle his curiosity at finding a woman asleep in the chapel.

I struggled to sit. "God give you good day, sir. I do apologize. I only meant to rest a moment, but it seems I slept a good long while."

The man clasped his hands. "And here I fancied you an angel who had grown tired of flying and alit on the bench. Of course you haven't any wings. And that dress . . . ." He brushed his hands across his nose. "Human, yes, indeed human. I can't imagine . . . ."

"Good father, may I interrupt you. My name is Dandelion. Dandelion . . . Dering. You seem the kindly sort, and I am in dire need of help." I placed my bare feet on the floor.

He came closer. "Yes, well I suppose that much is true."

My stomach growled, and I pressed a hand against it. "I haven't eaten in days, sir. Might . . . ."

"Why of course, of course. I dare say, we aren't in the habit of rescuing foundlings, but I'm sure we could find you some food." He looked into my eyes. "Yes, indeed. I wanted to be a knight once, you know. This might be my opportunity to rescue a true damsel in distress. Come. Come with me." Beneath his soft, brown tonsured hair, he wore a perpetual startled look on his smooth, pale face, and ushering a fallen angel yet deeper into the interior of the cathedral made it worse.

He sat me at the large kitchen table and served me a cup of wine with a bowl of tepid porridge. "My apologies. We broke our fast hours ago."

"No, this is perfect. Truly." I dug into the bowl with zeal.

In rushed another priest with a sharp, narrow face. Upon seeing me he squealed, and his hands fluttered about him. "Good Lord, what in heaven is going on here, Frederick?"

"I was coming to find you, Brother Cedric. I apologize for the surprise. The lady was distressed and came to the cathedral in search of solace. I found her sleeping beneath our Blessed Mother. She looked like an angel, and I thought it a sign. I hope you aren't displeased."

Brother Cedric clasped his hands together to stop their fluttering. "Well, it is highly unusual. Francis, Brother Francis. Come here at once," he hollered.

In rushed yet another priest, effeminate and jolly looking, this one plump as Cedric was thin. "What in the devil is this?" he shrieked.

Brother Cedric cleared his throat. "It seems young Brother Frederick has taken in a stray."

I continued eating and staring down into my porridge, content to let them squabble over my fate while I attacked the food settling so pleasantly in my empty belly.

Frederick moved to shield me from their stares. "But she needs help, and she has a name. It is Dandelion."

"'The poor and needy you shall always have with you,' Frederick. Besides," Francis whispered loud enough for me to hear, "she stinks."

Brother Cedric craned his neck to better gape around Frederick. "But look at her closely, Brother Francis. Her dress is expensive, and

159

I think she might be quite attractive under all the filth."

Frederick turned then to take another look as well. The three men stood side-by-side observing me. Had I not been the center of their little circus, it might have been amusing.

"Are you thinking what I'm thinking?" said Brother Francis with delight.

"We could all stand a little favor with the bishop. I think he could earn quite a good bit from this one." Cedric took a step closer to me.

"Yes, he's always in search of lovely little wenches for his brothel." Francis stepped forward. "Perhaps she is a gift from heaven after all."

I squealed through my porridge and looked aghast at my new friend Frederick.

Frederick returned to his defensive position, this time with arms spread wide. "Absolutely not. That is most certainly not why she was sent to us."

"And why, most certainly, not? I think she would do very well," said Francis. "You aren't used to women, my innocent Frederick. They are vile and sinful creatures designed for such a service."

I sputtered and coughed with shock. When I recovered myself I said, "Gentlemen, I am sitting right here."

"Heavens, she's been listening all along." Cedric's hands were all aflutter again. "Don't worry, my child. Francis exaggerates. It is not a sin. Unless you're married. You aren't married are you? The bishop has pardons galore for pretty girls like you. The brothels serve a righteous purpose in keeping men from committing even greater perversities."

I stood up as indignation welled through my sleep-clouded brain. "Surely you jest. Not twelve hours ago I ran through those streets to the safety of this church, and now you want to send me back."

"Please, Dandelion, calm down. They shan't make a harlot of you on my watch," said Frederick, my gallant protector.

"Actually, now that I hear her speak, she may in truth be destined for something better." Brother Cedric leaned in for yet a closer examination. "Francis, have you heard the rumors that the Cardinal is in search of a new mistress?"

Francis joined him. "Indeed I have. Do you think?"

Cedric crooked his head to one side and then the other. "Look at her carefully. Why, she's exquisite."

"You're absolutely right," said Francis. "I'm not typically an admirer of female flesh, but even I cannot fail to notice. Little wonder you thought her an angel, Frederick."

"Again, gentlemen." I smacked my hand against the tabletop as anger seethed hot in my chest. "I am standing right here. Please do not discuss me like a cow gone to market."

"In all fairness," said Frederick, looking me in the eye unlike his cohorts, "mistress to the Cardinal is quite an honor—practically nobility."

"Well, I am not interested in being the Cardinal's mistress, pardons or no. I've been down a similar path and shan't be making that mistake again." I sat back down and straightened my smelly skirt. "Perhaps you gentlemen can direct me to a group of Holy Sisters. It seems you are grossly inexperienced at dealing with ladies."

"Oh, I do apologize." Cedric backed up a few steps. "I had no idea you intended to be wed to Christ. Why, He trumps even the Cardinal, I suppose. Pity though," he said, studying my features once again, "quite a waste." He continued his perusal to the specifics of my figure, and I rankled under his gaze.

Snapping my fingers, I called his attention back to my face. "I do not plan to become a nun, but I was hoping to find assistance from someone who did not view me as a chess pawn."

"I apologize for our manners, Dandelion," said Frederick. "I for one still believe God has sent you to us for a purpose." He settled himself at the table across from me. "How can we be of service?"

I relaxed and took a moment to collect myself. It seemed this conversation was ready to take on a saner tone. Cedric and Francis also sat down and looked at me, waiting for my reply, as if I were an actual human being capable of rational thought.

I tucked my unruly hair behind my ear. "Well, I was hoping you might direct me toward some gainful employment."

"In that case you will need to give us a list of your credentials," said Brother Francis. "Mind you, we are not in the habit of finding work for destitute women."

I picked up my goblet for a bracing sip. "Unless they are prostitutes," I mumbled into my wine.

Francis's eyes popped wide. "Pardon?"

I smiled politely. "I'm sorry. I was saying I am skilled at cooking and cleaning and sewing. I could work as a seamstress or a maid. I can also read and keep accounts if that helps."

"What would help would be references from a previous employer," said Brother Cedric. "Do you have those?"

"Sadly, I do not."

"That's all right, Dandelion. We trust you," said dear Frederick.

Cedric gestured toward me. "Goodness, Frederick, she could be a thief or worse for all we know. We cannot in good faith recommend her for a job."

Frederick grimaced and nodded. "Dandelion, if you want us to help you, you must tell us the truth."

I had not much choice. "I was recently lady's maid to the Countess Catherine Worthing."

"Heavens." Francis clapped his hand to his cheek.

"Surely not." Cedric echoed Francis's gesture.

"No, it is true," I said. "Unfortunately, her lover fancied me, and she was terribly jealous. She fabricated outrageous charges against me and banished me. She ordered me dumped into the gutters of Southwark. I ran away from the brothels and came directly here. Can you help me?" I looked at them with huge, pleading eyes.

"Heavens," said Brother Francis again. "Why should we believe her?"

"Because we do," said Frederick simply.

"Yes," said Cedric with resignation. "We do."

Francis thought for a moment. "I've heard tales of Lady Worthing since I was a child. Isn't she the one who tried to kill the old queen?"

"I thought she murdered someone for trying to seduce her husband," said Cedric.

I smiled. "That certainly sounds like Catherine."

"Yes," said Frederick. "I think she tried to poison the queen but somebody stopped her. Wasn't she banished from court?"

No one knew for sure.

Francis shook his head. "She does have a ruthless reputation. What if she discovers we helped the girl?"

"Well, she hasn't been back to London since," said Frederick.

Francis did not look convinced. "Yes, but isn't her son often at court?"

I nodded.

They sat and thought some more. It was Brother Cedric who jumped up and made a declaration with his finger pointing to the sky. "Giovanni Sabatini!"

This time Francis mimicked Cedric's gesture. "Giovanni Sabatini. Why didn't we think of him sooner?"

"It is perfect," said Cedric. "He's rich as Midas, but has no ties at court."

"Who is this then, another Cardinal in need of a mistress?" I eyed the good brothers with suspicion.

"Hardly," said Frederick. "He is indeed the perfect solution, Dandelion. He is a sweet and charitable man, a merchant from Italy. He attends mass faithfully and brings alms for the poor. Only last week he was mentioning his housekeeper ran off with some traveling musician. He had to rush back early from Florence because his home was in disarray and the butler in a panic. Giovanni is precisely the person we need." He smiled.

And I believed him.

Chapter 25

London England – 1333

What a lovely view. I gazed out the window of the narrow, upright townhouse. Granted, I could not see a forest full of trees in their handsome autumn coats, but the holly bushes lining the streets made of rare cobbled stone held their own sort of charm. The few sapling trees dripped leaves like gentle rain in a soft and floating descent. Over the past three years I had grown accustomed to city life, no longer startled by the throngs of humanity, no longer intimidated in the narrow alleys and lanes.

I poked my head outside to better hear the rhythms—the rumble of wagons, the clip clop of horse hooves, the bark of vendors, and the squeal of children, all so energetic and vibrant. Even bickering spouses and shouted warnings followed by splashes of waste from overhead were amusing refrains in the city's cadence.

I ran my fingers across the mellow mahogany side table beneath the window. They left lines in the light film of dust. I needed to speak with the maid concerning this. Furniture attracted grime in homes along the crowded thoroughfare, but it was, after all, her only duty to see the house remained spotless.

Giovanni and the priests agreed we best concoct a whole new name and background for me when I became his housekeeper. I left Dandelion Dering, Dandelion Westover, and an entire history of joys and triumphs, heartaches and struggles far behind me on that day. I was now Dame Mullens, the widow from the Isle of Wight, and it suited my current image just fine.

"He should be back by now," the butler said, catching me musing out the window.

I smiled to reassure him. "I'm sure it won't be much longer."

My newfound universe rotated around the central point of Giovanni Sabatini. He spent half the year in London and half at his home in the Italian city-state of Florence. He was as sweet and kind and good as Frederick described him—a man in his middle years with a cheerful demeanor. At certain angles he reminded me of Friar John, but in fact a handsomer version with his pleasing olive skin and straight, thin nose. His hair similarly circled about the shiny, bald crown of his head, but rather than sticking out in stark white tufts, it fell in gentle waves of reddish-gold peppered with gray.

The similarity extended also to his light, jovial spirit, although he was far less theatrical. He had no cause to be either hypocritical or sermonizing like Friar John. In fact, while his works bespoke strong Christian character, he rarely discussed religious matters at all.

The butler joined me at the window. "He's never this late. I certainly hope nothing's gone amiss."

Giovanni sailed during spring and fall when the seas were calm. His childhood sweetheart and wife of twenty years, Francesca, would not be joining him. Indeed, she never traveled. Giovanni claimed she had the ethereal face of an angel with the fragile health to match. He said it with admiration in his voice. I wished to meet her someday.

I ran my hand across the windowsill. "I'm growing impatient, as well, but try not to worry," I said to Robin, the butler.

When the city was hushed and tucked away against the cold, Giovanni brought the house to life with jokes and cheerful smiles. Not born of nobility himself, he ignored traditional lines between servant and master, preferring the term staff. He oft played the lute and sang, encouraging us to dance along. The other workers would laugh and twirl about, but I felt safer tucked into a corner, watching the fun.

Having discovered my interest in his extensive library, Giovanni gave me lessons in Latin and Italian during my free time. However, most evenings supper guests kept me occupied late into the night. With Mistress Sabatini far away in Italy, I played hostess to Giovanni's friends and associates. Among our frequent guests were the three bumbling "holy" brothers, still close friends.

Each year as spring returned, Giovanni wished us a bittersweet farewell. He loved his Italian homeland and longed to reunite with his wife. We in turn enjoyed a lighter schedule but missed him sorely. His departure ushered in warmer weather, country picnics, and wagon rides. I loved to explore the expanding city, its markets, pubs, bridges, and ships. Surely, there were areas as dirty, stinky, and disease-ridden as William mentioned, but many others were as pleasant and appealing as the wealthy neighborhood I watched through the window.

"I'm bored of tournaments and fairs." The butler brought me back again. "It's time we all get to work before we're spoiled entirely."

The cook overheard my conversation with the butler and came to watch out the window too. "I could do without the tournaments. But I wouldn't miss the fairs and watching Robin win at feats of strength for all the world."

She and I laughed as the flighty butler turned red. Most assuredly some secret source of power hid in his small wiry arms.

"Why don't we admit it," said Cook. "We all miss Giovanni terribly."

I turned my back to the window. "Well, he shall never arrive so long as we stand here waiting for him. Back to work, both of you." I waved them away, but cast one last glance through the glass.

Although my employer, I missed Giovanni so. I longed for a friend who knew my real name, my actual past. I was somehow adrift without him.

"Look, there it is!" shouted Robin.

Swaying pennants in a rainbow of colors rose over the crowd. We made our way through the entrance and lined up along the lists in the fields. Everyone was welcome at the tournaments. The better seats on the raised platforms behind us were reserved for nobility, but when the jousts began, the peasants gasped with just as much excitement as the royalty in the grandstands. The place was every bit as romantic as Lady Jane had described it.

The staff had decided to fit in one last outing before Giovanni returned. The gentle man never did much like the violence of the tournaments, but as for me, I could never get enough of the vibrant energy crackling through the air. I had yet to witness a knight perish in mock battle as Giovanni once had, and I prayed I never would.

To each side of the dirt ring, knights in glinting silver armor checked their horses and lances. One wore a surcoat of green and gold over his breastplate, and the other was bedecked in blue and gray. Their horses featured long coverings to match, and each was followed by a retinue of banners and flags.

"It's the young Lord James Tallanger." Cook pointed to the green and gold knight.

Jamey Tallanger. Oh, I would have so loved to meet him. I stood on my toes for a better glimpse. He held his helmet under his arm, and I got a clear view of a face not unlike Thomas Worthing's in its aristocratic features and freckles. But the resemblance ended at Jamey's head of flaming hair.

He pulled the helmet on and climbed upon his horse, taking the long pointed lance from his squire. Holding it straight up and down, he led the retinue into the ring. The herald in the center called out the names of Lord James Tallanger and his opponent. As the crowd cheered their hearty approval, a nobleman in the stands stood and waved them into action.

The two horses separated back to their sides. The knights took their places on opposite ends of the rail. They tilted their lances to the horizontal position.

"Green and gold. Green and gold." Robin started up the chant, and a crowd soon joined them.

Excitement brimmed inside of me, but I pushed it back down. I was no longer the old, wild Dandelion. I was staid Dame Mullens. Instead of pressing forward and taking up the chant, I took a few steps deeper into the throng. If James Tallanger was about to joust, might not Thomas Worthing be close by?

The two knights rushed at each other in a thunder of hooves, their lances steady in their strong grips. They met in a shower of splinters at the center of the ring, as the lances exploded into fragments. Both kept their seats as they dashed off in opposite directions once again.

I gripped my hands tight together. No, the old Dandelion may have whooped and cheered, dancing at the raw intensity of the battle. But not Dame Mullens. Instead, I pulled my veil tighter over my face and checked that every blonde curl was tucked safely out of sight. I straightened my dowdy gray tunic in place.

The old Dandelion was long gone.

Housekeepers were a no-nonsense lot, strong women with backbones of iron. As Dame Mullens, I must preserve appearances and guard my bothersome good looks. They had caused quite enough trouble for one lifetime. I appeared every inch the prim professional, feeling safe in my stoic costume—as reserved, quiet, and resourceful as I had once been merry, chatty, and saucy.

The knights took their places once again, new lances secure in their gloved fingers. This time as they surged toward each other, Jamey pulled in tighter on his lance and caught the inside edge of his opponents shield. The lance glanced off to the side, catching the blue and gray knight in the chest and flinging him off his horse before shattering.

"Whoo! Whoo! Whoopee!" Robin shouted.

"He did it. Green and gold. Green and gold," yelled Cook.

The other servants huddled together, slapping one another on the back and hugging, as if they themselves had wielded the lance.

"Good job, Jamey," I whispered into my clasped hands.

Jamey Tallanger pulled a handkerchief in his green and gold colors from his collar with a snap of his wrist. He trotted to the stands as it billowed in the breeze. There, he gallantly offered it to a pretty young noblewoman in a sheer pink wimple and silken gown encrusted with jewels and gold braid. I couldn't help but miss such attention. I recalled a young knight who once offered me a token at Lady Catherine's Christmas party. Would a man such as Jamey Tallanger notice me if I were to discard this ugly old frock?

A deep booming voice broke over the crowd. "Go, Jamey. Good job, man! That's the way it's done, old cousin."

I hadn't heard that voice in years, but I knew in an instant. Although I couldn't see him, Lord Thomas Worthing hid somewhere in the crowd. My hands began to tremble. The air seized in my lungs. I wobbled forward to Cook and grasped her arm.

She turned and took in my ashen face. "Dear lord, Dame Mullens. What is it? Have you seen a ghost? Whatever is wrong with you?"

I managed to gasp out the words. "Lord Worthing."

"He's here? Now? Oh, my. Let's get you home at once."

Until that moment I had remained a picture of crisp efficiency, but something in my eyes, my voice, must have given me away. Cook ventured to put a motherly arm about my waist. She gathered up the household staff, and they escorted me back to the house like my own retinue of faithful guards. They knew some trouble had come my way at the hand of Lady Worthing, but my reaction told them the matter was far from closed.

Late that evening I awoke from a dream screaming in a pool of sweat and gathered the covers around my neck. I wished Giovanni would arrive home soon. His comforting presence never failed to ward off my nightmares.

A month later we received word of Giovanni's return and a request for the carriage to meet him at the dock. I waited by the front door, in no way attempting to hide my impatience under a professional guise at a time like this. As they rolled up the lane, John, the footman, wore a glum expression. When Giovanni stepped out the carriage door, the look on his face said it all. It was not so much sad as dazed. The low dip of his head and the slump of his back spoke volumes. When his valet, Roberto, looked up toward me and shook his head, it made perfect sense.

They led Giovanni to the house. I greeted him in hushed tones, placing my hand on his back and directing him toward his favorite chair in the study. Next, I sat him down and removed his cloak. Taking charge, I ordered Roberto and the footman to carry his luggage upstairs, ordered Margaret to bring refreshments, even ordered Giovanni to lift his cup and drink. He looked for all the world like a little boy lost.

I whispered to Roberto in the hallway, "How did it happen?"

"Her health was always fragile. His poor Francesca caught some sort of fever and never recovered. She looked like an angel to the very last moment."

I gave him a comforting pat on the shoulder. "Why ever did you rush back? We could have managed without him. What matters the state of his London business when his dear wife is dead? He should have family around him at a time like this."

Tears filled Roberto's eyes. "He couldn't stay. Everywhere he looked, every sound, each nook of the house reminded him of her."

"Oh. I am so sorry. What shall we do?"

"Take care of him for now. Listen when he is ready to talk. He will survive this thing."

In truth, Giovanni did somehow maintain his serenity through it all. We may have reminded him to eat and drink and bathe and dress, but each day, his eyes focused a bit more, and he walked with more purpose in his step. He spent much time at the church, and late at night he knelt in prayer before a candle by his bedside. I heard him mutter the phrase *la gioia viene di mattina*, "joy comes in the morning."

When he asked why the Christmas decorations were not hung, we were quite surprised. We were a household deep in mourning, but he insisted life continue, that our Savior's birth was cause for celebration despite his sadness, that Francesca would have wanted it that way. On Twelfth Night he further surprised us by handing out gifts near the fireplace in the main living area. "Everything was purchased and ready to go before Francesca took ill. I'm so sorry I forgot about them when I arrived." It was so like Giovanni. He lost his beloved wife, and yet he apologized to us.

He actually smiled when he handed my present to me. "Dame Mullens, this is for you. My sister recommended it."

I ran my hand over the cloth wrapping in loving tribute to the mistress I never met and untied the string. Inside sat a book. I never owned a book of my very own. Tears sprang to my eyes, but I managed to control them. I turned it over in my palm and read the title. *The Divine Comedy*, it said in Italian, by Dante Alighieri.

"Oh Giovanni, it is too much," I said. The other servants received the typical gloves, hoods, fabrics, soaps, sweetmeats, and such. I held in my hands a treasure that my parents couldn't have afforded after years of work in the field. The staff uttered the appropriate "oohs" and "aahs" over the extravagant gift, but did not seem at all bothered.

Giovanni grinned at my delight. "Forgive me. I could not help myself. It is all the rage of Italy right now. I thought the subject would interest you. We shall read it together, so it is a gift for both of us."

Speechless, I gave him a spontaneous hug. The others had never seen me so affectionate.

Our foray through *The Divine Comedy* proved to be a time of healing for Giovanni, perhaps for me as well. Sitting across from each other next to the wall of books in the study, we read the potent words aloud. It was my turn tonight. We both related with Dante's journey through hell in the Inferno, feeling we had passed through similar journeys in our own lives. Giovanni began his trek mid-life in the throes of despair just as the narrator. He took great comfort in our exploration of the afterlife, feeling confident his angelic wife enjoyed the pleasures of paradise. The vivid imagery of the poem brought him closer to her with each reading.

I learned much both from Dante's journey and from Giovanni's. Although he had never been given to spiritual discussions, the narrative provided a natural starting place for Giovanni to share his thoughts about God. Might he be the worthy man with whom I could discuss the amazing concepts found in Samia's poetry?

I dared to pause from my reading and share my favorite quote, the one Richard had so quickly judged and dismissed. Giovanni listened with an open heart, pausing a moment to weigh each word against his own understanding of God and of life. "The thought of God adoring man is a bit surprising," he said, "and yet the concept of God being wed to mankind is well supported by both the Bible and church traditions. It is a beautiful picture, the bridegroom and the bride, the lover and the beloved. In such a wedded state of oneness, I could almost imagine a sort of mutual and communal adoration. It is indeed profound."

What a gift those words were, a priceless glimpse into the faith that sustained him. I longed for it, as well, and for the first time ventured to hope I might one day have it for myself.

We shared so much during those fireside chats—stories of our childhoods, feelings, even hopes and dreams as we both dared to hope and dream once again. Giovanni was someone with whom I could trust my secret self.

One night in early spring when the weather was gentle and the windows were open to allow the breeze, Giovanni pulled out a surprise. "Dandelion, I received a most interesting letter today. I thought you would enjoy reading it." He spoke to me in Italian now. After so much Dante, I was almost fluent. He handed me a sheet of parchment.

It smelled vaguely of flowers, and the handwriting was so pretty. I stared and enjoyed it for a moment before attempting to decipher the language. It was addressed, "To My Dearest Brother in Flesh and in Christ." I knew it must be from his sister, Reverend Mother Maria Scholastica, living in a convent not far from their hometown of Florence. Giovanni oft spoke of her. She was the inspiration behind his spiritual beliefs.

I can only imagine how you must be feeling. Know that my

prayers are with you day and night. I hope you remember our parting words and that morning has come, bringing joy to your heart. Francesca's loss has affected me as well. It inspired me to write many new poems. I included one here for you with references from the book of Ecclesiastes. It is amazing how when you think you are starting to understand the nature and love of God, He reveals an entirely new level and leaves you breathless and searching once again.

> *With Love and Prayers and My Deepest Sympathies,*
> *Maria Scholastica*

She sounded precisely as I imagined her. I paused from my reading and smiled. "I should like to meet her someday."

"Read on," Giovanni prompted me.

> *Longing to push beyond the borders*
> *of skin consumes my days.*
> *I feel a prisoner in this finite space,*
> *eternity buried deep in my core,*
> *beneath layers of muscles and bones.*
>
> *My only desire is an ever-increasing ache*
> *to be shattered into ethereal fragments,*
> *to be at last united with my one true love.*
>
> *And so I play out my days,*
> *sojourner on this planet of testing,*
> *watching time unfold,*
> *the sifting sands,*
> *still chasing after the wind,*
> *waiting to be made beautiful.*

There were tears in his eyes. "My Francesca has been made beautiful."

As joy and sorrow battled within my chest, I began to weep. "I want this, Giovanni. I want this hope. I want this intimacy with God."

"It's much like the poems from your past, is it not? I thought you would like it. I didn't mean to make you cry."

"I'm sorry." I swiped at my tears. "It brings back so many old memories . . . old memories and longings."

"Would you like to talk about them?"

"Not yet," I whispered.

Chapter 26

To our surprise Giovanni chose not to sail to Italy in spring. With the warm weather, he enjoyed walking in the early evenings, and often I joined him for that peaceful interlude between the busyness of the day's work and the night's social obligations. We strolled up and down the lanes, arm in arm, relishing the whirl of the city around us. I still wore my hair covered by a dowdy wimple, but I no longer took the precaution of veiling my face. I felt safe with Giovanni by my side.

On such a night, we were ambling along when a sweet little puppy trotted up the street toward us. I bent down to pet him, and he surged at me with glee. Running my fingers through his silken curls, I fought back tears. His moist tongue against my palm stirred a well of emotions long forgotten. His high-pitched whimpers made me swallow down a lump in my throat. With one last rub of his head upon my palm, the busy creature dashed off.

I watched over my shoulder with a hollow void forming in my belly as he continued along his way. He was not white nor terribly puffy, but he was tiny with long brown hair and a familiar impish twinkle in his eye.

On a sudden whim, the pup darted onto the road. Two gigantic horses ran straight toward him, pulling a rumbling carriage. The hollow in my stomach filled with heavy dread.

Having not a second to spare, he yelped and hopped out of the way.

He stood immobilized and shivering on the side of the road as I ran to him, my heart pounding in my chest with the ferocity of a blacksmith's anvil.

Then everything melted into a daze of thumping heart and rushing blood.

I heard myself yell, "Cloud, no, Cloud," as if floating outside of my body. Unable to process the overwhelming emotions, I grew numb and acted on instinct. I scooped the puppy in my arms and fell to the street side. Clutched him tight to me. "I'm so sorry, Cloud."

Giovanni lifted me off the ground and guided me away from the traffic. He sat me down upon a set of nearby stairs. Before I registered what happened, both the puppy and I were shaking and covered in my tears.

Two boys dashed up the street. One of them shouted, "There he is." They stopped short in front of us, looking at each other and then at Giovanni.

Giovanni laid his hand upon mine. "I think the dog belongs to these young men."

I stared into their confused faces. "I'm sorry. He was almost run over. I had a puppy once. He's all right, though," I said through my sobs, not at all sure I was making sense. I loosened my grip and began to hand over the dog. Having no real desire to give up the warm, lively bundle in my arms, I halted and held the puppy mid-air. "Take good care of him. Promise me."

"We will, ma'am," said the older boy. "We promise." Once he took the pup in his grasp, they ran away, leaving Giovanni to cope with the sobbing mass upon the steps.

At home Giovanni directed me to my room, removed my shoes, and wiped the city grime from my wet face. Settling me into a cushioned armchair, he tucked a light blanket about me. Then, Giovanni sat at the foot of my bed and waited. He waited as I cried myself out. He waited as I stared into empty space. He waited until my eyes focused and searched him out in the semi-darkness.

"Are you ready to talk?" The question applied not only to the evening, but to the entire spring.

The barrier around my pain was demolished during that instant lasting an eternity, as I waited for the little dog to be smashed beneath the hooves of the massive stallions. The puppy survived the ordeal, but my defenses were gone, and I was flooded by emotions held at bay for years. I wondered at the fate of my own little dog. It all came back in an instant. Cloud. Catherine, Richard, Gottfried. My mum, my da, my brothers, and Sadie. Worst of all, William. I left so much unresolved, so much unfinished in Arun Village, and there was truly no going back.

I shuffled over to the bed and slumped next to Giovanni. I laid my head on his shoulder as he placed a supportive arm around me. In hushed tones, I spoke reverently, as if I told the story of someone's death. I talked for hours, weaving the tale of the girl who had once been Dandelion.

Yes, much like Giovanni and Dante, I had been to hell and back. These last years in London were a sort of purgatory—a place of waiting and preparation. I was ready to look at it all and to hope there might be a paradise waiting for me somewhere on the other side.

Giovanni took every shocking detail in stride, never once loosening his grip, never flinching, never drawing away. He allowed me to weave my tale without interruption. It concluded with Catherine's guards dragging me toward the dungeon. After a few moments of silence Giovanni prompted me to continue. "What happened then?"

"Well you know the rest." Twisting my hands in my lap, I looked up at him. It was dark, but our eyes had long since adjusted. "I was banished. I ran to the cathedral, and I ended up here."

"Of course," Giovanni said. Yet those two words suggested the issue was anything but resolved.

I stood beside Giovanni at the noisy Smithfield Market, examining a speckled gray amidst the pushing crowd. The sun shone warm overhead as I ran my hand over the horse's firm flanks. He responded well to my pats. The gray looked right at me and bobbed his head, confirming my decision.

"Strong and lively, but kind and obedient. He's a fine specimen, Giovanni. I think he will do well for your warehouse." I nuzzled the gentle horse. He nickered his approval and nuzzled back. Warmth flooded me at his touch. The scents of manure and hay wafted about me, reminding me so much of home.

"I don't know." Giovanni rolled his eyes toward the owner.

Ahh, so he would bicker the man down.

"He's a bit old." Giovanni pushed back the horse's gums. "I've seen better teeth."

"True." I managed to pull a step back but winked to my new equine friend.

The owner in ragged attire stepped forward and pressed his hands together, all but bowing as he spoke. "I assure you, sir. You'll find no finer in Smithfield Market."

"Well." Giovanni walked around the gray for one last inspection. "I suppose if the price is right I might consider it."

While Giovanni negotiated the price with the horse's owner, I resumed snuggling with the lovely animal. Then I stood on tiptoe to whisper in his ear, "I'm going to get you a treat, sweet boy."

Turning to the men who were busy haggling, I called, "Giovanni, I'll be back in a moment. I'm going to the fruit stand."

"Of course, Dame Mullens."

I slipped into the jostling crowd. Several weeks had passed since the awful night of the puppy incident, and life had returned to normal. Today I accompanied Giovanni and some friends here to the market north of the city. I attempted to decline, feeling I should stay home with the rest of the staff and prepare for the evening's supper, but all the men were taking their wives, and they requested I come along as well. It seemed Giovanni and I were viewed as somewhat of a couple. We had made a day of it, buying food from vendors and picnicking under a shady tree. The ladies discussed fashions and court gossip while the men talked business. We would meet back with them soon.

Standing on tiptoe to better see past the throngs, I scanned the colorful carts about me. I had noticed a fruit vendor somewhere near the entrance but was having difficulty locating him again. Moving forward with determined strides to the next area, I rounded a corner and ran right into a rock-hard chest.

I stepped back and rubbed my nose as pain radiated from it to my eyes and cheeks.

The man grasped my shoulders to keep me from stumbling. "I'm so sorry."

I was still seeing bright bursts of light as I blinked my eyes. "No, no. I'm so sorry. It was my fault. I was busy looking for apples." As the stars cleared, a set of familiar features stunned me. The man looked as if he recognized me as well, but couldn't place my face.

I pulled away, mumbling, "So sorry," one last time before darting into a nearby crowd. I stayed in the middle of the throng and then ran around to the back of a stable, pressing myself against it and breathing hard as my heart raced. My face turned cold, as if all the blood had drained from it. Paying close attention to my surroundings this time, I sidled my way back to Giovanni.

I grabbed him by the arm. "We have to go. Now."

He did not question me. "I'll gather the others. Go and wait in the carriage. I'll tell them you're not feeling well. You certainly don't look well at all."

Back at home Giovanni settled me in his study and had Cook fetch a drink. He canceled supper, since after all, I was supposed to be sick. In truth, my head still pounded from the close call.

He closed the door to the study once Cook left. "What precisely happened?"

"I ran into Lord Worthing—quite literally. I wasn't paying attention and turned a corner and smacked directly into him." I rubbed my nose at the memory.

Giovanni gave it a quick check for injuries. "Good gracious. Did he recognize you?"

"I'm not certain. I think he was still trying to remember who I was when I dashed away." I took several bracing sips of my cider.

"I'm so sorry. It is my fault." He stood up and wrung his hands. "I should have been more careful. You came to me from the start looking for protection, but we've grown too comfortable."

"It is not your fault, Giovanni. I can't live in fear forever. I'm sure it will be all right. Lord Worthing is a good man, one of the king's most trusted advisors ever since the coup. It was a shock. That's all."

"Well, we shall be more careful in the future," he said.

Later that night I awoke screaming. Within seconds Giovanni burst through my door, relieved to find I was not under attack. Physically I was safe, but I must have looked a fright nonetheless with damp blonde curls plastered to my face and terror in my eyes.

Once again he was at my side with a comforting arm about me. "Bad dream?"

"Yes." My teeth chattered.

"Have you remembered more?"

"Yes," I said, and then a few moments later, "I had almost forgotten." Still he waited.

Burying my head in his chest, I closed my eyes as I spoke. "The dungeon—it was so dark. I was so cold. There was no food, no water— it went on for days. The smell—it smelled so horrible. I gagged and vomited—until there was nothing left. After a long time someone brought me a blanket and water, but I couldn't keep it down, and Lady Worthing came in and yanked the blanket away—she kicked me—she kept kicking me. Then the rats—oh God. The rats came." I buried my face in his chest.

"Shh." Giovanni rubbed my arm to soothe me. "It's all right. You're safe. It's over now. But tell me everything. You must let it all out."

I tried to focus my mind, to remember what was left. "There's something else. The rats were biting me. I remember that—and the skeleton. There was a skeleton in the corner. I dreamed it chased me. It laughed at me." I tried to recall that moment. I felt the panic, the constriction in my chest, the lack of breath.

Once again I was overwhelmed with the sickness in my stomach, the clanging in my head, the walls closing in upon me. In that rush of sensations, the memory came. "No, wait. It was Catherine. She threw the skeleton on me, and she was laughing. She said I should get acquainted for I would soon be joining him. I thought I was going to die. I believed she was going to kill me." I shivered. "I hate her."

I thought I had drained myself of all the hurts and sadness and disappointments already, but the panic, the fear, the hatred—they had still been lurking. They were there all along, coloring every single day of my life in London, every breath I took in this place.

Giovanni spoke over top of my head. "You must forgive her."

I gaped up at him.

He had been so kind, hearing of my betrayal toward William and never judging, listening to the story of my infidelity with Richard and saying not a word. In fact, Giovanni had never before in all these years ordered me to do anything.

"Forgive her?" I muttered, confusion overtaking me.

"Do it, Dandelion. Trust me. Right here and now as you feel everything, choose to forgive her, Dandelion, for you—not for her. Let it go. Simply give it to our Heavenly Father. Trust Him with it."

I sat confused, grappling with my thoughts for a few moments.

And then, in a moment of childlike obedience, I did it.

I handed it over to my Heavenly Father as Giovanni instructed.

For a moment I was tempted to grab a hold, to draw it back to me. My fingers clutched after it, but I stopped myself and released it all. I purposed in my heart to forgive Catherine and wish her well. She no longer held any sway, any power over my life. I understood, perhaps for the first time since arriving in London, how safe and far from her grasp I was.

A light, renewing sense of peace washed over me, as powerful and overwhelming as the flood of pain I so recently experienced. I clutched to Giovanni, but when I caught my breath and looked up, he knew. We smiled at each other. He stroked the sticky hair away from my face. He laid me back down against my pillow and tucked me into bed.

The next morning when I awoke, the world was a different place. The sun was bright and golden, the sky a most amazing shade of blue. The birds outside my window sang a greeting just for me. I had learned to make do, to find joy in the small things, but on this morning I felt alive and tingling again; I felt like Dandelion again. I brushed the knots out of my hair as quickly as possible. I searched my closet and found nothing but tan and brown and gray. I would remedy that soon enough. I threw on a tunic and dashed down the stairs in time to catch Giovanni on his way to the cathedral for morning prayers.

"Coming with me?" His smile was warm and welcoming.

"I wouldn't miss it," I said, prancing down the cobblestone lane at his side.

Chapter 27

Twirling before a mirror, I stared to make sure my eyes did not deceive me. Today I not only felt like the old Dandelion, I almost looked like her as well. Cosmetics were no longer appropriate for a woman of my station, but I wore a pretty lavender mantle over a crisp white linen kirtle. My hair was not a wild jumble of curls, but neither was it dragged back or covered by an ugly old wimple. It was brushed and styled, so that it hung in an orderly braid down my back. A simple linen headband held a gossamer white scarf in place. My cheeks wore a healthy sun-kissed glow now that I no longer hid behind veils all the summer long. Yes, it was indeed the old Dandy, perhaps matured and tamed, but her eyes were shining and alive like I remembered. I was happy to see her again.

That night we dined with the good brothers of Southwark Cathedral. Their visits were always merry occasions. They looked quite shocked when they walked in the door.

"Dandelion. Whatever is this?" Frederick took me by the hand and twirled me once in a circle. "Finally, you look like the angel I always thought you to be."

"Indeed." Cedric clapped his hands. "Of course modesty is commendable, but gracious was I tired of your dowdy frocks. The nuns have better fashion sense than you."

The brothers always wore robes of the finest cut and fabric. I was glad they approved. The evening was full of their typical catty gossip, ribald jokes, and zany antics. We heard tales of the Bishop's latest mistress.

Frederick leaned over his roast foul. "Her name is Cicely. She is pretty and mysterious with dark hair and even darker eyes. I fear she looks rather sad."

Cedric corrected him. "Not so much sad as spooky, if you ask me. She's pale as a ghost from the nether regions, and seems to float about as silent as one."

"What a pair of romantic buffoons you are." Francis paused from devouring his giant goose leg. "All you need to know about the Bishop's precious Cicely is this—she eats far too many onions, and she has bad breath. I for one do not like her or her onion breath one whit."

I couldn't help but laugh at that. "Well, I for one am quite glad I am not poor Mistress Cicely. Good Lord, I would hate to hear what you say about me when I'm not present."

"Why your breath is always quite lovely, Dame Mullens," said Francis, gazing about and feigning innocence.

"That's true." Cedric took a swig of wine from his goblet. "He never speaks of you smelling badly, only of your ugly dresses."

"Unfair." Francis wagged his finger at Cedric. "For I shall no longer have any reason to mock her clothing."

Frederick looked me in the eye. "May I say that I for one have never mocked you?"

"I never doubted you, Brother Frederick," I said. "My only question is, whatever shall Francis find to gossip about me in the future?"

"Oh, never fear, I shall come up with something." Francis wiggled his eyebrows at Giovanni and me. "The lovely young widow living with the widowed, wealthy merchant finds a penchant for fashionable clothing and flattering hairstyles. Why, I don't think it shall be difficult at all."

"Oh hush." My cheeks grew warm.

Francis ate until he could barely stand, and Cedric drank far too much wine. Giovanni took in the foibles of the others with smiling patience and humor, as always. They actually were good-hearted, if somewhat misguided individuals. I wished Frederick would leave them and join a devout group of friars or monks where his sincerity would be better cultivated, but he was the third son of a powerful duke, and his family would not hear of such a plan. I could only hope he would manage to maintain his pure heart, and someday rise in the church to effect some positive change.

We played chess after supper and had much fun teasing Brother Francis. He was terribly competitive and a horrible loser. However, the evening took a more serious turn when I mentioned my encounter with Lord Worthing at the Smithfield Market.

Francis, Frederick, and Cedric all looked up and passed messages to one another by raised eyebrows and subtle head nods. Frederick spoke out loud. "Yes."

"No," countered Francis.

It was Cedric who settled the matter. "I think we must this time."

Frederick spoke up first, but the others chimed in once the ball began rolling.

"Lord Worthing came to the cathedral looking for you last week."

"The minute you ran away he knew who you were."

"That was a mistake; you should have played it as though nothing was out of the ordinary."

"Well, of course, things are always clear in hindsight, but how was she to know?"

"To the cathedral." I clasped my hand to my face. "How in the world did he know to look for me there?"

"Oh, they've stopped by for years." Francis waved it off as unimportant. "Yes, that Richard fellow, now he's a charming devil. I could tell he was trouble from a mile away. We never told him a word. Denied having seen you each and every time."

They started speaking one on top of the other again. "Poor man, he looked rather wrecked up about the whole thing."

"But we didn't trust him. He said Lady Catherine sent him to fetch you home."

"We didn't want to see you hurt. We thought you safest here."

"But this Lord Worthing, he was different."

"Yes, and he'd seen you with his own eyes."

"He knows you're somewhere nearby. He'll not be as easily deterred."

"But he'll not learn anything from us, unless you want us to tell him of course. Couldn't blame a young lady for wanting that handsome, young gentleman to find her." Francis took a breath and gazed wistfully toward the ceiling.

"Francis, focus." Frederick snapped his fingers. "I wanted to tell you this time, Dandelion, because he seemed sincere. He said his mother is eaten away with guilt and wants to make things right by you. I thought you should know."

"I wouldn't trust a woman like that if I were you," said Francis. "She deserves to suffer."

"I don't want her to suffer," I whispered. "I've forgiven her." The room grew quiet. "But I don't trust her either, and I have no desire to go back."

Giovanni put a protective arm around me. "You did well to keep silent, gentlemen. We are in your debt."

The summer fairly flew by. We took great care to avoid Lord Worthing, and he did not trouble the good brothers at the cathedral further. Autumn was approaching and Giovanni announced he should begin preparing for his return to Italy. He was not looking forward to it as he always had. There would be no Francesca awaiting him this time. Despite his busy preparations, Giovanni and I still found opportunities to sit in the candlelit study and ponder the status of the universe.

We had already finished *The Divine Comedy*, but Mother Maria sent us more poems to read. Over the last few weeks we pondered several of her masterpieces—so simple, yet so profound. There was no rhyme, no verse, just powerful portraits of one woman's encounters with the divine. I was copying my own little booklet of them.

I am giddy with the words of God that flow like amber wine.
They are honey sweet, delicately spiced,
each one a world to itself, alive and teeming, sparks flying,

Glimmering in multi-faceted rays,
a rainbow of truth to touch each heart
with the idyllic shade of light.

Otherwise, too bright, white hot,
like gazing into the sun.

Her sentiment that God revealed Himself through His word in a unique way to each of us inspired our conversation for days. We were determined to borrow a book of scriptures from the good brothers at the cathedral soon. Hearing snippets in church during the liturgy left us craving so much more, as had this poem about God's love called "The Bride."

Oh, this fathomless love,
how can it be?
This zeal, is it even true?
It's too amazing to believe.

Yet, all I know is this:
I have felt the touch of His lips.
He has saturated my soul.
I am fully aroused to the depths of my being.

I've never felt so full,
yet so devoid of self,
as if I am of clay—a pitcher
empty but for that fiery life.

I was so relieved to learn I did not need all the answers in order to fall madly in love with God. I found myself falling for Him years before, but thought I wasn't worthy of the honor. It brought new depth to my earlier insights. I remembered the feeling of crazy love as I pranced through the fields as a little girl. I had indeed felt the touch of His lips. At the time I did not recognize it, but now I knew, and I could share in the zeal and direct it to its divine source.

Tonight we read "My Psalm of Praise." My favorite lines were:

I am overcome by a bursting of radiant song.
The words that pour from my mouth,

they are mine and then some.
I can almost watch their luminous extension.

My tongue, my hand, my foot
begin to sing and flow.
My whole body is his choir.

My spirit erupts into dance,
burgeons into embodied praise,
releasing the heavenlies,
even here, even now on earth.

My voice was barely passable, yet I longed to sing a song of praise. I so wished I could think of one. I had only heard chants sung in mass. They didn't seem quite the joyous tunes this author had in mind, but I could indeed sing a song of praise with my feet. I had done so throughout my childhood. A part of me wanted to get up and dance a little jig to the tune in my head there and then.

However, Giovanni looked rather pensive as he sat meditating. It was not the response one would expect from the poem. I deduced his mind had wandered back to his travel plans. There was much to arrange with his traveling six months off schedule. He had spent most of supper fretting the details.

"It will be fine, Giovanni. You'll find the right ship. These things have a way of working themselves out."

He snapped back to the present and took a moment to decipher my meaning. "I'm sure you are right, my dear, but I had a different issue on my mind."

"Oh, is it Francesca?" I closed my book to give him my full attention.

"Actually, no."

"Oh."

He looked uncomfortable as he spoke. "Actually, I've been thinking about you."

"Me. Whatever for?" I attempted to catch his gaze.

"Well, to begin," he said, "I hate to leave you here and vulnerable when we know the Worthings are searching for you."

"Yes, that was disturbing. But in truth, with Lord Worthing involved I am not overly worried. It was Lady Catherine who frightened me, but I'm feeling much better since we talked everything through."

"Still, I feel a responsibility toward you. I shall worry about you while I'm in Italy." Giovanni turned his eyes away from me and stared into the fire. "I shall worry about you, but more than that . . . I shall miss you." After the words were out he glanced over to see my response.

I gave him a melancholy smile as impending loneliness tugged at my heart. "I shall miss you too, Giovanni. Our time together has meant much to me as well. I want you to know that. We've never been without you in the winter. It shall seem strange no doubt, but you won't be gone forever."

"I keep trying to imagine my time in Italy, and I keep seeing you there with me. I don't know if I can face it without you. I'm not sure I want to." He stood and paced. "There's so much I long to show you and share with you. I want to take you to Florence and to Rome. I want to introduce you to my friends and to Mother Maria. I want to show you my country villa. It's full of horses and little dogs the way you like."

I could almost imagine it. "It sounds like a dream, Giovanni, but we both know that is all it can be. You barely get away with escorting me to an occasional dinner here. You can't whisk your housekeeper off to the continent with you. It isn't done. I know this seems difficult, but you will be fine. Trust me."

"It is true I can't take you to Italy as my London housekeeper, but there may be another way." He looked oddly sheepish as he said it.

"What are you plotting, Giovanni?"

He did not respond immediately, but my own mind was spinning. Perhaps my Italian was good enough to manage a home in Italy.

He took a few fortifying breaths. "Well, I'm not quite sure how to put this. Where do I begin? I'm certain you know Francesca was the love of my life. There shall never be another like her. I have no desire for anyone to take her place—and yet, I've much living yet to do without her, and I have built a huge and successful business with no heir."

I was starting to follow him. His words were not at all what I expected.

Staring at the ceiling, he continued his speech. "Then there is you, Dandelion. It seems perhaps you have lost the love of your life in this William, but might you not still find happiness in being a wife and a mother?"

There was no denying the direction of his speech now. My mouth fell open in a most unladylike manner.

"Don't misunderstand." Giovanni seemed dismayed by my shocked expression. He came and knelt before me. "I acknowledge we don't quite love each other in that way. But Dandelion, there are many kinds of love. You are the closest friend I have ever known. You understand me in ways even my dear Francesca never did. It would make me so happy to have you by my side as a partner through the rest of life. It would bring me much comfort and joy, and I could give you so much in return. I want to give you the kind of life you deserve."

I sat stunned and silent. My heart raced along with my thoughts.

He took my hands in his. "Perhaps you still dream of true love. I shared it with my Francesca, and I would never deny you the opportunity to seek it. You are so very young. I realize you may not be ready to settle for what I suggest."

I gave his hands an encouraging squeeze, although I struggled to comprehend his words.

"But know this, Dandelion, I do hold much love for you, and I think we could have a beautiful life together."

I looked deep into his brown eyes—the eyes of my dearest friend. They were so sincere and caring, indeed so full of love—a different sort of love, but love nonetheless. Warmth flowed through me to my fingertips and toes. "I will give it great consideration."

His face brightened. "That is all I ask."

"May I think about it and answer you in the morning?"

"Take all the time you need, my dear." He lifted me to my feet and leaned in to kiss me on the cheek with his soft lips. He had never done so before.

My mind was still spinning as I settled myself beneath the blankets of my bed. My chest clutched in fear. There was something so familiar in what Giovanni offered, something so similar to Gottfried. Giovanni was the older man, the protector and provider. I couldn't help but experience some panic at the similarities, but then my more rational mind took over.

I've known Giovanni for years, not days. The man had not an ounce of violence in him. He opened the depths of his soul to me. He was nothing like Gottfried. He wanted to take care of me because of the true friendship we shared, not because of delusions or ghosts from his past. I admired him for his compassion and strength of character, not because of his broad shoulders and shiny armor. I loved Giovanni for who he was, not for who I dreamed him to be.

And he was right—we did share a love, a deep and abiding love. I always thought it more a familial type of love, but in truth what was marriage if not the making of a family? Tonight when he kissed me, I realized I did long for his touch, for the touch of a man. Like a starving child will learn to forget their hunger, I taught myself to ignore my desires. I felt them tonight, though, at his kiss. It may not have fired my blood like William's or Richard's, but it was gentle and sweet, and I longed for more.

I could not help comparing Giovanni with the men from my past. They were the only standard by which I could judge. Richard— gentle, charming Richard. He disappointed me so tragically, and yet we shared something real. He was all romance and sweet talk and dreams. I loved his humor and his wit. However, he never possessed Giovanni's strength. At the core he was a coward, a pawn. Giovanni and I shared an emotional and spiritual intimacy I never found with Richard. Why, I would take a good and honest and trustworthy man over Richard's steamy kisses any day of the week.

Good and honest and trustworthy, those words brought me to William. Was he in fact the love of my life as Giovanni suggested?

If indeed we only had one soul mate in the world, I feared William may have been mine, but I was not certain I believed in such silliness anyway. The truth was, we all had decisions to make. For as desperately as I still missed William, I did not regret my decision. Had I stayed with him then, I would have resented him forever. I would have blamed him and his God for my poverty and my lowly lot in life. I would have turned into a nagging fishwife and made us both miserable.

Regrets served no good purpose by my way of thinking. Living in the past, focusing on the "if only" had a way of murdering the present. Would I ever go back and give up discovering the poetry of Samia? What about that romping summer in the woods near Bath with the Tallangers, or my first glimpse of the sea with Lady Catherine? Could I ever wish away meeting Giovanni and coming into my own as a strong, independent, and capable woman?

My path in life thus far had been twisted, jagged, and rough, but it brought me to this place where I was free and coming to peace with my God and with myself. How could I regret that?

Giovanni was a big part of my growth and change. How could I regret being banished from Arun Castle and coming here to work for him? Yet I did not wish to accept him out of a misplaced sense of guilt or obligation. I certainly did not wish to accept him out of fear or a need to run from the Worthings once again.

For once in my life I longed to make a decision in the proper way. I wanted to choose the path that would best please God. I wanted to choose the plan that would bring me closest to Him. It seemed to me marrying Giovanni would be that path. Thank the good Lord I had put the old, wild Dandelion far behind me.

Chapter 28

Giovanni and I sat aboard a small rocking boat, waiting to be rowed to the ship and waving good-bye with misty eyes. We would spend a year in Italy and return in accordance with Giovanni's typical schedule. The entire household was gathered in the bustling warehouse district south of London, waving and shouting their farewells from land. Then they climbed into the wagon and rolled away, our friends fading to a distant blur. I wished I could say they were surprised by our sudden engagement, but they were not.

As I surveyed the passing shoreline, the fish vendors, the sailors, the merchants tallying their wares, I spied the strangest thing.

Could it be?

Why, of course not. How ridiculous.

But indeed, the man hauling sacks from a wagon to a waiting ship looked the mirror image of my William. His name sprang to my lips, and I swallowed it down. Whatever would William be doing near London? A part of me longed to yell to the oarsmen to turn around. Was this a sign? Was this marriage a mistake? Should I go back while yet I could? But where to? Lady Worthing had banished me from Arun. Even if my eyes did not deceive me, I could never run home with William.

The man lifted his head and nearly caught my eye. But then the sack of grain upon his shoulder stole my attention instead. Sensations of hunger and panic overtook me as always upon the sight of it. I forced a deep breath, shaking off the ludicrous notion along with the horrible feelings. Surely it could not be William.

Forward. Ever forward, never back.

Eyes focused ahead of me, I climbed up the ladder and aboard the giant ship.

As I stood surrounded by the scents of fish and water, looking anywhere but the shore, sailors dashed about me, barking orders. Within moments the vessel lurched. The boat had merely awaited our arrival. We slid into the flow of the River Thames. At the end of this river, we would pour into the fathomless sea, that same sea I saw with Catherine so many years ago. It was the greatest gift she ever gave me, and one she could never take away.

Giovanni and I agreed it was best for him to finish his year of mourning for his beloved first wife before we wed. We thought it better

DINA L. SLEIMAN

for his family to meet me as his intended and have time to adjust to the thought before the actual marriage. For the first time in years, I dressed in colorful silks and satins rather than functional wools and linens, today's kirtle a deep red. Thankfully, Italian fashion did not require married women to wear head coverings. Lord knew, I had never much liked them.

I anticipated a beautiful month sailing aboard the *Alessia*. On the vast expanse of water my mind would grow clear and open and ready to face each new challenge awaiting me in Italy. I fairly tingled with excitement as I watched the strong oars stroking through the water at my side.

Unlike the old days of galley slaves, the crew would only row us away from shore and later back toward it again upon arrival. The giant sails of the double-masted Genoan ship would carry us on the wind for most of the trip. In the past, the journey would have taken four times as long as the ship hugged the coastline and rowed to land each night for safety. The sturdy *Alessia*, however, was made to handle the open sea. Although a mere twenty-five feet wide, it was nearly one hundred and thirty feet long. The large crew now manning the oars would deter any pirates along the way.

A deep Italian voice broke into my thoughts. "Beautiful day for a sea journey."

"Beautiful day it is, Captain," said Giovanni. "Allow me to introduce you to my *fidanzata*. Dame Mullens, this is Captain Lucio Bartello. He came to me with the finest reputation after a long and exhaustive search."

The handsome, blond Captain Bartello bowed to both of us. "At your service."

I extended my hand, and the captain kissed it as was customary.

He caught my eye for the briefest moment before turning back to Giovanni. "I can only hope both I and my ship live up to your expectations."

"Well, I must say I'm quite impressed so far." Giovanni surveyed the fine vessel with a swooping gesture.

The captain tugged on the rigging. "As sturdy as they come, I assure you. Your valet is unpacking your baggage below deck. The apartment has been arranged as you requested."

"As you requested?" My mind was such a jumble of preparations and dreams of foreign lands. I hadn't stopped to consider life on shipboard.

"Yes, my dear," said Giovanni. "We're aboard a cargo ship, and I'm afraid Roberto and I are far from hardened sailors after all these years."

"The crew just sleeps where they fall, on the deck under the stars in fair weather, or below with the cargo," said the captain. "Passengers must make arrangements if they desire a sleeping chamber. Giovanni was very thoughtful in requesting two separate compartments side-by-side to preserve your modesty, my lady."

186

"Dame Mullens, if you please, Captain." I dipped my head.

He bowed once again. "Of course. Forgive my lapse, but you certainly do carry yourself like a lady."

"Quite true." Giovanni gave me a chivalrous little bow as well. "Ocean travel is not fit for a lady, but we shall do our best."

I turned to look out over the ship rail at the churning water. "I suppose I didn't realize the extent of this adventure."

"We'll make it as civilized as possible. I've taken on extra provisions and warned the sailors to use the chamber pots rather than relieve themselves over these rails as they usually do." Captain Bartello gave the wooden beam a sturdy pat.

My eyes grew wide, but I smiled. "Oh, it's quite all right. I rather enjoy a good adventure, and I grew up in the countryside with two brothers, so there is little your crew could do to shock me."

"I'm glad to hear it, Dame Mullens. Far be it from me to steal a young lady's innocence." Something in his tone made me doubt that.

"Well then, let's go and see where we shall be living for the next month," I said to my betrothed.

I was still smiling as Giovanni and I descended the stairs into the hull, but my smile faded. The air below deck was stale and musty. It was thick with dust, and the torch did little to illuminate our path through the huge crates of cargo. As I slid between them, it seemed as though they were shifting around me and closing in upon me, but I grasped onto Giovanni's sleeve and trekked onward nonetheless, determined not to be deterred on this grand adventure.

As we burrowed deeper into the bowels of the ship, I grew even more disheartened. The smell worsened, and the darkness deepened. Near the stern of the great ship was a small area partitioned off as sleeping quarters.

We pushed aside a curtain and entered. A cheerful Roberto was at work, at ease in this depressing place. True, the light glowed brighter here, and colorful touches abounded. A mirror hung on the wall, and a basin of water sat in a stand attached to the floorboards. I saw a small desk in the corner already covered with ledgers, pens and some of our favorite books.

Giovanni pushed aside a second curtain, and there was a bunk with my own coverlet from home looking snug and quaint. My sewing basket beside it overflowed with ribbons and threads. I had a mirror, washbasin, and chamber pot. Roberto had even laid out my comb. For all the effort put into making my room inviting, the walls and curtains were closing in upon me. I grasped even tighter to Giovanni's sleeve with two hands now. I couldn't find enough air.

"Giovanni," I said, my voice thin and breathy, "I know not if I can stay in this place."

No sooner were the words out than I heard a squeak, and two huge rats, perhaps five pounds apiece, went streaking across the floor and under my bed.

I screamed in earnest. I buried my head against Giovanni's chest, shaking. It was all I could do not to claw and climb my way into his arms. He sensed my need and lifted me onto his own bed.

"Dandelion, my dear, I'm so sorry. I should have realized. It's too much like the dungeon, is it not?"

Unable to form any words, I nodded my head furiously, still trembling. My heart threatened to explode right within my chest.

"Come then." Giovanni lifted me into his arms. "Let me get you out of this place."

Roberto buried his head in a trunk and continued unpacking as if nothing happened, but he couldn't resist a sympathetic glance as Giovanni carried me out of the chamber.

Safe on deck once again, I relaxed. Giovanni sat me down against the starboard side of the ship. "Don't worry, dear. We shall think of something else."

After a few moments, I felt like myself again. The fresh air was invigorating, and the wind teased my hair from its pins. I stood up and looked over the ship rail again. The day glowed in stark contrast to the dreary hull. The sun stroked my cheeks. All the air of the world was mine.

I took a deep breath. I spread my arms wide and couldn't resist spinning in a circle. "Now this is heaven."

"Yes, I see," said Giovanni, chuckling. "Far be it from me to drag you into the pit of Hades once again."

"Yes, keep me up here under the blue sky, and I'll have not a care in the world."

"Let me get back to Roberto then. Perhaps you and I can set up some sort of little tent here on the deck later today." He still looked unsure.

I gave him a nudge in the right direction. "Yes, please, go right ahead. I'm fine now, more than fine."

Coming up those stairs from the hull of the ship was much like the historical day I emerged from my parents' dreary hut into a vivid world of color. I hadn't danced once in the city of London, but here on the open water, my feet took on a life of their own, and I couldn't stop them from taking a few merry little steps. I longed to dance full out a romping jig of spins and leaps and stomps like I did as a child. I longed to dance a dance of praise for sun and air and sky and life—a dance of praise to the marvelous God who created them all.

It was then I noticed the captain studying me from his cabin door. I walked back to the rail and stood looking over it once again, trying to keep my eyes on the shoreline, but I sensed him as he approached.

He leaned against the rail alongside me and spoke in Italian. "So, you did not find the accommodations to your liking?"

I felt a blush rise to my cheeks.

He gave a roguish chuckle.

"My sincerest apologies, Captain Bartello. You have a lovely ship, but I cannot stay below deck." I answered in his language, hoping my grammar was passable.

"Call me Lucio."

"Lucio." I tested the feel of the new name against my lips and tongue. I hadn't fully looked him in the eye earlier. He was a handsome man to be sure, more like a pirate than a respectable sea captain. His white muslin shirt was open midway down his chest. Foregoing any sort of tunic, he wore the shirt over tight-fitting, brown hose, which were tucked into tall, shiny, black boots. A long, curving sword dangled from a black belt across his hips.

Lucio's pale blond hair fell in feathery wisps from chin to shoulders. His face was bronzed with sharp cheekbones. He wore a scruff of a beard, more likely from lack of shaving than any actual attempt to grow one. It gave him a roguish, devil-may-care appearance to match his chuckle. He towered over me, forcing me to tilt my head far upward to meet his gaze. He almost reminded me of William for a moment, but the resemblance stopped at his eyes.

Unlike William's warm brown orbs, Lucio's were green and fathomless like the sea. Mysterious—laughing one second and predatory the next. I shook off the spell and looked back out toward the shore.

"Don't you worry your pretty little head about it one bit," he said.

For a moment I thought my preoccupation was apparent, but then remembered with relief that we were discussing my aversion to the ship's hull.

The captain continued. "You won't catch me down there for more than five consecutive minutes either. It's dark and stale and rank. Give me the sunshine and stars and clean, clear sky. You should have seen your face when you came through that door. One moment you were terror-ridden and ashen and the next you were rosy-cheeked and dancing for all the world to watch. It's as if you were born for life at sea."

I couldn't help but giggle in agreement. "Or reborn after hell in the hull."

"Ah, and she's witty too. Dame Mullens, eh?" He shot me a swarthy sideways glance.

"Yes."

"The name doesn't quite suit you."

I turned again to look him in the eye. The breeze played havoc with my loosened hair. I swiped the curling strands from my face and held them back while I spoke. "Then I suppose, Lucio, you may call me Dandelion." It wasn't appropriate, but something about the water and this ship made me long to throw propriety to the wind.

"Dandelion. Hmm. Well that sounds a far cry better. I've never heard the name before."

I ducked my head. "No, I'm afraid my father was waxing quite creative when he came up with it."

He reached out and turned my head back toward him. It was unthinkably forward of him. "Does it mean anything?"

"Oh, it's a flower. Funny, I don't know the word in your language." Our entire conversation took place in Italian other than my name. "It's yellow and it grows in the fields. It turns all white and downy, and then the seeds float away." I demonstrated the way I would blow upon it as a child.

"Ah, yes. I know the flower you speak of, *Dente di leone*. Very appropriate. Wild and vital and free. It is at its most beautiful close to death as it dances in the breeze. It is a tragic and romantic sort of flower, don't you think?" His stare threatened to burn right through me.

"Most people find it common, crass even. Leave it to an Italian sea captain to turn it into poetry."

"At your service, my lady." There was a familiar sort of hum and crackle between us as we spoke.

I turned away and broke the spell once again. Lucio Bartello was a dangerous man. I would tread with care.

Relief washed over me as Giovanni emerged back on deck and headed our way. My dear, dear Giovanni, I would never let this striking sea captain come between us. I waved a cheerful greeting to him. He placed his arm around me and gave me a loud kiss on the cheek. It seemed the ship was having the same effect on his inhibitions as it was upon mine, and we hadn't even left the River Thames yet.

"She's looking well now, isn't she?" Giovanni gazed at me with pride. "It seems Roberto has everything under control below deck after all. He told me I was unneeded and sent me back."

Lucio tossed his sun-bleached hair away from his face. "I suspect this one has sea water in her veins, Signore Sabatini. You may well never get her off of this ship."

Giovanni chucked me beneath the chin. "Whatever makes my girl happy is fine by me."

"Quite a nice arrangement you have here." Days later, Captain Lucio caught me alone again. He plopped himself into a chair across from me and waved his hand in a sweeping motion to take in the colorful canvas tent and my little shipboard camp of a table and chairs.

"Yes, isn't it charming?" To a woman who grew up on the dirt floor of a makeshift cottage, the tent seemed a true luxury. "It reminds me of the tournament grounds where the traveling nobility and their retinues sleep."

"Hmm." Lucio fingered the patterned fabric. "Or the tent of a sheik on the Arabian Desert. You'd make a lovely little harem girl."

"Have you seen such things?" Ignoring his innuendo, I sat forward. My mind caught only on the mention of exotic wonders.

"Indeed I have. Why don't you and your *fidanzato* join me for dinner tonight, and I shall regale you with my tales."

"Oh, please!" I tore my eyes away from his intoxicating face, and corrected my rash speech. "Giovanni does so love a good story. He's resting below deck in his quarters, but should be up shortly."

"Sounds like a marvelous plan to me."

Yes, as long as I could keep my unruly thoughts in order. We sailed the open Atlantic now. My skin grew coppery and my hair faded lighter with streaks of cream. I oft spied Captain Bartello watching me. He never tried to disguise his interest. I told myself it was a captain's duty to keep watch over his passengers, though it certainly was not his responsibility to wink at them with a roguish grin. He would sometimes wander over to offer me a benign lesson about sailing or navigation, his eyes all the while offering so much more.

"What is that you're working on?" he asked.

I dared not look up from my stitching this time. "Just some gowns I'm making." For my new wardrobe befitting a Florentine merchant's wife, I reminded myself.

"The sailors aren't used to pins and ribbons. I do believe such domesticity on shipboard makes them homesick for wives and mothers. They've been behaving uncommonly well."

I flitted the briefest glance upward. "And does it make you homesick captain?"

"You tell me. Have I been behaving uncommonly well?" He ducked down to better catch my eye.

"Why captain, I have nothing to compare your behavior to. Yet somehow, I suspect not."

"Smart girl," he said with a knavish chuckle. He stood to his feet. "I shall see you at dinner then."

"If you promise to behave." I tied off a thread.

"Would you turn me down otherwise?"

I didn't answer, only gazed up with a wry smile.

He walked away still laughing.

"Tell me the story of your camel," I said to the captain several evenings later over a meal of ham and vegetables.

We dined with the captain in his wood-paneled quarters once again. He was witty, and I enjoyed our banter. Telling us amazing tales of his travels, he answered many of my questions about the orient, which Gottfried had never satisfied.

"Not that silly one." Lucio poured himself another goblet of wine.

"Yes, oh please, I love that story." I clapped my hands together over top the sturdy table.

Giovanni nodded his agreement.

"Well," said Lucio, weaving his magical yarn, "I once bought a camel named Malek, which means 'king' in Arabic. He was a fine camel, and I was quite proud of him. Then one day, I walked out of a tavern, where I had been eating a lovely lunch of hummus, tabouli, and flat pita bread, when lo and behold, I discovered my camel was gone."

"Where was he?" I feigned ignorance, although well I knew by then.

"I searched up and down the streets for my handsome camel, Malek, thinking surely he chewed through his ropes and was somewhere close by munching on flowers."

"But he was nowhere to be found," I said.

"But he was nowhere to be found." Lucio played along. "As I was about to give up hope, a young Arab boy came around the corner and gestured me to him. 'Sir, come with me,' he said in a hushed voice. 'I know where your camel is.'"

"Let me guess," said Giovanni. "You were so happy to hear it."

"Indeed I was so happy to hear it. I thought all my problems were solved. Until, of course, the young boy started looping me through the city streets—to and fro, back and forth, it made no sense at all, and I began to worry. Then we walked down a small dark alley and up a long flight of stairs. There waited no less than ten frightening men with turbans on their heads and long, curved swords at their hips. In the middle on a large chair sat their chieftain." Lucio imitated the chieftain's bow.

Giovanni and I bowed back to him.

Lucio smiled his devilish smile and continued. "'Good evening, my nephew,' he said in a pleasant enough way. 'It seems your camel has somehow made its way into our possession. We would be happy to return it, but naturally we shall require a small fee for our trouble.'"

"They were thieves." I shrieked with laughter.

"It seemed they were precisely that, although the kindest and most hospitable thieves I ever met. After I paid the ransom for my fine camel, Malek, they invited me to join them for supper. We smoked the argheli and danced the debke together that night. Before sending me off they wished me well and my children well and said with complete seriousness, they hoped to do business with me again someday."

It was a silly story, but I could listen to it all night long. Afterwards we played checkers, and Lucio taught me the names of constellations along with their legends and significance—Cassiopeia, the bears, mighty Orion with his arrows and bow. I never heard of such things, but he brought them to life and made me believe. Later, I bade Lucio farewell, yet hated to leave him behind as I hid myself away in my little tent.

The next night, once the sailors were well soused, they took out their fiddles and lutes and entertained us under the starry sky as they often did. Giovanni and I sat side by side on a crate in the streaming moonlight. Across from us, the captain clapped along to the strong beat.

The first time the sailors had played for us, I sat on my chair with demure toes tapping to the music, but as I grew more comfortable aboard the ship my hands had clapped and my shoulders swayed. By the third night, I stood up and performed several courtly dances, graceful and reserved, for a very appreciative audience. No one was more surprised than Giovanni, who lived with me for years without ever seeing a single dip or spin performed under his roof.

But on this night, for the first time in ever so many years, the music filled my soul and threatened to burst through my skin. I could no longer resist. Toe tapping and clapping were not enough. Patterned dances would not suffice. Throwing caution into the chilled sea breeze, I gave way to my instincts.

Rising to my feet, I allowed the tune to flow through my body in an irrepressible jig of stomps and spins, just as I danced in the fields as a child. My arms flew through the open air. My feet stamped hard against the wooden deck to the lively beat. My hair tumbled about me as I twirled in circles again and again. I kicked my legs high and leapt in time to the music, freedom overtaking me as I sailed weightlessly through space.

All this time in the open sea air roused the old, wild Dandelion from a long slumber.

When the music stopped, I stood and blinked from the center of the deck.

Whatever had come over me?

My cheeks felt warm and flushed in the cool night air. I clapped my palms over them.

The sailors cheered and whooped in response. The captain winked at me over the crowd. When I sat back down next to Giovanni, he gave me a hearty kiss on the cheek. He wore a look of wonder, tinged with confusion and a touch of fear. I turned my head down and closed my eyes, pretending to be lost in the music once again. I didn't need to ask what he was thinking, for the message was all too clear upon his face.

Whatever happened to the proper and stoic Dame Mullins who was his housekeeper in London?

Of course he would stare at me in wonder. How many times had people told me I was beautiful, mesmerizing, even mystical when I danced? Giovanni now witnessed firsthand the Dandelion known for her mischief and fairy magic throughout the shire. Giovanni loved me, and he had never before seen me truly free and happy.

Of course he was pleased.

Of course he was afraid.

I was afraid. I didn't know what to expect from myself anymore. I felt as if I watched myself in a dream, from the outside, unable to control anything, unsure of the outcome. Who was this Dandy, wild and spirited as the child, but with the body and mind and desires of a grown woman? I wasn't certain I could trust her.

After Giovanni went below deck still shaking his head, I tried to sleep, but slumber eluded me. I was too awake, too exhilarated, too frightened to sleep. Although I moved as if within the haze of a dream.

I pulled a wool kirtle on over my chemise within the shadows of my tent. Pushing up the flap, I exited and crept to the rail of the ship. The sailors didn't quite sleep where they fell as the captain claimed, but they did toss their pallets about the ship deck, and several were snoring as I tiptoed over them.

The moon was large and full that night. It glistened over the water in a flowing luminous pool, like a pathway of glimmering glass one could step out upon and walk away into the night. Surrounding the path were tiny rogue sparkles of light, sharp shards escaped from the glassy pool. I leaned against the rail and reached toward them.

The lap of water upon the hull splashed against my ears like a

194

lullaby. I pulled the air deep into my lungs and released it with a sigh. The aroma of the seawater enticed me as usual. I could lick the salt upon my lips. The sound and taste and smell of the sea soaked into my skin, into my very being.

I should have jumped and squealed when Lucio brushed past to settle himself along the rail beside me, but in that moment it seemed all too natural. We exchanged a long, lingering look in the flood of moonlight.

"That was quite a stimulating performance tonight. My most sincere thanks," he said with a bow of his head.

I smiled. "I suppose I should apologize for bringing your crew to such a frenzy . . . ."

"But."

"But it was wonderful." I sighed, looking back out over the water.

"I think you have a bit of the sea siren in you."

"At home they said I was a fairy."

"There is certainly something magical about you—like a mythical pagan goddess in a whirling dervish, like Salome dancing for the head of John the Baptist on a platter. You have me under your spell."

The wind played havoc with my hair once again. Lucio pushed it away to see my face. He laughed at my expression, and I wondered if I appeared as intoxicated as I felt. "Are you quite sure you are cut out for the life of a respectable merchant's wife?"

I chose not to answer. We stood side by side for a long time, sharing the blissful moment, a love for sea and sky and the magic in the universe.

"Well, good night then," he said and walked toward his quarters. He must have thought better and turned stealthily back, for the next thing I knew he pressed against my back and whispered, his voice ragged in my ear, "You shouldn't lean against the rail in such a way. It makes me want to do unspeakable things to you, Dandelion." Just as quickly he was gone, although the tickle of his breath against my skin lingered long afterward.

Chapter 30

*I*should tell *Giovanni*. Surely it was my duty to inform him of any untoward advances. I should tell him this instant and remove all temptation.

We must have looked the perfect couple at that moment, the making of paintings, stories, and songs. Giovanni studied his ledgers, and I sat by his feet upon a rug, sewing a row of genteel stitches for my new gown. I should have told Giovanni right there and then, but I did not. Perhaps I didn't want to hurt him. Perhaps I wanted to save us both from tension during our idyllic cruise, our lovely interlude on the sea. Perhaps . . . but I knew deep down I thought of myself and the fire that flowed through my veins at Lucio's touch instead of my dear, precious Giovanni.

"I'm not feeling so well, Dandelion," said Giovanni. "I might go below deck and lie down for a while."

The large ship rocked on the choppy water. I enjoyed it like a babe in a cradle, but until now failed to notice Giovanni's green tinge. A thin sheen of perspiration covered his brow, although the breeze was cool. However had I failed to notice? I put the back of my hand to his forehead, which felt cold and clammy to the touch. My brow crinkled in concern. "Certainly, darling. You're not looking so well, now that you mention it. Go and rest. I'll be fine."

A wave of sympathy washed over me, sure as those crashing around us.

Several times that afternoon I attempted to descend the stairs into the hull of the ship, but my feet betrayed me. The stale air, the squeal of giant rats, it was too much for me. I went back to my chair beside the tent and returned to my journal. I worked at translating some of Mother Maria's poems into English. It was slow going, trying to keep the subtleties and symbols alive while relating some sense of the musical language she used. I allowed myself several versions to get things right. I was lost deep in thought when a shadow covered my book.

"Good afternoon, Mistress Salome."

"Oh good, Captain Bartello, you are just the person I wanted to see. Could you please check on Giovanni? He went below deck to lie down. He wasn't feeling at all well. I suppose the sea is too rough for him today." I registered Lucio's disappointment at my request. I hoped my message was clear.

Lucio crossed his arms over his chest. "Yes, I saw him a moment ago. It seems neither he nor his servant Roberto have found their sea legs after all these years. They'll survive, though. I encouraged Giovanni to join us for supper. This weather will only be getting worse before it gets better."

"Oh, I suppose I must go check on him, then."

"I'm sure he would rather you remain here in the fresh air where you're happy. I'll have my men see to them. What's that you're working on today?" He snatched the book from my hand before I could refuse him.

"It's some poetry I'm translating."

"A heathen and a scholar, what a delightful combination." He opened the book. The poem was in English. He looked disoriented and disappointed once again, for he spoke little of my language, but then he rifled through the pages and found the original Italian verses.

I couldn't keep myself from enjoying the sensual beauty of his jagged beard against the hollow of his cheekbones or the devastating effect of emotions playing across his soft lips. I was able to search out the answer to the mystery in his eyes unheeded as he focused on my book. "As you can see, Captain, I am not a heathen. Quite the contrary."

He flipped through a few more pages. "Oh, I wouldn't be so certain." He tossed the book at my feet and sauntered away. I looked down to see what he meant by his parting shot. I read the words and gasped.

> *Yet, all I know is this:*
> *I have felt the touch of His lips.*
> *He has saturated my soul.*
> *I am fully aroused to the depths of my being.*
>
> *I've never felt so full,*
> *yet so devoid of self,*
> *as if I am of clay—a pitcher*
> *empty but for the fiery life.*

I looked over the pages. I hadn't noticed how sexual the imagery was until seeing it through Lucio's eyes. They were passionate love poems to God, but resonated with some deep and very human needs as well. I bit my bottom lip and regretted my mistake. Lucio viewed me more and more as a strumpet with each passing moment. I must leave that Dandy far behind me. I must make it clear to him—but first

I must make it clear to myself.

That night I donned a simple brown kirtle and modest mantle. I pulled my hair back and covered it with a wimple. It was cold on deck and beginning to sprinkle. When Giovanni did not emerge for supper, I settled myself amongst a group of quiet, middle-aged sailors. Lucio approached, and this time I was ready for him.

He leaned against the mast. "Dame Mullens, won't you be dining with me tonight?"

I stared down at my food. "No, thank you. I don't think it would be proper without Giovanni."

"As you like. Giovanni tried to come up and join us, but he looked so wobbly and miserable I insisted he lie back down."

"I do appreciate it, Captain."

"Of course."

I looked up in time to see him shaking his head as he walked toward his cabin. Now that was much better. A polite tone was precisely what was needed between us. Thank God he could not see my wildly pounding heart.

By the next morning a storm hovered upon the horizon. All day long waves crashed against the ship tipping us to and fro, no longer a gentle cradle rock. The sky grew darker until it covered us in a thick, gray blanket. Dusk seemed to linger from noon till night. I spent the day mesmerized by clouds, watching them descend and huddle about us in a purplish-yellow haze. The old Dandelion longed to rise up within me.

The Dandelion who had poached and danced.

The Dandelion who had fought her way to an education and a better sort of life.

Or was it better?

Those days now seemed so simple and carefree. The dangers of childhood so benign. I almost longed to return to them.

My mind wandered back through time of its own accord.

198

"Faster, Robin. We've almost got him," I yelled to William as we flew through the woods like three blurry phantoms. "Around that boulder."

William, still in the lead, made a sharp turn to the right with his slingshot poised. I heard a *whirr* and then a *whack*. For the past ten months we never entered the woods without catching some type of game. Today's fox, though sly and quick, would be no exception. Tim and I caught up and rounded the boulder as well. I gasped and pulled to a stop. There was no small dead fox at William's feet. Inexplicably, there lay a huge buck instead, the most beautiful tawny color, with no less than twelve sharp-pointed antlers sprouting from his head.

"Wow." Tim bounced about. "That's the biggest thing we've ever caught."

"But we can't keep him," I said. "It's too dangerous." After all these playful months, we had nearly forgotten the inherent threat of our child's game.

"Why not? I think he's lovely. Why, we could eat off him for a month." Tim ran toward the deer.

My heart sped. My hands shook. I caught him and pulled him back. "Stop. Enough, Tim, it's out of the question. We must get away from here."

William had yet to twitch a muscle or make a sound since the fateful *whack* a few moments earlier. He dropped the offensive slingshot upon the ground. "I don't know what happened. I turned the bend and did what I always do, and then it was too late."

"Come, William," I chided in my most authoritative voice. "Before someone sees us." The steward was still our secret ally but had warned us again and again to stick to the small game.

William remained steadfast in his spot. "We can't just leave him lying there. Look at him."

I let go of Tim and yanked on William with all my might, but to no avail. "Surely you jest. We may get away with stealing a few paltry squirrels, but this shall never go unnoticed. The guards will whip us for certain." I almost felt the cold, hard snap upon my back. Indeed, only our youthful ages would spare us from far worse a punishment.

William let out the saddest sigh.

I couldn't leave him standing there so forlorn, so moved by the great dead beast before him. I took a deep breath and gathered my courage. "All right, then, what do we do?"

"Well." William reached down to stroke the deer's long graceful neck. "He shouldn't have died for naught. He was proud and brave, and his life was a gift. I suppose, if he had to die, some good ought to come of it."

"But what?" I stooped next to him for a few moments while he thought.

William stood in triumph. "The nuns at the convent across the river!"

199

It took us near an hour to drag the heavy carcass the few furlongs to the shore, only to find the Arun River high and coursing that day. It would be hard enough to wade across, but there was little doubt the deer would be swept away by the strong current. The three of us sat at the shore, panting and perplexed.

Then I heard a snap.

A rustle in the leaves.

Pray God it was just a rabbit. I pulled Tim closer.

A figure moved through the dense forest.

The figure of a man.

I hugged Tim to me and grabbed William's arm.

A voice came through the trees. "Look what we have here."

"Run," I said. We were scrambling to our feet and out of danger, when uproarious laughter gave us pause. From the thick brush stepped the rotund figure of Friar John, the parish priest. For all his stern lectures about the evils of vice and sin, he was likely the worst sinner of us all. Yet he did it with such a jovial spirit and merry twinkle in his eye, few held it against him.

"Friar John." I stomped my foot. "You scared us near to death."

"The price of sin is death, my child. Surely a hot and fiery place awaits those who break our Lord's commands, unless we turn from our sins and run to the feet of Him who suffered death for us on the cross over a thousand years ago. Repent, I say. Repent, ye sinners, before it is too late. I stand ready to take your confession." His face, already flushed from too much liquor, turned even brighter red with his impassioned speech.

William turned to me with a smile and a roll of his eyes.

I proceeded from there. "Actually, we're so happy to see you, Friar John. We're in a bit of trouble. We were playing just over there in the woods when we heard some strange boys shouting to one another. It seems one of them struck this deer you see here before you. We knew the deer should rightly belong to his lordship. So William, being the brave and good boy that he is, rushed at them with a huge staff, screaming and hollering as fierce as could be. Well, I guess I don't have to tell a smart man like you that those cowardly thieves took off quick as lightning."

"Hmm, you don't say. This very deer right here." Friar John moved closer to examine the buck. "And I suppose, brave young William, this has nothing to do with the slingshot I've seen peeking from your tunic."

William's eyes grew wide. "Why, sir, whatever do you mean?"

"No, no, of course not." Friar John waved his hands with a flourish. "Clearly, you are to be congratulated for running off those ruffians. But why, may I ask, are you not returning this fine stag to his lordship, for whom you so courageously snatched it out of the jaws of hell?"

"Well you see, sir." My speech flowed. "Once the boys were gone, it occurred to us someone could misunderstand the situation and think we were the poachers, ridiculous as we all know that to be."

Friar John clutched his heart. "Ridiculous indeed, my child."

"Yes," said William, "so we decided God and justice would be best served by taking it to the nuns at the convent."

"Which is what we were doing, until we saw how strong the current is today. Now true justice may never be served." I managed to wring a few pretty tears from my eyes.

"And what do you have to say to all this, little one?" The priest directed the question to Tim.

"I still think it would make a lovely dinner." Tim kicked at the dirt.

"Ah," said Friar John, "but don't you think it would taste even better in the mouths of the poor and needy and the holy sisters?"

"I thought we were the poor and needy." Tim turned to William. "Right, Robin? Steal from the rich and give to the poor. That's our motto." He pointed to his chest with both thumbs.

Friar John gave Tim's hair an affectionate ruffle. "Well, my son, I do understand your reasoning, but it seems the hand of God is in young William's plan today. I was on my way to visit the holy sisters myself, and I would be pleased to help you deliver this fine stag to them."

"Oh thank you, thank you, Friar John," William said.

The priest slung the huge deer over his shoulder, and we started on our way. Once across the river, he continued the conversation, or lecture as it were. "It seems to me you three may have too much idle time on your hands. Why, idleness is a danger indeed, a snare of hell itself. Idleness leads us into the hands of sin, sin which most assuredly leads to death. Idle hands, idle minds, why, they are playthings in the hands of Satan. We must avoid idleness at all costs. The price of sin is death, my children. As I was saying on Sunday . . . ."

The price of sin is death, my children. The words echoed through my mind. I would do well to remember them.

That evening, lightning split the sky and rain poured down. The sailors dashed about "battening down the hatches." I ran for my tent. The oiled canvas had been attached that morning in anticipation of the storm.

As I listened to the tap of the raindrops above my head, I longed to feel them upon my skin. The powerful, vital, living entity of the storm drew me back toward the flap of my shelter. I pushed it up and peeked out my face. The cool rivulets caressed my skin. I left the protection of my tent and stood right in the middle of it, raising my palms to catch the downpour.

Once again I found myself returning to my favorite perch along the rail. The waves splashed high against the side of the boat, and the raindrops danced along the surface of the water. Lightning filled the sky with crisscrossing patterns, glowing long after each strike. Thunder roared over my head and resounded right through me. It should have been terrifying, but somehow I felt overwhelmed with life and all the wonders of creation.

"Dame Mullens, please miss, go back inside," the first mate shouted to me over the din of the storm.

I waved him away and continued my musings.

In an instant I felt someone press against me and saw two fists clench tight to the rail on either side of me.

Now I was afraid.

I knew the hands were Lucio's. No one else's could be so sculptured and strong. I felt him press in harder against the length of my body. I took a quick, sharp breath.

"I thought I warned you about leaning against the rail like this." He blew the words into my ear like a kiss.

I shivered.

He grazed his gruff cheek across mine. "It's amazing, isn't it? I can't resist a good storm. The air is so full of power and energy, rippling with just the right touch of violence. Can you feel it? The crash and the roar. Are you afraid?"

Chapter
31

When I turned to look over my shoulder, his face was barely inches away. "Of the storm? No."

"The storm is the least of your worries tonight, eh?"

I pushed against him to move away, but only managed to twist and face him in his arms. "I was going back to my tent."

His eyes flashed green even as they drank in the inky darkness of the sea. I couldn't drag my gaze away from them. My fingers screamed to reach up and run themselves through the wet strands of his hair, to graze the prickles of his beard.

He clasped my chin in his powerful grip. "Oh, I don't think so."

A huge wave came careening over the side of the ship and would have knocked me over if I were not locked to the rail between Lucio's arms.

In the next moment, he released me and turned all business as he shouted orders to his crew. Never had I seen him exert such authority. When a second wave splashed over the rail, I ran toward the protection of my tent.

"Dandelion, no. Go to my quarters. You'll be safer there."

"I'll be fine, truly," I said, as I fought the wind toward my shelter.

Lucio took three purposeful strides and covered the distance between us. He hauled me over his shoulder like a sack of cargo and marched me to his cabin. "I've no time to argue with foolish, stubborn women."

"Ohh!"

He kicked the door open with one foot. Crossing the room, he threw me onto his bed. "Right now I must deal with this storm, but I will be back to deal with you. Don't give me any trouble. This isn't a game. Lives are at stake." He strode back out the door and slammed it behind him.

I shivered on the bed. Though wrapped in a blanket, I couldn't sit and wait. There was no sitting to be done without clinging to something anyway, as the ship pitched vehemently. All around me were shouts and bangs.

Needing to see what was happening, I cracked open a shuttered window. Some of the men ran about frantically, while others lashed themselves to any stable part of the ship and held on for dear life. My shredded tent somersaulted across the deck. I watched it crash into the sea.

Lucio stood still in the midst of it all, feet planted to the floor as if they had roots, hands gripping the giant wheel, steering the ship like some ancient Viking hero. The gale whipped wildly at his hair, and lightning crashed behind him against a dark indigo sky, illuminating him with legendary power.

In the midst of it all, he wore an easy smile.

The gust threatened to yank the window from my grasp, so I snapped it shut and fastened the latch. I sat back against the bed and held tight to the post. I now understood the secret hidden deep in Lucio's eyes. He was as powerful as the ocean, as violent as the storm. He was somehow too massive, too compelling for everyday life. He was as fierce as the wind, as unrelenting as the waves, as brutal as the lightning.

I clung tight to the bedpost and prayed for mercy.

The worst of the weather was short lived. Afterwards, I made my way back to the window and looked outside. The sailors were on their feet now, cleaning up and repairing damages. The pilot was back at the helm. I didn't see Lucio. I rather felt his eyes boring into me, and turned my head to meet his stare. He shoved a handful of ropes toward a sailor and barked an order. He walked toward the cabin now.

Mercy had not come at all.

I pulled the window shut as he strode through the door. He caught me in his arms and ravished my lips with his mouth. I tried to push him away but never stood a chance. "Lucio, no." I shouted against his lips.

"Why not?" he said without backing away. He caught my bottom lip between his teeth and let it slip through, making it hard to think of an answer and even harder to verbalize one. His tongue invaded my mouth, complicating the situation further.

I managed to get out the single word. "Giovanni."

"You are not married yet. And don't pretend for one moment you feel for that shopkeeper one tenth of what you feel for me. So, I'm going to need a much better answer than that. Why not?" Lucio returned to his sensuous assault, this time traveling from my mouth to kiss my cheeks, my eyes, my neck.

Why not? *"Perche non?"* He spoke the words in Italian, and they echoed through my mind.

This thing with Lucio could not be love. I would never abandon Giovanni for this, and yet, surely he would not begrudge me one last indulgence. Giovanni would understand. He would forgive. I was no blushing virgin. Yet, never once had I consummated a passionate exchange with a man I truly desired. And, oh, how I desired Lucio. I needed this. I needed it, and more than that, I deserved it. I deserved it just this once before I vowed myself into a life of domesticity in Giovanni's very proper and religious Florentine home.

And where was God in all of this? Hadn't I so recently decided to make Him the center of all my choices?

But wasn't God everywhere? Wasn't it He who made the moonlight and the saltwater, who unleashed the fury of the storm? Wasn't it He who placed this molten blood in my veins? Hadn't He faced every temptation known to man? Surely then He knew. I struggled to convince myself. Surely He understood.

This one night is more than I can bear, I told myself, although I knew the scriptures said otherwise.

Just this one night, I thought. *Appena questa una notte.*

Just this one night, I said to myself as Lucio's fingers undid the ties at my bodice. Just this one night, I thought as his hand slid up my thigh. Just this one night, I vowed to myself again and again, until Lucio's hot mouth drove every last thought away.

I woke confused in a bed that was not my own. I jumped up with a start, clasping the scratchy blanket to my chest. Lucio was nowhere to be found, but what about Giovanni? Then I remembered the tattered shreds of my tent flailing through the wind and into the churning water. Surely Giovanni would expect me to be safe within the captain's cabin, but the fact made me feel no better about facing him after the torrid night spent in Lucio's arms.

I threw on my clothing and stepped out on deck. It was too late to hide anything from Lucio's sailors. I heard a few muffled snickers and saw a shy young boy look down at his toes as I emerged.

Lucio ran to greet me as if he hadn't a care in the world. He reached to embrace me, but I ducked away.

Instead, he ushered me by the elbow to the bow of the ship. "There's nothing to worry about. Giovanni's recovering, but he won't come up for hours yet. My men won't say a word. That would be nothing short of treason, and I've killed for less. Here, Giovanni sent you this note."

He handed me the scrap of paper, and I scanned it. Giovanni begged me not to come below. He swore he was on the mend and would be joining me soon. It sounded like Giovanni, always putting the welfare of others before his own.

I would not put up any fight today. Between the horror of the hull and the horror of facing Giovanni after betraying him with the first handsome man to come along, I was more than happy to stay on deck.

"All right." I handed the note to Lucio and walked away, but nothing could have been farther from all right.

I went back to the little area where my tent stood yesterday. Fortunately, I packed my book, finished dresses, and sewing supplies into my heavy trunk before the storm. It must have pitched about during the worst of it, but today it sat as it should. The tedium of stitching would be good for me. I had so much to think about, so much to sort out.

Hours later I realized I had sat there in a daze for most of the day with no more clarity than I had in the morning. Giovanni remained below deck. Lucio reported he and Roberto seemed to be coming down with something upon the heels of their seasickness. He assured me the crew's physician would take excellent care of them.

I thanked him and resumed my sewing with my mind still numb. I couldn't think, wouldn't think. I had no desire to reflect on the choices I had made or the choices I must make in their devastating wake.

That evening at suppertime Lucio returned and squatted down beside me. He took the dress out of my hands. "This is quite beautiful, Dandelion. The craftsmanship is excellent, but I see nothing here as mesmerizing as you've made it seem today."

I looked up at him. I could think of no quick retort, no witty comeback.

He spoke again. "Come and eat with me in my quarters. The physician says this thing with Giovanni could take days to run its course. You can't sit out here alone indefinitely."

He did not mention my missing tent. Both of us knew full well I would not be needing it. He hopped up and returned my sewing to the chest. When he reached for my hand, I gave it to him willingly, without a single word of protest. Denying him now would not make last night go away. When he pulled me toward his cabin, I followed meekly like a lamb to the slaughter.

Chapter 32

Half a week later I stood at the bow of the *Alessia* overlooking the sea in the same dazed state. Lucio was an inebriating wine, and I was already addicted. No man ever sent me soaring to the pinnacles of ecstasy and crashing back down like Lucio. It occurred to me God was being truly unfair when he designed this man, for what woman could resist his magnetism, his power, his ideal form? He was a living, breathing temptation if ever one existed.

The fiery orange daybreak was gorgeous as we sailed toward it. After the first week on the open sea I could sometimes spy the shore to the east as we looped around the Iberian Peninsula, but today I could spot it on both sides. We traveled through a narrow strait. To the north of us was Europe and to the south lay Africa.

Africa! The land of the long-nosed elephants. I never dreamed of seeing such a place, even as a shadow on the horizon. I longed for Lucio to steer the ship off course and let me set foot on the exotic continent, but I restrained myself from making the ridiculous request. What an amazing life he lived—out on the open sea, trotting about the world at will.

Sunlight glinted off the jeweled combs I held in my hand. I was afraid to slide them into my hair. Lucio gave them to me last night as we lay in bed, drunk on love. The combs themselves were made of bronze and shaped in a pattern of three arches. Each was inlaid with a mesmerizing swirl that changed colors with the light. Mother of pearl, Lucio called the rippling substance. The pinnacle of each arch was inset with one perfect, sparkling diamond. Lucio said he purchased them in Africa three years earlier, knowing that when he found a woman worthy of wearing them, he would have found a woman worthy of keeping for his own.

To slide them into my hair now would be to acknowledge I had given in, to acknowledge I was indeed his for the keeping. I was not at all ready to take that enormous step. Yet I did not refuse the combs. Taking them into my hands, I caressed them and marveled at them. Somehow, they represented the sea and all its splendor. They represented its beauty and grace—the pathways it opened to the wonders of the world. They represented its strength and vitality.

They represented its human incarnation in Lucio Bartello.

Which brought me back to a question he asked last week. That question haunted me every waking moment since. *Can I be a respectable merchant's wife?* My feelings for Giovanni had not altered, but they were eclipsed by the passion I shared with Lucio.

I should have gone to Giovanni long before now. My poor, beloved fiancé was sick with fever below board, and I'd offered him nothing more than a few jotted notes sent through the wiry little ship's physician. I swear I would have braved my fears to see Giovanni by now; it was my overwhelming guilt and confusion I could not overcome.

What is love? The second question haunted me on the heels of the first. Was love the companionable comfort I felt with Giovanni? Was it trust and safety? Was it security and belonging? Was it familiarity and understanding? Surely I had all of those with Giovanni. Why couldn't that be enough? He'd been my closest friend in the world for years, and I felt sufficient attraction to hope it may grow into something more.

But is that love? In light of my feelings for Lucio, I couldn't help but think it was not. My feelings for Lucio were a tempest, a whirlwind, a roaring fire. They were all consuming, irresistible, overwhelming. Knowing what I knew now, could I tie myself to Giovanni in good conscious?

True, I was yet unmarried, but would a piece of parchment keep me from falling into this temptation next time around? Perhaps powerful feelings were needed to hold a marriage together. Could I swear to be faithful without them? Perhaps next time I would see the signs earlier and resist. Perhaps I would grow to love Giovanni in a way that would give me the strength I needed.

Perhaps . . . but I never had a chance to finish the thought. I heard a loud splash from the port side of the ship. It somehow called out to me, oddly poignant in its pitch. I hurried toward it and arrived in time to see the human form, bound tight in canvas and rope, dipping beneath the surface of the water.

I froze, glued to the floor boards, unable to speak, unable to breathe, unable to move. Lucio threw overboard a chest and some bedding, then he stared over the side of the ship with a sincere expression of sadness. This was not a sea captain punishing a mutinous crew, nor was it a pirate in the throes of murder.

That could mean only one thing—someone had died.

These thoughts came to me slowly, one by one, as I remained a statue looking out at the sea. The next thoughts didn't want to come. They were too horrific, too unjust, far too final to emerge.

"I'm so sorry, Dandelion. We did all we could, but Roberto took a turn for the worse during the night." Lucio came to me, pulling my rigid form into his arms.

I melted and the tears flowed. It wasn't Giovanni.

"We thought it best to bury him at sea before the infection spread." Lucio rubbed my back before he spoke the next chilling words. "Giovanni is not long for this world, my sweet."

I gasped against his chest.

"I know it is a shock. We fully expected them to recover, but now we fear this is the horrid plague sweeping through the Far East. We heard tales of it in Crimea. The signs were the same—shallow breathing, pale as death, and a huge lump on the neck, speckled with dreadful black spots."

"I should go to him. I must . . . ."

Even as nightmare images of the hull flashed through my mind, Lucio interrupted. "No, Dandelion. It's out of the question. This plague is near surely fatal, and it spreads like wildfire. The physician insists Giovanni be isolated."

"Oh, but I thought . . . ." Did it even matter now? I should have done something. I should have been there with him. Once again I realized I was the worst sort of faithless wench. I betrayed William, I betrayed Gottfried, and now I betrayed Giovanni, as well. I thought I might yet redeem myself, that I might yet turn from my wickedness and fulfill my promise, but it was too late. All the questions I'd struggled with moments ago no longer mattered.

Lucio pulled back to study my face. He took my hands in his and noticed the combs still clutched there. He swept them from my grasp and slipped them into my hair at each temple.

"Not much to work with," I mumbled to myself as I surveyed the supper supplies—dried meat, a few colorless root vegetables. I tossed them into a boiling pot of water over the fire in the hearth.

Lucio's wooden cabin with its display of maps was my new permanent residence, my trunk finding its way there the very afternoon of Roberto's death. I could not keel haul or jib, row or swab floors, weigh anchor, or whatever tasks sailors performed. So, I took care of Lucio and his home as I would a husband—cooking and cleaning, tending his clothes. To myself, I continued to mourn Roberto's death and Giovanni's eminent demise, but I daren't let Lucio see. I had moped about the ship during the week of Roberto's loss, but only until Lucio sickened of it.

"Enough is enough, Dandelion," he said to me right in front of his crewmembers. "If I have to look at that ugly, pitiful face of yours for one more moment, I swear I shall pick you up and hoist you overboard. It disgusts me."

I pressed down my anger and rallied, unable to stand the thought of Lucio finding me ugly. Whatever guilt and questions remained, I brushed them from my mind and focused upon pleasing Lucio.

I learned all I could about him. His grandfather owned the ship we were on, along with a small fleet. I always thought him uncommonly young for a captain. He was a mere twenty-eight years old, but he commanded men twice his age. His mother was the only surviving child of her family, and he her oldest son. His grandfather adored him and planned to leave him everything someday. No wonder the arrogance, the sense of entitlement about him.

Lucio had stowed away on his grandfather's ship when he was but a boy of ten and lived on the sea ever since. He may have gotten his ship by birthright, indeed it was named for his own mother, but he kept it by being an excellent captain and demanding the best of his crew. I hoped he would value my hard work as well, but he showed no appreciation. He was a busy man, I reasoned. Why should I expect him to notice I cared for his needs instead of some novice sailor?

He burst into the cabin at that very moment, and I realized the soup had scorched and bubbled over while I daydreamed of him. "For heaven's sake, Dandelion. Have you straw for brains? How hard is it to properly cook a kettle of stew?" He lifted the lid and turned his head in disgust. "What an idiot I've gotten myself. My Lord, I think I shall vomit. Get it out of here. I can't abide the smell."

"That's entirely unfair. I've been caring for you for days with not so much as a word of thanks or a grateful smile. Now I make one small mistake and you rant and rave and call me names."

He lifted the pot from the fire and swung it in my direction. "This is my ship. How dare you speak to me so? Of course you are caring for the place. I would think you a complete sluggard otherwise. You live here now. Would you prefer I put you below deck as Giovanni arranged?"

"No I . . . I . . . ." I looked down at my hands.

"I shall leave you to think long and hard about this, you ungrateful little . . . ." I missed his choice of expletive, as he slammed the door behind him.

Lucio did not return to the cabin that night. I barely slept. By morning I was so miserable I ached. When I opened the door, he stood nearby but didn't even look my way. I ran toward him calling his name, "Lucio! Lucio!"

He turned to glare at me, but the instant he saw tears streaming down my face he melted and took me into his arms. Lifting me up, he carried me back to his quarters.

"I'm so sorry. I'll be better, I swear it. I'll do better. Just please, don't ever leave me again."

"Shh. None of that matters now." He quieted me with his kisses, and all was well in the world once again.

He never did say he was sorry, but merely having him back in my arms was apology enough. Wasn't he right, after all? He captained this ship. Who was I to oppose his authority? It would set a dangerous precedent. He was Captain Lucio Bartello. More than that, he was Thor, the god of thunder. He was Triton, all-powerful god of the sea. His entire crew knew it was true. Who was I to question him?

"What is to become of me, Lucio?" I couldn't help but ask one night as we lay in bed. We now passed close to Sicily and would soon be traveling around the heel of Italy's boot and north toward San Marino, the closest port to Florence. Despite Giovanni's impending death, there was still a small fortune of cargo to be delivered there. Even if by some miracle he did survive, there would be nothing but a limp shell of the old Giovanni to turn over along with the goods. "Whatever shall I do when we arrive in San Marino? I'm not even certain they know about me."

Lucio rested with both arms propped behind his head. "I could dress you up in one of those fancy gowns and walk directly to his family and say, 'Good afternoon, this is Dame Mullens, Giovanni's fiancée. He died of a horrible shipboard illness, but she was otherwise occupied making love to me, thus remains fine and plans to inherit his fortune.'"

I threw a pillow at his face. "You are needlessly cruel sometimes, Lucio. He is not dead yet, and I have no intention of asking for his fortune, but truly, I don't know what I shall do next. I don't know where I should go. What if they are expecting me?"

"If it comes up, I shall say you died along with Roberto."

It was an appropriate answer. Capable and dowdy Dame Mullens, the woman Giovanni proposed to in London, was long dead by now.

He reached over to stroke my cheek. "Stay here aboard the *Alessia* where you belong. I can hardly do without you now, can I? We are two of a kind—wild and lusty and heathen to the core."

I pushed his hand away. "I wish you would stop saying that. I'm only a heathen when I'm with you."

"Please." He reclined back on his pillow again. "Surely you jest, with your seductive dances and erotic poetry. You love the sea and the storm and the winds every bit as much as I. You worship with me at their pagan altars each and every day."

I sat up and looked out the window at the sparkling night sky. "No, Lucio, you are the pagan. I worship the God who created those things. I only hope He can forgive me."

"Forgive you, forgive you for loving me? Why not forgive you for breathing, my sweet?" He swooped me into his arms atop of him.

I did not resist this time. My traitorous body responded to his passionate embrace despite my anger. "So am I to stay aboard this ship and live in sin with you forever?"

"Perhaps, or perhaps I shall marry you someday. My family has been demanding an heir for years. They've all but given up on me. My mother would like you. She's a religious woman, as well. Let's see if you can produce me a strapping boy to bring home to them. Then I suppose I shall have to marry you."

"And what if I don't? What if you tire of me?"

He leaned up to kiss me on the tip of my nose. "Well then, my sweet, I shall simply throw you to the sharks."

I frowned at him. I wished I could be sure he was joking.

Chapter 33

Giovanni surprised us all by surviving the trip to San Marino. I was even more shocked when I looked out the cabin window and saw him stumbling up the stairs, assisted by two of his employees, on his own feet.

"Lucio, Giovanni is conscious."

Lucio looked up from the ship's log, rather unconcerned.

I leaned further out the window. "I must go to him. I must talk to him."

Lucio added a few more words to the log. "But we agreed to say you were dead, remember."

"We can't. It's not right. Besides, he might not believe it later. He might come after me."

That brought Lucio to his feet, and we both rushed out the door.

"Giovanni, Giovanni." I caught him halfway across the deck and looked into his foggy eyes. "Giovanni, I'm so sorry. I can't go with you. You deserve so much better than me."

He stared at me, confused. "I . . . I . . . who . . . ?"

"I am Dandelion. We were engaged to be married. Don't you remember me?" I spoke the words in English, not wanting to raise unwanted questions from his associates. Tears filled my eyes. This was not going well.

"Dandelion?"

He scanned the air above my head for answers.

Lucio approached and placed a supportive hand upon my back. I turned to shoot him a look of despair. His eyes locked onto mine, and I sank into their depths despite Giovanni and the weight of the moment.

When I turned back to Giovanni, it was as if the clouds had parted. "Dandelion—Dame Mullens. I am so sorry. I should have known better."

Indeed he should have known better than to get involved with the miserable likes of me. Certainly he was sorry. Surely he regretted everything, but I couldn't bring myself to speak the words. His eyes looked sad, yet sympathetic. He reached for my hand, took it in his own, and patted it. "It's all right, my dear. I understand."

No, I wanted to scream. *It's not all right. It's anything but all right.* But the words stuck in my throat.

"I so wanted you to meet Mother Maria." Then, the clouds rolled back over his eyes.

It made little sense to me, the last sentence slipping back into Italian as his mind slipped away.

He dropped my hand and turned back to the man on his right. "I'm so tired."

"I'm afraid we must get him to shore, Signorina." The Florentine was nearly as perplexed as his employer.

Lucio answered in my place. "Of course. I don't think he'll remember much of this later. If he asks about the . . . um . . . *woman* he brought aboard . . . ."

I turned in shock at the innuendo in time to see him raise a suggestive eyebrow my way.

He continued. "Be sure he knows she stayed behind with me of her own free will."

My face was steaming hot and surely bright red, but I managed to nod my agreement in their general direction.

"As you wish, Captain."

I watched three sets of feet shuffle toward the ladder, horrified by what I had done. Truly Giovanni did not deserve any of this. My stomach roiled. The tears in my eyes overflowed the rims and down my cheeks. I turned on instinct to the one place I should not, to the very source of my trouble.

Lucio gathered me in his arms and led me back to the privacy of his cabin.

The cabin was familiar territory for us. Lucio and I were enrapt in each other and rarely left it after dusk ever since that first night I meekly followed him to dinner. All problems faded the instant he closed his door to the world beyond. Who needed food or water when one could feast on love? During the day he captained the ship, but at night he was mine.

After I fell asleep in his arms, he would go outside to check on his ship before officially retiring for the evening. But on the night of Giovanni's departure, I could not sleep. Guilt crashed in upon me the moment Lucio walked out the door. I stared up at the wooden ceiling wide awake, as the ugly faces in their grain tormented me. Horrible, indicting thoughts threatened to drown me. I needed to escape.

The sailors played their instruments outside my door. Perhaps music might chase the guilt away. I donned my tunic and cloak and joined them under the stars. The air was balmy, the breeze clean and pure. It was the same song they played that first night I danced so wild and free. There was something about the tune I couldn't resist—the beat strong and lively, the melody unrestrained. I began to dance once again, twirling about the deck to the rhythm, throwing my guilt deep into the ocean, feeling giddy and light.

That is until Lucio jerked me by the arm and dragged me back to our cabin. At first I thought he was overcome by passion and unwilling to wait another moment, but one look at his face told me I was wrong, that I made a dreadful mistake and was about to pay for it.

He shoved me onto the bed. "You stupid strumpet. What are you thinking? Do you want my men to ravish you right there on the deck? Is that why you beg for it so? Never again, Dandelion. You shall stay in this cabin unless you are by my side."

"Lucio, that's silly. Your men respect you far too much. They would never dream of such a thing. You've slit throats for less." I rubbed my sore arm.

Lucio crossed to the window and fumed at his men. They scurried away from his glare as he slammed the shutters. "Ah, but Dandelion, some women are worth dying for. Surely you have discovered that by now. You did not see them salivating over you, and nobody knows better than I how easy it is to seduce you."

I squealed in outrage. "Then why don't you put me off at the next port and be done with the trouble?"

"Because I am doing the world a great service by keeping you hidden away aboard my ship. Lord knows you are far too beautiful for anybody's good. How many hearts have you broken along the way?" He crossed to the bed and leaned over me, trapping me against the mattress. "How many men have killed for you? How many have died?"

I wished to God it were farther from the truth, but memories of Henry's smashed skull, and the threats upon Richard's life flashed through my mind. I tried to hide my looks behind frumpy dresses and veils in London, and that had gotten me nowhere. Perhaps I was better off hiding aboard this ship for the rest of my life, or at least until I grew fat and wrinkled, but knowing my luck, that day would never come.

Lucio leaned over and kissed my lips. He crooned in my ear. "Don't look so glum *Dente di Leone*. I merely tease you. I keep you here because I can no longer live without your touch, without your smile . . . ." His kisses trailed down my neck and over my collarbone.

I offered a shy smile to the dark night. I would waste no more guilt on breaking my engagement. I freed Giovanni from a terrible burden. I never did deserve such a man. I would have ruined his life. In truth, Lucio saved him from a heartrending mistake. This ship was where I belonged. Lucio alone understood me, understood the depths of my wild heart and wanted me anyway. He thought me a fatal beauty. He couldn't live without me. What more could I possibly want?

"But you will stay in this cabin." He broke off the kisses and turned harsh again. "I wasn't teasing about that. You may come and sit outside by me while I'm at the helm."

And so it was decreed.

Hidden away in the cabin, my mind wandered even as my mouth continued to tell a story to my new companion, Christopho. He was the shy young boy who looked down at his toes the morning after the storm, a twelve year-old lad who missed his family terribly. They lived on the outskirts of Genoa in a poor neighborhood. Jobs were scarce, so he worked onboard the *Alessia* to help support them.

I was glad he had found honest work in relative safety. Christopho was now assigned to bring my food, run my errands, and escort me to Lucio at appointed times. Because of his age and his timid demeanor, Lucio judged him fit company for me.

Christopho and I spent much time together in the captain's cabin fashioned out of warm redwoods. Lucio's bed wore a beautiful silken quilt, purchased from the orient in a patchwork design of bold colors. Everywhere my eyes fell reminded me of Lucio. I surveyed his desk, his dining table, the wardrobe where he hung his clothes. Each carried memories that made me blush.

Last night as I sat upon his lap in the armchair, Lucio whispered in my ear. "I love you, my pretty little Dandelion." He said it in thickly accented English. It was the first time he spoke my native language to me, saving it, I supposed, for the special moment. I could live and die in Lucio's arms listening to his broken English and never ask for more.

Yet I did have more, I realized as I looked over at my new friend, Christopho. The boy with his dark hair and eyes reminded me of Tim at that age. In fact, Tim hadn't been much older the last time I'd seen him. Something in Christopho's mannerisms always brought Timothy to mind, as if I had my baby brother back again, reminding me I once planned to seek a better future for him.

I found much packed away in my trunk to amuse Christopho along the voyage. I read him stories and poems and taught him to play chess. The idea of play seemed a novelty to him, and I was thrilled to introduce it. Lucio fashioned a ball for me, and I taught Christopho a favorite game from my childhood in the afternoon out on the deck. Perhaps I might teach him to read and write in the days to come. I continued with today's story until Lucio burst in the room.

He looked at me with disdain. "Brush your hair, woman, you look a fright."

"Why? No one is allowed to see me anyway."

Lucio busied himself rifling through the papers at his desk. "I have to see you, and so does Christopho." He looked up and grimaced at the two of us lounging on the big bed. "For heaven's sake, Dandelion, he may be a lad, but a little decency is still in order. You treat him as some sort of eunuch, a pet slave from Africa."

"I treat him as I treated my younger brother." "He's the son of an indigent, so what then does that say about you?"

Little did he know.

Lucio shook his head and stomped away.

"Why do you let him speak to you so? He's inexcusably rude to you, miss," said Christopho. "You should run away when we come to shore."

"I'm not his prisoner."

"Then why do you stay?"

"I suppose I have been drugged by love." I closed the book and sat it on the bedside table.

"Then I shall pray love never finds me." Christopho made a face.

"Oh, it shall," I said rolling over wistfully. "Someday it shall."

"Drugged by love, aye." He crossed his arms with a huff. "I've seen what the opium tincture does to sailors. It can be good for surgery and saving lives, but it can lure you in and destroy you if you're not careful. It will suck the life out of you until there is nothing left."

"You're wise beyond your years, Christopho, but Lucio loves me as well, so it is different."

He picked up his ball and tossed it in the air a few times as he considered the thought. "The first mate says the only person Captain Bartello loves is himself."

I laughed. Christopho oft made me laugh. "Tell the first mate that people change."

"I highly doubt that," he said.

I laughed again.

"I still say when we arrive at the port you should pack up your bags and walk away." He tossed the ball at me.

I caught it and shook it at him. "But wouldn't you miss me? Who would play ball with you then?"

"Well, I hadn't thought of that. Perhaps I shall run away too. I miss my family ever so much."

"You shouldn't run away from your commitments." I tossed the ball back to him. "I thought you were a good churchgoing boy. You should know such things."

"So should you, if you'll forgive my saying so. This is no life for you, miss."

"But what would I do?" I threw my hands in the air. "I have no money, no place to go. Everything depended on Giovanni, and now he is gone. A fine pair we would make begging for our bread."

"You could always dance on the street corners. That would be sure to earn us some supper, and I can play the fiddle. Or, we could go to a nunnery." He tossed the ball up and clapped a few times before catching it.

"So, it comes back to that again, does it?"

"Pardon, miss?"

"Nothing. No, I'm hardly suited for a nunnery, and you may play the fiddle, but you do not own a fiddle." I playfully poked him in the belly. "This will work out for me. Never fear."

Christopho looked into my eyes with great sincerity. "I wish you wouldn't let him treat you so."

"It's just Lucio's way. He doesn't mean anything by it."

"I hope you are right, miss."

I hoped I was right, as well.

"Good afternoon to you, Mistress Bathsheba," Lucio said to me as he entered the room to check his navigation charts. I was glad to see him in a better mood, for it made life so much easier. He once again permitted me to roam the shipboard. I had paid my penance for my wanton dance in front of his sailors, and Christopho was never far from my side. Lucio trusted me more and more. I would be careful not to betray that trust.

"So I am Bathsheba today. Whatever happened to Salome? Has she been reprimanded and sent to her room, as well?"

"Yes, it seems Salome has been duly chastened, but I'm thinking she's been supplanted by Bathsheba—a woman whom men will stop at nothing to attain, a woman whom men will kill to possess." He walked out of the cabin, a wicked laugh trailing behind him.

What did he mean by that? It was the second time he brought it up. Was I being naïve? Roberto had died and Giovanni nearly so. Were they truly sick or was foul play involved? Why would he torture me? It was cruel and uncalled for, but that was typical of my captain. Perhaps he hadn't noticed the insinuation. Perhaps it was my imagination. Lucio may not be overly kind, but he was a respectable sea captain. Everyone said so. I banished the ridiculous thoughts from my mind.

Chapter 34

After eight weeks aboard the ship, my favorite perch was still leaning against the rail, looking out over the sea. Was it possible so little time had passed? It felt like a lifetime. I lost my betrothed and gained a lover. I viewed the shores of Africa and Italy. I visited my first foreign city of Trieste on Lucio's handsome arm. He showed me a beautiful Orthodox cathedral and took me to dinner at a lovely tavern, but the city itself was a disappointment. I don't know what I expected, some sort of enchanted world, I suppose. There were small architectural differences to be sure, and the people spoke a mixture of Italian and German. All in all, though, it looked much like London or Bath.

Lucio promised we would travel to Tripoli and Jerusalem come spring. They would be more like I imagined. According to Lucio, everything would be unconventional in those lands. There would be no grass that time of year, but palm trees and spiky cactus plants instead. He would take me on the mountains with snow-topped peaks in the summer, and we would travel on camels down a road where Jesus once walked. He would show me domed mosques with windows shaped to match. We would see veiled women and turbaned men. Everything would be as exotic as I wished.

I looked forward to it. More than that, though, I thrilled to hear Lucio speak of our future together so casually yet with such certainty. I turned from the sea to watch him at the helm. He was as beautiful as the Mediterranean. I could stand and gaze at him all day.

"Enjoy him now, miss, for he's not so pleasant close up." Christopho sat on the deck beside me, practicing writing his letters.

"Wise beyond your years, Christopho."

He squinted up against the sun to better examine my face. "So the drug has not yet worn off."

"No, I'm afraid it hasn't." My nights with Lucio were still blissful. It was during the day when he was caught in the business of being "Captain Bartello" that he tended to be cruel.

Christopho shook his head. "It's an illusion. If you would get away from him for a while, you would be able to judge things more clearly. You should see the men when forced to quit the opium tincture. They shake and sweat and shiver in their beds for days in utter misery, but it's the only way to stop. You must stay away from it entirely."

Away from it—from Lucio, never! I ached for his touch, his scent even at this distance. Just last night Lucio had massaged my skin with sandalwood oil from Egypt, as if I were an empress and he my personal slave. I could not explain this to Christopho, so I did not even try. "Why ever would I want to go through all the pain?"

"Because the longer you are locked to the drug, the longer it takes to overcome. Eventually it will kill you altogether."

I pushed my windblown hair out of my face and gazed at Lucio in a new light. There was far too much truth to Christopho's analogy.

He put down his book and stood beside me. "One more week, and we'll be back to Genoa. We could get help. Keep it in mind. I'm certain deep inside you long to be a better person than this."

I felt an unexpected tear spring into my eye. "A nun perhaps?"

"Why not? You told me yourself Giovanni's sister fascinated you. Nuns are incredibly forgiving. You could go to her."

"I should never have read those poems to you. You're starting to know me too well." I hadn't thought of that before, actually.

What was it Giovanni had said? *I so wanted you to meet Mother Maria.*

It didn't matter, though. That was water passed under the bridge. I was a woman adrift, both metaphorically and physically. There was nothing left for me in London or Arun Village, and no longer anything for me to look forward to in Florence. Lucio was all I had these days. Yet Christopho was right, sometimes his cruelty went too far.

"I'm glad you read the poems to me. They were beautiful," Christopho said. "They show a whole different side of God that I never saw before."

"You're a good boy, Christopho. Perhaps it is you who should join the church."

He waved his hand across the horizon. "I have all the church I need out here on the open sea."

"So then you do love it after all?"

"Yes, I miss my family sometimes, but I do love it. I think it is the life for me."

I examined the heavens above me. "The captain says I'm a heathen because I worship the sun and the sea and the sky."

"Why should that make you a heathen, miss, for didn't God create them all?"

I turned toward Christopho's probing gaze. "That's precisely what I said. I don't know, though. I do not worship the gods of the air, but I'm afraid I've been all too quick to bow down before the altar of Lucio Bartello."

He placed his hand over mine. "Like I said, deep down you long for something better."

"But I'm afraid it's very deep these days, Christopho."

"You'll find your way, miss. I have faith in you."

I was cutting vegetables for supper at the table in the cabin, when Lucio's razor-sharp knife slipped and sliced into my finger. A dark red line formed upon my skin. I grabbed it to me and pinched it in my apron before the blood could flow in earnest.

"Christopho, Christopho, come quickly," I shouted through the window.

"What is it, miss?" he said, running into the cabin.

I showed him my finger. He found a clean cloth and wrapped it for me. Blood soaked through in an instant.

"Perhaps we should call the physician." I clutched my finger to my chest. "It seems quite bad."

"We don't have a physician, miss. I'll fetch Captain Bartello. He rinses wounds with seawater and presses against them until the bleeding stops. It should be fine. I didn't see through to the bone." He left to find Lucio.

My finger was forgotten as his words echoed in my mind. *We don't have a physician, miss.* What of the wiry little man who tended Giovanni and Roberto? I sought to remember his face. Who was he? Likely some random deck hand. Had anyone tended to Giovanni and Roberto at all, or had Lucio left them to suffer and rot? Had there even been a mysterious illness?

He lied to me before, but somehow this time it felt so much worse. Our entire relationship seemed based upon deceit. He may very well have murdered Roberto and poisoned Giovanni to keep me away from him. Lucio was a man who knew what he wanted and let nothing stand in his way.

What he wanted was me in his bed.

Even if he swore he hadn't done it, I would never be certain.

The very first night of the storm, did he know? Did he plan it? I remembered the note Giovanni sent me. Was it even in his handwriting? I was in such a haze that day. I couldn't picture it. I couldn't remember.

Lucio rushed in. "Christopho told me . . . are you all right? Look here. Let me see your eyes. That's good at least. They look normal, and your color is fine."

My finger, of course. I looked down. The cloth was soaked through, and blood puddled atop my dress.

"I need to stop the bleeding. Give me your hand. This may hurt for a moment." He squeezed my finger with one hand and pressed hard against my wrist with the other. I didn't feel a thing.

"There's no physician on the ship," I said.

"Of course not, that would be a huge expense. I've had some basic medical training. I know what I'm doing."

"You told me the physician took care of Giovanni."

He looked at my face. "So that's what this is about. You needn't slice your finger to get the truth out of me. I'm not as stubborn as that. Good grief, you imbecile, you could have cut it off."

"You told me there was a physician." My lips trembled.

"Yes, and I also told you the disease was deadly and contagious. I would have said anything to keep you away from them," shouted Lucio.

"So then, who took care of them?"

He jerked away and raked his fingers through his hair, abandoning my wounded finger. "Dandelion . . . you don't seem to understand. We all could have died. You're a God-fearing woman. Accept this was God's will and be thankful Giovanni survived."

I shouted back at him, "I will not accept it. This was not God's will; it was Lucio's will. Every move, every breath on this ship is according to the will of the almighty Lucio Bartello, and I'm sick of it. You killed him. You killed Roberto as sure as if you slit his throat. You drugged Giovanni to keep me in your bed. Did you plan to murder him too? Was his survival merely an unfortunate accident? You villain!"

"I most certainly did not kill Roberto, and I did not poison Giovanni. It was the plague, I tell you. I was not about to risk my entire crew to make their last hours on earth a little easier."

"You should have told me." I hiccupped through my tears. "You shouldn't have lied. How could you? How could you, you selfish, arrogant pig?"

"See here now, woman, that's quite enough. This ship is my domain. I will do as I please, and I will not be questioned by you or by anyone else." He paced before me, violence in every step.

"You blackguard. You murderer."

"Tread lightly, Dandelion, or you may be sleeping in that dead man's bed tonight."

"Better than with you." I spat the words at him.

Lucio took a long, deep breath, all the while clenching and unclenching his fists. "I should leave and give you some time to cool off, before that cut becomes the least of your injuries." He stormed out.

The bleeding of my finger had stopped, but what of the bleeding in my heart?

"I've brought the saltwater." Christopho was back. "Let me see your finger again."

"Christopho, when Signore Sabatini and his valet were sick, did anyone other than the captain see him?"

He poured water over the wound. "Yes, ma'am. I brought them food and water twice, and some of the other sailors, as well, but not after we spotted the plague signs."

I barely registered pain as the water soaked into the cut. "Did anyone other than the Captain see the lumps?"

He looked me straight in the eye to better read my thoughts. "He's bad, miss, but he's not that bad."

"So someone else did see him?"

"One of the deck hands tended Giovanni. I'm sure of it. Giovanni never could have survived otherwise."

Likely the same wiry man who passed himself off as the ship's physician.

Christopho took a deep breath and blew it out. He lifted my finger to wrap it with cloth. "Captain Bartello may be a ruthless scoundrel, but he takes his responsibility as captain very seriously."

"Thank you, Christopho. You've been ever so helpful," I said as he finished bandaging. "I think I should lie down."

"Yes, that's what Captain Bartello instructed."

I climbed onto the bed and closed my eyes. So perhaps Lucio was not a murderer, but he was ruthless and cruel, selfish, and arrogant. What in the world was I doing with him? How could I share my life with a man like that? Plan a future with him? Dream of marrying him, of carrying his children? What was wrong with me?

Maybe Christopho was correct. I needed to get away from Lucio. I could never fight this insane attraction while living on the same ship. It was a madness in my blood. I should take a lesson from yet a different Bible character and flee this temptation like Joseph.

There was that other danger, though—me, me and my blasted, beautiful face. I could never outrun that. Perhaps I should do humanity a favor as Lucio suggested and stay aboard this ship forever. Perhaps I was destined to be with Lucio. Perhaps we did deserve each other.

Somehow, there must have been a solution, but I had no clue what it could be. For the first time in my life, I got on my knees beside my bed and prayed.

I awoke early the day we pulled into the port of Genoa. I awoke with resolve and determination. Everything was clear—crisp like the cold November wind. A mere two days earlier Christopho begged me to reconsider and run away, but still I was not sure. It would serve Lucio right, I reasoned. He had made me sleep out in the freezing winds the night I berated him. My skin was still chapped and my nose still ran.

I bemoaned making this decision now, instead of while in San Marino close to Florence. Christopho, astounded by my lack of geographic knowledge, informed me that Genoa was nearly as close to the inland city of Florence as San Marino, merely on the other side of the peninsula. Still it was not enough to settle my mind. This morning, though, the port called to me loud and clear. The gracious Lord supplied the sign I needed, and I knew beyond a shadow of a doubt. I would leave the *Alessia* today.

Christopho entered with a tray smelling of bacon and found me packing only my favorite belongings in a light satchel. I knew not yet how I would travel to my destination, or even how far it might lie. The scent of the meat further sent my stomach to roiling.

"I'm so proud of you, miss. You'll not regret this, but I'm afraid there's a bit of a problem now." He sat down the tray.

My heart clutched. "What is it?"

"Captain Bartello decided to anchor far from land. You'll not be able to slip over the rail and swim ashore without notice."

I ceased my packing. "Why ever would he do that?"

"It's common enough, especially in the winter when the port is full."

"But still, we've always anchored close to land before."

Christopho shrugged. "I suppose it is an unusual choice for the captain."

He must know. Last night, something in my kisses, something in my touches gave me away. Lucio knew me better than I realized. "Well then, what shall I do, Christopho?"

"Let me think for a moment. I'm good at devising plans."

We schemed for a few moments, like I had as a child back in Robin Hood's merry band of thieves.

Then I winced and clutched my head. "This is ridiculous. I'll not go slinking off this ship like some sort of criminal. I shall walk off with my head held high, and Lucio himself shall row me to shore if I so choose."

"What about me?" Christopho picked at some imaginary lint on the quilt.

I wrapped his hand in both of mine. "You shall come with me and visit your family for a few days and then return to the ship as you should."

"Do you truly think it will work?" He looked up with hope.

"Yes, I do. I am resolved, Christopho. I am leaving today, and nothing Lucio can say shall stop me." I gave his hand a firm shake.

And so, when the first boat of cargo was being loaded to row ashore, I stood at the rail with satchel in hand waiting to get aboard.

"What is this, Dandelion?" Lucio called up at me from the smaller vessel.

"I am going to shore." I tossed my satchel to him.

"You've somewhere to go?" He placed it on the floor without tipping the boat an inch. "Have you decided to declare yourself to my parents on your own? You needn't take your bags, for even I shall be sleeping aboard ship."

I hoisted myself up on the rail and draped my feet along the outside of the ship. "In fact, I do have somewhere to go—to Christopho's family, not yours. I shall be needing my bags because I won't be returning to this ship—ever."

Lucio gripped his hands upon his hips. "I hope you aren't expecting me to stop you, for you will be sadly disappointed."

I climbed down the rope ladder. The boat bobbed beneath my feet as the sailors helped me into it. Looking Lucio straight in the face, I said, "No, in fact I was hoping you would not try to stop me, but I'm prepared to fight you if I must."

"Fight me? Please, you will be crawling on your belly and kissing my feet by nightfall."

I picked up my bag and sat upon a cross plank. "Think what you like, Lucio."

"Do you have any idea what sort of rat-infested hovel his family lives in?" Lucio gestured to Christopho, who nimbly made his way down the ladder. "Besides, we both know full well you will never again be able to live without me. You are worthless without me at your side, you pathetic little harlot. You haven't the strength to survive on your own. Giovanni will never take you back. Surely he's glad to be saved from a conniving strumpet like you. I'm the only thing worth a single farthing in your life. No one else will ever put up with your wanton ways. You should be falling to your knees and thanking the good Lord for bringing me into your life."

I clung tight to my satchel. "Think what you like, Lucio. I'm leaving."

At last he looked shaken, but he retained his pride. "Do as you please, you fool." He pointed at Christopho. "But he belongs to me."

I slipped the combs from my hair, running my fingers over the glistening mother of pearl one last time. "Fine, then, these should more than pay for several days of his indenture." I handed them to Lucio. "Christopho will be visiting his family during that time. He misses them terribly, but he shall return to fulfill his commitments. Christopho is a man of his word."

Lucio glared at us both, then turned his back and barked the command to row toward shore.

Once on land in Genoa, Christopho and I began our long trek to his home upon a dusty road. We were quiet, each of us lost in our own thoughts. After much walking, my feet felt heavy, but my heart felt light. Every step took me further from Lucio and closer to my new destiny.

Christopho broke the silence. "Why did you do it, miss? Why did you give him the jewels?"

My aching feet kept moving forward. "Because you are worth it."

"But they cost a fortune. I'm little more than a peasant, not worth nearly so much. I could have waited to see my family."

That stopped me in my tracks. I cocked my head sideways. "The jeweled combs were his to begin with, Christopho, and now he has no excuse to come after either of us. Besides," I said cryptically, "I may have given him a small fortune, but I took from him something far more valuable."

He looked sidelong at me but did not say a word.

Chapter 35

Italy – 1334

"Can I help you?" A pretty, youthful face peeked through the bars. The cheerful girl wore a simple creamy tunic.

Thick tan stone walls surrounded the complex, but I was able to glimpse more women through the gate. I saw them at a distance— young women with quick energetic steps chasing after a lively group of children, old women sitting still and quiet on a bench, a woman pruning a bush with merry snips, and another one strumming a lute as she strolled past. Beneath a tree on a blanket sat a group sewing a quilt on this temperate winter day, and unless my eyes deceived me, yet another dangled upon a tree branch above their heads, deep in contemplation.

"Maggio tutto che entra nella gioia del ritrovamento." *May all who enter find joy,* read the arching words atop the gate, and despite the stoic black habits the nuns wore, it seemed they were true.

Yet I almost turned and ran away, my courage faltering at this very sight. I so wanted to do right for once in my life, yet wasn't sure I possessed the courage to face all I must bear within those walls. The compassionate eyes of the young woman peering through the bars bolstered my spirits.

I tossed caution to the wind and spoke. "Yes, I wish to see the Reverend Mother Maria Scholastica."

"Of course." She swung wide the gate. "May I offer you some refreshment while you wait?"

"That would be lovely." I gaped in awe as I entered the convent. This woman's world struck me as an anomaly, a paradise, a hidden haven from the world beyond the gates. I saw it, nay, more than saw it. I felt it the very moment my feet crossed over to the anointed soil. It was just what I needed, exactly what I wished for. If only by some miracle they would let me stay.

After spending a week with Christopho's family, I mustered the resolve to set forth on my journey. I sold the extra fabric intended for my Florentine wardrobe to pay for the trip. Christopho's father found a roaming band of players with whom I traveled. They performed wonderful mystery and morality theatricals in every village we passed.

The young woman escorted me into the convent and toward a cozy parlor to await the Reverend Mother. She brought me a generous tray of bread and juice. All too soon, I heard a disembodied voice calling, "Yes, my child, you wished to speak with me."

With the distinct feeling of one walking to an execution, I approached the curtained metal grille full of guilt and shame.

"Do I know you, child?"

I knelt before the grille. "No, Reverend Mother. My name is Dandelion Dering, of Arun, England, but you would probably know me as Dame Mullens."

There was silence for a moment, then the grille swung aside. Mother Maria's habit covered all but her elegant face and hands. I was not in the least comforted by her pronounced bone structure and long straight nose. Her reserved features brought Giovanni to mind. When her eyes met mine, however, I felt at ease. They were Giovanni's as well. Deep brown eyes—warm, forgiving, and utterly accepting.

"Come in. Come in at once." She ushered me down the hall and gestured for me to sit across from her at a wooden table.

Tears filled those warm brown eyes. She gripped the table ledge before her. "We've been praying for you night and day. It took several weeks for Giovanni to find his right mind. The poor man did nothing but shake and sweat, and the doctors thought he might yet die. Once he came around, though, the first words out of his mouth were of you. He had a hazy memory of you and the sea captain together, but he still feared those sailors might have stolen you away."

Her kind words stung like a slap. Dear God, I wished they were true. I wanted to tell her all, to confess everything, but the explanation shriveled within my throat. She shouldn't be so caring. She was concerned about me . . . me, Dandelion Dering, the cottar's daughter. It was too much. I began to weep.

"What is it? Come to me, child."

I rushed to her side, falling to my knees and burying my face in my hands.

She reached out to touch my head, lightly as a blessing. "Was it so bad as all of that?"

"Oh please, Reverend Mother," I said through my tears, "please don't be so kind. I cannot bear it. I do not deserve it." Then I was overwhelmed and could say nothing at all for a long while.

She shushed me like a mother whispering to her child, "It's all right, dear. Let it out. That is why we're here."

"No, no, you don't understand. I don't deserve this. I have no right to feel better. I am the worst sort of faithless sinner. Once I tell you, you shall no doubt cast me from this holy place."

"That is not how it works, my dear. All have sinned and fallen short of God's glory. You are no different than any other woman who calls this convent home."

"Oh but I am, Mother. I am worse. I am so much worse I can hardly bear to tell you." But after a few more moments of bitter tears, the entire story poured forth.

I spared myself none of the vile details. I told her of Lucio, of my wanton behavior, of my betrayal. "I never did hear confirmation of this so-called plague, but the story you told me about Giovanni's recovery sounds remarkably like opium sickness. It's all my fault. It's—all—all—my—" I disintegrated back into sobs.

The Reverend Mother waited patiently, allowing me to spend my tears. She escorted me to the straight-backed chair across her desk before returning to her own. "Dandelion, I know this will be hard for you to accept right now, but I forgive you."

I looked up in wonder but rejected her words, my hands pushing them away. "No, don't. You can't forgive me. I betrayed your brother. He nearly died, and I did nothing to help him. A man lies at the bottom of the sea, and I may as well have thrown him there myself."

"That is not true. It is a lie from the devourer who seeks to destroy your soul. The important thing is that you are alive and safe."

"I shouldn't be alive. I don't deserve to live. I would trade my life for Roberto's in an instant. Why ever would God spare me and not him? I am the sinner." I clutched my head in my hands.

"He was ready to meet his maker, Dandelion. Perhaps you were not. God does not hold your sins against you, nor does Giovanni. Indeed he hoped you had fallen in love with the captain and weren't taken against your will. I'm sure he has forgiven you. In fact, you may find this difficult to believe, but I think he will blame himself."

"Blame himself." I bolted upright.

"He was thrilled you agreed to become his wife, but he felt guilty and selfish at the same time. He so wanted to care for you and show you the world, but he knew he was not being fair."

My sobs mellowed into sniffles. "Not fair?"

"He knew you did not love him in that way. He thought you had yet to truly find yourself, and he would only be preventing you. I'm sure he'll be glad to know that you are here and safe. He realizes now that he was not the right man for you. Do you feel the same way?"

I fidgeted in my seat. "Absolutely, but not for the reasons you might think. Dear Giovanni, I was never good enough for him. I hope he finds someone so much better than me."

"Your goodness is not in question, Dandelion, only your love."

Wringing my hands in my lap, I said, "In truth, I did not love him the way a wife should. But still, I was so evil, Mother. I decided in London that I wanted to please God. I wanted to follow His paths for my life. I was so inspired by your letters and those poems. How is it I failed so miserably? You may have forgiven me, but how shall I ever forgive myself?"

"Dandelion, you are but a babe in Christ. Shall a toddler berate himself for falling down when he attempts to walk?"

My continued fidgeting in the face of her serenity made me seem a babe indeed. Though her speech was eloquent, the essence was so simple—too simple, almost absurd. "But how can I do better the next time?"

"We can never be better on our own. You must learn to lean on Christ's strength."

"I don't know how to do that."

"It takes time, my dear."

"Oh, I see," I said, although I did not.

"You must give His word time to grow deep within you, and water it well with prayer. Let it soak in the sunlight of His presence."

I chuckled for the first time in our meeting.

"What is it, my child?"

"You are just as I imagined, Reverend Mother, too good to be true."

"Not nearly so good as you may think" Mother Maria hid her hands within the deep sleeves of her habit. "I suppose the question remaining is where you shall go from here. I'm sure Giovanni would be happy to pay your fare back to England, or we will help you find employment in Italy if you prefer."

I took a deep breath. "In fact, I wondered what would be required of me in order to stay here, Reverend Mother?"

"Here at the convent?" Surprise filled her voice.

I leaned forward. "Yes, I want to do all those things you mentioned. I want to be like you and those women I saw out in the courtyard."

"But, Dandelion, you needn't become a nun to serve God, nor even to learn more about Him. What makes you want to stay here?"

"I've been longing to be close to God for some time. I can't say for certain I've felt God's call to become a nun, but may I at least stay here for now?" I clutched my hands together like a prayer. "There is so much in this place I need. All I'm good for in the outside world is getting myself into trouble. I need to make a radical change, and this is the only way I can think of."

Mother Maria nodded. "One cannot move forward while running from the past, yet I think you do belong in this place. You need time to discover God's plan for your life. It may be to remain with us as a Holy Sister, or it may be to rejoin the world and glorify Him there."

"Well, before you welcome me, there is something else you must know, something which might change everything." I stood up and moved to the window, my stomach plummeting. I gazed out at the lovely convent.

"What is it, my dear? Have I not told you all have sinned?"

"Yes, but this is different." I paused to gather my thoughts and my courage. "I am carrying a child, Reverend Mother."

It was true. I knew my cycle was late, but it was the morning before we arrived at the port of Genoa that I vomited thrice in the chamber pot and noticed the swelling in my breasts. It was the sign for which I prayed. I was overwhelmed with love for the miniscule human in my womb. I would do anything to protect the babe, and I knew in a flash I could never allow selfish and cruel Lucio Bartello to be a part of my child's life. What I tolerated for myself, I would never tolerate for my baby. Christopho was the only one who knew, and I swore him to secrecy.

I turned back to look at Mother Maria. "I don't suppose there are many pregnant nuns about the place?"

She laughed outright, a merry laugh with no derision. "No, that would not be permissible. However, many young girls have come to us in such a state. You are free to stay as our guest. You may begin working and studying among us. It is a bit unusual, but not outside of our discretion to permit. However, the vows of a nun allow no worldly ties. Once the baby is born, if you do feel the call, we shall find a suitable family to adopt it."

I paced a few steps. "And if I do not feel the call? If I choose to keep the child?"

"Well, we shan't toss you to the street, but eventually you must choose, the child or the convent. Guest is but a state of limbo. You would find no fulfillment in that."

I returned to my seat and ducked my head. "And what if I choose neither? What if I'm not strong enough?"

Mother Maria narrowed one eye and studied me. "I doubt it will come to that. We try not to tell women what to do here, Dandelion. We've all faced far too much of that already. We only ask that you do your best to follow the plans God reveals to your heart. Trust him day by day. You needn't figure everything out right now."

Warmth flooded me. "Oh, how I would love to stay."

"Then we would love to have you. I will write Giovanni immediately."

I bit my bottom lip. "Perhaps I should see him."

"I think it's best if you settle in and focus on God for a while."

"Thank you, Mother Maria."

A novitiate escorted me to one of three large dormitories and assigned me to a small guest cell with only a bed, a row of pegs, and a small side table. Next door I heard whistling and left my unpacking to investigate. It was the inquisitive young woman who met me at the gate. She introduced herself as Agnesse. Her dark eyes glimmered from an impish, heart-shaped face surrounded by long black hair. Chirping like a songbird, she welcomed me with stories of life at the convent. The promise of a lasting friendship blossomed from a place I had not opened in a long time.

She was a guest as well, only eighteen and come just a week

earlier to escape marriage to an older man she did not love. Many of the women came here to outrun the dictates of their families, she whispered to me as I continued unpacking my few belongings.

"So you do not feel the call of God on your life?" I placed my hairbrush on the table.

Agnesse titled her head. "I didn't at first, but perhaps I am beginning to now. One can hardly help but feel it in this place."

It comforted me to learn I was not the only one to come to the convent uncertain of any great and supernatural "call" upon her life, that in fact this was a place of refuge for many of the women around me.

"What now?" I asked as I hung my empty sack upon the wall hooks.

"Well, you arrived during recreation time. Most of our day is far more structured. Next, you shall eat supper with me in the guest refectory. Be glad, for the sisters must dine in total silence, and their food is much plainer. Then we shall go to vespers. From vespers to morning mass the convent remains silent other than organized prayers. I suppose as guests we are permitted to whisper, but I would feel odd doing so. The sisters are so very reverent here."

"I'm not good at silence, but I shall do my best." I sat down on my bed beside her.

She patted the mattress. "Be glad you get a full night of sleep. The sisters shall rise every three hours for prayers."

"Hmm, and you think you may be starting to feel the call?"

"Ugh. Don't remind me."

We muted our giggles.

Before long we left the room for supper, and afterward Agnesse led me to the chapel. We crossed through a sculpted garden along our way. Even in the winter twilight I could picture it bursting forth with the first blooms of spring.

We entered an inviting building at the center of the complex. The simple chapel lacked any sense of architectural design. Only an iron cross adorned the top and signified its purpose. Yet it was imbued with its own special beauty.

As we walked inside, I spied a single stained glass window high above the altar, designed in a bright tree of life motif covered with colorful fruits. The other windows were shuttered with a thick candle illuminating each one. The flickering glow bounced off rough-hewn tan stones, filling them with undulating warmth. We passed by walls gracefully painted with biblical scenes from a female perspective—a dove descending upon a frightened but willing Mary, wise Deborah judging beneath a palm, Miriam dancing with a tambourine, David singing psalms with his harp to a flock of fluffy white sheep, the Lily of the Valley, the Rose of Sharon, a risen Jesus resplendent in His glory.

Spicy incense filled me like an inebriating wine.

I stopped and made the sign of the cross to Christ's symbol on the wall before taking my place in line beside Agnesse and the sisters of

232

this joyful convent. Although my long journey had ended, I somehow felt it had just begun.

Chapter 36

On a pleasant spring afternoon as I passed through the elegant sculpted gardens again, they were indeed bursting with colorful life as I imagined on the day of my arrival. Agnesse walked with me. We had finished our midday meal, and having a few moments to spare, we sat down on a comfortable bench surrounded by the sweet scent of rose blossoms.

Agnesse flounced her skirt. "I received a letter today from my brother, Anthony."

"How nice."

She turned her lip into a pretty pout. "I wish he would visit instead of write. What I wouldn't do to see a male right about now, even if he were my own brother. You should meet him, Dandelion."

"The ever-so-handsome Anthony? I doubt Reverend Mother would allow me within a hundred paces of him." I grimaced.

Her hands fluttered like a butterfly about her head. "No, no, Leonardo is the handsome one, almost prettily so. Anthony's been in too many fights to be truly handsome, although now that I think about it, he's still quite good looking. Heavens! All my brothers are handsome devils. Little wonder I didn't want to marry a middle-aged banker."

A nun cleared her throat in warning from a bench hidden by the bushes.

Agnesse lowered her voice but continued. "Truly, though, Anthony has the most charming friend, Dimitri. Why couldn't they have chosen Dimitri for me instead? I might be home planning a wedding at this very moment."

"Dimitri? Isn't he the one who gets Anthony into all those fights?" I clicked my tongue.

The bell rang for afternoon prayer. The older sister stood and walked toward the chapel, shooting us a disapproving eyebrow as she passed. Once she rounded the bend we dissolved into fits of giggles.

I wagged my finger at Agnesse. "Why, you are horrible. You shall get me into trouble one of these days."

She smiled and leaned back, tipping her head to enjoy the sunshine on her face.

We may jest, but we were growing accustomed to the spiritual rhythms of the convent. Morning mass was a beautiful ritual of prayer and consecration, the Latin words ringing so pure and true in this land of their birth. I enjoyed starting the day with God upon my mind and sealing it at vespers in songs and prayers. I never did so much praying in my entire life as I did in my first week at the convent. It took my knees a month to become accustomed to all the kneeling.

Other than their scheduled prayers, the rest of the day was spent in the nuns' chosen areas of service. Being a large convent, there were nearly as many duties within as outside its walls. Although obedience was expected, Reverend Mother Maria Scholastica generated an odd sense of grace and freedom, and a mystical reliance upon God's leading I never before dreamed possible. I was certain I would manage to muddle the system entirely. This afternoon, I planned to meet with Mother Maria to discuss my future.

"Mmm," said Agnesse after a moment's relaxation, "we haven't taken our vows yet. What's the harm in a little joking?"

"You can afford to talk that way, Agnesse, but truly, I should not."

My belly displayed to the world that I was no innocent. It was expected we live a holy life here at the convent, but in truth, spending so much time in worship and prayer made sinning rather uncomfortable.

"I must admit." Agnesse flipped her waving black tresses over her shoulder. "I sometimes wish your dashing sea captain would come for a visit. How romantic would that be?"

"Agnesse. Stop it this instant. Don't you dare wish for such a thing!"

Looking into my eyes, she saw the truth. "Oh, Dandelion. I'm so sorry. It was thoughtless of me to say." She closed her mouth, giving my mind a moment to wander.

During the first few weeks, I did struggle with thoughts of Lucio. He particularly haunted my dreams in the throes of defenseless sleep. I would find myself in that place between slumber and consciousness craving his touch once again. Of course, morning mass left me feeling chastened.

In time, though, just as my passion for Lucio once eclipsed my love for Giovanni, my passion for God overwhelmed every human encounter I ever knew. He showed me new heights, new pinnacles of ecstasy, pure and holy ecstasy, and left me tingling and glowing for days to come. It was as if God was inside of me, and then expanded until He was all around me, until, in fact, I was inside of Him.

Just yesterday afternoon during recreation I met with a group of sisters in the garden to spend more time worshipping God in a relaxed and spontaneous fashion. Singing songs from the Psalms and Revelation, our voices wove in intricate harmonies, accented by the trills of pipes and the mellow strands of harpsichords, until it seemed the angels descended to listen.

"Holy, holy, holy is the Lord God almighty. Heaven and earth are full of your glory. Hosanna in the highest. Blessed is He who comes in the name of the Lord. Hosanna in the highest." We gathered into circles and moved in praise as well.

We began with simple steps in unison, but as the music expanded and transcended the predictable chants and psalms, so did the dance. One by one we blossomed forth from the circle. I flowed in my own unique rhythm and pattern, unleashing the heavenlies within through my fingers and my feet. I offered a dance of praise before the very throne of God.

I danced not only before my Lord it seemed, but with Him. I did not worry if I was too wanton; such a word lost all meaning dancing with the divine. Safe within our cloistered convent, I expressed my heart in full measure.

"It's about time." Agnesse pulled me back from my musing. "We should get going, or I shall be late. I can hear Sister Theresa now. 'Those vegetables won't plant themselves.'" She held up her calloused palms for my inspection.

We stood and headed toward the chapel.

My calluses were on my fingertips. The most rigorous aspect of my training here at the convent was biblical transcription. Knowing I was skilled at Latin and had begun studying biblical texts with Giovanni, the Reverend Mother assigned me to transcribe at least three chapters a day, beginning in the New Testament. Writing the scriptures in one's own hand was of great importance. Not only did it help to better know God's word, it helped to preserve the Holy Book for future generations to come. Both my hands and my knees did much aching in my first days at the convent.

"Did you bring your poem to share with Mother Maria?" asked Agnesse.

"No, I felt shy."

"Why? It's one of the most beautiful things I've ever read. You certainly spent enough time writing it. You should be proud."

"Pride is a sin, Agnesse," I reminded her gently. Though, I must admit I was pleased with the results of my hard work.

I had learned so much from the creative sisters in the areas of poetry, music, and even art. I had first stumbled upon a collection of the nun's paintings in a back room of the library while searching out a manuscript. Unlike the simple biblical scenes in the chapel, these were quite visionary and mystical. A picture of a nude woman bathing in a pool of blood drew me, appearing almost pagan, but all the more stirring because of it.

Understanding dawned. Christ died for me, paid the price for my sin. Perhaps I too could be washed clean in His blood of forgiveness.

I bade Agnesse farewell and headed to Mother Maria.

Walking through the hallway to Mother Maria's study this time, a pleasant aura of anticipation surrounded me rather than a heavy weight of guilt and shame. I tapped on the doorframe, and she bade me enter. "Good morning, Reverend Mother." I dipped a curtsey.

"Good morning, my child." She seated us on two comfortable chairs in the sunshine of her open window. Heavenly sounds of the rehearsing choir drifted into the room. After some polite greetings, she inquired if I had any questions about what I'd been learning.

"Well, in fact, something has been plaguing me. I was reading a verse I found many years ago. 'Now faith is the substance of things hoped for, the evidence of things not seen.' I was wondering, can this scripture work even if our faith isn't in God, Reverend Mother? The first time I saw this verse, I teased my friend I did have faith and gave a long list of selfish wishes, things I dreamed of all my life. I spoke them like some ancient oracle. Then three years later—almost to the word—they came true. What does that mean? Was it faith? Was it evil—some sort of witchcraft?"

The Reverend Mother crossed her arms over her middle. "Let me ask you this—if you jumped off a rooftop, but didn't believe you would fall, what would happen?"

I thought before answering. "I would fall anyway, of course."

"I have found the laws of the spiritual world sometimes work independent of what we believe as well. You have stumbled upon the concept 'you will have what you say,' or put into other words, 'as a man thinks in his heart, so shall he be.' There are many more of these laws. 'Give and it shall be given unto you.' 'Do unto others as you would have them do unto you.' These concepts have found their way into many of the world's religions," she said.

My face must have shown my confusion.

She continued her patient explanation. "I've heard of a religion from the Far East with a concept much like our sowing and reaping, and another that encourages long hours in quiet meditation seeking to lose all desires, similar to our idea of dying to the flesh. Even the Moslems give alms and pray five times a day. Each of these religions has found some pieces of the truth."

I put my hand to my mouth. "Reverend Mother. I thought you were the consummate Catholic. Isn't that a bit scandalous? Do you even believe Christianity is the truth?"

She sat serene despite my shock. "I absolutely do, and yet, I'm not afraid to be a little bit scandalous. God and His Word are so vast. I think most people create their own much smaller version of God fitting what they choose to believe."

"Couldn't that sort of talk make a heretic of you?"

"I care only about pleasing my Heavenly Father."

Her comments gave me courage to ask another question I had wondered about for years. "Back in England I read some poetry written by a Moslem woman. She seemed so close to God, so passionately in love, so intimate. I felt jealous, until I came here and found it for myself. But still I wonder, if what I'm learning here is true, does that mean she could not have known God?"

"I don't think it has to mean that. Don't misunderstand, I do believe the shed blood of Christ is the only assurance we can have of salvation, and yet I wonder how many Christians have gone beyond that and actually met God."

I leaned forward toward her. "But the writer, Samia . . . do you think she may have met God? She wrote with the same passion as you yourself, Reverend Mother."

"I think anyone who fervently seeks after God will find Him. God has many ways of revealing Himself—through nature, through visions, through dreams, through intuition. It sounds like your poet may well have found God."

I opened my mouth to ask another question.

Mother Maria cut me off with the answer before I could even speak it. "But, I believe our Christian scriptures are the ultimate revelation of God. The roots of the Moslems are violent, as well as much of their fruit," said the Reverend Mother. "Our scriptures alone embody the entire truth and vastness of God's Being. The God of the Moslems may seem like ours upon the surface, but He is strikingly different in character. Jesus said, 'I am the way, the truth, and the life, no one comes to the Father except through me.' I wouldn't trade Christ's sacrifice for all the beautiful poetry in the world."

"So then, what of eternity?" I asked. "Will I see Samia in heaven someday?"

"Far be it from me to decide who does and does not deserve heaven." She smiled at the ridiculous notion. "At the end of the day, my dear, God judges the heart. I doubt this Samia would have rejected Christ had she the chance to discover Him. Some surprises may await us in heaven."

I pondered her words a moment. "Why don't they teach about this in church, this intimacy, this passion, this heartfelt relationship? It's what I've been searching for my whole life."

"People like simple formulas. Be baptized. Attend mass. Observe the sacraments." Mother Maria ticked off the steps with her eyes, although her hands remained still as usual. "They want a list to complete so they can get on with their lives."

"Well, that is true enough."

"They're babes, suckling the milk of the word of God. But milk alone will never satisfy your hunger, Dandelion, and that is why God brought you to us."

"Thank you, Mother." I folded my hands in my lap, attempting to mirror her stillness.

"So, my child, do you think this might be your calling—to be a poet, to put into words and song this intimacy you so desire?"

"I don't know yet. I think it must be 'a call' on my life, but is it 'The Call'? I'm not sure. I don't think God has spoken to me on this issue yet. I must admit, I'm terribly afraid I shall never hear His voice and wind up disturbing the balance of this lovely utopia."

"This place is not as fragile as you might think."

I remained uncertain but kept my opinion to myself.

"And how is the babe in your womb?"

"Growing, to be sure. I was tired at first, but seem to be regaining my strength. Truth be told, I almost forget the babe is there some days. It's easier that way." I resisted the urge to pat my belly.

"That shall not last for long. In a few more weeks it shall begin tumbling about and making its presence known." She gave a deep chuckle. "I hope you can find a way to treasure this time, Dandelion. You are bringing a fresh new soul into the world, no matter its origin. There shall be months when you will be the only person in the world to understand the secret you carry inside. You will get a sense of its personality long before anyone else is even aware it is an actual human being."

"I hadn't thought of it that way." I could neither ignore the babe nor my decision much longer.

It wasn't until I lay in bed that night replaying the conversation that it occurred to me Mother Maria knew far too much about pregnancy for a proper virgin nun. The notion gave me pause. What an unusual day. The meeting was not at all as I expected. I felt as if I were entering a new chapter in my stay at the convent.

Chapter 37

Surely enough, soon after my meeting with the Reverend Mother, I found myself loading into an old wagon on a warm spring day to go and minister to the needs of the poor. I wanted to stay far away from humanity, to keep hidden safe within these walls, but God was changing my desires.

Until now I sewed dresses for little girls as my charitable contribution. I made each special by embroidering a uniquely beautiful design upon the hem or the collar—butterflies, bumblebees, dragonflies, birds, flowers. Suddenly, I longed to meet the little girls who wore my dresses, poor little girls like I had once been. I longed to feed hungry mouths, to fill empty hands with bread.

The timing was odd, just as my belly became obvious. I hadn't even been sure I would be permitted, but Sister Ernesta, the nun in charge of charitable outreach, approved. She instructed me to wear loose dresses covered with an apron, and if anyone did notice, well it wasn't what people thought, but what God thought that mattered.

I mentioned my fear about my looks, but she smiled that sweet serene smile that was so common at the convent. "God has given you the gift of beauty, Dandelion. You must use it wisely, but you should not feel ashamed. Those children will take one look at your face, and they shall believe in angels for the rest of their lives."

It had been kind of her to say, but trepidation still overwhelmed me as I boarded the wagon and sat upon the soft hay to leave the convent for the first time in months. It helped that Agnesse came along and folded herself cross-legged beside me. After a lifetime in the city, Agnesse discovered a love for farming and spent most of her afternoons working in our community's large vegetable garden. This project of delivering food and clothing to the poor brought our interests together.

Agnesse's classical dark Italian looks overshadowed my golden-blonde prettiness. I hoped she might detract attention from me. I wore a wimple to cover my extravagant curling hair, but it did nothing to hide my face.

The only men I'd seen since late fall were the priests who came to perform mass and an occasional monk in burlap robes trading grain for our fruits and vegetables. I couldn't help but feel afraid. I was certain God placed this new desire in my heart, and yet I wasn't sure it was a wise plan, as I did not yet trust myself.

I shared my thoughts with Agnesse.

She slid closer in the wagon. "Well, you might not trust yourself, but it seems our Heavenly Father does. Besides, I've been told most men prefer their women with flat bellies."

I batted her on the shoulder for the comment.

"Seriously, Dandelion, there is something I must tell you." She whispered the words although no one appeared to be listening.

"What is it?"

She lowered her voice even further. "I have heard the call."

"Oh, Agnesse, I'm so happy for you." Instinct told me to offer a hug, but I restrained myself. Nuns reserved their affections for God, and Agnesse would soon become one. "Tell me how it happened."

"Well, I was working in the garden yesterday, and I heard my name as if it were whispered on the wind. 'Agnesse, Agnesse.' I looked around, but no one was there. 'Lord, is that you?' I asked. Then I heard it again, 'Agnesse, Agnesse, will you be mine?' I knew in that moment He was calling me to become His bride. I answered at once, 'Yes, Lord, I will, with all my heart.'"

"Goodness. What does it feel like?" We went over a rut in the road, and I grabbed a hold of the side of the wagon.

"I wish I could explain it. To be in love with love itself, why there are no words to capture that feeling. I thought myself in love a hundred times over with every handsome boy that came along, but this. How could I ever have been foolish enough to imagine those feelings love? I'm so happy, Dandelion, I might explode with it. I've never felt so happy. I can barely wait to take my vows."

"You shall still have a long novitiate period to go."

"Yes, but I hardly feel I need it. I've never been so sure of anything."

I saw the certainty in her eyes. "I'm so happy for you. I long for the day when I feel such assurance about my own future."

"Perhaps once the baby is born you shall hear the call as well. I hope so." She offered an encouraging smile.

We sat in silence for the rest of our trip. Agnesse would need to accustom herself to silence. Nuns spoke no frivolous words and devoted much of the day to quiet contemplation. She looked ready to undertake the task. Silence left one alone with one's own thoughts and with God.

More silence would benefit me as well.

The moment we arrived in the neglected little village, the needs of the poor consumed my mind. If a handsome farmer passed by, I did not notice. I could barely believe it as we rolled to a stop and the dingy peasants in the tattered tunics, so familiar to me, stretched their skeletal arms over the sides of the wagon. Their hungry eyes screamed out at me from within their worn leathery faces. A toothless mouth gaped at the stack of bread and vegetables. A child pushed past. Arms crowded in from every side, crisscrossing atop one another, empty hands clawing the air. I grabbed the food as fast as I could, filling those hands in desperation, hoping against hope to fill their empty eyes as well. A bunch of carrots, a loaf of bread, how could it ever be enough?

Helplessness washed over me. I began to shiver. I gasped for breath. My own hunger bellowed for me to fill yet more hands, feed yet more mouths, but all too soon, the wagon was empty.

As we bounced away in our merry little cart, a moan of disappointment taunted my ears, not a hearty wail, or an indignant cry, merely a heart-wrenching moan. Still shaking but now able to breathe, I wept for them, and for the dear little Dandelion too weak for tears.

Sister Ernesta climbed back to sit by me. "I'm sorry, dear. I know it's hard the first time. You must focus on the ones we were able to help and let go of the rest."

"But I can't. I can't, Sister Ernesta. I was one of those children. I don't think you understand. I don't think anyone at the convent understands. If they did they would surely drop their paintbrushes and their prayers and run directly to help those children in every way possible. We could do it, Sister Ernesta. I will talk to them."

"My sweet child, your heart is right, but your words are rash. We cannot fix the entire world. We can only be responsible for what God has called each of us to do and trust Him to take care of the rest."

"But did He not say to his disciples whatever you have done for the least of these you have done for me?" Tears streamed down my face.

"Yes, dear, and we've been about that business for hundreds of years, but we can only accomplish what He sets before us day by day." Sister Ernesta offered me a handkerchief from her huge sleeves.

I took it and dabbed my eyes. "But they were right before us, Sister. They were right before us with hands outstretched, and we turned them away."

"I know it's difficult to understand, my dear. Even if we worked day and night, we could never care for all the poor in our district, but maybe, just maybe our prayers will soften the hearts of their liege lords to lower their taxes and tend them. Those who work on transcriptions ensure these same needy people will have the rich heritage of God's Word to feed their spirits as we feed their bodies, not only today, but for generations to come."

"What of the artists? What of the musicians? I've wasted so much blasted time writing poems. I'm so ashamed. Whatever was I thinking, piping away on my foolish little flute while people are dying from starvation mere furlongs away?"

"Why, Dandelion, the arts provide food for our souls. So many nights I've gone home weary, exhausted to the very core of my bones and ready to give up, but the paintings and the songs, they renew me. They give us little pieces of God right here on earth."

I managed to cease my crying.

She took back her handkerchief and pushed it up her sleeve again. "My dear, we are all one body in Christ and each serves an important function. Each of us represents some facet of the Father."

My logical mind heard the truth of her words, but my long-broken heart could not accept it.

I sat under a shady tree one afternoon in early summer embroidering and still meditating upon I Corinthians 12, as Sister Ernesta had recommended. It helped, as did watching each of the sisters go about her daily tasks with love and devotion. My own pain and bad experiences did not serve to erase God's truth, and I would have to let them go and allow Him to heal my heart so I could better know and accept Him as He is. I winced to realize my thoughts sounded much like the pious words William once spouted at me. That's what comes of living in a nunnery, I told myself with a wry smile.

I had continued ministering to the poor until I became too heavy with child to be of any real help. It ended the day I nearly tipped off the wagon while reaching a loaf down toward a tiny boy. At least I could sew beautiful dresses for the girls, and I found much joy in doing so.

I wished I could say I found much joy in my pregnancy, as well. I put aside my sewing and encircled my womb for one of those brief treasured moments Mother Maria described, but no sooner did it come than reality crashed back in upon me. I still knew not what I planned to do with this child. I was learning to hear God's voice, but about the baby I could sense only a thick cloud of confusion. How could I allow myself to enjoy her when she may not even be mine? How could I face the world alone with her, hear her called a bastard? Could I find a job to care for her? I could never let her suffer as I had. Then again, how could I ever part with her?

I loved living at the convent. The questions that drove me my entire life seemed meaningless in these walls. Where shall I live? What shall I wear? Whom shall I marry? What title shall I hold? None of it mattered. In this place I could work the fields like a peasant and play the harp like a lady born all in a single day. What could possibly be more meaningful than loving, worshipping, and serving my creator? It would be so easy to settle in and take my vows, but would it be easy to watch someone else rear my beloved babe?

I did not think giving another woman the priceless gift of a child could satisfy the deep ache in my soul.

But was I being selfish? What if I returned to my old sinful paths? Oh, I was certain to mess this all up. Either way, my heart might break in two and never recover. It was the same endless cycle of thoughts, and it was easier not to think about her at all.

Instead I turned my thoughts to the very first time I had visited the convent near Arun Village. Even then that female domain had been a place of wonders. The Italian garden around me slowly melted away into the Sussex countryside as I hiked up the knoll with my childhood companions.

The kindly nuns welcomed William, Tim, Friar John, and me through the grille at the front gate of the convent. They ushered us inside, making an appropriate fuss over our generous gift of the deer slung across the friar's massive shoulders. Once it was deposited safely near the kitchen, we were led into a fancy room for greeting guests filled with soft, colorful furnishings. I had never before seen such a place.

There the Prioress met us warmly. "Brother John, what is this! Have you been out hunting again?"

"Me, no, no never. These youngsters here saved this deer from the very clutches of Satan. 'The wealth of the wicked is laid up for the righteous,' unless my Latin fails me," the friar answered with a wink.

"Why, William Ashby, look at you. How you've grown." She gave him an affectionate nod, but her hands remained clasped and hidden within her long black sleeves. "My, your mother must be proud of you, young man. How has your reading been going? Seems to me it's been quite a while since your mother has visited our library on your behalf."

"I've been awfully busy, ma'am, but it's coming along nicely I think. Thank you again for all of your help."

I shot him a look of shock and awe, but was too shy to say anything in front of all of these strangers. We passed a pleasant half hour with the sisters, chatting over milk and biscuits, a rare treat for Tim and me, but it wasn't until after the last farewell that the pressing question fairly burst from my mouth.

"William, can you truly read? Why didn't you ever tell us?"

"I don't know," he said sheepishly. "I suppose it just never came up."

My jaw dropped for a moment. "Reading, my heavens, that's astounding. How? When?"

William strolled down the path as if nothing were amiss. "In the evenings when my mother returns from the castle, she reads with me. It's difficult to bring up, you know. It's highly unusual."

"But how did she learn?" I turned to walk backwards, so I could better study his face while he spoke.

"My mother was reared by the sisters at the convent. You knew that."

I brushed over the subject of his mother. She had never much liked me. "But reading, William." I grabbed hold of his shoulders and stopped his progress. "I thought only the nobles could read."

Friar John came up behind us with Tim at his side. "Well, how do you like that? What about me, young lady? Where do you think I get all those fine sermons, if not from reading a book now and again? William has a point, though. Not everyone would look kindly upon a peasant family reading."

Friar John led us on our way down the path as he continued his speech. "Lady Worthing herself can do little more than write her name and look over the household accounts, and that spoiled son, George. Ruled by the flesh that one is, ruled by his own sinful desires. Won't keep his head on his shoulders for long. 'The price of sin is death,' as the holy book says. There is a hot and fiery—"

"But what about the older son, the new Lord Worthing?" I awaited the answer with dreamy-eyed expectation.

William glared at me.

Friar John, lost in the joy of his own voice, failed to notice. "Ahh, now young Thomas Worthing, he's a different story. Takes after his father, God rest his soul. 'Growing in wisdom and height and favor with God and man,' like our very own Lord. Such a waste, he's off campaigning in Scotland. I hear he was an incredible student, which gives me a thought." The priest paused for dramatic effect.

"What, what is it?" shouted Tim.

"Well, clearly you all have too much idle time, and truth be told, so do I. Perhaps I should tutor you boys. William, do you know Latin?"

William eyed him. "No, sir."

"Would you like to learn?"

William took a few more paces, considering his answer before he spoke. "Well, I've always wanted to read the scriptures firsthand."

Friar John startled us with a loud clap. "There, you see? A divine plan. I'll need a good man to take over this flock someday. Why, I could teach you sums, and we could work on your writing. What about you, Timmy, would you like to read?"

"Oh yes, sir, very much." Tim slipped his small hand into the Friar's huge one. "Do you have any books about Robin Hood, sir?"

"Well, I don't know about that." The friar smiled down at him. "But I imagine I could find some interesting stories for you."

"What about me, sir?" I rushed ahead to block his path and looked up expectantly. "I'm a quick learner."

"Merciful God in heaven, first peasants and now peasant girls. Why, I'll be burning at the stake before sunup." Friar John laughed at the outrageous suggestion. "Although, I suppose if you were watching over Tim, it wouldn't be my fault if you picked up a thing or two. I've kept my eye on the three of you for some time. There's something different about you. Some even say you have . . ." he dropped his voice to a whisper, " . . . fairy magic."

"Don't look at us." William held up his palms. "That's Dandy's specialty."

"Yeah," said Tim, "don't look at us. We're just the poachers."

I was lost in my own thoughts as the others laughed at our private joke. *I'm going to read. Miraculous. Why not walk on water?* I wagered not even our ancestor, the brave Saxon chieftain Dering, knew how to read. Unthinkable. Utterly ridiculous. I'd never even touched a book. Oh, how my fingers ached to get a hold of one, to be a part of the world of castles, furs, and silks, where people did magical things . . . like read.

I patted the tiny creature in my belly. I wanted to give my daughter that sort of magical life. And I did feel quite certain the child was a girl. The Reverend Mother was correct about knowing the babe's personality even before she was born, and to be certain, I never met a boy as stubborn and contrary as the little creature in my womb. Naturally, she was sleeping since I was busy at work. She would wait until late at night to tumble about like an acrobatic court jester.

I took my hand and removed her bony little heel from my rib, but she returned it with several sharp kicks to punish my bad behavior before settling back to sleep. At least I could be thankful she didn't have the hiccups as she did every morning during mass. They were so strong I kept waiting for someone to shush me.

This time was special, and it should be treasured. If only it did not fill me with such unease. I focused upon my meditations, driving those thoughts from my mind.

By June when I met with the Reverend Mother, my life had transformed nearly as much again as during the first three months.

"You're looking well," she said. "You must have given up on single-handedly feeding the whole of Italy, or you would not have that rosy glow to your cheeks."

"Yes, I'm not much help these days anyway. I suppose I shall have to serve the world with my needle and quill, after all."

"And how has your transcription been going?"

I tipped my head slightly. I was becoming skilled at the subtle gestures of the nuns. "Well, Mother, I feel I know you well enough now to speak the truth. I have come to the books of the Pentateuch. I must be honest. They are mind-numbingly boring. I don't know how much longer I shall be able to stand it. All those lists, all those numbers. Smear the blood, sprinkle the blood, rub the blood on your ears, burn the fat here, burn the flesh there. I swear I've written the same paragraph twenty times over. I keep thinking it must be some sort of prank, that at any moment the entire scriptorium will break into hysterics."

"Only twenty times over, then you must have a long way to go. No, it's no joke, dear, although your perspective is quite amusing." She raised one side of her mouth. "Believe it or not, some of our sisters love those books more than any others. They love the order, the reverence, the holiness of them."

I lifted my eyebrows. "Truly? I shall try to continue on with an open mind, but I can't imagine those being anyone's favorites."

"Have you ever seen a rainbow? Light hits the mist and the next thing we know shatters into a myriad of colors. God is light. Each of us sees the light, feels the light, but many relate to only one or two of His colors."

Typical Mother Maria. "I do believe someone wrote a poem to that effect." I couldn't hold back a giggle.

Her eyes glimmered at the jest. "Yes, these sort of things do seem to keep popping up. Don't they. Speaking of things popping up," she said looking at my enormous belly. "Have you been enjoying the baby?"

"It's difficult. I start to, and then I remember she may not be mine to keep."

"Yes, I understand, and once you see her, it will only get harder. Not much longer now I would guess by the look of you. Have you felt any pains yet?"

"No . . . ."

"What is it dear?"

"Well, you seem to know an awful lot about these things, Reverend Mother. Did you work as a nurse or a midwife at some point?" I tipped my head again.

She sat for a moment before looking into my questioning stare. "Is that truly what you think, Dandelion? Come, child. Ask me what you wish to ask."

"I can't. It is too ludicrous. I'm too embarrassed. It just seems . . . ."

"That I have been with child before." She spoke the words for me.

"I'm so sorry. I don't know why it should have occurred to me. I have such errant thoughts sometimes."

"It occurred to you because it's true."

"What? It is? Do the other sisters know?" I pressed my hands in my lap to keep them from flying about.

Her nod was nearly imperceptible. "The ones who have been around long enough do. We don't gossip here."

"And your child?"

"He was given to a wonderful God-fearing family who reared him as their own. He is a fine young man, studying to become a physician in Venice."

"How . . . however did it happen?"

Mother Maria smiled. "Oh, in the usual way, I suppose. No virgin birth here. There was a boy, a blacksmith's son. I fancied myself in love with him. I was arranged to marry a storeowner at the time. My father thought we should rush the wedding and try to cover things up. He even suggested I take a potion to rid myself of the baby. It was my mother who thought of sending me here, God bless her soul. Not many convents would have accepted me."

"But what about the blacksmith's son? Didn't you miss him?"

"Oh, for a few months I did. I believed I was in love, but in retrospect, I think it was more about defying my parents."

"That must have been hard."

"Most people considered it the lowest point of my life, but look where it has brought me." She cast her eyes about the room.

"Yes. I had a childhood sweetheart once," I said, my insides churning despite the peaceful environment. "We truly did love each other."

"And what happened to him?"

I looked down at my hands. "I suppose my sins were pride and greed. I didn't think him good enough." Wanting to change the subject, I chatted about my poems instead. In the back of my mind I kept thinking, by the next time we met, like it or not, I would be a mother.

Chapter 38

It was a hot day in mid-July when I first felt the painful tightening of labor. I was well tended by the nuns throughout my pregnancy, and the midwife came straightaway to my little cell with its tan stone walls to check on me. The pains were far apart and lasted for no more than a moment or so. I could fairly laugh my way through them. The midwife said when the baby was serious about making its entry into the world, it would no longer be a joking matter, and encouraged me to continue with my daily tasks.

My labor was not a quick one, and by early on the second morning, I knew what the midwife meant. I was tired from being woken so oft. Then with little warning the pains came one on top of the other— radiating pains starting in my back and working their way around my belly, where sharp talons threatened to tear my womb in two. Thrashing upon my bed, I sent Agnesse running to fetch the midwife once again.

The midwife stayed with me this time. She rubbed my back, making soft soothing noises. She claimed it was not so much pain but the feel of hard work.

Easy for a virgin nun to say.

When I could no longer withstand the pain, she told me it was time to push my baby into the world.

The pushing felt good, for I was able to exert myself toward speeding the process along. The midwife placed hot compresses on my bottom and applied counter-pressure to prevent tearing. The baby burst forth in a gush of life. I reached toward her instinctively, pulling her from the midwife's grasp.

I laughed then, laughed in ecstasy and hugged the sticky little bundle to me. I kissed her head and stroked her belly, and all the pain of the last hours faded from my mind.

I am a mum.

No wonder women did this again and again, suffered through the heartburn and the flatulence, the distended belly and the backaches, the hours of pains. Look what came at the end of it.

And look I did. I looked at her perfect little lips. I counted her tiny fingers, so long and thin I thought they might snap. I inspected the set of matching toes. I gazed into her deep and soulful eyes. She wailed furiously, yet I laughed joyously, almost hysterically the entire time.

The midwife washed the babe as I held her and examined her in my arms. "She's hungry, dear. Why don't you try feeding her? It will help along your healing process."

The first time those tender rosebud lips touched my breast, I gasped. It felt so odd, but the little creature knew what to do and before long was suckling contentedly. I never felt such a rush of emotion as I felt at the birth of this child. I accomplished this thing. I grew this perfect little being in my own body. I knew in that moment I would hold tight to her for all eternity and never let her go.

God help us both.

"Lily," I said without preamble.

"Pardon, my dear?" The midwife paused to look at me.

"Lily. Her name shall be Lily. I want her to feel pure and clean before her God as I have come to feel. It is she who brought me to this place."

Summer was nearly gone, I realized as I attempted to call the children to order. My, how it flew past, much like the wee ones dashing and squealing about the room. Working in the convent orphanage, I at last had the opportunity to try something I suspected I would be good at for many years.

Teaching.

Imparting to others the education that was so invaluable to me, teaching them reading and writing and arithmetic, it was as if I doled out priceless treasure each and every day, so much better than a mere dress or a loaf of bread. A dress could brighten a year of one's life, two at the most, a loaf of bread only a day, but an education could change one's entire destiny.

"Guiseppe, Katrina, sit down this instant." I gathered the unruly bunch into a circle and settled in a chair before them. The children were so innocent, so curious, so eager to learn. The older ones were my favorites, for they sat so nicely, and we could discuss my favorite topics of poetry, philosophy, and history, but these smaller children brimmed with vibrance and joy. I awoke each morning with a renewed sense of vigor and purpose, even if my physical body was tired from Lily's nighttime forays.

I peeked over my shoulder to where she now cooed and kicked her feet in a woven basket. In fact, she slept well for a newborn, waking only to eat and then drowsed or played quietly beside me. Our nights may not have been perfectly restful, but I was happy for her company. After holding her in my womb for nine months, I would have felt lonely without her at my side.

"All right, quiet now, children. Let's begin our lesson. Who can remember what we read about yesterday?"

Guiseppe's little hand shot into the air.

"Yes, Guiseppe."

"Jesus walking on the water."

"That's right. Can you recount the story for us?"

Guiseppe recited the tale with childish purity.

When I met with Reverend Mother again, I would be able to say with certainty I felt called to teach children. It was the most certain I felt of anything in years. I was, however, not yet certain of my future beyond that. I knew I would never be far from my precious Lily, but where to go or how to manage on our own, I still had no idea. Oh, how I dreaded making the wrong decision, but now was not the time for such thoughts.

I held up my slate. "Who can read this for me?"

It was late in the fall when the Lord spoke. I was in the scriptorium copying the book of Jeremiah, when a portion of one verse branded itself into my mind.

> *Stand at the crossroads and look;*
> *ask for the ancient paths,*
> *ask where the good way is, and walk in it,*
> *and you will find rest for your souls.*

I pondered the verse for days. I could not shake it. It seemed to follow me everywhere. It echoed from the very walls of the chapel, on the whistle of the wind, in the rustle of the leaves. Yet several nights passed before I knew what to do with the words.

Then came the dream, a dream most vivid and clear. I saw myself upon a road, wide and open and smooth. I wore a bright blue kirtle and held Lily upon my hip. She seemed older than the child who slept beside me, with white-blond hair already wisping past her ears. To the side of the wide, clear road, I saw a path. It was an old and rugged path, patched with rocks and stones, but as the path stretched onward it seemed to expand and glow and end in a bright luminous sun. Against the sun stood the silhouette of Arun Castle. I saw a giant hand reach down and point to the craggy trail. Then I heard the words once again, not in a faint whisper, but in a bold and powerful voice. "Return to the ancient paths."

I awoke at that moment, the dream sharp in my mind. *Return to the ancient paths.* It could not be more clear.

By December I was ready with my answer when Mother Maria said, "Do you have any plans for the future, Dandelion?"

"God has instructed me to return to the ancient paths. I shall return to my home in England." Lily wiggled upon my lap, showing no regard for Mother Maria's preference for stillness.

"To London?"

"No. There is nothing for me in London." I took a deep breath. "I shall return to Arun Village." I wished I felt as certain as I sounded.

"Wasn't there some danger in Arun? I recall that's why you ran to London in the first place."

"Yes there was. In fact, I was banished entirely. All I know is that God told me to return to the ancient paths." I nuzzled Lily's head, drinking in her milky scent. "I must trust somehow He shall arrange the details. There is much I left unfinished."

"Like the childhood sweetheart."

"Well, yes. I did William a terrible wrong, but I'm not sure I shall be able to fix it. Return to the ancient paths was the first verse to guide me, but then there was another that burned itself into my mind. It said, 'He despised the oath by breaking the covenant. Because he had given his hand in pledge and yet did all these things, he shall not escape.' I don't know why I never thought it significant before but, Mother, I was married once, to a man named Gottfried Westover."

"That's odd. You never mentioned it."

Lily made a cooing baby sound.

I shushed her. "No, I never believed it mattered. The wedding was not quite legal. It was a rash and sudden decision. When Lady Worthing burned the marriage certificate and declared it null, I believed her, until I read that verse. Something about it took hold of me. I made a covenant before God. No law, no earthly authority can nullify it."

"But what of the husband? Will he take you back?"

"I know not what he shall do. I know not if I shall be thrown in a dungeon or whipped before I can even speak with him. He himself might yield the axe for my beheading."

Lily stuck her bored little fingers into my mouth. A secret part of my heart whispered, *What if I misunderstood?* I was so new to this.

I removed Lily's fingers. "There is no way to tell the future, but I know what I must do. I must go back and try to set things right. Else I shall never be able to move on." I hugged her tighter to me.

"She certainly is a handful, isn't she?" Mother Maria smiled at my daughter. "Do you want to go back to this husband if he will have you? Is this Gottfried a good man?"

"I'm not sure. When we parted I thought him evil, but looking back, perhaps not. The first thing you taught me is that all have sinned. Were his sins truly so much worse than mine? He was a sad man, a man damaged by his experiences. I didn't know how to help him, but perhaps this time I can do better. Deep down, he was a dear soul. If not, I pray God will spare me and release me from my vow. It seems it is biblical sometimes at least to separate."

"Goodness, Dandelion, you have grown into a confident and courageous woman under my very nose."

Lily's wiggling increased. *What if I fail her?*

A greater part of my heart whispered back, *Hush!*

Lily tugged at my wimple. I laid her upon the rug at my feet to scoot around and explore.

"Not so brave," I said, my heart fluttering at that very moment. "I shall be begging you and each of the sisters for your prayers. It shall not be an easy path, but if I dreamed true, it will turn out well in the end."

"My nephew plans to sail to England in the spring. I shall ask him to arrange your passage as well."

"Not Giovanni?"

Mother Maria's eyes shot open, then her brows tightened in concern. "I wasn't certain if I should bring it up, but Giovanni is on a honeymoon trip. He married a dear friend of ours from childhood. Sonia spent most of her life tending her ailing father and so never wed. Giovanni wants to show her the world she's been missing. He shall meet up with his nephew in London later in the year."

Tears sprang to my eyes at the news. "I'm so happy things have turned out well for him."

"As they will for you, my dear."

Lily had scooted to Mother Maria by this point. She picked her up and allowed the child to investigate the trinkets upon her desk. I caught Mother Maria nuzzling her sweet baby hair as we concluded our conversation.

My precious baby, I pray we shall be all right.

Spring arrived more quickly than I ever imagined possible. The good sisters did not allow me to leave without a fuss. Meeting us by the convent gates, they stockpiled my trunk with tokens to remember them by. I would miss this convent—mass, vespers, the library, the scriptorium, dancing in the garden, the ever-present incense floating in the air. I would miss my friends, Agnesse most of all. She now wore the simple habit of a novitiate. Unbeknownst to me, she copied all my poems into a beautiful little book and tied it with a bow.

The most precious gift came from the Reverend Mother, though.

She waited until Lily and I were about to board the wagon that would carry us to the ship bound for England. She handed the gift to me wrapped in paper. I untied the strings, and the contents stunned me. It was the Holy Bible written in my very own hand.

"You shall be needing this more than we shall," she said. "Use it to teach those precious children back in your village."

I walked away and swiped the tears from my eyes. Only Mother Maria followed, the rest of the women allowing us a moment to say good-bye. "So here I am headed right back to where I started, and I can't help but wonder. Why? Why has all of this happened to me? Was it God seeking to punish me? Satan seeking to destroy me?"

"Oh Dandelion, you do complicate things. Sometimes there are simply paths we must follow. Were it God, I would call it not so much punishment as gentle wooing. Were it Satan, well certainly he seeks to destroy, but he cannot do so without our willing complicity. He tempted you to be sure. Life handed you everything you wanted, and yet in the end it was not enough. You were sifted as wheat, my dear—refined in the fire, but what came out was nothing short of gold."

I so hoped she was right.

"I shall miss you, dear, but God has great things in store."

I brushed some stray tears from my eyes and took a deep breath. I handed her a letter with a Genoan address and asked her to send it for me. I climbed into the wagon before I could change my mind.

As I passed through the gates for the last time I read the words once again, "*May all who enter find joy.*" I did find joy in that place. Holding Lily upon my lap with one hand, I fumbled through my sack with the other. I pulled out my book of poems and thumbed through it. There it was, my very favorite.

After a long and shady path
she pushed back the last branch,
opened to a bewitching scene,
a small paradise, a pool that sparkled in the sunlight,
a waterfall streaming down the sandstone walls.

THE POOL GLISTENED
not crystal, but ruby—a deep red pool,
and the falls a bloody gash against the rocks,
flowing from a wooden cross atop the cliff.
The entire vale suffused in an odd crimson glow.

She felt herself drawn, drawn forward, slowly, mesmerized.
Against all reason she was drawn, against all shame.
She felt her fingers running down her dress
and freeing the ties. She felt it sliding to the ground,
then each garment, one by one,

254

as her feet caressed cool moist earth.

Until she stood at the bank,
dipping her toes into sticky warmth,
watching the blood drip, and it felt good.
Oh so good, and she was running,
she was splashing, and dove headfirst into spilt life,
immersed in it, one with it, and she was swimming.

She was swimming through it to that fountain.
climbing the rocks to be washed,
to watch her body painted red again
and again within a smooth, clean sheet of blood,
that left her feeling white as snow.

She opened her mouth to drink deep,
and whispered up so inadequately, thank you.

I took a deep breath, hugged Lily to me, and focused onward.

Chapter 39

Arun Village England — 1336

It was just as it looked in my dream. I stood on the rugged little path to my village. The road ran directly into the descending sun, the outline of Arun Castle sat in silhouette against the fiery red-gold ball. Lily rested upon my hip, nearly a toddler now. Already she had been crawling about the ship's deck and pulling herself up by the rigging to stand on her wobbly feet. Her hair did indeed flow in wispy strands past her ears now.

It boded well.

I started down the hillside toward the small village in eerie quiet. I walked unheeded right up to my parent's door. I knocked, but no one answered. I pushed the door open, but no one was inside.

"You'll not be finding them there, miss." A small girl I had not noticed spoke. The child was dressed in the rough, brown, flaxen fabric I remembered so well, her clothing more of a sack than a proper tunic, but her coppery red hair belied her dreary attire.

"Are they at work in the fields?"

She skipped over to me. "No ma'am. They no longer work, except to help with planting and harvest. They have a new cottage at the end of the lane."

A cottage?

"Would you please take me to it, young lady?"

Her cheeks blushed an appealing shade of pink. "Oh, I'm no lady. I saw a lady once, a real one. You almost look like you could be one, but never me."

I bent down to look her in the eye. "I beg to differ. Being a lady is about who you are on the inside. If you are kind and gracious and considerate of others, then you may yet grow to be a great lady."

She shuffled her feet. "I don't know if I'm all those things, but I shall try if you say so, ma'am."

"Indeed, I do say so. What is your name, child?"

"Gwyneth."

"Well, isn't that lovely."

Gwyneth?

Could it have been the name my brother, Robert, and his betrothed, Daisy, once talked of naming their child? The babe was not yet born

256

when I ran off to the castle. This girl looked to be about seven or eight.

"It's Welsh. My mother's family is from Wales. Come, I shall take you to the cottage." She took my hand and led me down the lane.

Daisy's family came from Wales, and her hair was bright red as well. Could this girl be my niece?

I had missed so much.

We approached a tiny but sturdy cottage, large by our village standards. The timbers were neatly cut and filled with waddle and daub. It stood in a crisp rectangular shape. The roof rose far above my head and featured a proper chimney. "Do you know the family who lives here, Gwyneth? Do they go by the name of Dering?"

"Yes ma'am. That's them, and of course I know them. They are my granny and pappy."

I stood speechless.

"You have a pretty baby, ma'am. I like her." She reached up to stroke Lily's silky locks. Lily cooed and giggled and grabbed a hold of Gwyneth's finger.

"It seems she likes you too," I said, my voice wispy.

"Well, shall we go in?"

"Of course."

Gwyneth opened the door. "Granny, Pappy, there's a pretty lady and her baby come to see you."

I followed her inside. My mum turned from the fire, where she cooked a hearty stew that smelled of beef. Da sat in a chair carving a wooden stick into something that looked like a child's toy. Goodness, but things changed in a few short years. They were still small, wrinkled peasant folk, but they looked so well and rested now.

Mum gasped, dropping her wooden spoon upon the timbered floor. She let out the most gut-wrenching wail. For a moment I feared she was upset to see me until she hobbled over and grabbed me to her in a desperate embrace. "Child! They finally got word to her, Da. She's come home. The Good Lord has heard our prayers. After losing so many of our babies, He's brought one home to us."

"Looks like m-maybe He's brought two," said my da. He struggled to stand. I couldn't go to him, as Mum held me locked to her breast, but Gwyneth ran to help. Before long, we were one massive hug. Even Gwyneth joined in the happy reunion, although she did not yet know why.

I pulled back to watch their joyful faces. "Da, you don't seem surprised to see me."

"Nay, I h-had a dream, you see. I knew you were coming. Whatever took you so l-long?"

"Well, that is quite a story." I hoisted Lily higher on my hip. "But first I must tell you I never did receive your message. Indeed, the Good Lord sent me. What babies have you lost, Mum? Why is it so quiet here? How is it you live in this lovely little house now?"

"So much has changed. We tried to send word to London. We've lost so many souls. It pains me to speak of it." Mum shook her head.

We all had so many questions, but Gwyneth's shrill young voice demanded the first answer. "Wait, all of you. I must know. Is this my Auntie Dandy, and is the baby my cousin?"

"Yes, yes. Yes to both, my sweet." I kissed the top of her coppery head. Her features looked like a young Robert. "I am sorry I've been gone so long. I shall make it up to you, Gwyneth, I promise."

Later I sat snapping peas with my sister-in-law Daisy in the small yard behind my parent's new home. We watched the children playing and smiled at each other. This was just as things should be. Lily toddled after a ball Gwyneth rolled to her. She laughed and clapped her hands, falling on her well-padded rump. Peter and Cole, the three-year-olds, squealed and chased each other about. I wished the rest of the cousins could be with us to make this scene complete.

Only last summer a pox had swept the Sussex countryside. It brought fever and chills and spots, and many died from it. Mum and Da survived a similar sickness when they were children. The disease did not touch them this time around. It did, however, steal Sadie, Gilbert, Gilbert Jr., and their daughter Caroline. The baby of the family, a sweet-faced boy named Peter, pulled through and now lived with my parents. Robert, Daisy, their children Gwyneth and Cole, and my brother Tim survived as well, though the illness wiped out nearly a third of the shire.

I wasn't ready to ask if anyone at the castle had died. It did not occur to my parents to mention it. We always knew little enough of castle life here in the village anyway. For now I was satisfied to be back with my family and embraced once again into the fold. I would deal with one thing at a time.

Daisy and Robert welcomed me with as much joy as my parents. I had so much to share with them. My life was an exotic adventure none of them could have imagined in their wildest dreams. I regaled them with tales of London, Italy, and the sea. I taught them songs and dances I learned at the convent and the castle. I'd had little opportunity to catch up on happenings here in the village, but I was in no rush. They were clearly happy and healthy and living a better life than we ever hoped. If I learned one thing at the convent, it was patience.

I had yet to face Tim or William. They were both away on some business and expected home soon. The villagers elected William their new reeve several years earlier. Perhaps that explained the improved living conditions. Although I was glad to hear he was doing so well for himself, I knew his prosperity would be the final nail in the coffin of our friendship. He was not good enough for me as a peasant. I would not insult him by attempting to renew our relationship now.

And I was eager to see Tim. Once upon a time I vowed to make a better life for my little brother. It was still not too late. I looked forward to discussing his future, certain Giovanni would find a position for him in the city if he liked.

One of the best pieces of news to greet me upon my homecoming was that Friar John at last returned to his true calling and became an actual friar, vows of poverty and all. I hoped to visit him as soon as possible. Alice lived with and cared for her aging father, the miller of a small town west of Arun. For now our village made do with the itinerant priests who traveled about the countryside.

Yes, I would accustom myself once again to life here in the village and enjoy my family before facing the harder issues. I did long to contribute, however. I could start even while I waited for the rest to unravel.

I looked up from my snapping. "Daisy, are there many children near Gwyneth's age left in the village?" I tossed a few more peas into the pot.

"Yes, a few. About twelve between the ages of five and ten, I would say."

"I thought I might start a little school for them. Do you think it would be permissible?"

She nearly tipped the peas as she jumped. "Goodness, do I think it would be permissible? Why, it would be a dream come true. William has been longing to bring education to the village, but with Friar John gone, there hasn't been much progress."

I straightened the pot. "So can they be spared from the fields, then?"

"Well, certainly the younger ones. Perhaps by winter we could organize a time for the younger adults, as well. They need their earnings from the field, but likely many of them dream of moving to the city and finding a better life."

"If only it was so simple," I said with a snap of another pea.

She picked up another handful herself. "What do you mean?"

"I mean if only it was so simple for any of them to walk away from this place with no consequences."

"But it is. Haven't you heard? We are all paid workers now, free to come and go as we please," said Daisy.

"No, I hadn't heard." I paused for a moment to digest the surprising news. "I suppose a part of me is afraid what I might learn if I ask too many questions too fast. Paid workers, my goodness, will wonders never cease? William talked Lady Worthing into that? She's not the heartless taskmaster we all thought her to be, but she's a shrewd businesswoman and not much given to innovation." I halted my rambling speech.

Daisy had stopped snapping peas and stared at me with the oddest expression on her face. "Dandelion, Lady Worthing is dead. She was one of the first to go. We all assumed you knew, else you would never have returned."

Tears welled up in my eyes, tears of relief, but I realized as the thick lump settled in my throat, I was also terribly sad. "Lady Catherine's gone?"

"Yes, I'm so sorry. I thought you would be glad. No one wanted to mention the banishment. We assumed it was painful for you. Boys, stop that this instant." She ran off to break up their tussle, coming back a bit disheveled.

I barely noticed any of it as I sat recalling my tumultuous relationship with Lady Catherine. "It was. It's complicated."

"You returned without knowing?" She straightened her pretty red hair. "But why? You could have been beheaded."

I didn't answer. It no longer mattered. Catherine was a dear friend once. I hoped she did not die lonely. Somewhere deep down I suppose I wished I might reach out to her, help her, perhaps even reconcile her to the Heavenly Father. She needed Him so badly and never even knew. I went back to snapping my peas with so many questions on my mind.

The next afternoon, as I returned from the well with water, quite a ruckus met me. I was thinking of how much I missed indoor pumps when I heard the fray coming from my parents' home. The door crashed open and out dashed Tim holding Lily upon his back for a horsy ride. Spotting me, he stopped dead in his tracks. He tossed her around to hold her against his hip. He swiped at his eyes before breaking into a run once again and swooping me into his strong arms. He was half a foot taller and twice as broad as the last time I saw him.

I found myself crying as well. The heavy bucket of water sloshed to the ground. "Oh, Tim, how can I ever tell you how very, very sor—"

He reached his hand up and pressed it against my mouth. "None of that matters, now." He hugged both Lily and me to him and held on tight for even longer than the first time.

He looped his arm around my shoulder and walked me to the house. "William is inside, Dandy. Are you ready to see him?"

"As ready as I'll ever be, I suppose."

It took a moment for our eyes to adjust upon entering the dim cottage. The windows were open, but the overhang of the thatched roof shaded the whole place. Then, I saw William bent down and playing with the boys near the hearth, every bit as strong and handsome as I remembered him.

"William, will you look what the cat has dragged here," said Tim.

He stood and attempted a smile. "Welcome home, Dandelion." His deep voice reached out to me and strummed a chord in my heart. A part of me longed to run to him. But so many others held me back.

"Thank you, William." I made my own conciliatory gesture by walking to him. I stood on tiptoe to kiss his cheek. The moment was indeed stiff and awkward, but quickly over.

"Your daughter is beautiful," he said. "You must be very proud of her."

"She is a gift from God. Thank you." Silence strained the air. "And you," I said, "reeve of the entire village. It looks like you're doing a wonderful job."

"I certainly try. Lord Worthing deserves as much credit as I do. You just missed him." William nodded toward the door.

I turned to stare at the empty doorway, surprised to hear Lord Worthing mentioned so casually. I hadn't yet heard he was back, although I guessed as much with Catherine deceased. Words escaped me once again.

Might he prove to be my greatest temptation yet?

William, Lord Worthing, it was all too much.

Tim took over with his energetic chitchat. At least some things never changed.

He went on for near an hour with funny stories about the children and the neighbors. Daisy and Robert joined us for this family reunion. William sat on a chair by the kitchen table with Sadie's Peter snuggled on his lap. The picture of them as father and son tugged at my heart. Gwyneth and Cole played near his feet on a rug made from rags.

William remained part of the family after all these years.

I slapped my knees to gather everyone's attention. "So Tim, stories aside, what are you doing with yourself these days? I have a friend in London who owns a trade warehouse, and I wondered if you might be interested in a job. I know you don't want my apologies, but I feel there is so much I should make up to all of you." I couldn't help but look at William as I spoke those words.

"Well, actually, as wonderful as your offer sounds, I've somewhat of an announcement to make." Tim stood.

Everyone stopped to listen. Mum put down her cooking, and Da stopped carving.

Tim cleared his throat. "Lord Worthing and William did have some business to attend, but that wasn't the true purpose for our trip. We stopped and visited Friar John along the way. Arrangements have been made. I shall study to become a priest and return as soon as possible to take over the parish."

Daisy was the first to rush over to him. She put the back of her hand to his forehead. "Quick, fetch a healer. He's delirious."

"Goodness, Tim," I said. "Here I was enjoying your stories and feeling thankful some things never change, and you throw this at me. I thought you hated studying, and since when are you interested in church?"

He chuckled. "Oh please, Holy Sister Dandelion. Do you think you are the only one capable of change? Why I nearly fainted when Mum told us you had come straight from a convent."

I grimaced. "I stand corrected. You will make a wonderful priest. Why, if your sermons are half as entertaining as your stories, the entire countryside shall be lining up for church."

Everyone congratulated Tim on his fine decision.

William jumped up and pulled Lily away from the fire she toddled toward.

I took a deep breath and braced myself. "William, would you care to take a walk with me? I have something to ask you."

He didn't look at all certain, even as he said, "Certainly," and stood to join me. Mum grabbed up Lily before I even had a chance to ask.

William and I started down the lane we knew so well. The familiarity was bittersweet.

I chanced a quick sidelong glance at his chiseled features and waving, sandy brown hair. However had the man remained unmarried after all these years? And now reeve of the village. Surely every lass in the shire must be near daft chasing after him. I longed to know the reason, but had given up my right to ask on the day I rejected him. So much time had passed. So much had changed. And that was not the reason I had brought him here today.

I spoke before I lost my resolve. "When I was at the convent, my main objective was to find God's path for my life."

A memory assaulted me from nowhere. *"Dandy, I'm going to say this once, knowing full well you'll never understand. This is not about duty, or guilt. It certainly isn't about selfishness. I'm doing this because I prayed long and hard, and I know this is God's path for my life. I truly hope that you are a part of God's path for my life, as well, but you have a decision to make."*

Regret at my choice of words knocked the air right out of me. Tears sprang to my eyes. It would be easy to have nothing but regrets where William was concerned. I swallowed hard and started again. "What I mean to say is, I had opportunity to try a variety of vocations. I did a lot of sewing. I transcribed the entire Bible. I learned to play the flute and write poetry. When all was said and done, though, I realized what I longed to do more than anything was teach."

For the first time since we left the cottage, William looked directly at me with his warm brown eyes that were still familiar to me after all these years.

"Of course, the next question was where I should teach. It would have seemed simplest to stay at the convent, but the more I prayed, the more I realized that was not the plan at all. It was frightening to return here. I had no idea Lady Catherine had died. I truly thought my life was at risk, but that aside, there were many ghosts for me to face here." I stopped again.

This was so hard. "I have so much to repent for, so much to make right. I'm trying, William."

"I see that." He scratched his head. "But you have yet to ask your question."

I held my hands tight against my chest. "Yes, of course. May I start a little school here? I would like nothing better than to educate the children of our village. It seems fitting."

He gaped at me for a moment. "I agree entirely. I've been praying for such an opportunity." William couldn't stand still. "By all means, begin tomorrow if you like. You may have the children in the afternoons. I'm sure they can be spared for a few hours. They run amuck and get in trouble anyway." He chuckled as he said it.

It brought back so many memories of our own childhoods.

"Do you need supplies? I could speak with Lord Worthing."

My head was reeling, but I managed to answer. "I've some ink and paper donated from the convent. I shan't need those in the beginning anyway. I imagine it will be a while until we're past the basics. I also hoped after harvest I might find some time to work with the young adults."

His smile traveled from ear to ear. "That's certainly ambitious of you. If you're up for it, we shall find a way to make it work."

I clapped my hands together and matched his smile, relaxing with him. "Thank you. It's more than I ever expected."

We turned to head back toward the house. I could see a new future for William and me in that moment. I could see friendship and mutual respect. I could see us working together to give our community the opportunities we were blessed with so many years ago. "I shall have much praise to give in my prayers tonight."

"I'm glad. I only ever wanted for you to be happy, Dandelion. I hope you've found it in your heart to forgive me after all these years."

My heart twisted. "Forgive you. William, you did nothing wrong. It is I who need forgiving, but I fear it is far too much to ask."

He stopped for a moment. "Well, then let it be said. I do forgive you, and I don't blame you for anything. We were both young and foolish. I held in my anger for too long. If I had spoken to you sooner, things might have ended differently."

A pleasant shiver ran through me.

"You always deserved better than I gave you." I longed to reach out and cup his cheek in my hand but reminded myself I was a married woman. I hadn't thought in those terms for many years. "Sometimes I wish we could go back and start over. I'm so sorry it's too late now."

He looked surprised to hear me say it. He clenched his jaw before he spoke. "It's all right. All of that is long past. We're different people now. Of course it would be ridiculous to try to go back. Circumstances have changed. No, I wouldn't want that at all."

"I'm just glad we can still be friends." We walked the rest of the way in silence. The conversation should have been gratifying, and yet I felt oddly dissatisfied.

So now I would become a teacher, but what of Gottfried, of William, of Lord Worthing? Whatever might be in store?

Chapter 40

I sat in the shade of the big tree little more than a week later. The children were already hard at work practicing their alphabets. They carved their letters with small sharp sticks into the dirt patch behind the house that once belonged to Friar John. Lily, Cole, and Peter played nearby as well. Daisy offered to watch Lily while I taught, but to my surprise, kept the children mere feet from the lessons. I assessed Daisy longed to read and write more than any of them, but was too shy to say so.

Having the little ones nearby did add some chaos, but I was happy to see Daisy scratching her letters in the dirt side by side with Gwyneth as they giggled at their poor attempts.

If I traveled a month by sea and risked my head only to teach my niece to read, it would have all been worth it. The look on her face when she stumbled through her first sentence, "A cat is fun," was worth every sacrifice. Indeed it was one of the finest moments of my entire life.

I was supposed to be choosing a passage of scripture for part of our daily lessons, Bible study and a few moments of contemplative prayer. Some of the children tried to beg their way out, but on this issue I would not budge. I knew firsthand what little use worldly education proved without the guiding principles of God's word to balance it. It might take years before any of them could read Latin, but they could sit and listen to me translate a few verses each day followed by a short time of silence to meditate upon them.

Yet I was distracted. I kept turning toward the banging of construction down the lane. My parents were one of the first families to receive a new home, but eventually all the villagers would move into larger and sturdier cottages with wooden floors. Mum and Da were given priority since William knew how Da suffered from swollen and aching joints during the winters. The warm floor made all the difference for Da.

Again my eyes were pulled in the direction of the hammering. William pounded away at the floorboards of a new cottage wearing only his breeches and open shirt on this sunny spring day—my same old William with his same big heart.

In all these years, he barely aged. Only his tawny eyes looked older and wiser, perhaps a bit sadder. And as for that well-muscled physique I had long admired . . . I chided myself for the tenth time.

I had no right thinking about William this way. I had yet to deal with Gottfried. These were sinful thoughts, surely. Life was so much simpler at the nunnery. I sighed. All the more reason to focus on the scriptures in front of me.

Besides, I reminded myself, William made his feelings amply known. That part of our lives was far behind us. We were different people now. He wouldn't want that at all. He was quite clear. William may have forgiven me, but he surely would never love me again.

Ugh. "Stop it this instant." I scolded myself aloud, causing several of the students to straighten up and work harder. No harm in that. I chuckled.

And then I did manage to focus on the scriptures. I Corinthians 13 would be my text. I, more than anyone, needed a solemn reminder this day about God's view on love.

Staring at the scripture, I failed to notice anyone approaching until Gwyneth shouted, "Auntie Dandy, look!"

I raised my head to the oddest sight. A large man walked down the lane from the castle, leading a massive black horse with a blur of white bouncing by his feet. I thought my eyes played tricks and waited until I could see them clearly. Within moments, I could no longer deny it was indeed Lord Thomas Worthing himself bringing Roman and Cloud down the lane. I didn't flinch a muscle. Such utter shock overtook me.

Cloud led the way. Dashing past Lord Worthing, she bounded toward me. She stopped for only a moment to twist her head sideways and stare at me, and then yipped and jumped all over me, kissing me and rubbing her head against me all the while. I bent down and hugged her warm, wiggling body. "Oh Cloud, I missed you so." She pulled away and looked at me again. This time her angry bark punished me for my long disappearance before she snuggled into me and licked my arms some more.

Lily toddled over to inspect the little dog. Before long Cloud was tumbling about with the children in the grass. Daisy herded them all a small distance away as Lord Worthing reached me.

"I tried to wait for you to come to me on your own, but Cloud would have none of it," he said.

I rose and walked to Roman. I pressed my face into his hay-scented mane. He nickered, remembering me after all these years as well. I turned to Lord Worthing, although my eyes remained downcast as I curtsied. "I'm sorry, m'lord. I should have reported to you immediately. I have no right to be here without your permission."

Lord Worthing stood close, holding the reins. "What rubbish is this? You have every bit as much right to be here as I. It seems both of the prodigal children have at long last returned."

"But m'lord, I was charged with so many crimes. Surely you knew."

"Yes, Mother told me everything. She even sent me searching for you."

I tilted my head against my horse's warm neck and petted her. "The good brothers from the cathedral told me as much."

Lord Worthing gave the horse a rub as well. "Which reminds me, you led quite a merry chase through the horse fair that afternoon."

"Which reminds me, my nose hurt for days." Finally, we looked each other straight in the eye and laughed.

"Losing you changed my mother, Dandelion. When I came home and told her you had sailed for Italy, she broke down and apologized to me."

"Oh, Lord Worthing, were you here with her when she died? I've worried about that so. She was such a lonely person."

He threw back his head. "Will you listen to this? I suppose the rumors of you spending time in a convent must be true. After all she did to you, you worry about her feelings? You are a saint indeed."

"I hated her for many years, but once I was able to forgive her, it felt so right. She was a sad person underneath it all."

"I *was* with her when she died. I wasn't living here, but I came straightaway when the sickness broke out. Father John was with her too. She had much to confess upon her deathbed."

I made the sign of the cross. "I pray God had mercy on her soul."

"Perhaps He did. In truth, I never heard my mother so sincere as she was on that day." Lord Worthing broke the dismal mood by straightening Roman's saddle. "Come. Sit upon this fine horse and let me take you to the castle. We have business to attend at the tower."

"Of course." I mounted Roman for the first time in over five years. It was kind of Lord Worthing to include him in this reunion. The familiarity was soothing, but I was not so happy about where he was taking me. I looked over to Daisy and the children still playing with Cloud.

She waved me away.

I sucked in a deep breath. "I suppose facing Gottfried is long overdue."

Many curious stares met us as we entered the gates. Lord Worthing tied the reins near the entrance to the tower and lifted me down. We climbed the stairs to the apartment that had been my home once upon a time. The place was nearly bare, except for the table and chairs and a stack of crates by the fireplace. I ran to the window. My old friend Gerald stood guard on the crenellated walkway. He winked at me, but remained otherwise still and professional.

"I think Gottfried passed peacefully as well, Dandelion."

I stood gaping in awe, and then once again to my surprise, I cried. "Why didn't anyone tell me?"

"Why didn't you ask?"

"I don't know." I sank upon the boxes.

"Nor do I." Thomas opened one box and took something out, then came to sit beside me. He wiped a few tears from my cheek, then took my hand in his and patted it. "I found him with this lying on his chest when he died." Placing it into my hands, he said, "Mother asked me to return it to him only a week earlier, before she herself passed away."

I stared down at the charred remains of Samia's poetry book. Had he truly been reading it when he passed? "Did he suffer much?"

"I don't think so. I don't think he fought at all."

"Poor, dear man. He had nothing to live for."

"And everything to die for."

I looked up at him. Unlike William, Thomas had aged. He might have been nearly as old as Gottfried when we first met. How time did fly. Yet Thomas still had the same sky blue eyes and freckles, giving him the boyish charm I noted over twenty years ago, even if a neatly groomed beard now graced his face. His hairline receded at both temples, but his dark hair still fell in an endearing flop over his brow. I thought once again with wonder how things changed, yet stayed the same. On that day so long ago Thomas gave me the priceless piece of pink candy that transformed my entire world, and today . . . this.

He opened the book and handed it to me. "This is the page Gottfried was reading in his last moments."

I dream of the day that I die,
when at last I am held
within God's ecstatic arms.

Distance will fade, our hearts pour together as one.
I will cup His cheek in my hand
with passionate disregard.

I dream of the day
when He shall adore my exquisite beauty,
and at last I may meld into His flesh.

I hugged the book to my chest. "Perhaps Samia was there to greet him."

Thomas returned my smile, although he couldn't have comprehended my meaning.

"How can I ever thank you, Thomas?" I realized after the words were out that I failed to say "Lord Worthing," as I should, but somehow it seemed far too formal in this intimate setting.

"Don't thank me yet, for we are just getting started."

"I don't understand."

He swept his hand around the room. "Well, to begin, we have all of these boxes to deal with, and we must decide if Roman should be kept here with the horses or in the village with you."

"Whatever do you mean? Please, Lord Worthing, stop speaking in riddles."

"Were you not married to Gottfried?"

It took a moment for me to recover from that statement, so many confusing thoughts flooded my mind. "Yes, I suppose. I'm not sure, to be honest. Not according to your mother."

"Ah, I see. Perhaps this will clear the confusion." He pulled a piece of parchment out from inside his surcoat. Thomas was full of surprises. I untied the parchment and rolled it open. It was my wedding certificate signed by Father Hayworth's own hand. Thomas seemed to be getting far too much enjoyment from my confusion.

"But . . . but . . . it's not possible. It can't be true. I watched her burn this paper with my own eyes." I held it up to the light and turned it over to inspect it further.

He pulled it down to look at me. "You of all people should know about Mother and her tricks, Dandelion. She always did like to keep her options open."

Tears threatened to spill over my eyelids yet again.

Thomas pulled one leg up to his chest in a relaxed manner, settling in to tell his story. "Gottfried confessed to me how sorry he was for the way things turned out with you. On the day you were banished, as he stood over top of you, whip in hand, he couldn't do it. It all became clear, and he understood how he had wronged you. He could not deliver even one stroke. His only regret was that he never got the chance to make it up to you. He seemed to know his end was coming, though. He asked me to give you all of this if I ever found you. He also asked that I deed to you a piece of land my father promised him decades ago. He chose a plot he thought you would like."

I stood and paced about the room, surveying it all. "It's too much. Oh, Lord Worthing, I don't deserve all of this."

"Gottfried believed otherwise."

I gazed out the window at the village far below. "I can't. I can't take it."

"Well, you needn't decide today. Think about it. This is what he wanted."

"I don't know. Perhaps I should. I do have my child to think of."

Thomas stood and pried the lid off a nearby crate, allowing me to peek inside. "Almost half of these boxes are full of books. If you won't accept them for yourself, then take them for the students at your school."

A book of philosophical essays I adored sat atop the stack. "Of course, of course you're right. I will at least take the books, and

269

perhaps some of the furniture for my parents' home." I was growing accustomed to the idea already.

He stood up and looked through the boxes once again. He took out a lovely bolt of yellow fabric. "Might not this make some very pretty dresses for the village girls? Mother mentioned you were an excellent seamstress."

"All right, all right, you win. I shall take it all, but for the good of the whole village, not for me."

"All right then. I always win, by the way," he said with his boyish grin. "I've been hoping for years to challenge you at chess. Why, you are legendary about these parts."

"Oh! Whatever happened to Richard?"

"I believe he is living with an elderly countess somewhere in Northern England."

"Poor Richard." I plopped down into a chair.

"Gracious, woman. How can you be so insanely forgiving?"

"When one has been forgiven much, it is easy to forgive."

Thomas crouched down in front of me and scrutinized my face. "And were you always this way?"

"Not at all." I offered a twisted smile. "Perhaps you would like to come to supper some night, and my family will be happy to tell you all sorts of stories about the old, wild Dandelion."

"Oh, Tim's shared a few already, so you can imagine my surprise. But I will take you up on that supper."

I hugged Samia's book to my chest once again, my head light and buzzy. When I dreamed of returning to the village, I surely never dreamed of becoming an heiress and inviting the local lord to supper. I purposed to be patient with things, and yet still they came flooding in far too quickly.

Gottfried died last summer.

No wonder God had not spoken to me of His plan until the fall.

"I should get you back," Thomas said, extending his hand. "You look like you need a rest."

When Thomas opened his palm to me, I feared he offered more than just assistance to my feet. Oh, surely this meant trouble. Would I somehow manage to wound yet another good man and bring disaster down upon all of our heads?

Thomas waited a few nights before surprising us all by popping in for supper with his chessboard and deck of cards. The whole family seemed at ease with his presence. William heard the commotion and stopped by as well. I was surprised to see he and Thomas were particularly close. I knew they must work together managing the estate, but I had no idea they were friends. They teased and spoke with the familiarity of longtime chums.

I was out of practice with cards, not to mention a bit distracted. Things between William and me remained cordial but strained. Although he said nothing unusual, the tension reached new levels that night. Thomas managed to beat me twice. The rest of the family watched with interest, and he took time to teach them all. I was glad, for it would help them learn their numbers. Once they were busy at their own round of cards, Thomas and I took the chess board along with a blanket around back.

It was a beautiful summer night, and the moon was huge and full. The little ones were already dozing on a pallet in the living area. I was thrilled to escape William, but as I gazed up at Thomas's handsome face, I feared I may have chosen the greater threat. Cloud trotted beside us and settled herself down for a rest between the two people she loved best. She was as excited to see Thomas after their three days apart as she was to see me after five years.

I made my first move. "So, Lord Worthing, tell me about coming home after all this time. I think I know why you stayed away, but still, I'd like to hear the story from you."

He tapped a few of his pieces before sliding one forward upon the board. "Well, I imagine you expect my mother was the reason, which is partly true. She made it easy to stay away, but there was more. Becoming an earl at age fourteen was frightening. I spent as long as I could running from the responsibility of it. I was happy to play at court, and I loved being a soldier, but running a manor, it was not for me." By the time he finished speaking it was his turn again.

"So what changed?"

"When I came home and saw things such a mess, I was shocked. Mother hadn't taken proper care of the place in years. Then of course, everyone was so sick. It hit me. These people need me. Somehow I never realized that before. I thought only of the duties, of the land, of the weight of the title. I hadn't thought about the people." He shook his head. "I saw a similar epidemic in Scotland and had some ideas about how to help. I ran to Friar John immediately, and we went to work. We were able to save many of the sick, Tim and Daisy among them. We contained the sickness too. It barely spread after that. When it was over, I realized I had never done a single thing as important in my entire life. I wasted twenty years doing what? Nothing at all. Nothing of consequence. Oh, I killed my share of Scots, but why? I don't even remember."

I had paused with my knight still lingering in the air as I listened to his rich cultured voice. "Quite an epiphany." I placed it on the board in its designated spot.

Thomas took a moment to focus on the game before continuing. "Yes, well it had been building for a while. A year earlier, I rode into a Scottish village and all the children went shrieking in terror to the farmhouse of the local laird. A young woman dashed out, little more than a child herself. She covered the children with her own tiny body like a human shield. Something about her bravery struck a chord in me. 'Who are you with,' I said, 'England or Scotland?' She looked at me with such fire in her eyes. 'I am with whichever side will leave these children safe, and let us live in peace.' She fairly spat the words. 'What?' I said. 'Care you not who rules over you?' I'll never forget her answer. 'All we want is a normal life free of war and death and fear. Whoever can grant us that, we will accept with open arms.' I turned and rode away. I was mystified. Her words took all the fight out of me." He chuckled at himself. "I suppose it sounds a bit dramatic in retrospect."

"Perhaps, but very true, as well."

"After the epidemic, William and I got started at once making serious changes. I've been happier in the last year than I've ever been before."

I smiled deep into his eyes. "I'm so glad, Thomas. At the convent I spent much time praying for the peasants of Arun Village. It's good to hear you haven't let them down."

"Only in taking so long."

"No point in regrets. The journey is as important as the destination."

"Very true."

I eyed the board. A distraction technique was needed. "So I suppose you shall be quick about providing them with an heir now. They shan't be secure without one."

"Are you offering to help?" he asked with a devilish gleam and wiggle of his eyebrows. He made his move.

"Not at all," I said. "By the way . . . ."

"Yes?"

"Checkmate."

Chapter 41

"**M**ilk?" I shrieked in wonder.

Friar John chuckled over top of our midday meal. We had met at Alice's cozy cottage and split the travel between us. I thought perhaps he would look old, as he was middle-aged throughout my childhood. Surely he must be reaching his elder years, but the mendicant life suited him, and he looked the same spry, merry soul as always.

"Ahh, lass, I've given up strong spirits for good, along with my other sinful vices. Thomas was there. He remembers." The friar nodded to my traveling companion. "I've said the rites at many deathbeds over the years, but there was something about seeing so many in a short time, about hearing so many heart-wrenching confessions in that brief span. I realized the season for hypocrisy had ended. I did not want so much regret on the day I met my maker."

Thomas nodded. "I do indeed remember. Those days changed me as well."

Whatever animosity once existed between Friar John and me was long gone. "I'm so happy for you."

"So now, tell me more of this Italian convent where you stayed." The friar listened with rapt attention to my tales.

By the end, his blue eyes misted over. "Ah, my dear, I wish there was such a place for me in my youth. Perhaps I would have been a better man."

I reached over and took his hand in my own. "Well, you are now."

He gave it a squeeze. "I wish in truth there was a better place for Tim to study. He's already sent me a letter about the corruption he's seen. It's hard to focus on the Heavenly Father when His earthly representatives are so sadly flawed."

I clapped. "Why didn't I think of it sooner? It's been on my heart all these long months to do something special for Tim. I can't believe it never occurred to me. I have a dear friend who recently took the parish in Dover. I sent a letter to him from London and received his reply only last week."

I could barely stay in my seat. "Father Frederick is just the one to train our Tim. Never have I met such a pure-hearted priest. His spirit is much like Mother Maria and the nuns at the convent. How he ever survived Southwark Cathedral with his innocence intact remains a complete mystery. Why, I would be so happy for Tim to study with him. I'm certain Father Frederick would do this favor for me."

"That's a splendid idea, Dandelion," said Thomas. "I shall dispatch messengers straightaway. If, of course, you approve, Friar John."

"Approve? Why, I've been praying for such a miracle."

I had a moment alone with Alice as she packed us a picnic for the trip home. "So tell me true, Alice, do you miss him?"

"Some days I do, but he visits frequently." Gray had overtaken Alice's hair, and she had more wrinkles than I remembered, but she looked merry and healthy and pink-cheeked.

I took the warm bread from her and tucked it in the sack. "I thought he gave up all his sinful vices."

"Not those sort of visits, you naughty child." She swatted me on the shoulder. "We're too old for such nonsense anyway."

I was glad to see she could joke about such things.

Once we were loaded down with food, Alice and John bade us farewell. I could hardly wait to dispatch the letter to Father Frederick.

Thomas and I traveled on horseback at a relaxed pace through the lush Sussex countryside. I stopped for a moment to allow Roman a nibble of clover and give him a pat on the neck. I could hear water nearby rushing over the rocks. The weather was warm, and I was glad to be dressed in a simple blue kirtle and hair scarf instead of the fancy gowns and wimples I wore while riding in the old days. I gazed over at Thomas's manly frame and kind face with new eyes. He had proven himself both a faithful friend and an entertaining companion.

As we headed back toward the village, I thought of all the crates there still awaiting my attention at home. Thomas had moved Gottfried's things into my parent's old hut for me to sort. Perhaps I should sell off what I could and tuck away a savings for Lily and me. The villagers were happy to send spare milk and eggs my way in thanks for teaching the children, but I still had no steady income. There might be a few items in the boxes that would bring a bit of coin. The task seemed overwhelming, and I avoided it until one afternoon last week when I found good reason to deal with them.

The children and I had all sat huddled in the shade on that hot afternoon, watching the men tote buckets of water back and forth from the stream to the fields. It was only a hundred yards to the nearest patch, but others stretched far to the east, and watering in that weather looked a miserable task. I wiped the sweat from my own brow, although I was sitting still under a tree, not laboring in the scorching sun. We were long overdue for rain, and the crops would never survive without water.

That's when an image flashed through my mind—a black and white sketch of pipes flowing from a stream to a field of barley. Where had I seen it before?

Why, in Gottfried's books, of course.

I jumped up. "Daisy, watch the children for me," I said over my shoulder even as I ran toward my parent's old hut. It took near an hour for me to sort through the crates of books, but by the end I found six of them chock full of farming innovations, including the one with the picture of the irrigation system that had flashed through my mind. I ran out to the fields in search of William to show him the wondrous books.

"William, William," I shouted, panting and short of breath by the time I reached him.

He flinched when he saw me running toward him.

"Look," I said, turning right off to the picture.

He took the book from me skeptically, but his face changed as he studied the diagram and read the description beneath it. "Where did you find this?"

"There's more, William, so much more. I wanted to share these with you years ago, but forgot about them until now."

He flipped through the books, his countenance growing more stunned. "Truly, Dandelion, wherever did you find these? I've never heard of such ideas. Why, these are priceless to me." He gave me a big hug of thanks. If I clung to his arms a moment too long, he did not notice in his excitement.

"They belonged to Gottfried. I suppose they are mine now, although I intended to put them in a library for the villagers."

Gottfried's name washed over William like a bucket of cold water. "Thank you, Dandelion," he said. "I shall read them all from cover to cover. It's fitting something good came from your marriage, I suppose."

An apology sprang to my lips yet again, but what purpose would it serve? "You are most welcome. I hope they help," I said simply and turned to walk away.

The very next day I saw the men working on the new irrigation system. It remained unbearably hot for all the chopping and cutting they did to prepare the pipes, but now there was an end to the tedium in sight, and they worked with renewed vigor. *I should have done this years ago*, I thought as I stood watching them. My insufferable pride had stood in my way. William looked the most joyful of all as he waved his sketches directing the endeavor.

I understood why he stayed to work the land. He had chosen well.

"Shall we stop over there and eat?" Thomas startled me back into the present. He pointed toward a small glen reaching clear to the riverbank.

I managed to respond as if I was thinking about his company the entire time. "Of course. It's lovely."

We let the horses roam free, and Thomas placed a thick blanket on the grass in the picturesque vale. A huge willow tree rained branches halfway across. We sat in its billowing shade beneath the whispery leaves. Patches of wildflowers grew about, all the flora of my childhood in a rainbow of colors. Those nostalgic sights sent my thoughts floating back to William yet again.

"So let's see what treasures Alice cooked up for us today." Thomas opened the sack to roasted pheasant, cheese, bread, fresh milk, and a large apple pie.

I squealed with delight. "I haven't eaten one of Alice's pies in years." I ignored the main course and grabbed for a slice of the treat with no sort of manners whatsoever. I bit into it and sighed. "You know, Alice is the one who taught me to cook, but she must have held back some secret about this pie. Here, try." I reached the slice toward Thomas's mouth.

He lounged on one elbow, amused by my enthusiasm. Leaning forward, he took a bite right out of my hand, grazing my fingers with his lips in the process.

I blushed as I realized how flirtatious I must seem.

Thomas tossed back his head and laughed outright. "Does your passion oft surprise you, Dandelion?"

"You've met Lily, I suppose," I said.

"Well, I for one like a woman with passion." He stole another chunk from my pie, catching my finger in his mouth this time and letting it slide between his teeth as he released it.

My cheeks grew even more flushed. The skin of my hand tingled. This was old and dangerous territory.

"I suppose it can be a good thing, but it certainly causes its share of trouble." I shoved away the disturbing sensations and polished off the treat despite my embarrassment.

Thomas was still chuckling. He took my hand in his.

I should have pulled away, but I felt so at ease.

"You are an astonishing woman—truly an original. I knew it from the first time I laid eyes on you."

I glanced up at him.

"Oh yes, I remember. That was one of the saddest days of my life. My father was dead, and I was being announced the new earl. I could hardly bear it. Then I looked across the crowd and saw a scowl of scathing outrage on your tiny pixie face. Why, if looks could kill George would have fallen dead that instant. You were all skin and bones and eyes with huge hollow cheeks and scraggly blond hair, but you had the spunk of a woman ten times your size. Passion blazed through you even then. For all you looked like a ragamuffin, you were the prettiest little thing ever."

I smiled at him. "I thought you would have forgotten."

"Never, and if that was not enough, the look on your face when you tasted the candy was even more memorable."

"It was my first."

"I imagined as much. I wondered about you often over the years—wondered what sort of woman you grew into." He stroked my wrist with his thumb.

"Do you remember visiting when I was twelve?"

"Ah, you were growing into more of a stunning beauty than I even imagined. I just couldn't resist that wink. But, you were so young still. I admit from time to time I thought about traveling back to see what became of you."

I ignored the shivers moving up my arm. "So what stopped you?"

"Well, in my saner moments it sounded rather absurd to spend weeks with mother for the chance of a quick glance at a pretty maiden."

"I used to dream you'd come back for me. It made William ever so mad."

"Yes, you and William and Tim were quite the threesome, weren't you?" It seemed Thomas didn't know William was my sweetheart.

"Then of course, one day I got a letter from mother that said 'Grumpy Old Gotty' had gone off and married some 'brazen blond strumpet' from the village. I thought it must be you."

"Oh!" I giggled.

Thomas turned bright red. "I didn't mean it that way. I don't know why you came to mind. Who else would Gottfried have chosen? We may have had our differences, but the man had exquisite taste."

"I imagine it must have been painful for you." I laid my other hand over top of his.

"You know that bit of history."

"Yes, I dragged it out of your mother late one night at the Tallanger keep near Bath. I never looked at her the same way after that night. I know she regretted telling me."

We both sat in silence.

"And what about the day at the horse fair?" I turned to see his face better. "Did you remember me right off?"

"Actually, no. Why, I hadn't seen you in ten years or more. You were looking rather tame that day too, if I remember correctly. But those eyes." He grazed his finger across my cheek and cupped my face with his hand. "I could never forget those eyes. It was only a moment before it came to me, but you were already dashing through the crowd. I managed to follow you for a few minutes; then you vanished into the air."

"Well, if I knew how sweet you could be, I might not have run off."

"Then one day I look out the castle window, and there you are. The loveliest lady I've ever seen sitting under a tree with a gaggle of children about her, teaching them to read and write. It was in that moment I knew you had grown into a woman I could truly admire. Nay, not only admire, cherish."

The last words trailed away. He pulled my face toward him and our lips melded into a kiss as sweet as honey. He pulled my whole body into an embrace. I couldn't resist dipping my lips for another taste of his. His hands roamed, strong but gentle, across my back.

Then unexpectedly, he rolled us both over till he was on top, resting his elbows to each side of my head and staring down at me.

"Marry me," he said it emphatically, as if it were an order.

I pushed him off and sat up, shaking off the kiss induced haze. "Are you daft?"

"Not at all. In fact, this may be the sanest thing I've ever said. Marry me, Dandelion."

"Why, you are daft. Really, Thomas, that's the silliest thing I've ever heard."

"What's so silly about it? We admitted we've dreamed of one another our whole lives. Why not? This must have been in the back of my mind all along. Perhaps that's why I never did settle down."

"They were silly childhood dreams, all mist and fairy dust. That sort of nonsense doesn't count for a thing in the real world." No, I could never fall into that trap again. I had left my ambitions far behind at the Italian convent. I would follow God's will. Not childish dreams. Not my own determination.

Not even my fickle heart.

He leaned in close to me. "Why not? Why couldn't we let it count for something? Why shouldn't we marry?"

"Goodness, there are surely a thousand reasons. Must I list them all?"

"Let me do it for you, and I shall refute each one. Let's see." He held up his pointer finger. "First, I am an earl, and you are but a peasant girl. Ah, but no, not so at all. As I have so recently given evidence, you are the widow of an aristocrat, a brave and honorable man, a dear friend of my father."

I pushed his finger down. "Well, be that as it may, it's not the same. He was the third son of some minor gentry, not the powerful Earl of Worthing. Surely the king would never allow it."

"Eddie, why he's a pal. The poor man falls prey to every pretty face at court. I'll have to fight him off to keep you for myself. He'll be utterly smitten by you. My father married beneath him. Why can't I?"

I shook my hands in the air. "This is ridiculous. What about Lily? How shall you explain her? Shall you adopt my bastard daughter as well?"

"Couldn't you say Gottfried came to visit you in London before you left, or that you thought the marriage annulled and married someone else who met a tragic end?"

I frowned at him. "I shan't lie for you, Thomas. That is no way to start a life nor to please my heavenly father."

"Oh, don't be like that." He pushed the corners of my lips into a smile. "Fine then, we shall flaunt it to all the world, and I shall claim her as my own. She will be the bastard daughter of my wife the nun. It will be roguishly trendy."

"Thomas . . . please stop this nonsense." I closed my eyes and pressed my hands to my ears.

He pulled them off and held them between us. "Why, because you don't think I shall truly do it? Are you afraid to hope only to have me change my mind and break your heart? I'm not that sort of man."

Was that the reason? It wasn't as if I would betray William this time around. William didn't want me. He made it clear again and again. "I don't know. It's so odd. You offer all my childhood dreams."

"Isn't that a good thing?" He leaned in to sneak another quick kiss.

"You don't understand. You must know the truth. It wasn't so much you. It was that castle, that life I lusted after. It was all you represented. What if this is a temptation to lead me astray?"

"Are you tempted?" Concern filled Thomas's eyes.

"By the castle, the title?" I searched the sky for the answer. "No, not for me, but I have Lily to consider. I won't let her suffer as I did. It confuses me. I do still long for love, though, and I do adore you. I imagine I could come to love you—the real you, not the fantasy in shining armor."

He brought my hands to his lips and kissed my fingers one by one. "I imagine we could both grow to love each other with little effort. And it's only right that you should worry about your daughter. Will you consider it then?"

"I . . . I suppose I will. But I must tell you, I won't make any decision until I feel sure God's hand is upon it."

He continued kissing my fingers. "Think of all the good you could do as a countess, Dandelion. You could care for the entire shire. You yourself mentioned the importance of an heir. You could rear that heir as a righteous man. You could influence the English court. You could sup with kings. You could make kindness and compassion fashionable throughout the land. Might not God have a hand in that?"

He made an excellent point, yet somehow it did not sit right in the pit of my stomach. Perhaps this was what God had in mind all along. I never did glimpse His plan past my initial arrival in the village. Surely I could choose to love Thomas. "Perhaps. I don't know. I shall have to pray about this long and hard."

"I'm not a young man, Dandelion. Don't keep me waiting too long."

"Oh Thomas, you've waited all these years, what will a few more hurt?"

279

He clutched his heart. "Cruel, cruel woman."

We laughed and finished our meal. We traveled back to the castle talking and joking all the way. I was relieved my hesitation hadn't strained our friendship. I had enough strain already with William.

Chapter 42

Whatever it is, God, please just tell me.

The day was dismal. Rain poured all morning, turning the fields to pools of mud. One lone speck of a man continued hard at work in the distance. I sat upon a hillside midway between the village and the castle, determined not to return to the cottage until I made my decision.

Weeks had passed. I owed it to Thomas to make up my mind. Damp grass tickled my ankles. My wet dress clung to my body, but the day was warm, and I felt so much closer to God beneath the expansive sky.

Too many decisions had nagged at me for far too long. Would this journey never end? It would bring such relief to accept Thomas and secure a future for Lily and myself. My daughter deserved a decent life. How dare I, an unwed mother, an adulterous woman with nothing but an empty plot of land to her name, turn down such an offer?

What if another famine hit? It could happen. What if this incessant rain didn't let up in time for harvest? Could I possibly endure watching my little girl starve before my eyes?

And what of the village?

Not only Lily and I were in danger. Things had improved so much, but Thomas still had not secured an heir. One accident, one bout of sickness, one mindless battle could end it all. What if his relatives were the barbaric sort of lords who abused their people while they lived in luxury? How could I ever forgive myself if such a thing happened, and I had given up my power to prevent it?

Oh, this cursed proposal. Was it the ultimate gift, or the ultimate test? What if this was God's plan, and I was too afraid to accept it, unwilling to trust myself with such generosity? What if I followed this path, and it led me away from my Heavenly Father and back to my old wicked ways?

What if I betrayed Christ just like I betrayed everyone else?

I swallowed down the awful thought.

The lone man in the field caught my eye.

Of course it was William. Who else would be hard at work in such weather?

What about William?

I wasn't sure if the words came from outside of me, or from somewhere in my own head, but as I stared at him laboring away,

281

traipsing through the thick mud, I began to shiver. Could I ever win him back? My stomach grumbled. Would it even be worth it? The air turned smoky around me. Could I ever bear it? The sky itself threatened to fall in upon me.

Then I was in that other place. My childhood hut surrounded me upon a thin film of mist layered atop the actual world.

I awoke in gray light, Mary's cold, hard form pressed tight along the front of me.

"Mary?" I poked my sister, but her rigid flesh did not yield.

"Mary," I shouted, sitting up, shaking her.

"Mary." I screamed as my eyes locked to her fixed dead stare.

Sadie and Robert awoke, joining in my screams.

"No," Da moaned.

He just sat in the corner, head in his hands.

"No, it c-c-can't be! God in heaven, where are you?" He struggled his way to our pallet and lifted Mary's stiff body.

He shuffled under her weight to the door. Slammed it behind him.

"Da, don't leave me." I ran to the window and threw it open to the razor teeth of the winds. "Da, come back."

Something in the finality of his trudge made me think he never would.

I sank to the floor. "Da," I screamed. "Da," I screamed again and again until all strength seeped out of me.

Sadie and Robert stood crying at the window.

Baby Tim whimpered along, unheeded.

I crawled my way to Mum, knees chafing on the cold, grinding dirt.

"Mum, Mum, Mum, please. Wake up." I shook her. But she'd been caught in the same strange delirium ever since Tim's birth.

I pushed her. Clawed at her arm. Smacked her face. "Mum, wake up!"

She opened her dead, glazed eyes and shrieked like the demons within her. "Get away. Get away." She thrashed her arms and legs. She whacked the back of her hand across my face and sent me reeling to the center of the floor.

This time I did not get up.

I crushed my cheek, white-hot and throbbing with pain, against the cold dirt. Cold, cold, always so cold. There were no tears left to cry. The room spun around me. In a moment the walls would collapse and smash me. Smoky air smothered me. Baby Tim whimpered in the background. It would all be over soon.

Relief flooded me.

It would all be over.

But it never happened.

Instead the vision thinned, and I could see lush green hills through the transparent spinning walls. "God, help me. Speak to me. God, please!"

I heard Giovanni's voice in my mind. "Just forgive them, right here and now as you feel everything. Just choose to forgive them."

I gazed at Da again, shuffling away with Mary's body in my mind's eye—hopeless and weary, obsessed with finding food, unwilling to steal one more morsel from his children's mouths. "I forgive you, Da."

I saw Mum, my kind, loving mum, caught in her strange delirium. Trapped by some forces we may never understand. I looked again into her eyes. The Mum I knew wasn't there. "I forgive you, Mum. I forgive you everything."

The walls of the vision hut dispersed, and I saw clear to the dingy snow-covered village beyond, a benign victim to the capricious weather.

I looked up to the gray looming clouds, but they were not to blame.

I gazed past them to the heavens.

A knife thrust into my gut. I doubled over and hugged my knees to my chest. "Ahh," I screamed in my throat, and it came out a garbled whisper.

I expelled the words from my mouth. "I . . . forgive you . . . God."

What a ridiculous thing to say! But somewhere, I had, I'd blamed Him all along. "I do. I forgive you, and I trust you . . . I trust you with my deepest self. I don't have to do it on my own. I place my life and my future in your hands."

I gazed into the eyes of my beloved. "Oh, Father, I love you so, so, so much." Rivers of healing tears rushed down, blurring the scene before me.

The images faded.

The feelings subsided.

I sat at peace.

Before me stood the village, stood the fields, stood my William hard at work to make a life for us all.

So is that it, God? Must I stay here? Might he take me back?

But, after all I had experienced that day, God remained silent.

I answered myself. There was too much between us, too much hurt, too much heartache. My betrayal cut too deep. We could never go back. I would always love him. Love was an action. A decision. Even a state of being as my mother once told me long ago. Yes, a part of me would never stop loving him. I would ever seek to bless and support him as a friend should.

But I would expect nothing in return.

"Lord Worthing." I called from my yard, stopping him one day as he returned from the fields.

"Yes, my darling. How can I be of service?"

I scooped up Lily and jogged to catch him. "I was wondering if you might take me to see that land."

"The land Gottfried left you?"

"Yes."

"Well, I'd be happy to, but why the sudden interest? Weighing your options before you accept my proposal?" He gave me a satiric grin.

"You needn't make it sound so mercenary. It's just that I've been praying and praying for weeks about this, and I'm still so unclear. I feel as if I'm missing a piece of the puzzle."

Lily tugged at my hair.

I freed it from her petite hand. "I need to find the answer. I searched through all of Gottfried's boxes and found nothing. I thought, perhaps, this might help."

"Then by all means, let's get on with it. The sooner you say yes, the better for me. I'm available now if you like." He bowed to me.

"Don't be smug, Thomas. Is it far?"

"Less than a mile. Gottfried said you played there as a child."

"Let me run Lily to my mum, and then we'll go."

"A woman with a mission, I see."

"The sooner the better for you, aye. I think only of your well being, m'lord." I curtsied and carried Lily in to Mum, stopping a moment to straighten my hair and collect my thoughts. I still wasn't sure why I held back my answer. I wasn't afraid any longer. The more I pondered it, the more I did want to marry Thomas. There may be some social challenges to face, but society aside, we could make a sound marriage based on friendship and respect . . . and a healthy dose of attraction to round it off.

Did I still dream of love? Surely we could build it together.

I stopped to kiss Lily on my way out the door. "Bye, bye, darling."

"Bye," the little beauty said, curling her tapered fingers and releasing them. This decision affected her fate as much as mine.

I swept her into a fierce hug before returning her to the wooden toys Da had carved. I straightened my periwinkle mantel over a simple ivory kirtle. Swiping at my eyes, I walked through the door.

"I'm ready," I called before I noted what Thomas was doing.

He stood discussing something with William. Why must William always show up at the most inopportune times?

"Far be it from me to keep a lady waiting." Thomas offered me his elbow.

I tried to smile at William as I passed. I wasn't sure I managed a reasonable facsimile of the expression. His answering grimace suggested I had not. I focused on the lane before me, although I'd walked it a thousand times before.

When Thomas turned down a wooded path, I tensed. This trail led straight in the direction of the river. It let out not thirty feet from what I long referred to as kissing rock. Why ever were we heading this way? I expected Gottfried had chosen the meadow past the fields where I danced in the wildflowers as a child, or somewhere along the path where we hunted as Robin Hood's merry band—not the river—never the rock where I discovered love in William's arms.

An ache settled upon my chest as we traveled down the path where William and I first held hands after he helped me over that fallen log. Gracious. It was still there. I stepped over the crumbling wood and frowned. And what of the day we walked down this trail for the very last time? There to the left was the little clearing where we sat and fought, where we both cried and yelled, and where he made his marriage proposal, that violent proposal sounding more like a threat than a promise. My eyes tightened and lingered on the spot long after we passed.

Thomas took notice of my mood. "You're very quiet of a sudden."

"I . . . I . . . I wasn't expecting to take this path." My voice came out soft and shaky.

"Are you all right? Shall we continue?"

"I'll . . . be fine. Let's keep going."

After a few moments he could not contain his curiosity. "Do you plan to explain what's happening?"

"There's a lot of history on this path. Good and bad. Can we please discuss it later?"

"Of course. Of course." He shook his head.

We continued until we emerged from the woods near the coursing Arun River. "What the devil is this?" Thomas shouted.

I saw it first, and hoped for a moment he was responsible, or that it was some sort of delusion, but his shocked outburst put a quick end to those hopes. What lay before my eyes was the most horrific, the most puzzling, the most amazing thing I ever saw in my entire life.

It sat on the hillside across the river. The water was too high to wade. For now we stood at the bank and stared, both speechless for a long while.

"What the devil?" Thomas said again. "Squatters, here on my land? But why would they choose the one plot belonging to you? It makes no sense at all."

I stood frozen.

"It must have taken months," he said when I did not respond. "Maybe more. Why, I was here less than a year ago. They must have started shortly after."

I still said nothing.

"I mean, it is a beautiful spot. No doubt that's why Gottfried chose it."

Still nothing.

Thomas put an arm about my shoulder. "Don't be upset, darling. I'll take care of this. It doesn't change anything." He sounded worried.

I still stood frozen and speechless.

In front of me sat the prettiest stone cottage.

It reminded me much of the charming cottage in the woods near Bath where Catherine lived as a child. It was larger than any peasant cottage—far too large, far too lovingly crafted to be built by squatters. I would be more inclined to believe elves magically placed it there, that fairies formed it out of sparkling dust.

The stones were gray and rounded, each a similar size. It must have taken forever to collect them. It had a timbered roof, covered with fresh thatch, and shuttered windows carved from wood. There were flowers growing in a ring about the house, the wildflowers I so adored, transplanted from the meadow to this sunny patch on the hillside—cornflowers, poppies, foxgloves, and buttercups, even fluffy white-topped dandelions. Bees and butterflies danced merrily side by side.

Someone was building a bridge along the far shore. If all that weren't evidence enough, the perfectly spaced row of cobblestones running from the doorway to the river was the final hint. The cottage was placed precisely where he said he would build it for me the same day we first kissed on the rock.

"Please, Dandelion. Say something."

My gaze remained locked to the cottage. "Did you ever tell William this land was deeded to me?"

"Well, I suppose I must have. We surveyed the entire area together last fall. I haven't been back since."

"Then I have my answer." My voice was filled with wonder and awe. My heart soared.

William had never stopped loving me.

Thomas looked at me, confounded.

My heart crashed back down.

"Thomas, I cannot marry you." I could barely believe it myself. "William..." My throat strangled around the word as I took in my dear friend's fallen countenance.

Pain filtered into Thomas's eyes.

"William is the one you love." He said it for me. "What a dolt I have been."

"Thomas, I'm sorry. I'm so sorry. I do adore you but . . . ." I wrung my hands before me.

He scratched his head. "But you've loved him since childhood. I should have known. How could I have been so blind? He built this for you himself." He waved to the cottage. "Did he not? Looks as if he's loved you all this time as well. I've seen it in his eyes a hundred times. How could I have been so blind?"

His words echoed the thoughts battling in my own mind. "Oh, Thomas."

"Go to him. What are you doing standing there, woman? Go to him."

"But—" I couldn't just leave Thomas pining at the riverbank.

"But nothing. I adore you, Dandelion. I saw a future for us. A good, solid, practical future, but nothing to battle the emotions churning in those beautiful periwinkle eyes of yours."

I reached for his arm. "Perhaps it is not too late to search for that Scottish lass." I smiled up into that face I had grown to cherish.

Thomas threw back his head with a hearty laugh. "No, perhaps not. Perhaps it's time we both seize love while yet we can."

He gave me a playful shove toward the village. "Now go, truly. I shall be fine." He pushed me again, harder this time.

Looking back only once, I dashed into the woods. I ran the entire way back to the village.

Chapter 43

When I found William, I literally leapt into his arms. He caught me in spite of himself. I started kissing his face madly, again and again. "Oh William, why didn't you tell me? Why didn't you say something? Oh William, I love you. I love you. I have always loved you, and I will keep loving you forever, long past the day I die."

"What are you talking about? Where is this coming from? I thought Lord Worthing proposed to you. Isn't that what you wanted all along?" He clutched me tight despite his hesitation.

"No. No. Of course not, you silly toad. I only considered it because I thought you stopped loving me. You are the one I love, William. How could you doubt that?"

"But you said it was too late to go back. You said you wanted to be friends. I felt sure you stopped loving me long ago."

"William, oh William." Tears streamed down my face now. I stroked his cheek. "I'm so sorry. I thought Gottfried was still alive when I said those things. I thought I was still married. I thought you were the one who stopped loving me."

"Never. I wanted to. Oh how I wanted to, but I never could. I gave you my pledge." He buried his face in my hair.

The day of Sadie's wedding. He had spoken his vow. The truth of it struck me, and I gasped. William was a far better man than I ever imagined. "That's why you built the cottage." I whispered in awe. "You must have started collecting those stones years ago. You never did give up on me."

"The day I saw you boarding the ship. I knew I had to do something to keep my hope alive, so I began searching out the stones and putting them aside. It was you, wasn't it?"

I nodded but couldn't find my voice.

Oh, if only I had turned back when I had the chance.

Or on that day in the castle before Richard kissed me in the wine cellar.

But no. No point in regrets.

I was not yet ready for him then. This time, everything was right. My heart had healed.

This time, I was ready for love.

He still held me tight, high off the ground, and I kissed him all over again.

"Wait, wait, wait one minute, Dandy. Let me get this straight. Lord Worthing did propose to you, correct?"

"Correct." I said, punctuating it with another kiss.

"And you turned him down?"

"Correct. Utterly rejected him, his absurd little title, and his drafty old castle." I punctuated it with four kisses this time.

"But won't you regret it?"

A melancholy smile settled upon my lips. "I hated hurting him. He is our friend, after all. But he saw the truth in my eyes. He's the one who sent me to you."

"You're entirely sure about this?"

"Yes, yes, yes, a hundred times yes, William." I kissed him some more to prove my point. "You are the love of my life. I know I turned you down once, but if you can find it in your heart to give me a second chance, I will spend every day for the rest of my life making it up to you. I am ready for love now. William Ashby, please say you'll marry me."

This time he did the kissing. "There is nothing in the world I would rather do." We kissed long and hard then, like two people dying in the desert who found water. William broke the kiss. "But shouldn't I be the one to do the proposing?"

"You already did, silly."

"In that case, yes, of course I will marry you, Dandelion." He pressed his forehead against mine, and we stared into each other's eyes.

A yipping ball of white fur jumped about my feet and broke the spell. We looked up to realize we had drawn quite a crowd. Robert held Daisy to his side, and Lily toddled toward us. Many of the villagers paused from their work and stood leaning upon shovels and hoes. These people knew us all our lives. When Robert let go of Daisy's waist and clapped his hands together, they joined in with applause and whoops of approval.

I leaned down to scoop up Lily. She belonged in this happy reunion scene as well. Cloud jumped up right alongside her, and William put his arms around all of us. I was struck with an odd impulse that something was still missing from our family portrait. Looking back toward Robert and Daisy, I saw my nephew Peter, Sadie's orphaned child, peeking from behind Daisy's skirt. William noticed the direction of my gaze.

He held out his hand and hollered, "Peter! Peter, come and join us. We are off to explore our new cottage."

The little boy ran to us and hopped on William's back.

The day of our autumn wedding dawned bright and clear,

reminding me so much of the day when Sadie married. Lord Worthing offered the castle great hall for our wedding, but we declined, wanting to be married in the village like our families always had. We did, however, accept his offer of minstrels for the party afterward. If ever there was a day made for dancing, it was today.

I wore a creamy silk wedding gown. I sewed each and every stitch, dreaming of William the entire time. Lily and Peter were dressed to match in cornflower-blue finery. They walked up the church steps hand in hand, and I followed close behind with a bouquet of wildflowers in my hands and a coronet of them upon my head. William stood waiting for me on the porch. He wore a handsome velvet tunic of deep midnight blue. Although I designed the suit myself, William's regal appearance left me gaping.

Friar John made a special trip to officiate the ceremony. Remembering how much I loved his sermon at Sadie's wedding, he repeated it for mine.

"What is love, my dear friends? I tell you with more confidence today that I have never felt before, 'Love is patient and kind, it is not prideful, it is not selfish. It bears all things, believes all things, forgives all things, hopes all things, and endures all things.' Yes, this is indeed the true nature of love, and our marital love is but a beautiful symbol of God's own love for His bride, the Holy Church."

He paused and winked at me. "We are to be a bride without spot or wrinkle that He will come to claim someday. So be ready, and remember through the love of William and Dandelion, His incredible love for you. 'For, we see darkly, as a poor reflection in a mirror, but someday we shall see Him face to face. Now these three remain,' I tell thee, 'faith, hope and love, but the greatest of these is love.'"

When he began our official wedding vows, I warmed with pleasure.

"Hast thou will to have the woman as thy wedded wife?"

"Yes, sir," William said.

"May thou well find at thy best to love her and hold ye to her and to no other to thy lives end?"

He said again, "Yes sir."

"Then take her by your hand and say after me. I, William Ashby, take thee, Dandelion Dering, in form of the Holy Church to my wedded wife, forsaking all others, holding me wholly to thee, in sickness and in health, in riches and in poverty, in well and in woe, to death us depart, and there to I plight my troth."

William repeated the words aloud as I whispered them in my heart.

"In the name of God and the Holy Church, I now pronounce you man and wife."

ACKNOWLEDGMENTS

I drew inspiration for this novel from a number of eclectic sources. The idea for the plot came from an old Eugene O'Neill play I read in high school. Dandelion's quest for the true meaning of love was driven by a book called *Love Life for Every Married Couple* by Dr. Ed Wheat, and her inner-healing moments were guided by the principles of theophostic prayer counseling. I was led to my own ecstatic experience with God through the teachings of Mark Virkler, and the spiritual elements of the book drew from the experiences of my favorite medieval poets. My daughter, who was six years old when I first had the idea for this book in 2000, inspired the childhood version of Dandelion and her ethereal dances through the fields.

Of course, I owe much thanks to my family, church, and many friends who helped make this dream a reality. I would like to offer special acknowledgment to those who had a role in guiding my journey. My husband Dani Sleiman encouraged me to pursue my passion, although I worked for no pay for five years. My close friends Angela Andrews and Kim Upperman helped launch my career with our short-lived but pivotal writers group. Craig Von Buseck convinced me to give Christian publishing another look. Steve Laube's kind rejection steered me to a whole world of writing experts and resources while still giving me hope. Donna Fleisher guided me in turning my book better suited for the 1950s into a marketable novel for today's audience. Kate Lee, my "nun2be" friend found on Godtube.com, helped me tremendously with the Catholic elements of the story. Siri Mitchell gave special attention to me as a new author and directed me to networking with the American Christian Fiction Writers. The Hiswriters and HEWN groups taught me more about historical accuracy and this time period than I ever dreamed possible. Without ever knowing it, Donald Maas showed me how to develop a decent plot into a stellar one. My former agent, Janet Benrey, believed in this book and kept my dream alive. And my good friends at Inkwell Inspirations cheered me on to the finish line.

I would also like to thank WhiteFire Publishing for stepping outside of the normal CBA publishing box and taking a risk on this new author and my crazy book.

This novel takes place in the early 14th century and adheres faithfully to the historical period while still portraying fictional characters and settings. The famine of 1315 occurred during what some call the "Little Ice Age" in Europe. The culture and lifestyles of the characters are historically accurate to the best of the author's understanding. The names are true to the Sussex area of England. The name Arun is now used for a local government district along the Arun River. Arun Castle is fictional. However Arundel Castle is a restored medieval landmark in Sussex. The title, Earl of Worthing, is fictional and named after an area of West Sussex.

Edward II ruled England from 1308 to 1327. He led an ongoing campaign against Scotland and Robert the Bruce. Edward III succeeded his father in 1327, when Edward II was murdered. The reign of Edward III is known as a time of the emerging middle class in England.

Robin Hood legends existed during this period, although they were recorded in the 1400s. The plague known as the Black Death officially ravaged Europe in 1348, but there are accounts of it in the Far East as early as the 1330s.

The great Sufi poet Rabia Basri of the 8th century inspired the character Samia. Reverend Mother Maria Scholastica and her convent draw on the rich experiences of medieval mystics such as Hildegard von Bingen, St. Catherine of Sienna, and St. Theresa of Avila.

Slight inconsistencies in biblical quotations merely portray that no standard English translation of the scriptures existed at this time.

A note on language: The Middle English language of the 1300s would look like an original excerpt from *The Canterbury Tales*. Most contemporary readers would be unable to glean more than half the meaning. Since recreating the original language was not an option, the author chose a slightly archaic, slightly British form of English to convey a sense of the era, while still providing an enjoyable reading experience for her audience.

1.   In what way does the idea of feet and path recur throughout the book? What are some of the forces that guide Dandelion's feet and determine her path? At what point does she take control of her own destiny? At what point does she turn it over to God?

2.   What does the bee symbolize? How do Dandelion's feelings toward the bee change throughout the book? How does the presence of the bee come into play during her fight with William?

3.   Dandelion refers several times to walls closing in upon her, the smell of smoke, clanging, rapidly beating heart, lack of breath, etc. In contemporary terms, what phenomenon was she probably experiencing? Why?

4.   Did any of the poems in the book speak to you? If so, which ones and why?

5.   In *Theophostic* psychology, when God's light is shed upon old memories and feelings, we are able to experience forgiveness and healing, and see things clearly. What are examples of such moments in Dandelion's life? In what way was she changed after each of those experiences?

6.   How is color used throughout the book?

7.   What gifts do the various men in Dandelion's life give her? What does each symbolize?

8.   In the biblical Greek, there are many words for our one word "love." How do these different types of love apply to Dandelion's relationship—love that provides security and a sense of belonging, romantic love, friendship love, brotherly love, familial love, passion and desire, unconditional Godly love?

9.   How do you feel about Dandelion's relationship with each man in the story? Which types of relationships have you experienced? Which types do you desire?

10.   In what ways was Dandelion's relationship with God at the convent similar to what you have experienced? In what ways were they different?

11.   Name some of the ways God speaks to Dandelion and those around her at the convent? Does God speak to you? If so, how?

12.   In your opinion, what is the single most significant change Dandelion undergoes at the convent?

13.   How is life at the convent similar to what you would have expected? How does the convent compare to Dandelion's experiences with the church in England?

14.   What might be some of the reasons that God withheld His plan for Dandelion's life until near the end of her stay at the convent?

15.   Compare and contrast the seventeen-year-old Dandelion who left the village with the twenty-five-year-old Dandelion who returns.

16.   When Dandelion returns to Arun Village what new heartaches and hardships does she face?

17.   What do you think Dandelion's life will be like after the story? Do you think she will remain so close to God, or is this just a "mountaintop" or "ecstatic" phase with God that will fade in time? Do you think she will live happily ever after? Does such a thing even exist?

ABOUT DINA L. SLEIMAN

Dina Sleiman writes stories of passion and grace. Most of the time you will find this Virginia Beach resident reading, biking, dancing, or hanging out with her husband and three children, preferably at the oceanfront. Since finishing her Professional Writing MA in 1994, she has enjoyed many opportunities to teach literature, writing, and the arts. Also look for her novels, *Love in Three-Quarter Time* and *Dance from Deep Within*, and her Valiant Hearts series coming with Bethany House Publishers in 2015. Dina serves as an acquisitions editor for WhiteFire as well, and she loves to represent them at writers conferences throughout the US. Join her as she discovers the unforced rhythms of grace. For more info visit her at http://dinasleiman.com/

ALSO BY DINA L. SLEIMAN

Dance from Deep Within
(WhiteFire Publishing, 2013)

Love in Three-Quarter Time
(Zondervan, 2012)

The Valiant Hearts Series
(Bethany House - Beginning March 2015)